THE BOSS THRONE

THE BOSS THRONE

G. W. Hixon

Copyright © 2006 G. W. Hixon
The moral right of the author has been asserted.

Apart from any fair dealing for the purposes of research or private study, or criticism or review, as permitted under the Copyright, Designs and Patents Act 1988, this publication may only be reproduced, stored or transmitted, in any form or by any means, with the prior permission in writing of the publishers, or in the case of reprographic reproduction in accordance with the terms of licences issued by the Copyright Licensing Agency. Enquiries concerning reproduction outside those terms should be sent to the publishers.

Matador
9 De Montfort Mews
Leicester LE1 7FW, UK
Tel: (+44) 116 255 9311 / 9312
Email: books@troubador.co.uk
Web: www.troubador.co.uk/matador

ISBN 1 90523762 6

Typeset in 11pt Stempel Garamond by Troubador Publishing Ltd, Leicester, UK

Matador is an imprint of Troubador Publishing Ltd

For Carol

To Mike
Hope You Enjoy

Prologue
Origins of Badad

An age ago, long before the events set down in this book, a hunter wandered too far into the wilderness. Realising he was utterly lost and abandoned, he sheltered for the night in a cave cut into the hills, against the soaring mountains of Tragara. He had tried to light a fire but could not, so simply huddled and cowered in the corner and watched the entrance with an eager and fretful eye, for in these forested hills were wolves.

He was tired but he could not close his eyes for the briefest moment for he knew that if he allowed himself to drift into sleep he would not wake up. So he sang to keep himself awake: a song his mother used to sing to him; a cheerful tune to make him smile, but it did not work quite so well here and now. As he sang the wind roared outside the cave and as the wind roared the wolves howled to compete. Then the last speck of slender daylight was gone and the cave was so dark that he could not tell whether his eyes were closed or not. They were, and, as he thought, he did not open them again. His name was Marrock.

The Lady Pannona came to the cave that same, fateful night, and touched his frozen face with her warm hand and kissed his lips and breathed fresh life into his lungs. But he did not wake there and then. Instead, he lay comfortable and warm for a long while. And as he slept he dreamt and as he dreamt he learnt all that was to know about the ways and the wants of mortal men. He gained knowledge of all manner of things, things that were not worldly or would have been understood by anyone except for the servants of Pannona, Mistress of the Druids. And as he slept he learnt all about what it was she expected him to do, for all of her Druids' were given a task. His task would prove to be the most difficult of them all.

Then he woke up at last and ventured out of the cave. At once his eyes widened in wonder and incomprehension for the world had changed a great deal from when he had crawled inside. He found himself standing on the edge of a lake; still and silver, with wooded hills all around, rising to snow-capped mountains in the distance. As he breathed in the cold morning air he was happy just to be alive. However, he was not the man he used to be...

One
The Siege of Bosscastle

It was dusk on a freezing cold, mid-winters day and the sky had a strange salmon pink glow about it as the sun plunged behind the huge stone keep at the fortress of Bosscastle, on the eastern coast of the land of Geramond. It had not snowed during the course of the day but the snow that had settled the previous night had frozen solid so that the archers along the castle walls struggled to keep themselves from sliding one way then the other as they loaded their bows and took aim. Below them, the gateway to this mighty fortification was being repeatedly pounded by a battering-ram so long that the end of it disappeared into the furrow of the valley; shaking the gatehouse and threatening to shatter it into a thousand pieces of stone.

Between every battlement stood a longbow man, firing down on the rebels as quickly as it took them to reload. Every arrow finding its target and so quickly that before too long the ram crashed to the ground. It was not, however, abandoned as there seemed to be an endless supply of volunteers to rush forward to take the weight of this immense piece of wood, and thump it again into the gate. Arrows reigned down upon them too, and when they were the next to perish, replacements kept on arriving, stepping over their bodies and ignoring them as they writhed in agony beneath their feet. And on it went for two hours.

Whoosh! Arrow after arrow, soaring high into the sky before showering down on the helpless rebels like iron hail. Then: screams and yelps of despair. Those that had replaced the fallen fell themselves; condemned to die at this loathsome place; their bodies, like those beneath them, trampled into the mire.

Whoosh! Arrows in eyes, bellies, arms and legs; blinding them or crippling them or both at once. Every arrow caught a man, and more arrows now than at any time during the attack, slaying the rebels so rapidly that it was not too long before there was no-one left at the front of the battering-ram, and it crashed to the ground for a final time and sank quickly into the morass of mud and snow. This time, no-one rushed forward to retrieve it, the back end was forsaken and the rebels at the gate withdrew into the forest, thus bringing an end to this squalid and deleterious attempt to break the Western Gate.

Fogle Winnersh had been watching from the relative safety of a clearing in the trees. His fur cloak was heavy on his shoulders; his head soaked to the scalp and his face frozen with horror. His rebels were coming back towards the forest and formed a column of wretched souls that stretched back to Bosscastle. Broken men; exhausted and daunted by the concept of leaving their companions to die in the mud. Faces that were pale and haggard; clothes that were torn and covered in red sludge; souls lacerated. And Fogle forced himself to watch as this army walked by, and his heart was so heavy that it threatened to plunge every step they took. For here, too, was a broken man; woebegone and sorry that he had ever suggested that such an attack could work.

Had these men been genuine soldiers, equipped with the sharpest swords and their bodies covered with armour, whose job it was to follow such instructions to fight and make war, therefore accepting the effects of defeat; and had Fogle been a proper general, designed to give instructions and send men to war and then look on dispassionately when they returned nursing their wounds it would have been so much easier to look them in the eye as they turned their heads to him: cast a compassionate glance that would lessen their pain, instead of lowering his face to the ground or turning away when one of them looked at him.

These, though, were not soldiers but ordinary folk, thrown together in an extraordinary situation that had brought them to Bosscastle. Among them: farmers, bakers, thatchers and innkeepers. Tradesmen and grafters all, but not one ounce of warrior in any of them. Yet, they had followed Fogle for over a year now. Simply downed their tools and abandoned their homes and marched with him through valleys and over perilous mountain passes. Had endured the worst winter any of them could remember; blistered their feet and chapped their skin, exchanged blows with each other from time to time, but followed him still and went where he lead them and did what he told them. It had been Fogle's idea to attack the Western Gate. A good idea, they all agreed. No-one said so now.

As he watched them pass he asked himself why they had been willing (he did not know if they still were) to forsake their comfortable, if humble, lives and rally to his cause with a fervour that would make any general proud. He reasoned with himself aloud before the answer came to him. When it did, he remembered that he had asked himself the same question once before, at the very beginning. He muttered the answer to himself again now. Their lives, however normal and customary, were anything but comfortable. The portion of life allotted to every one of them was impoverished and muffled. The land they farmed was not their own but the Governor's; the water they drank was tinged with the bitter taste of betrayal; the trees in the forests bowed to the force of an ill-fated wind. These were not happy, contented people at all, for the days when they had sang and danced to the tunes of the Northern Pipes or the Miffel Drums were long gone and but a distant memory. This, then, was a race of conquered men, and they were all the more wretched because of it.

Reassured, Fogle was able to lift his head again and look upon his men with renewed pride as they passed. He had remembered why they had been willing to come here. Sixteen long years had passed since the day those forty ships first appeared off the coast of Bodmiffel. Sixteen years almost to the day since Fillian guided his troops ashore at Bossiney. Everything changed after that first footstep. Until then, the island of Geramond had existed alone in the cruel Northern Ocean, untouched by foreigners and uninfluenced by the ways of the southern lands, and the people were the better for it: true to who they really were and the culture to which they belonged. Life was onerous, especially during the winter months, and a living was hard earned, for the land could be pitiless and unyielding at times. Yet in some ways they had forged a community that was more advanced than the opulent societies of the south. In other more crucial ways they were as wild and unrefined as any race of men in the world.

Three tribes coexisted: the Bodmifflians' in their forests, the Shiremen in the Middle Lands and the Tragarans' (the smallest tribe) in the frozen mountains of the far north. All belonging of this island of Geramond, yet each one different from the other, in mind and in heart. Had fought against each other for so long that the cause of the conflict was lost in the mists of time. And all the while they had been unaware that another island race had the ascendancy over them all. The vigour of this nation, the might of its armies and the mercilessness of its leaders, had occupied vast swathes of the world and now turned to Geramond to fulfill an insatiable quest to empire-build.

Only the Druids, when such men existed and when such men were listened to, gave warning of the impending danger from the south. "Beware he who would be more than a man," warned Badad, at a time when he was the last of his kind. "For he seeks to conquer, and by so doing shall mesmerise his own people whilst binding us all in chains!" And they listened and they waited.

Geramond had not been explored fully by any foreigner, be it a conqueror or a voyager. Men from distant kingdoms and regions had certainly visited; trade had existed between Geramond and the south for centuries; but they had barely set foot upon the shore before they withdrew to their ships. Men had seen Bosscastle and returned to their homelands to tell of this mighty fortress, but none had dared to venture too far inland, and none ever got as far as the Shirelands. Foreigners, therefore, knew nothing of the place and in the absence of the truth they created myths and legends. And so many that to most people Geramond was a ghastly place full of wondrous beasts, sorcerers whose magic and trickery held sway over the people; a place where misbehaving children were sent, never to be seen again. However, only the part about the magic had an element of truth, though not as commonplace as a storyteller would have a man believe.

As a child, Gauin Fillian had heard most of the tall tales that subsisted about the land at the end of the ocean. And like most children, when he behaved badly, his father would threaten to send him there. Unlike most children, however, this particular one longed for it to come to pass.

In adulthood it did. When Fillian landed at Bossiney and brought his army inland, cutting a swathe through the great forests of Bodmiffel as though they were not there, it was the start of a ferocious war of conquest that would ultimately see this timeworn land enslaved within his regime of tyranny and brutality. Bodmiffel fell first, then the Shirelands, though he stopped short of crossing the mountains into Tragara, assuming that he had gone far enough. He had been right, for once he had conquered Threeshire he had conquered enough of Geramond for it to be annexed and absorbed into his country's empire.

For sixteen years it remained so. Hate-filled years of torment and fear, when the spirit and true being of this place was crushed into the dirt; the people repressed so as to master them once and for all but instead had installed a loathing in them so profound that for the first time since the very first age of Geramond the people of the island were united in their despair. And while the Governor of this fledgling province grabbed his taxes, he did not notice that the hearts of the men of Bodmiffel and of the Threeshire or Tragara in the north were drubbing so angrily and loud that what was to follow had been inevitable from the very first step Fillian took upon the shingle at Bossiney: rebellion, and more, heartfelt rebellion, the bloodiest kind. Such stirrings in a man and he would gladly be slain so long as his cause was progressed. The chains that bind a man are only as strong as the man himself, and will decay with time, until the day when he tugs and draws with such strength that they snap and fall to the ground.

What started at Bossiney seemed destined to end here, at Bosscastle, just five miles along the coast. Bosscastle: the last bastion of Repecian rule, of tyranny and oppression, where chains were forged and linked in the first place. Yet, this great fortress was the incarnation of Geramond itself, built by the men that first built the nation, and witness to the time it took for that virtuous realm to splinter into three parts. Here was the seat of the kings of Geramond during the first age; noble men with good purpose and an idea of how a life should be lived; of the lesser kings of Bodmiffel during the second, darker age of distrust and suspicion; of a Governor of a malevolent empire during the third age. Rebellion, surely, would bring in the forth age of a ripened country. Freedom above all else, and with that freedom an end to strife. Peace was all that these men desired, and why they chose to fight those that would deny it to them.

"And here we all are, at the gate of Bosscastle," Fogle uttered to himself. All his life he had longed to see it. He had been within sight of it for a month and yet he suddenly realised that he had not seen it at all. He took his gaze away from the retreating army and placed it upon the stones before him. Cold, grey stones that had been put together to form a structure so remarkable that he could barely believe it.

Yet he had studied it for the past month; he knew that the main gateway led into an inner courtyard that housed the barracks, giving way to streets and alleyways that delved deep into the bowels of the place; that the wall was as thick as a man was tall and that the Great Hall at the far side was actually the hub of the place and not the huge Bossmilliad Keep in the centre. Fogle probably knew as much about the arrangement of the castle as the men who built it; had examined it for so long that his eyes had grown weary of the dull, grey stones. Only now, at this precise moment, was he looking at it in the way he was meant to.

Although engulfed in a thickening mist he could see as much of the outline of the fortress as he needed to and allowed his powers of retention to bring her out of her entanglement. Her? It had to be a woman for nothing this valiant and beautiful could ever come of being manly. And as the mist set in it served to add to her exquisiteness, as though she was hidden beneath a delicate gown that allowed only glimpses of her true beauty. This, without a doubt, was the most extraordinary building he had ever seen, and the only one built entirely of stone anywhere on Geramond.

Then a strange thought occurred to him. His purpose here had been, and still was, to bring about the fall of Bosscastle, and by so doing dismantle the last veneer of Repecian rule on the island. And to achieve that he would have gladly torn it down brick by brick with his own hands; willingly become known as the man who broke Bosscastle, and been more famous for that feat than for anything else he had done besides. He realised that the castle was as much a slave to the regime as any man could be, not its servant and certainly not its accessory.

The mist engulfed the castle entirely; the arrows had ceased to fall and the tail end of the retreat passed him before disappearing into the forest. Fogle leaned back against a tree and rubbed his weary face with his hands. He had not noticed that someone was standing beside him, so when that person spoke he jumped out of his sodden skin, jolted forwards and put a foot in a pool of mud.

"Galfall, you young fool!" he blazed. "What are you doing creeping up on a fellow like you mean to do him harm?"

Galfall was the youngest of the rebels; barely eighteen and here against his father's wishes, who thought him too young to fight and told him that he would impede the rebellion rather than assist it. Galfall, though, seldom listened to his father, and here he was now, standing next to the rebel master as though he had every right to be. He was a tall, gangling youth at the age when he considered himself to be a man even though every one else still thought of him as a boy; certainly as broad as a man but with the reddened flush of youth and eyes that were lastingly open like he was startled by everything he saw or heard.

He sneered to himself as Fogle shook the mud off his boot and shook his head angrily. "I've been watching, Fogle, from up that tree," said Galfall.

"Watching what?" asked Fogle, irritably.

"Watching you. You had no idea I was up there for I was as quiet as a leaf. But mostly watching the attack. I told you it wouldn't work, didn't I? If the Western Gate could be breached by thumping it with a battering-ram then it would have happened long before now, by an army much stronger than yours."

Fogle was annoyed by the youngster's tone, but more than that he was drained and tired and had not the need nor concern to listen to him. Galfall stepped away to look across the darkening valley towards the black shape of the castle. "But there must be a way," he mused.

"If there is then I don't know it," replied Fogle, tiredly. "Nor do I wish to waste any more time … lives … trying to fathom it out." He drew a sharp intake of breath before continuing, as though he was trying to muster the courage to say the words. "We have spent too long here," he mumbled. "And lost enough men already."

Galfall, sensing Fogle's fragility, moved to stand beside him. The youngster was irritated. "Then you mean to give in, Fogle. It has all been in vain."

"We have done enough, boy," roared Fogle, finding renewed vigour with which to defend himself. "The Repecians have been expelled from Threeshire … and from Bodmiffel too, apart from this one rocky out-crop. And they were never in Tragara in great numbers!"

"You promised us that Geramond would be free!" Galfall replied, his voice crazed and his eyes like glass.

"And so it is!"

"It can never be free until we have taken back Bosscastle."

If Fogle had a reply he did not offer it. Instead he stepped back and looked deep into the boy's face. There was something about him that was absorbing. A fervour and boldness that defied his years. He was truly his father's son, not just in image but in substance too. He wondered that if Gringell were alive to see him would he be proud or angry? A boy at the beginning had grown solid in body and mature in mind at the end. This war; the sight, sound and smell of it, had changed an innocent, idealistic mind so that here was not a boy in the midst of men but a man like them, and better in some ways; more robust but just as forsaken.

But there seemed to be a doggedness about Galfall Gringell. A sense of having achieved nothing; like he was living in this solitary moment. A spirit born to dwell in the darkness of the forest or a shrub to blossom only here and now, in the mist at Bosscastle. Fogle concluded that Gringell would have indeed been proud of his son if he were here to see and listen. Then he recalled the moment when he had witnessed his own son as he slipped into manhood. The finest day he had known, and the foulest.

He jolted himself out of his private thoughts and finally offered his reply. "Bosscastle has not been routed since the day its final stone was laid. I was a fool to think that my army would fare any better than the countless others that have come here."

"Then why did you bring us?" Still, Galfall was reluctant to accept any form of explanation.

Fogle pulled his heavy cloak further over his shoulders and nipped it around the neck, observed his breath on the air and shivered as though his blood had suddenly turned to ice.

"So many ghosts here," he said, quietly, almost fearfully. "A thousand years of ghosts all gathered in the one place. And now there are hundreds more to join them."

"Marrock says that if we don't take Bosscastle the Repecians will keep a foot in Geramond," said Galfall. His quarrelsome attitude was beginning to fray Fogle's already fragile nerves.

"Marrock! What would he know?" snapped Fogle, and so strongly that Galfall, at last, was taken aback. "It was Marrock who suggested that we should come here in the first place. And I was foolish enough to listen to him. Give me a man whose arm is strong and can hold a sword firm to one whose tongue makes idle comment. I need fighters, not thinkers. And definitely not talkers."

Young Gringell, despite being a nuisance, had impressed the rebel leader thus far, but now said something that completely took the breath from his lungs. Quite calmly Galfall replied: "Do you think a war can be won by merely fighting? Does an army not need its thinkers too?" And at once Galfall, as young as he was, was propelled ever higher in Fogle's estimation, for the elder man could offer no argument. "Not every man can fight. And not every man can think," Galfall concluded.

There was no reply that Fogle could give. The truth was that he was neither. Instead, just a simple man that had led a simple life. So his thoughts naturally turned back to that simple life. "I'm tired of it all, Galfall," sighed Fogle, so pitifully that it must have been true.

"What vicious times these are. When a man is not true to who he is but is what others want him to be." He grasped at his cloak even further to shut out the biting wind. "This isn't me. Not really. I am not a general or a leader of men. I am a blacksmith. A good blacksmith. The best blacksmith in the whole of Woldshire." He smiled fondly, thinking of his old furnace and his little cottage. "But

I am not a general and have never proclaimed to be. I have done my best, but it's over now. I think it's time Fogle went home, to what he knows and does best."

The cloak around his shoulders was now so frozen that it was like having the whole boar weighing down on him. Galfall, he noticed, was trembling with the cold, too. Their breaths formed a cloud of gloom on the black air and the full moon, scattered across the tops of the trees, threatened at any moment to come crashing down upon them. It was time to return to the camp.

Despite the darkness, as he turned to follow the others, Fogle caught sight of something out of the corner of his eye; a sight so terrible that it made him stand stock still. He glanced quickly at Galfall and was glad that the youngster had not seen it too.

"Go back to the camp," he said, quite calmly but in a way that suggested he expected no argument. "Tell them to build up the fires."

"But I will walk with you, Fogle," Galfall replied.

Fogle looked all around him but whatever he had seen, whoever he had seen, had gone. "Go now, boy," he barked, and with an urgency in his voice that left the youngster in no doubt that he was to return to the camp without him. Fogle watched as he disappeared into the trees until he was satisfied that he was alone again. "I've seen you," he said, then louder: "I can hear you!"

What he could hear was breathing. A deep, almost laboured breathing that first seemed to come from one direction then, in an instant, from another, like he was being stalked by a wolf or some other creature of the forest. But Fogle had caught a brief glimpse of what it actually was and knew that it was something much more spine-chilling than a wolf or a boar.

He spun around on the heels of his feet several times to try to locate where the breathing was coming from and when he stopped spinning he realised that the correct route back to the camp was gone. The mist had thickened so rapidly that it now overwhelmed him completely; Bosscastle had vanished and the forest had been shrunken down to just one tree, himself and whatever it was that was with him. "Come out," he demanded, his voice risen with panic. "Step free of the mist so a man can see you."

The breathing got louder and louder until the little man could feel that foul breath wafting against his face. He carefully tilted his head away from it. "I am not afraid," he stammered.

"Be afraid, Fogle," said a voice from one side, then from the other. "I would be afraid."

"Who are you?"

"An old friend, long gone."

"A friend would not torment a man so," Fogle shivered. "A friend would not hide in the trees and whisper like a ghoul!"

"Then perhaps I do not wish you to see me."

"I will not believe you are there until I do."

So, emerging from the mist and with mist clinging to him like he was part of it, appeared the outline of a man. A very tall man with his arms by his side and coming forwards. As he came closer, the mist was left behind and Fogle could see him clearly at last; when he dropped his head forwards for he could not believe his eyes so chose not to look.

"You are afraid now, Fogle," the man said. "So afraid ... or disgusted ... that you dare not look. I don't blame you. I would be afraid if I could see me."

Nothing could have prepared Fogle for what he was seeing. He warily raised his head and looked again and his eyes at once filled with sorrow and his heart began to thump against the caverns of his chest, for the vision before him was not one of menace or threat but anguish and pity. It was covered in blood, its own blood, from head to foot, so that his blackened eyes seemed to be detached from the head. It lifted its head to reveal a slit across the neck that was so wide and deep that the head was barely joined to the body; the blood in the wound had clotted and turned black and clung to the bottom rim and trickled down like sap from a young tree. Fogle, bolder with each second that passed, looked closer at his eyes. They were yellow with traces of red, like a spider had crawled over them to leave a trail. The eyes told this man's story better than the wound on the neck.

"Come back to the camp," said Fogle, stepping closer and stretching out his hand.

"My wounds cannot be healed by your fire, my friend," the

spectre replied. "Even the Druids of old could not help me now."

"Then I have truly lost my mind, for I can see you but you are not real."

"Is a dead man any less real than one living?" It brought its scabby hand to the side of Fogle's face. "I could touch you if I wanted to," it said.

Fogle had actually believed that his old friend was still alive after all, yet could remember holding him in his arms as he had died. The last battle, Tangelwitt, came to mind. The bloodiest of the entire war. He remembered looking on helpless as two Repecian soldiers rounded on Gringell and cut him down with a slice and blow. Almost the final act of this ruinous battle. And that fact, more than Gringell's actual death, was the hardest to take. Shortly afterwards the two soldiers retreated with the other Repecians into the shadowy shelter of the forest.

Fogle examined the spirit more closely now that his mind had adjusted to the fact that it was there. "I had forgotten how deep the wound was cut," he said. "But for weeks afterwards it had stayed with me … haunting my sleep. And yet here you are. Here I am, looking at you."

"Those soldiers knew who I was. As they pinned me to the ground they spoke to one another and said that although the battle was lost the Governor would look kindly on them if they could take the head of the Rebel Master back to Bosscastle." It therefore pushed back its head with its finger to reveal a vast, grotesque gash.

"They had a good go, but didn't have time to finish the job." It chortled. "Luckily for you. A headless corpse is worse in a dream."

"Why are you here, Wilfren?" asked Fogle in a gentle, inquisitive manner. Not a trace of fear in his voice. "Why have you come to me this night of all nights?" It seemed that after all that had happened during the course of the day it mattered not that the ghost of his old friend was with him now, as night set in.

"Because I have never felt so helpless as I do now that I am dead!" The spirit carefully lowered its head so that it was once again sitting upon the neck. It drifted towards Fogle and went past him, disturbing the mist so that it swirled on the cold, damp air like a silent windstorm. "Don't believe them when they tell you that a dead man has found peace," it said. Then turning: "Chances are he won't have. More likely he is roaming the earth cursing his luck and asking himself how it came to pass, and scheming his revenge on the fellow that did for him with every ounce of energy he has left." It coughed and spat out a large clump of clotted blood. Instinctively, Fogle looked to the ground to see the blob, but stood in it instead, confirming that Gringell was here with him and not just an apparition.

Momentarily, Fogle was disturbed by the ghoul's outburst. Long had he believed that a dead man was relieved of all his worldly burdens; hoped to be relieved of his own one day. Death, by whatever means, had become a favorable alternative to this bloody war over recent weeks. Indeed, his one comfort had been his belief that his dead soldiers were at peace again. But it seemed that they were not after all. Gringell, here and now, was evidence of that. So he wondered how many more restless spirits were roving through these Ingelwitt trees, or those at Tangelwitt or on the plains of High Cleugh. And of his own kin, one in particular, back in the yard in front of his house.

"Then you have come back to seek revenge?" asked Fogle, quivering in the cold.

"Ah ... I'll leave that to those who did not deserve what they got," Gringell replied. "But I was a soldier. What happened to me was a hazard of the job. I would have done for both of those Repecians had they not got to me first, so I mustn't grumble."

Fogle was puzzled. "A farmer, Wilfren ... that's all you were. None of us are soldiers. None of us deserve to die like soldiers."

The spectre sniggered, apparently amused by Fogle's innocent remark. Then its jaw was clenched shut, its blue lips pursed together; cheek bones protruding as though the skin had been stretched over them as an afterthought; eyes so cold that they were like balls of ice, puncturing Fogle's calm performance to see that he was really quite terrified. "There is more of me that you do not know than the little that you do!" it said, coarsely. "It is barely a year since I first lay eyes upon you." It strolled towards him and Fogle backed away.

"Although I doubt whether you remember our first encounter.

You were too wrapped up in your own grief. Poor old Fogle." Now it was standing next to him, breathing its foul breath once more upon his face. "You were very vulnerable then. Easily led."

"I would have followed you to the end of the earth!"

"You liked me and trusted me because I was kind to you and said the things you longed to hear. And like a fool you followed me wherever I took you."

Gringell's tone was menacing now as he revealed himself to be a threat after all. And he was so close to Fogle that as he spoke specks of blood splashed onto his face. "I was not the man you thought I was," it continued. Then walked away. "You would have trusted me less had you really known me. And not liked me at all."

Then he vanished into the mist. Fogle stepped forward to follow him but stopped himself. The mist now was so dense that he could not even see his hand as he held it out, and decided that the best and safest thing to do was stand as still as stone. He tried to focus his eyes against the dull mist but could not see any sign of Gringell anywhere, or hear anything or smell him anymore. Pure fear prevented him from stepping forwards or backwards so he collapsed to his knees. "You have come back to torment me, Gringell. But why, I ask. Why?" He clambered back to his feet. "There is nothing you can do or say that can make me more miserable than I already am."

Abruptly, Fogle's neck tightened and he was forced back until he was pinned against a tree, and he knew that Wilfren had returned to torment him some more. Overpowered and gasping for air, the spirit's hand grasped him so tightly that he thought his throat was about to be torn away. Unhurriedly, Gringell's spirit appeared again: its spindly, terrible face so close to Fogle's that it was almost touching him; and cold, foul air wafted against his skin.

"Then let me end your misery," it said, in a sinister whisper.

"Like a twig underfoot could I snap your neck if you would just will it. And then you and I would be the same again. Partners in death as we were in life. Oh, what fun we could have. What do you say? What do you say!?"

Fogle was filled with horror and pure panic. "We were never partners, Wilfren," he stuttered, and coughed as the spirit let go of his throat.

"What was that?" Gringell demanded, affronted and cross.

"You were ever the true leader of this rebellion. I merely made up the numbers like the rest of them." He looked on relieved as Gringell walked away. "The men trusted you and loved you and I can only ever imagine what that must be like, for they have no respect for me at all. You were the general … master … of this army. All the decisions were made by you."

"So you're jealous…?"

"No…! You made the right moves. The war is won. Had it been left to me we would not have got this far. We would not be here now."

Gringell turned around. It seemed that with every passing second his body became more decayed for he looked far fouler now than when he had first appeared out of the mist.

"Where are we, Fogle?" it asked, gliding back towards him as though floating, with not so much as a suggestion of movement in his legs.

"We're here …" Fogle answered. "Ingelwitt…! Bosscastle…!" He paused, for he knew what he wanted to say next but needed to call upon sufficient courage first. "At the end," he concluded, with a zest in his voice that confirmed his belief in the assertion.

Gringell was not convinced at all and was irritated that it had even been said, and gnashed his teeth from side to side to contain his fury. Then the same thought glanced through minds of both the man and the spirit. A thought that only the two of them could share. It was a private reflection.

Fogle was the first to touch upon it. With his voice risen with purpose and poise he said: "I promised you that I would bring the army south to Bosscastle, and I have," hoping that it would be enough to appease the raging spectre.

It was not. "You promised me that you would free Bosscastle, which is not the same thing at all and has not yet been achieved," the spirit replied. "Until it is this war can never be over. Until it is over you cannot go home."

Poor Fogle took a sharp intake of breath and released it with one burdensome sigh that temporarily parted the thick mist in front of him. And as Gringell stepped away, perhaps preparing to leave once and for all, he went after him. "What more can I do?" he bellowed.

Turning, Gringell said, quite plainly: "Fulfil your promise to me."

"How…?" Fogle persisted.

The spirit continued to walk away. "Set Bosscastle free."

"The men are exhausted …"

"Push them harder, you're the general now."

"They are starving. We have no food." He was walking at his side, almost running to keep up with him for he had to rely on his stumpy, aching legs. "We have been reduced to scavenging on the forest floor for grubs and berries … !!"

"Do you find them?"

"Yes, but that's all we find."

"That is enough!"

As Gringell continued on his way, Fogle stopped and fell behind to catch his breath. "Moral is very low, Wilfren," he said between breaths, leaning forward to rest his hands on his thighs. "The men are beginning to splinter into two groups … the Bodmifflians and those of us who aren't Bodmifflians." His face sank as it took on a look of torment and dread. "Gonosor is stirring again, as you threatened he would." It was enough to stop the spirit from floating further away. "His kind take heed of what he says. The rest of us are wary of him."

"As well you should be," Gringell replied.

"He has made it his business to undermine everything I say or do. They taunt me and those close to me. Yesterday, he warned us that we had no right to be here and that we should go back to the Threeshire. I think he's right. This isn't our homeland."

Gringell turned sharply. "You are afraid of him?!" He asked the question in a manner that implied surprise and part disappointment in Fogle, as though he had no reason to be fearful of anyone or anything.

Fogle let out a nervous snigger. "Look at me, Wilfren." He straightened himself and held his arms aloft to reveal his full, podgy body. "He's thrice the size of me." He lowered his arms and stopped sniggering. "There is nothing I can do or say that will make things any better. But I'm not bothered. If Gonosor wants to take control then I say let him and I hope he has better luck than I've had. I'm so tired, you see. I thought that I could do this thing without you by my side, but I can't."

"I never thought of you as a naysayer, Fogle," said Gringell, regretful and dreary, as he came back and stood in front of him to look directly into his drooping face. "You really do mean to give in, don't you?"

"I'm tired. All I can think of now is my old workshop back home ... my own bed ... hot rabbit stew ... a full jug of ale in the Shireman...!"

The spirit smiled. "We would all like those things. Some of us cannot have them." Then, something remarkable happened. Even more remarkable than the spirit being there in the first place. Fogle returned its gaze and watched in silence and wonder as the spirit began to change. After just a few, intense moments Gringell's vicious wounds were gone, colour came back into his face and his eyes were as blue and clear as they ever were. As the mist cleared slightly and the air warmed, the fearsome ghoul had been banished and in its place stood the Wilfren Gringell of old; as fit and full of heartiness as the days before the war. Fogle was fearful no more for his old friend had returned. To authenticate the fact he stretched out his hand and with one finger touched this new, refreshed face. "How can it be?" the little man gasped.

"Is this not what you want, Fogle?" asked Gringell, stepping away. "To return to days of old, before this wretched war, when the world was well and men were contented and happy."

Fogle nodded enthusiastically. "All I want now is to be free to live a simpler life." As he spoke, he half believed that Gringell was able to grant him his wish, and waited eagerly for the spirit's next deed. He followed as Gringell turned again and walked away but this time with more interest than trepidation. "Where are we going?" he asked. "We may lose our way, Wilfren. We mustn't stray too far from the others."

"I thought you wanted to stray, Fogle," said Gringell, striding along at a swift pace. "You said you wish to live a simpler life. You said you longed to return to the Shirelands."

"Yes, yes ..." Fogle stuttered.

"Then come with me, my little friend, for that is where I am taking you."

Gringell strode and Fogle trotted behind for what seemed like a considerable distance, until the trees cleared and they were standing on the brim of the valley. The mist cleared forthwith and the winter night suddenly became day as the sun burst into the sky and shed light over the land. This, unmistakable to Fogle's eye, was the Shirelands, just as he remembered them, bathed in autumn sunshine and so colourful that it was hard for him to remember where he had been just a moment before, a step or two back.

"Welcome home, my friend," said Gringell, and smiled as Fogle's mouth fell open and eyes widened with cheer and delight.

More specifically this was Woldshire. The city of Woldark itself was huddled snugly amidst miles of rolling hills, with smoke bellowing from the chimneys that punched the sky, and the thatched roofs of the houses shimmering below like leaves falling from a tree. Looking more closely, and with eyesight better than he could recall he had, Fogle sought out his own house and gasped with fondness when he found it.

"Life, once, was good, wasn't it?" said Gringell. "Men, once, were free. A time when war was for distant people and did not touch our lives." He placed his hand on Fogle's shoulder. "We shall go closer."

"What's happening?" asked Fogle.

"Be still, be calm, my friend. Wait and see."

Suddenly the smallholding, Fogle's little house and the workshop beside the spinney, were nearer, and the rest of the city was lost behind the hills. But something had changed. The air had turned fouler. A youth appeared out of the workshop. "Callarn...!" gasped Fogle, and he began to go down the hill towards him, only to be held back by Gringell. "My son!" Fogle protested, pulling his arm free.

"But you know what is to follow. What came to pass."

Fogle was anxious again. Beginning to realise that he was being deceived, he became angry. "What sorcery is this?"

The sound of horses. Then they came into sight around the bend in the lane. Four of them, with riders dressed in black. Callarn greeted them. Fogle turned away. "Take me back," he demanded.

"Will you not stay and watch?" asked Gringell.

"I will not," Fogle replied, with his back to the scene.

"You cannot watch," said Gringell. "I don't blame you. I would not watch if it had happened to my son."

"I have seen it before," Fogle slurred.

"You were there that fateful day a year ago when the taxman called."

Fogle paced back towards the trees to leave this dreadful scene behind, in the past where it belonged. But the closer he got to the edge of the forest the further away from him it went, and he realised that he could not flee quite so easily as he had got there, so he stood still and bowed his head, and turned to look down upon his old homestead with eyes that were only half open.

"Like most of the Woldark men you had fallen behind with your payments to the Governor," said Gringell. "His coffers and his patience fast running out, he sent north his collectors and a cohort of legionaries to take what was rightfully owed to him. You were one of the first to be paid a visit. But you didn't have the money, did you?"

Fogle shook his head, ashamed and embarrassed. He observed as his son struggled to prevent the tax collectors from entering the house, and watched himself trying to pull Callarn away from them.

"They would take payment in kind. Anything … anything at all that was worth something. Watch, Fogle. They're in the house now, turning out draw after draw. Ah, here they come. They've found your treasures. You have lost everything that you held dear. What little money you had left, those trinkets of gold left to you by your grandfather, your wife's wedding band that you promised her you'd pass to Callarn in time …"

"Take me back," Fogle pleaded, shielding his eyes.

But Gringell continued regardless. "Now they're taking your horses. Look, Fogle, Callarn is trying to stop them…!"

"I will not look!"

"The cart you borrowed off Toggett Took … they're taking that too. They will need it to carry all of the things they have stolen from you. Now Callarn is fighting with one of them. A knife is drawn!"

"Enough!" bellowed Fogle. "Please, Wilfren. Enough."

Gringell smiled compassionately. Suddenly, without moving and in the blink of an eye, they were back in Ingelwitt Forest, in the damp, night air. The sunshine had gone and so too had the Wilfren of memory; his spirit had returned and that foul smell that went with it. Only, the body seemed to have decayed further in the few moments that had passed.

"Sometimes things happen that change the world of a man forever, whether he would have it so or not," the spirit said, quite calmly for he had made his point, he thought. "And all he can do is pick up the pieces of his life and carry them with him until such a time comes when he is ready to put them back together. You must ask yourself, has that time come? Or is there work still to be done?"

He stepped closer and bent down to look into his face. "Do you remember how this war started? You came into the Shireman Inn that very day, wracked with grief and trembling with rage. I was there. I saw you. Your friends saw you, and together we marched to your homestead and avenged the murder of your boy. And so it started there, for all of our lives had changed after that. It would come to be known as 'the Battle of Fogle's Field'. The first battle in this war for independence."

"ARRRRRRAGH!" Fogle let out a vast roar that, when trapped within the confines of the trees, traveled upwards to be caught in the wind and taken for miles, to the walls of Bosscastle. Then he settled again. "Tell me what to do, Wilfren."

The spirit moved away. "Unless it finishes here, the only place it can finish, things will be a thousand times worse than before the war had even started. We have done well thus far, no-one can deny us that. So well that Fillian's vengeance will be terrible. He will send an army so vast that everything will crumble in its wake. And he will bring it to Bossiney, for he knows there is nowhere else safe enough to anchor so many ships. He has been here before, remember?"

Fogle was sad at the revelation. "Then it has all been in vain. So much death and violence and for what...? For it all to be repeated. On and on it will go, until there are none of us left and it doesn't matter anymore."

"Everything must have an end."

Fogle looked the spirit in the eye and returned its gaze. "Will we ever be free?" he asked.

"It will come to pass," Gringell told him. "But only if our hearts are strong and our minds are one and the same. And when it does, we will have a country of our own again."

Fogle wrapped his arms around the spirit and pulled it close to him and clung to it as though he was certain to fall if he let go. And the spirit at first was taken aback, but then allowed it to happen naturally. They were one and the same for a few, brief moments.

"Come back to the camp with me," Fogle whispered.

"My time is done," Gringell replied. Then he loosened Fogle's tight grip and pushed him back. "Finish it here and now, and let tomorrow take care of itself." The spirit smiled. "Go now, Fogle, my little friend. Be with the others for they need you, and you need them."

The mist lifted, not just in this thicket but all around, so that Bosscastle was exposed again on one side and the camp fires shone like beacons on the other. Fogle knew it was time to leave. And as he turned he got a whiff of camp smoke and inhaled it as though it was a breath of renewed hope. The spirit had been right to say that the others needed their leader, so he set off to be with them.

Gringell watched him go, then collapsed to the ground and decomposed instantly. Then, emerging from the shadows, the little Druid appeared.

"Rest in peace, Wilfren Gringell. You deserve no less," he mumbled to himself. "You task is thoroughly done. Now it's my time. The hour of the Druid is approaching."

Two
The Arrival of Badad

The forest of Ingelwitt was just a poor imitation of what it once was. It clung to the Bodmiffel coast for eighteen miles, north to south, and at places threatened to leap over the cliff to contend with the crashing sea below; reached inland as far as the banks of the River Bod and had trees so tightly packed that they competed against each other to grow as tall as they could as quickly as they could to reach the sun, to render the forest floor a dark and foreboding place.

There had been a time, not long ago, when Ingelwitt covered the whole of the Miffelwitt peninsular, and the mighty Bod, rather than forming its western boundary, cut right through it until finally converging with the sea. A time when Ingelwitt was a place held sacred; where spirits danced across the tops of its trees and wolves roved freely and owls and bats held sway over the dark, winter nights. A track and a trail existed only in the mind of the man who knew it was there. Pathways through the brushwood from north to south and east to west, twisting one way then another to coerce a befuddled voyager deeper into the trees until he found himself misplaced, unaided and forsaken to the hungry wolves therein. So a discouraging place, and not so long ago to be forgotten, for it dwelled in the hearts of the men and women of Bodmiffel, who once lived within its confines and sought solace in its ancient laws and wisdom.

Now the forest was giving up its secrets again, not to the wandering Bodmifflians of old but to a form of man not seen in these dark recesses since days of old: patriots of Geramond; men of Bodmiffel, of the Shirelands and of Tragara. Here to fulfill a task begun by Fogle and Gringell of the Threeshire; to right a wrong and in so doing avenge the slaying of a boy. To set free a proud land.

The rebels had come to Ingelwitt during the darkest, coldest part of the winter. The battle of Tangelwitt was won, and one final journey south, deep into Bodmiffel, through its dense forests to the sea, to Bosscastle, was all that was necessary to bring the war to a close. That was the promise. That was what brought them here in such numbers. They had travelled down the old North to South road and turned onto the coast road. It was called a road but was in truth a dirt track and wide enough for only four men to walk side by side, which meant that this army of rebels had stretched for miles, and when the front column first entered the forest the back was still coming down from the mountains in the border lands.

A dirt track that a thousand feet had churned into a mud track, that sunk beneath their weight and stuck to their boots and their legs, making this the most arduous part of the whole odyssey. The men of the Threeshire were gloomy and dragged their spirits behind them, made more grouchy by the Bodmifflians' songs and the slow, repetitive beat of their Miffel Drums, that could have accompanied any type of song but was especially suited to the one they sung: a lament for Gringell and all the others that had fallen at Tangelwitt.

In his heart his journey's young,
And the road before him finely spun.
Along the road each man must leave,
And hope for him the trees will grieve.
Will bow to gusts of men long gone,
Come to bring the forest's son.

That carries him west on ancient breath,
So in green hollow he'll heed to death.
And set him down when roads are done,
Upon stony knoll where all would come;
To kneel before the mortal tree,
And ask the son of which forest was he.
When mortal skin at last will shed,
In that valley among the dead.

Then Gonosor heard them and commanded them to stop. It was

a sign of his eminence among them, and his reputation, that they did as they were told.

At first Ingelwitt was kind to them. Its trees were widely spaced to allow them access, but the further they rummaged the tighter they became, until the forest closed in on them completely, pulling them ever deeper, so deep that the light of day did not follow and it went as cold as midnight. The wind, however meagre, was enough to stir the senescent trees so that they merged as one above their heads; a whimsical roof on top of a dark, unfathomable world. A world where the dark and the night belonged not to them but to other creatures, heard but seldom seen. Where a forest during the day became a place unworldly in the darkness.

They settled on a camp on the forest's eastern fringe, in a strange clearing in the trees aside the old road. The road continued across the valley to Bosscastle and the coast, so from here they could control who went in to the fortress and who came out. But no-one ever did. And so many of them that the camp was divided into two parts: the Bodmifflians and those from elsewhere. Two huge fires burned, and dozens of smaller, more intimate ones, scattered across the ground like fireflies across a still lake. And here they stayed for over two months; a buoyant yet untroubled place where the sound of laughter competed with the noises of the night.

Two months passed quickly. It was the morning after the attack on the castle gate, and all was not well. The fires burned so dimly that they were barely alive. It had started to snow again: thick flakes that settled on the ground in no time at all, and on the men too if they stood still for long enough. The wounded amongst them, and there were many, had been set down on the ground close to a fire, protected from the weather only by makeshift shelters of furs and leafage, supported by delicate frames of sticks and offshoots, that looked likely to collapse with the next strong gust of wind.

Stricken men in bloodstained bandages wrapped around their slashed limbs; faces blue with the cold and frosted hair; frigid eyes that watched those fires struggle and longed for their aching bones to thaw. Austere, remote eyes that still belonged to the day before; unflinching as the new morning brought with it a fresh burst of activity. Logs were brought to the fires by anyone able enough to carry them; huge cauldrons of broth were stirred by the cooks and dished into small bowls and taken first to the injured, who gobbled it up as though it contained the cure to what ailed them. It did help to warm them and gave the better off among them a sudden, however brief, burst of energy. It was accepted that those who were too weak to eat the broth were not long left in this world and that nothing could be done to stop them from joining the others that had perished at the castle gate.

Fogle was sitting on a stool beneath a canopy of leafage, in the company of four others: young Galfall, son of Gringell; Toggett Took, of course, for wherever Fogle was the old man was with him; the Tragaran, Marrock; and Gonosor, a prince of Bodmiffel. They were huddled around the small fire that burned and cracked between them, and only the Bodmifflian – an immense, thickset man whose face was almost entirely covered in hair save for the highest points of his cheekbones and the area around his eyes – was standing, next to the exit of this make do shelter of furs and sticks, as though he was prepared to walk out at any moment. Certainly, there was an ill-feeling between him and the others, like they were intimidated by his size and presence.

Marrock was sitting closest to the fire with his back to Gonosor. He was a short, chunky man without a hair on his head, a reddened face and kindly eyes. Apart from that, nothing else was known about him. He was wise and judicious, but where he had come from and why he was here was a mystery, and none of them had ever had the care to solve it.

"Come closer to the fire, Gonosor," said the Tragaran. It was an irritated request rather than a good gesture. "Warm yourself with us, your friends."

"That fire would barely warm a cat," Gonosor retorted.

"It will burn hotter in time," Marrock said.

Gonosor fixed his gaze on Fogle and at first the little man was anxious and uncomfortable, and bowed his head the longer the stare continued. "You wish to say something, Gonosor?" Fogle asked, returning the look at last.

"How much longer will you allow your people to suffer?" asked the Bodmifflian, in a heated tone.

"Until the job at hand is done," Fogle replied.

Gonosor came towards him but stopped short. "It is already done. Your lands are free, go back to them and leave us alone with ours."

"We came south to take back Bosscastle," Marrock said.

"Take it back for who?" snarled Gonosor.

"For us all," said Fogle.

"Then you are deluding yourselves. Bosscastle will not be broken by this army or any other. Many have tried it. All have failed. Enough men have been sacrificed at the castle walls, most of them forest folk. I will not stand idly by while you decide to send more of my people to their deaths."

"We have lost plenty of our own, too," Toggett snapped. "I reckon a hundred or more Shiremen perished yesterday, and a horrid way to go. I mean, this isn't even our homeland, but we came here to try to finish it, like Fogle and Gringell said we should. A little bit of appreciation wouldn't be amiss, Gonosor … if you don't mind me sayin' so…?"

Toggett's mistake was that he had not heeded any of the warnings Fogle had given him regarding the Bodmifflian: hot-blooded, capricious and violently arrogant. When Gonosor gave him a look that could have scared a stone, the old man remembered this warning in the nick of time. Backing down quickly, Toggett concluded: "What I mean is … we've all lost people we think some't of to those damn Repecians, ain't we then? Fat Fogle over there's lost his only son at the beginning … young Gringell lost his father just a few months back…." His voice was rickety with nerves for the Bodmifflian was coming towards him. "… and me … me oldest friend Miggel Thrull the butcher, taken by an arrow…" He looked at Marrock but did not know enough about him to comment, so continued. But Gonosor was upon him, casting him in his shadow. "And you've lost both your sister and your young cousin, for he is missing Fogle tells me…?"

Gonosor stretched out his arm and wrapped his huge hand around the old man's scrawny neck and squeezed it so tightly that his face drained of colour and his lips went blue. "Never … never again will you dare mention my sister in the same breath as the butchers and bakers of the Threeshire …!" the Bodmifflian grunted, clenching his teeth as he lifted the old man off his feet. Fogle moved to stand between them. "A sweeter thing, more gentle yet courageous, will this world ever see. So dear and neglected that I cannot allow her memory to be spoiled here, amidst such wretched men."

There was no doubt among them that Gonosor intended to kill Toggett Took there and then. To throttle the life out of the little man so that he could never again utter another word let alone another insult. And he was killing him easily; his eyes were swelling and his tongue was lashing at the air for a wisp of breath.

"He meant no harm," said Fogle, calmly taking hold of the Bodmifflian's arm to prise it off Toggett's neck. "So let him be."

"My sister has been slighted. Her honour will be restored here."

"Gonosor, let him be," said Marrock. Gonosor looked at him sharply. "Your quarrel is not with the old man. Let him go."

With a superior sigh, he let Toggett down and released his grip so that he could breath freely again, then walked out of this enclosure, pushing Galfall against the fence as he passed.

"Was it something I said?" asked Toggett, gasping at the cold, morning air, genuinely bewildered.

"Marrock, take him away will you," said Fogle, "before I throttle him myself."

The meeting was terminated once and for all. Fogle turned his back on the others and went to fetch some wood for his meager fire. Marrock escorted Toggett, shaky and unsteady, out into the open. Galfall turned to leave as well but stopped in his tracks and went back.

"Do you see my father like I do?" he asked.

Fogle was taken aback. "What kind of stupid question is that? A question I should expect from a young fool like you." He knew fine well what the youngster meant, and had his answer ready on his tongue but for the lack of inclination to give it. What concerned Fogle most of all was the way in which the question was asked, as though Galfall knew of the encounter in the forest the previous night. "Your father is dead!" he said.

"I see him, be he dead or otherwise."

Fogle was suddenly interested, nay concerned. "Where? When?"

"At night."

"In your sleep?"

"No. I am never asleep. And you?"

The rebel-master paused before deciding to continue. "I have seen him just once, in the forest. I thought that I was going mad, until he touched me and I felt his cold flesh against my own skin."

"What did he say to you?"

"He urged me to finish the war here, at Bosscastle. But then that's Wilfren Gringell … never did know when to let things be to the minds of others. What does he say to you, may I ask?"

"That's the strange thing. Always the same, word for word. 'Look out for your brother and protect him from the war…!' I don't understand it at all."

"How does he look? Like the day he died?"

"No, not at all like that. He looks like he used to, before the war … on the farm, bringing in the beasts."

"Before I knew him," Fogle mused.

"When he was happy," Galfall replied.

Fogle tried to remember the last time he had been a happy man. Not just joyous or giddy like he was at Ribble Bridge or Tangelwitt, but a time when his heart was steady and his life humdrum. A time when he was a mere blacksmith in his own shady corner of the Threeshire, long before embarking on his grisly journey, long before becoming the rebel-master he was now. A thousand years ago, it seemed; another lifetime. And as he watched the dreary snow fall and settle around the camp, he remembered the view from the terrace on the front of his house: the whole of Woldshire was to be seen to be believed from there, wallowing in the late summer sun, the Shire River meandering through its meadows of green and yellow; rooftops of Woldark and Aldwark glistening like sycamore leaves floating on a silver lake, with the occasional plume of smoke rising from an eager chimney to remind him that this was still the Threeshire.

"We were all happy men once," he said, turning to stoke his fire, abandoning his memories and returning his thoughts to the troubles of the here and now. "Go now. I wish to be by myself."

The snow stopped falling a little after noon but the temperature had dropped even further so instead of the snow melting away and disappearing into the little beck that skirted the camp, it stiffened and froze beneath their feet to create a carpet of ice. Gonosor spent the rest of the daylight searching for his lost cousin, at first around the camp, then into the forest and finally on the open slope into the depth of the valley and halfway up the other side, sneaking as close to the castle walls as he dared. He finally gave up with the setting of the sun and headed back for camp. And then he found him, under a bush of thorns a little way up the forest slope: face down in the mud, and when turned over, his skin was blue and his hair and beard frozen solid, so that when Gonosor lifted the head into his hand the ice cracked and soaked his sleeve.

He carried him back to the camp. The Bodmifflians – who were separate from the others – made a pathway between themselves as the body was brought towards the fire. They bowed their heads in respect as Gonosor passed. Those in helmets removed them and swords were drummed against shields. No-one spoke or made any sound to break the silence, but they could not help the wind whistling through the trees. Once the body had passed, the pathway collapsed and they walked behind it.

Effortlessly, Gonosor lifted the corpse into the air, his strong arms uncurling. The others gathered around so that he was standing facing them with his back to the fire. He took a sharp intake of breath and cleared his throat.

"It is the law of the forests, whenever anyone dies, and longer are his bones held together by flesh, that they be taken by fire, and a scorched body will set forth a soul, that drifts as black smoke into the Valley, and like in dreams will it walk with the ancients."

Then the carcass was tossed into the flames, that ravaged it instantly so that for a moment, until the better part of it was burnt, the fire turned from an obedient thing into a brutish thing. Flames turned blue and it made a noise like a dozen wolves, tarring at the flesh until there was nothing left of it. And the smoke did turn black, swirling into the trees and filtering through into the evening sky above, going ever higher to hang over the camp like shadow.

Galfall, Toggett and Marrock had observed the ceremony, such as it was, from the far side of the camp, the Shire side, around a small fire beneath a cover that had actually been made by Toggett so belonged to him.

"He'll be warmer on there, so he will," the old man chortled, and pushed some tobacco into his long pipe, and chuckled again as he drew on it.

Marrock leant inwards. "If Gonosor hears you, old man, he will finish what he started earlier, but for better reason."

Toggett blew smoke into his face and showed his yellow tooth as a sign of impudence, then looked to Galfall for support. But the youngster seemed distant; troubled by the events across the camp, his eyes predetermined on the body burning on the fire beyond their own, then skipping across the crowd that gathered around it, upon one in particular.

"I've seen them do that before," he said, quietly. "How can they do it to the people they love…?"

Marrock leant forwards. "Many a wiser man than you, Galfall Gringell, has fallen foul of the theory that because we are all native of one island we are the same. We are not. You may have already figured that out for yourself? And nothing detaches one group from another more than the means they have of disposing of their dead. In the north, Tragara, we bury ours in the deepest recesses of our mountains … in the Threeshire you bury yours beneath your blessed turf … and here, in Bodmiffel …"

"They burn the blighters…!" Toggett said, interrupting.

"Upon a pyre of wood from the forest of a man's birth," Marrock concluded, suitably annoyed by the intrusion. "It is deemed, when all is done and only ash remains, that a man is at last fused with the trees."

"I have never been to Tragara," said Galfall, interested.

"Thou ain't missing much," Toggett told him. "Now't there but mountains and wild men…!"

"Yet deeper, immeasurable wisdom does resound there," Marrock said. "And such splendour that those that dwell amidst the mountains will never leave them…!"

"You did," said Toggett. Then put his pipe back in his mouth, folded his arms behind his neck and leant back against his rock, happy and smug to have corrected the Tragaran.

Marrock smiled. "Then I am not as wise as my countrymen."

Galfall was not listening. His mind was elsewhere: across the camp with the Bodmifflian contingent, with Gonosor, and as that giant of a man moved amongst his own people, laughing with them and encouraging them to laugh with him, the youngster was puzzled at his ability to recover so readily from the loss and cremation of his cousin; whose body was seething in the flames, cracking and spitting still. Gonosor was laughing so rowdily that the whole camp could hear him.

"I fear him," said the youngster. He had meant to think it and was ashamed that he had whispered such a statement, looked at his friends and dared to hope that they had not heard. But they had. Of course they had. How could they not? Toggett's ears were as wide as they were long, equipped with long, grey hairs to pull in any secret whisper.

Marrock dragged his short, dumpy body forwards like a crab on a beach. "And you are right to fear him," he said. "You are a Shireman, and Gonosor of Baladorn does not care much for your sort."

"Why not?"

A thick, blue cloud of smoke came out of Toggett's mouth.

"Because he envies us, that's why," said the old man. "He envies everything about the Threeshire, though you'd never hear him admit to it…!" He rested his pipe on his knee and turned to glare at the Tragaran. "And what's with this 'your sort'? You make us sound like vagabonds … thieves…!"

"To Gonosor, that's precisely what you are …"

"What've we ever nicked of his?"

"His pride, Toggett, that's what. Not to mention his sister."

Suddenly, like someone had grabbed hold of his head, Galfall's attention was pulled away from the far side of the camp, back to this small, intimate discussion. "Who was his sister?"

Toggett released a long, satisfied sigh. "The most graceful, the most handsome woman of her time. Of any time, at that."

"If Gonosor hears us talking of her he will fly into one of his rages. The mere mention of her name is enough to stir in him such sentiment the likes none of us will ever know."

The comment prompted Toggett Took to rub his still tender throat.

"Why must we not talk of her?" asked Galfall, genuinely mystified.

"Tell the boy the story, Marrock, you know you want to." The old man drew on his pipe and enjoyed it so much that his eyes rolled in his head. "I would meself, but baccy's scarce these days and I intend to enjoy what I've got left...!"

Marrock fidgeted to make himself comfortable. "Very well," he said. "As you seem so keen to know."

"Gonosor's sister was Henwen, a woman of unsurpassed beauty and elegance. But her beauty defied her true self for she was also a great warrior woman, as ferocious when she had a mind for it as any man. Henwen was the fifteenth ruler of this land of Bodmiffel, and its first queen, who mesmerised her people with her charm and loveliness, so that they would follow her wherever she went and do whatever she asked them. They say, even now, when the forest is still and quiet, her gentle laughter can be heard coming through the trees on the breeze ..."

"What became of her?"

"When Fillian invaded Geramond and landed at Bossiney, he came first to Bosscastle, only to find it abandoned to its fate. Henwen's army was in her mould, robust and loyal, but no match for the Repecians. And she knew that her people functioned best amidst the trees of the forests, and led the retreat deep into Ingelwitt, from where she sent word to her brother in Baladorn, telling him of the invasion and calling for his assistance.

Gonosor settled on the idea of helping her, and brought his army up the Old Road and was reunited with his sister at Gwal, where the road forked east towards the sea. No-one knew the forest tracks better than these two, and that for Fillian to come further inland he would have to travel the Coast Road. So they encamped their combined army among the trees aside the road, and waited for old Ingelwitt to entice Fillian further inland until he was ensnared in their trap. But Fillian was as wise as Henwen was beautiful and

Gonosor was strong, and gave the charge for his soldiers to burn the forest to the ground. And Bodmiffel was conquered from that moment on. The trees, as they burnt, made a sound that was like an entire race of people screaming."

Galfall was enthralled and sat forward so that he did not miss a word of what the little Tragaran was saying. And while he listened he glanced at Gonosor for he was beginning to fear him less as the story unfolded. Here, after all, was a prince of Bodmiffel. He had never seen a prince before.

"Then the Repecians invaded the Threeshire?" asked the youngster.

"Not straight away," Marrock replied. "You have to bear in mind, Galfall, that when Fillian first came here he did not even know that the Threeshire or Tragara even existed." He stretched out his dumpy legs to warm his feet against the fire. "But he had a foothold on Geramond and was content with that at first. So the Repecians continued to destroy the forests, clearing the ground for their camps and new settlements. This forest of Ingelwitt, and Tangelwitt further north, are all that remain of the ancient forest that once covered all of the Miffelwitt Peninsular, and had lasted for thousands of years."

"What did Henwen and Gonosor do?"

"Henwen, as Queen, was certain that the only way for her people to survive was to lead them north, across the mountains and into the Threeshire, and dare to hope that the Shire folk would give them a safe haven in these troubled times. Gonosor went with her for Baladorn, by now, had fallen. When this news reached him he was said to have wept."

"There was once a song," said Toggett. "We used to sing it when such songs were permitted." He searched his memory for the words but they were not forthcoming.

Marrock knew them.

"Northward bound the warrior Queen;
Where mountains rise but never seen.
Wheels of stone at last begone;
Beyond the sky where deed be done.

In middle lands of green and gold;
A place of kings with blood of old;
And set ye down at noble feet;
To bring forth peace that all would greet.

In middle lands a union born;
Of blessed field and scared horn.
On the shore of the forgotten lake,
A king of Geramond at last they make."

Toggett Took was quietened at last, until he sighed heavily and said: "I've not heard that said for years."

"I've never heard it at all," said Galfall. "What does it mean?"

"A tale to be told, lad," the old man replied. "But not here and not now." He abandoned his pipe and placed it on the ground between his feet. He was fidgety and fretful for he was looking across the camp at Gonosor: as loud as a man could be and bouncing on his feet like a flame in the wind, pointing at the Shiremen and encouraging his people to mock them like he was doing. "Don't say anything else, Marrock, for Gonosor is getting excitable again."

"Are we now oppressed by the Lord of Baladorn?" asked the Tragaran, audaciously.

"Baladorn is free again," said Galfall. "He should be happy that it is, like we are happy the Threeshire is free … and Tragara…."

"At the village of Celwig, in the land of hills and mountains, Henwen set her people down and told them to rest. The Mor Pass was behind them and this was a foreign country, so they must wait for permission to venture any further. Gonosor, of course, was resolute that his people should not be here. This was a foreign country and a hostile one, and he urged them to return to Bodmiffel to fight for the liberation of their own lands. A futile effort, and death was certain, but a noble death was better than this shameful exodus across the mountains."

"In those days Gonosor hated the Threeshire even more than he does now," said Toggett. "Why?" asked Galfall. "I don't understand why anyone should loathe the Threeshire. We are decent people. He may not understand our strange laws and customs but that doesn't make them wrong...!"

"Remember, Galfall, that the emptying of the forests came at the end of a great war between the two countries that had gone on for over four hundred years. This newfound peace was threatened by suspicion and doubt, and peppered with accusations and insults. It was perhaps understandable, if not desirable, that Gonosor felt uneasy at this time. He thought that his people and his country were on the verge of being wiped out entirely."

Marrock held his hands against the fire.

"For four hundred years, every king that came to the Shire throne proclaimed himself to be the one, true heir of Calamthor, and rightful king of all Geramond. It was a good, solid claim, and few in Tragara ever disputed it. But there were those who did. Between the fall of Calamthor, the last king of Geramond, and the rise of the Shire Kings, the people of the southern, forested lands came together to forge their own country, and were bound to it by their strange customs and existence, so long shunned by those that did not understand. The early kings of Bodmiffel, rejecting the concept of Geramond as a nation in its own right, closed their borders to interference and influence from the north. And so began the Great Unease.

"The problem was that the kings of the Threeshire, at the same time as declaring themselves kings of Geramond, sought to prove it by sitting upon the Boss Throne, in Bosscastle, in the land of Bodmiffel...!"

Galfall's ears were pricked again.

"I've heard it mentioned before ... by my father ... but just in passing," he said, then grinned contritely upon realising that he was interrupting.

"Legend has it that only the one, true king of all Geramond, he of solid ancestry and pure blood, can sit comfortably upon the throne. For if he is not he shall meet his end, if not there and then, shortly afterwards.

"And each new king brought an army south to reclaim the old castle for themselves. Some never even got across the mountains in the border lands, some got as far as the castle walls, but none accomplished their charge." Marrock now smiled proudly. "The stones of Bosscastle had been set securely by the founder men … steadfast and durable, and no army that the Shire Kings could muster would fracture them. But that did not stop them from trying. Indeed, with every failed attack the mission became ever more pressing and splendid in its accomplishment.

"And on it went, age after age, king after king. Then, quite out of nowhere, something extraordinary occurred. Vercingoral, the seventeenth king of the Threeshire, came to the throne …"

"He was our greatest king," said Toggett.

"Yet there were those in the Shire Lands that would have him remembered as a traitor," Marrock replied.

"Why?" asked Galfall, more and more eager.

"Recognising the futility of waging war with the south … upon realising that his own people were war-weary and worn-out … Vercingoral came to Bosscastle not to make battle but to make the long-awaited peace, and signed a pact with Sodric, King, that Geramond would never have a king unless such was the will of all the people."

"And so ended the war?" quizzed the youngster.

"Yes, so ended that particular war. Sodric and Vercingoral dined that night amid great celebrations. It was then that the Shire King first laid his eyes upon the daughter, Henwen … and hers were laid upon him. Sodric, if no-one else, saw what was bound to happen. A young woman, fine-looking and prudent, and the young king, full of promise and enterprise, surrounded by old, argumentative men. The days that followed they walked with each other through the gentle groves on the castle slopes, and talked about the shady forests of Bodmiffel and of the gentle, rolling hills of the Threeshire. And as they walked and the more they talked they began to fall in love. Yes, old Sodric was wise but he did not need to be so wise as to see what was happening to his beloved daughter before his own eyes.

"More than anything, it was this new love that conserved the newfound peace. And when the time came for Vercingoral to return to the Threeshire, he did so with a heavy heart. I think really that he would have preferred to stay at Bosscastle …"

Toggett frowned in protest. "He would never have abandoned the Shire Lands," he said.

"If men are brave or wise, it is for the love of a woman," Marrock replied.

"Go on, Marrock," Galfall urged him.

"Sodric was as wise as any king of any age. He knew that the peace was a fragile, precious thing indeed, and vowed to uphold it. Barely a month had passed since the departure of Vercingoral, and the old king banished his troublesome son and heir to the distant backwater of Baladorn, never to see him again.

And when Sodric died, Henwen, daughter, was made queen, and all was well at last in the land of Bodmiffel. And in the Three-shire too, for Vercingoral, King, was a man possessed with love for the foreign woman …"

Toggett spat out some tobacco. He had a disbelieving, almost disapproving glower on his face. "How do you know all o' this?" he asked. "Who died and made you the know-all…? I know that you're a Tragaran, and they reckon strange folk live in those mountains, but you're talking as though thou was privy to it all."

"Yes, how come you know so much, Marrock?" Galfall added, though in a much less demanding tone.

Marrock smiled cunningly. "Men are renowned or remain unsung."

Toggett almost choked. "What the bleedin' 'eck does that mean…?" he spluttered.

Marrock snapped himself out of his private, intimate thoughts.

"I would tell you how I know, old man, young man, if I thought for a moment you would both believe me." He said no more, and warmed his face against the fire.

Across the camp trouble was fermenting. Gonosor was so spirited and fiery that the men standing close to him could not help themselves being swept along on his giddy breeze. And so rowdy was this group of Bodmifflians, that it made the rest of the camp uneasy and unsettled. There were men here still hurting and some were fighting for the lives, but it was as though Gonosor and his companions barely gave them a thought, like they were hardhearted and indifferent to their plight. Perhaps they were. And yet they had all fought together at the castle gate, at Tangelwitt and Ribble Bridge. Gonosor had fought bravely, had lost his own kin to a loose arrow. But now, men that had fought next to him and had drawn on his strength, lowered their heads or simply looked away for they cared not for what they were seeing.

Suddenly, laughter. Unrestrained laughter so loud and unexpected that it seemed that the entire camp jolted away. The burst of laughter was followed by a chant of 'Gonosor! Gonosor!' as the man himself was hoisted into the air by a dozen arms and countless hands. Then a cheer so loud that it was like a clap of thunder, and those that had looked away were compelled to watch, if only out of the edges of their eyes.

"Now Gonosor has returned," said Galfall. It was more a statement than a question.

"Yes," replied Marrock, sadly. "He has indeed."

Men held up their arms and stretched their fingers as far as they could so that Gonosor would touch them as he was conveyed amongst them on the shoulders of his supporters. Two Bodmifflians' held their swords aloft to form an arch for Gonosor to pass beneath, and had to stoop to avoid his head being scalped.

All the while his people applauded him. Not a gentle, respectful clap but a firm rackety din that must have made their fingers shudder it went on so long. One of them, close to the front, started to sing. And a tune that was barely heard on the lips of a solitary man resounded the length of the camp when taken up by all of the Bodmifflian contingent; far into the forest and perhaps even to the walls of Bosscastle.

Galfall, the only foreigner daring enough to observe the scene without restraint, edged his body forward to catch a word or two of the song, but it was difficult to hear. A clamorous rendition but not a very tuneful one. 'Hail! Glory! King!' And when the song was finished it was followed by the loudest cheer of the evening.

The noise was enough to bring Fogle out of his quiet seclusion. He walked amongst the Shiremen, who fudged and fidgeted to allow him to get to the front. The sight of the rebel master was a relief and it calmed their jittery hearts and a thousand pairs of eyes followed his every move. Fogle stepped between Galfall and Toggett, who promptly rose to their feet when they saw him come. These two were his closest companions now. The oldest and the youngest of all the rebels. Toggett he had known all his life and longer still, it seemed. He knew the old man better than he knew himself; his ways and characteristics, even what thoughts were passing through his old head; like a son would know a father, say, or a bird in flight would know the wind.

He looked at the old man and released a quiet, caring chuckle beneath his breath. Here was a frail man, with a face worn with a lifetime of misfortune and a body at the crooked stage, with puny arms barely able to lift a sword let alone use it with any purpose; and yet he was his greatest asset. Not in a practical sense, for what the old Took knew about the ways of war was not worth knowing; but in a much more important way: whatever happened, however this campaign twisted and turned for and against him, Fogle knew that if he had no-one else then he would always have Toggett. And as he looked behind him and saw hundreds of familiar faces he realised at once that he did not truly know any of them. Not really. Not like they were old friends. Good men, he was sure, but not his own kind. Shiremen, indeed, but not patrons of the old 'Shireman'.

"I was sleeping," said Fogle, groggily. "I heard the noise. What's been going on?"

"Gonosor's getting excitable over there," Toggett told him.

"They were singing," said Galfall. "But I couldn't make out the song or what it meant."

Marrock, his face sagging and ashen, rose to his feet.

"The Anvil of the Forest stands staunch upon the ground,
and the smith hammers out the sword.
Delayed in glory, pensive from the burden, the trees bring
Home the child born to shake the sword, and with it protect
The laws of the forests. Hail Gonosor, son, brother, king!
Hail Gonosor, by right of birth, guardian of the forested lands."

"What does it mean?" asked Fogle.

"Gonosor has just been proclaimed king of Bodmiffel," replied Marrock, sadly. Fogle was at once filled with shock and fear in equal measure. That turned quickly to rage.

"Bodmiffel has no king," he said. "It needs no king now."

"Tell that to laughin' boy o'er there," said Toggett.

This, surely, was the real Gonosor of Baladorn. The man of legend, feared by an entire race of people, performing as himself at last. When Fogle first met him, at Tangelwitt, he regarded him rude and arrogant, but was not as fearsome as people had told him he was. He saw a man, he thought, as desperate to be rid of his captors as the rest of them. Whose hatred of the Repecians went far deeper than could be imagined, to form a loathing that utterly consumed him, and when harnessed within the framework of the rebellion, made a warrior so menacing that the undertaking could not falter so long as he was a part of it.

'Beware Gonosor,' men would warn him. 'A dangerous man is one that is denied what he truly believes is rightfully his.' But Fogle ignored the warnings and would reply: 'Like his freedom.'

Whatever Gonosor was, be it warrior or ogre, his people, it seemed, adored him now, and lavished upon him all of the attention and adulation that had been denied him in the past and that he had for so long craved. They seemed to be mesmerised by his drunken, oafish performance. As he drank they cheered. As he ranted they laughed. And when the wind suddenly stopped and the forest went still, the fire cracked and was like a tree falling to the ground, and the revelry and jollity from the far side of the camp was as threatening to those who were not a part of it as an army on the march.

"We are but intruders to a private party," Marrock mused. "Interlopers in a foreign land. Less welcome than a fox in a chicken-run!"

"Must we leave?" Galfall asked.

"Gonosor will insist on it," replied the Tragaran.

"It cannot end like this," Fogle insisted. Marrock seemed pleased to hear it. "We will not leave until we have completed our business here." He seemed personally affronted and outraged. "And Gonosor is as bound to that task as any of us are. Gringell told me not to trust him but I did, like a fool." Now he was chastising himself in his troubled mind. "Before admitting his mob into the rebellion I told him about our cause … liberation from the

Repecians … the routing of the Governor … an end to all wars in Geramond. And he agreed … gave me an assurance of his good intentions. Gringell said that too much water had passed under too many bridges for him to be trusted, but I urged him to forgive and forget Gonosor's past recklessness. Why didn't I listen to Gringell?"

"Do not blame yourself for the actions of others, Fogle," Marrock told him. "Gonosor of Baladorn, it would seem, has been pursuing his own agenda, that does not include the Shiremen or the men of Tragara…!"

"What must I do?" Fogle asked him.

Marrock's answer was instant. "What would Gringell do if he were here now…?"

Fogle could hear his old accessory speaking to him. Indeed, he looked to his right then to his left to determine whether or not Gringell had returned again.

"He would say that Gonosor is a bully, and there is only one way to deal with a bully."

"Don't be a fat fool, Fogle," Toggett blasted. "He'll kill you if you go over there. Wait 'till he's simmered down a bit."

Fogle longed for Gringell to be here now more than at any other point since his demise. Then, turning his head slightly, he saw the boy: the image of his father and with his spirit too. It was enough to stir the little man into action, and he set off across the camp. "Stop him Marrock," urged Galfall.

"Your father was an exemplary rebel," the Tragaran replied. "Now it is Fogle's turn to be."

Gonosor and his tribe were behaving in an ever more frenzied way, guzzling back ale as though they may never taste it again, and all the louder through its influence. When Gonosor saw the little man approaching, he choked on his ale, marvelled at Fogle's boldness and was rendered temporarily speechless. Temporarily.

"Here comes the Rebel Master…!" mocked Gonosor. "All hail the Rebel Master…!" The others laughed. One shouted: 'The Shire Master!'

"There are men in this camp stricken with injury, trying to rest," said Fogle. "How can they rest with this din?" Suddenly, Gonosor erupted in laughter. Genuine, gut-wrenching laughter that was so contagious that it quickly spread amongst the others, but stopped just as quickly as it had occurred.

"Will you not kneel and bow your head, Shireman?" asked a Bodmifflian.

"Why would I do that?" Fogle replied.

"You are in the presence of a king," the man insisted. Gonosor studied Fogle carefully to measure his reaction. But Fogle remained quite calm; outwardly, inwardly trembling with fear.

"I see no king," said the little man. He drew a deep intake of breath before continuing. "The age of the kings of Bodmiffel has passed."

It was a strange thing to see such a giant of a man tremble with utter rage and contempt. And as Gonosor's face strained with anger and he stumbled back and had to steady himself against one of his associates, Fogle breathed out as discreetly as he could. He was waiting for the Bodmifflian's response. The fact was that Gonosor was so taken aback and so filled with fury that he could not concentrate his mind to find a response, or when he did, train his lips to say it. All the while Fogle kept him in his eye.

"Or, whether Bodmiffel shall have a king is not for you alone to decide. And certainly not now. Not while there is work still to be done."

With a twitching mouth Gonosor asked: "If Bodmiffel does not have a king, what will it have…? Have my people fought to rid themselves of one oppressor to be suddenly oppressed by another…? Long have the Shiremen sought to subdue and suppress these southern lands."

"Not this Shireman!!" Fogle insisted, crossly. He pointed to his compatriots. "And not them either!" And for a moment at least the Lord of Baladorn was stunned by the little man's behaviour.

"We needn't have come this far south, you know. For us the war could have ended after Ribble Bridge, when the Repecians had been cast out of the Shirelands. We chose to come here to help your people unfetter Bodmiffel as they had helped us set free our lands. Gonosor, we came here to liberate not to conquer. We came here to help. And in so doing we would end a petty, pointless war between two countries that are actually one country, and always have been." He paused to catch a breath, before concluding, sadly: "If you don't know that then it has all been for nothing...!"

Eyes turned again to Gonosor. He took a pause before offering up his reply. "Geramond!" he said, softly, before repeating it louder: "Geramond...! Why is the Threeshire so possessed by the ghost of this long dead place...? Geramond means nothing to me or to my people. It never has."

"Then at least let us help," Fogle said.

"Help us to do what?"

"Finish the war. Let us help you free Bosscastle. Only then will Bodmiffel be let go. And if it is decided that, after the war, Gonosor will be king of Bodmiffel, then let it be with a mighty clamour ... not a whimper. Witnessed by all, not the few that are here. And let me witness it then. I would offer my allegiance gladly. Then, I would kneel before a king. But not now. Not like this."

Gonosor stepped away from his people and lowered his face to the side of Fogle's head, and whispered: "Do you know how it feels to be brought up believing that one day you shall inherit a country, and to dream of what you will achieve, only to be denied it at the last moment and given something in its place that you do not desire? Worse than that ... helpless but to observe as that country ... that dream ... is destroyed...?" Fogle lowered his head sadly and shook it. "I am Gonosor of Baladorn!! The son of a dead king and brother to a childless queen. King by right!" He looked upon Fogle with such contempt that his eyes almost spat. "Curse you, Fogle Winnersh! I know what you're scheming!"

Yes, this was the true Gonosor of Baladorn. A man whose fists and brawn did his bidding. And as he pushed Fogle to the ground he towered over him, and put his mighty boot into the side of his writhing body. And such was the impact of the kick that Fogle was turned completely around so that when the little man dared to open his eyes the people he saw were his own: Toggett and Galfall and the others. Just a blur, but he could identify each one.

Another kick. Then another. Fogle was being turned over and over in the dirt. Savage strikes to his guts from the pointed toe of a solid, leather boot. And then blood began to seep from the side of his mouth and he closed his eyes for what he thought was the last time. As his sight was lost his hearing became ever greater. He could hear the grunts of the assaulter as blow followed blow. Heavy, almost excitable breathing to accompany the grunting.

"What should we do?" Galfall asked, fearful and jittery. "What shall we do, Marrock?" He felt sure that Marrock would have the solution, but as he looked to his side he realised that Marrock had gone.

A roar now, like thunder, but continuous. The wind rose again. Not a gradual breeze but an instantaneous gale that ripped through the trees above their heads like someone had put a hole in the sky and burst the world. A screaming, violent wind that went through the trees as though they were not there, disturbing them so much that one clashed into the one next to it, like dragons were fighting and clashing their necks to gain superiority. Huge branches, halves of trees, fell to the ground to send people scattering like seeds in the breeze.

But the roar was not the wind and did not sound like the wind. That was a familiar sound in these parts, this was not. It was like nothing any of them had heard before, and it panicked them and they all shot like horses across a haunted moor. Fogle remained on the ground and rolled himself onto his side to look into the camp fire. For that is where this new, startling clamour seemed to be coming from, as though the fire had been starved of air and now was suddenly breathing it in greedily and ferociously. The top of the fire went as high as the lowest branches of the trees above, and spread into them thereafter and across. The whole of Ingelwitt was engulfed by flame, it seemed, and the forest, so long dark, was as light as a summer morning. The noise of the fire got louder and deafened them all. Then they stopped running for they wanted to look at it to see what was happening.

Flames as high and as mighty as the trees, travelling on the wind then darting down to singe their beards before returning to the sky. The ground beneath their feet was as hot as fading embers, and cooked their toes. But the noise was the worst. Like a thousand screaming souls hanging around their ears. Then, flames swirled in the air, when free of the fire and with lives of their own, poked and burnt their backsides and circled their feet so that none of them could move now if they had attempted to. Mischievous little flames that shot up their trouser legs then back down to scorch their feet, to make every one of them hop and skip on one foot then the other.

Then, as quickly as it had been roused, it was over. The wind eased and the fire shrunk back to what it should have been all along. And all of the rebels were left stricken and scattered, looking at each other in utter bewilderment. Fogle struggled to his feet and looked into the trees and only when he saw the charred and burnt branches did he truly believe that it had happened. Looking all around he saw that the camp had been completely destroyed: littered with burning embers, their tents and shelters flattened.

He was pleased and thankful to see his two friends, Toggett and Galfall coming towards him, side-stepping the smouldering ashes underfoot. The old man's face and beard were covered in soot and dust so that only his yellow teeth and the whites of his eyes could be clearly made out.

"What was it?" asked Galfall.

"I've seen many an odd thing in me long years, but now't like that," added Toggett. "And if I live as long still I doubt that I'll ever see it again...!" And the three were reunited.

It quickly occurred to the Rebel Master that everyone had come together amid the chaos. One integrated group of baffled men, not two or three. Nor could he tell who was a Bodmifflian and who was a Shireman or Tragaran, for all of them were covered in dirt and dust. His eyes searched for Gonosor, but he was dismayed when they found him. However, he looked less threatening covered in dirt, and it did prove that he was just as fallible as the rest of them.

"Fogle Winnersh!" The voice was just as thunderous as ever it was. "What Shire devilry did this...?" A flame had burnt the Bodmifflian's trousers so that one leg was half gone and barely covered his hairy knee.

"I am as baffled as you are," Fogle replied.

A thought suddenly passed through Gonosor's mind.

"It was the Repecians!" he said, his voice risen with a renewed urgency. "We're under attack!!" Louder: "Men of Bodmiffel, come quick and gather around your king...!"

None of them responded. There was movement though, as a pathway opened up amidst them. Along it, having emerged from the forest, came a wolf. Clearly, not an ordinary wolf, for it was as white as snow save for its sullen, flame-red eyes. And it seemed only to have an appetite for Gonosor himself.

"Kill it! Kill it now!!" he looked at Galfall. "Kill it," he repeated, desperately, then sighed as he realised that no-one was going to.

The wolf stopped in front of the Bodmifflian. Everyone else moved out of its way. Gonosor drew his sword from its scabbard but the wolf pounced on him before he'd had chance to use it, and with such force that it pushed him onto his back. As it looked at him with those malevolent eyes, Gonosor squealed like a kitten.

The wolf opened its jaws to reveal its full armoury, and a blood-red tongue slavering between its black teeth, and released a roar so terrifying that there was a collective gasp of horror and men ran away. Fogle watched the eyes; not the wolf's, but Gonosor's: as wide as they could be and glazed with fear while fixed on the beast. Another roar, louder and sharper, more like a scream. And as the wolf lowered its jaw onto the Bodmifflian's face he writhed so much that a wall of dust rose from the ground, and so straight and high that no-one was able to see through or around it.

Screaming and yelps of despair from within the dust. And then they stopped but were replaced by the growling noise the wolf made as it finished its grizzly task. Then that noise ended too. It was over. The deed was done. When the wall of dust settled and the air cleared, Fogle and the others saw a scene ever more distressing than the one they had expected. Not a body half consumed, not even a white wolf covered in blood: an old man, five foot tall with hair as wild as a thorn bush, straddling the casualty and holding his gory tongue in the palm of his hand. Blood dripped down the front of his grey garment, and so thickly that it barely moved.

A murmur; chattering. The old man looked all around him and observed them all. Then he leant forwards and roared like the wolf, so they all stepped back in awe and incomprehension.

Looking to the sky, the old man muttered: "Give me more strength, my lady. I have suffered the worst trial of any of your kind. And I tire of these men. They heed not my will, and yet I would do them no harm. So give me more strength, and more still, for I tire. I tire…!"

And the lady Pannona of Fa-Noodar replied as but a quiet voice in his head: "I alone know what is coming, all of it exactly, for not a single evil can reach me unforeseen. And you must bear the fate allotted to you as best you may, for you cannot fight the will and the want of men. But if you look for the true heart of a man you shall find a thing of great resource and courage. And when you do all will be well beneath the open sky. Your lot, Master Druid, is to win your freedom after countless pains. Until then, what you must ask yourself is, have you less power than they…?!"

The old man stepped away from the body and held the tongue aloft, not afraid to let the blood drip onto his long, white beard.

"This tongue will speak no more of the kings of Bodmiffel. Vile, mindless words of forest dwellers. Nor will any tongue speak of the kings of the Shirelands, or those of Tragara…! Badad will devour them too, if he needs to."

The name was as familiar to them as the taste of water upon their lips, and at once, despite his deed, they were relieved and excitable. Yes, of course this was he. They could see it clearly now; the wild, unfathomable hair, the beard that went down to his knees and his clothes as old and as worn as time itself. Eyes, not flame-red anymore but bright and kindly.

The little Druid stepped onto a rock and was suddenly seen by them all. "Remember Henwen?" he asked. Men nodded but none replied with words. So he repeated his enquiry much louder and firmer and brought out of the Bodmifflians a resounding 'Aye!'

"Remember Vercingoral…?" he asked. The Shiremen, one and all, replied, only louder than the others. "Remember then their love, that was forbidden?" His voice, when raised as it was now, was high-pitched and screechy. "Forbidden because one was the king of the Middle Lands and the other the Queen of the Forests. A love that repulsed those that watched it form, and forbade it thereafter." He looked at the tongue in his hand. "A cruel thing is this that would deny its kin her chance of true being and desire. Badad of Kaw did not forbid this love, and saw it for what it was and what it would yield." Then the old Druid stopped talking and silence prevailed at last over this troubled camp.

Gonosor stirred and turned onto his side. Everyone waited for Badad to finish what he had started but it seemed that his business with Gonosor was done. Instead he ignored him as he groaned and writhed in pain upon the ground, and continued. "I have come back to you now when you need me most," he said, wallowing a little but sincere enough to keep their attention. "And with good tidings at last. At Kaw a union was made once and for all. A union between two warring lands that bore fruit soon after. You have all heard it rumoured, well I can tell you now that it is true. A boy as fair and as pure as the water in the river was conceived. A child born not to be king of the Threeshire or of Bodmiffel but king of all Geramond…! And once we have taken back Bosscastle, Badad will fetch him and show him to you…!"

Fogle moved forward to emerge from the hub of the gathered crowd. When Badad saw him he smiled fondly and stepped down from his rock. "Fogle Winnersh," he chuckled. "A man whose heart is as solid as his belly."

"You are welcome, Badad of Kaw," Fogle said to him, holding his side for it hurt still. "Most welcome. But I must tell you that we have tried and better tried to storm the citadel, without a single speck of success."

"Yes, the founder-fathers built it strong."

"Tell me how we can do it," Fogle asked. "I have tried to think of so many ways but always come back to the most obvious one, that has lost us many fellows."

Badad detected Fogle's deep shame and grief in the tone of his voice, but was benevolent to him with his reply:

"Fret no longer, my fine friend. Badad knows how to do it. But I will not tell you now as you will sleep not for thinking about it. And tonight we must all sleep. Tomorrow we shall take back our fortress." But Fogle, haunted by his own demons, pursued the Druid to provide the answer to a question that had lingered long in his mind. "The Repecians are few but they have the castle well defended. As soon as we get close enough to the walls the Governor unleashes his archers. We are helpless against them."

This time the Druid was quite firm. "Fogle, fret not about things that are done. You must concentrate on what is yet to be accomplished."

"But I have not been a good general, Badad," Fogle said, forlornly and sincerely. "I have made many wrong decisions, that have resulted in …."

Badad put his hand to the little man's mouth. "Dear Fogle, listen," he whispered. "The wind blows still, does it not? There are no souls in this forest that bid you ill. You have shown respect for your dead, and so they for you. Your decisions have brought your army here, and from here the road turns in a new direction."

"But to where?" asked Fogle. "For my own peace of mind I need to know." Badad was quite clear with his answer. "To better things. I am here now. You are not alone anymore."

Galfall emerged from the throng of the crowd. He seemed bothered by something. "Marrock has gone missing," he panted, searching frantically through the faces all around.

"He must be somewhere," Fogle told him.

"Everyone's somewhere, Fogle, you fool," Toggett scoffed, coming by. "But the boy's right … the Tragaran's disappeared."

"What have you done with him?" Galfall grabbed hold of the Druid's robe. "He was beside us until you appeared!"

"Wait a minute," Toggett mused. "When fat Fogle started to kick off with Gonosor, I turned to ask Marrock what we should do to help him. After all, he seemed to have all the answers. But, he wasn't there. I thought he must have crapped himself and done a bunk."

"Not Marrock," Galfall asserted. "Not him."

Badad tugged the sleeve of his gown free of the youngster's grasp. "If you're so sure, master Gringell, go and find him. Search everywhere. Even deep into the forest if you must. Search your heart and you may yet see him again."

With that said, and upon realising that Marrock would not be found while he was standing idly by with the others, Galfall broke away and veered into the darkness of the forest. Fogle made a move to follow him and try to stop him but Badad held him back.

"Ingelwitt holds no fears for a youngster like him," the Druid said.

"Where is Marrock?" Fogle asked, for he knew that the arrival of the little man had something to do with his disappearance.

"Look at me, Fogle," Badad said. "Look at me and look beyond what you see."

So Fogle looked at the old Druid and saw familiar eyes, a familiar face and for a moment at least he saw the Tragaran. It was the shiny eyes that gave him away.

"Then he is still here," he said, quietly, without Toggett hearing.

"There is nothing left here for a man like Marrock," replied Badad. "He was … is … too gentle a soul for the battles that lay ahead. A man can be wise and sound, but those qualities are not what are needed now. Besides, whom would you have by your side, Rebel Master, for you cannot have both."

Fogle smiled.

"Galfall will search all night in vain," Badad replied.

"Never be it said that men with me will live a wasted, dreary life."

"You have been here all along. At the side of the main events."

"Well," said the Druid, almost bashful. "Your intentions are good and your heart is strong, but you don't think I would have let you get this far without keeping an eye on you, do you…?"

"I'm pleased you're here, Badad."

"I'm pleased you're pleased," the Druid replied. "Now, to bed we must all go. Tomorrow we have a castle to take." And louder, to them all: "To sleep, dear friends. To sleep. I am here now. You have seen terrible things, and agonies, many and strange, but nothing that the Lady did not intend."

Galfall searched through the forest until it became too dark and immeasurable. But he did not find his friend Marrock.

Three
The Wanderer at Dawn

The chaos and upset of evening time gave way to a still, windless night, when sleep was had by all. Well, not quite all. The injured were still hurting and could not find peace, and those that tended to them slept only when they were not needed. For Galfall, too, it had been a restless night. Previously, when he had not slept well, it had been because of old Toggett's snoring and hawking; tonight, though, the boy had barely noticed that he was laying next to him. Nor had it been the screeches and the squawks of the creatures of the forest that had troubled him: those noises, now, were as familiar as Toggett's laboured breathing. What troubled him was what was in his mind.

How could he sleep after what had gone on? How could any of them sleep after an evening that had been disturbed, not by an enemy infiltrating their forest lair, but by evil things brought upon themselves. And those that did drowse did not care about any of it, he thought; or were they stronger minded than he was? He asked himself if his restlessness was borne of his fear for the night and what would have come in his dreams. Had he closed his eyes and settled into slumber, would he have seen his father again? This night, of all nights, he surely would have, and that is why he fought to stay awake. He did not want to see him again, not like he was. His father was long dead, and so his presence at the camp, at his son's bedside, was not right, in fact, quite wrong. When Fogle had told him that he too had seen Wilfren, he was reassured that he had not been the only one that had, and was not going mad after all. These were strange times, and the line between sanity and insanity was faint. If Galfall was mad then Fogle was too. And Fogle, tonight, had demonstrated that he was quite sane, and as brave and resolute as he'd always been.

He had, however, settled into his bed with the intention of going to sleep. Toggett was close by and Fogle not too far away either, and if nothing else then he was warm in his bed beneath his heavy, fur blanket. He had scrunched up his eyes and willed his mind to drift into dreams; tossed and turned until he was comfortable, then decided that he was not comfortable at all, and turned back the other way. And, at some point through the night, he must have gone to sleep, for he could not recall being awake. It was not for long, for the moment he felt his eyes were drowsy, the next they were as wide and as alert as an owl's, looking all around at the men lying nearby and at their foul, distorted faces and their slobbering mouths.

"Enough," he eventually told himself, and threw back his blanket and took himself off into the night.

It seemed to take an age for the dawn to break, and when it did it brought with it a stinging wind from the sea. He had walked through Ingelwitt not quite knowing where he was going and did not care, until he found himself at its edge where the trees were sparse, looking across the valley to Bosscastle. He had found a log and had sat on the ground and rested his back and neck against it. It had been so long on the ground that it was quite soft and offered a comfortable cushion as he gazed at the fortress at the far side of the valley. But he was cold, very cold indeed, and wished that he'd brought his blanket along. He'd be snug, then, and safe, and the others could have done what they wished, so long as they'd left him here. As he was, shivering and scrunched into a ball to keep warm, he would not be able to stay here for very long and would soon have to think about going back to the camp, where at least there was a fire.

"Ah, Bosscastle at dawn! The finest sight a man could wish to see. A view made by the Gods, for their own eyes, but offered to us as we're the only ones awake to see it." Galfall flinched and looked up to see the Druid sitting on the end of the log, and coiled further away. "A thousand times I have seen this place at this time of the day, and yet it's like this is the first. Privileged, then, you and I, to see such a thing as this." The Druid paused and looked hard at the youngster. "And yet, your eyes are filled not with wonder, but with sorrow and pain. What is it in your mind that brings you to this place and then not be in awe of it?"

Galfall knew his answer, but dare not give it. The Druid looked fearsome; his hair was wild and uncontrollable and his beard was the longest he had ever seen. A small man, yes, but with a presence befitting a giant. He had silenced the troublesome Gonosor of Baladorn, so what chance did he have? Then he decided that whatever the Druid intended to do, however he hurt him, he would not feel any worse than he already did, and decided to give his answer, whether the old man wanted to hear it or not. "When I look at Bosscastle, I feel nothing but contempt for the evil that exists within its walls." He had said it, and was glad that he had.

"It's the folk within that're filled with evil," Badad replied, but in a calmer manner than the youngster was expecting and preparing for. "The ancient stones bear no wickedness, and never shall."

"Bosscastle is the stronghold of the Repecians," Galfall insisted.

"But if it is lost to them, then we too are lost. Bosscastle, noble, irrepressible Bosscastle is the representation of everything that we are! As much a slave to the conquerors as us all! And there are good people within, as well as vile people, that we must liberate before this war is done. People like you and Fogle and the others, who have done no harm and want nothing more than to be free."

"Traitors and turncoats, I'd call them," replied Galfall.

"I'd call them servants and survivors, those that remain with breath in their lungs!" Badad eased himself off the log to stand on his feet, and now Galfall realised how short and insignificant he was. He approached the youth, and was barely as tall as his shoulders. "Those that have survived within Bosscastle, and have served the Governor and attended to his whims, deserve to be free and to smile again, as much as you do, for they are all born of this land, and hold it within their hearts! They know, and have always known, that the day would come when wrongs are set right, and evil is repelled once and for all …!"

"Will such a day ever come?"

"Oh, that it will, my boy," replied Badad, filled with joy and enthusiasm. "And what a beautiful dawn will bring it in, as lovely as the one we have now, but calmer and warmer, like winter had never been and the snow had never fallen. When bells will toll and birds will sing; like a sound that has never been heard, and folks will listen and be joyous at last." Badad looked across the valley towards the old citadel. "That day is close, Galfall. I can feel it swilling in my blood."

The birds, even now, were singing, but it was not a pleasant sound, for it meant that the morning had begun and that soon the others would be awake and on their feet. Fogle and Toggett would soon be searching for the youth, but he did not want to be found. Nor did he wish to be here anymore, in the company of the frenzied, aged Druid. He wished for nothing more than to be on his own; to feel the breeze in his hair and see his breath bellowing before him as he ran, as far away from this place as possible. To find a place where wars were not being waged and feckless battles were not being fought; and blood remained in veins and not spilt onto the ground like it was worthless. Home was such a place, and he longed for it now more than ever. From here, on the edge of Ingelwitt, it seemed such an ideal place to be, and he turned on his heels several times until he was facing the opposite direction.

"I must be going," said Galfall hesitantly, half looking at the Druid. "They'll be wondering where I am."

"Will they?" Badad asked, coming towards the youth. "Will any of them have noticed that you're not there? In fact, would any one miss you if you vanished completely?"

It was a strange question and Galfall was alarmed by it, for he knew not the intent with which it was asked. He looked at the Druid's face for a clue, but it was covered by a beard as high as the cheekbones, so that only his eyes were visible in this pale morning light, and they were giving nothing away. This, he was sure, was the man responsible for Marrock's sudden disappearance, and had certainly grappled with Gonosor despite being twice as old and only half his size. What chance, then, did he have? But the Druid's strange question was nothing more than a stalling device to stop Galfall heading back to the camp, for he had not yet done with him here. It was a question that had no intent and was uttered simply because the Druid could not think of anything else to say.

"Why could you not sleep, Galfall?"

"Nothing is achieved in dreams," he replied.

"Nothing, either, by a tired mind and body," said the Druid. "Later, when the others are awake and lively, you will be wearisome and of no use to anyone." He was standing close to the youngster now, and placed his hand on his forearm. "And frozen to death, unless you find warmth. Come, Galfall, and sit with with me for a while. The day has not yet broken this wondrous dawn and we have much to discuss as we gaze out at the mighty Bosscastle."

Badad set off walking back towards the log, but Galfall had no inclination to go with him. He turned his head away defiantly, but when he turned it back again he saw a fire burning and cracking as though it had been going all night, with the old man sitting on the log and holding his hands over it. It was certainly inviting, with high flames and a comforting glow that seemed to draw the youngster to it. An instant fire, though, ignited by sorcery, with the sorcerer guarding it and drawing heat from it, like fire belonged to him. "Come and warm yourself, boy," said the Druid, patting the log next to him.

"Fogle and Toggett, they would miss me if I vanished," Galfall said, reaching the log and resting against it, but far enough away to be out of the old man's reach. "And would come looking for me if I did not return. I reckon they'll already be searching the camp and calling my name."

Badad laughed, genuinely delighted by the boy's assertion. "You have no need to fear me, Galfall," he said. "I am your friend."

"I have no friends, nor desire them."

"Marrock was such a man to you. But now he has gone, and you are sorry for yourself."

"I'm sorry not for myself but for Marrock," Galfall replied instantly, for the reply was hovering on the tip of his tongue. "I think that harm has come to him. He would not have disappeared into the night without telling me where he was going or saying goodbye. Something bad has happened to him. I know it."

"And you believe me to be responsible, don't you?"

Now Galfall did hesitate. It was one thing to assume that this was the case, the thought was harmless, but another thing entirely to lay his opinion on the breeze, for the Druid to hear. However, the fact remained that Marrock had gone, and it outweighed any reservations the youngster may have had about offering an accusation. "One moment he was there, the next he was gone, and as far as I can see, the only thing in between was you, arriving like you did, with your tricks and wizardry."

"That does not mean that I killed Marrock," Badad replied, in a tone that was almost defensive.

"You grappled with Gonosor, and look what happened to him. He lost his tongue!"

Now the Druid was growing angry. And as his anger rose so too did the flames of his fire.

"A lament for Marrock is one thing, he was kindly and mild, but Gonosor's tongue…! I can't believe that any man would grieve at the loss of such a vile thing as that…! And by taking it Fogle's life was spared. A strange, dithering Druid this, that saves the life of one patriot only to take it from another!"

The Druid was right. What he had said made good sense, but that did not answer the puzzle of Marrock's disappearance. Badad, sensing that the youngster was satisfied with his reply, forced back his anger and it subsided, as did the flames.

"The fire obeys you, old man," said Galfall. "You commanded it last night, too."

"What I did last night I did for good reason," Badad replied. "This war is following its natural course, but sometimes fate needs a nudge."

Galfall moved up the log to get closer to the fire, and thus, closer to the Druid, and scrutinised him closely. Here was an aged man of a slight build, with hair as grey as the sea and a beard so long and shabby that he wondered if it had ever been groomed. His clothes were stained and torn in places and his hands seemed to be crippled with elderliness. Yet here too was a powerful man, for he had subdued Gonosor and brought peace to the camp where before there had been only discord.

"Who are you?" he asked.

Again, Badad tittered.

"There was a time when that would have been a foolish question. When every man knew of me and feared me hence." He looked at the youngster and his eyes shone like clear water. "Now, I am a relic of a lost age. The last of my order and the last of my kind."

"Your kind?" quizzed Galfall.

"The Wandering Druids!" The old man held out his hand and the flames came higher to give out more warmth. He seemed saddened and troubled now. "All things must change as time goes on, and things that were are no more. Men of faith and wisdom have been replaced by men of strength but little else, and those that had both strength and wisdom are lost." He looked directly at the youngster to conclude: "Gonosor, possessing knowledge and reason, would have been as great as any ancient king, and our island may never have been conquered and our ways of living not forbidden and lost. But he chose a path that served only his own selfish needs, and dared to call himself the King of Bodmiffel, when such a place no longer exists, and never can again if Geramond is to be reborn. He speaks not of Bodmiffel now, and those that followed him shall retreat into the darkness of the forest whence they came. And yet, had I not arrived when I did, and silenced him forever, your friend Fogle would surely be dead, and Gonosor of Baladorn more powerful than even he could have imagined."

"Fogle thinks that we have done enough," Galfall said, "That Geramond is free and that we should return to the Threeshire and back to the lives we knew."

Badad was provoked to anger at the statement. "And back to Tragara and Bodmiffel, so that Geramond is forsaken again! No, there can be no going back until the job begun by him is finished."

"I told him that."

"It will not be finished until Bosscastle is taken back, and our oppressors are vanquished for good."

"I told him that too," Galfall replied, excitedly, for at last the Druid seemed less threatening and spoke like he was of the same mind as he was.

"Fogle does not understand," Badad continued, scratching his chin through the dense beard. "He is a good man, yes, but not wise to the motive of this war. A war of liberation, of course. To unshackle the irons of Repecian tyranny; but in so doing we must use the ending of the war to end wars between ourselves, so that we are released from the grip of wickedness for all time."

He had a skill, the youngster noticed, of making extraordinary assertions while at the same time undertaking chores that were ordinary, and he scratched at his beard now as though something was crawling within the hairs. Galfall should have been paying attention to the Druid's assertions, but so enthralled was he by the intensity of the old man's itch that he momentarily ignored what he was saying to study his reaction to it. The itch moved upwards, it seemed, and the decrepit hand went with it, and slapped on whatever it was that was irritating. Concentrating hard, Galfall was sure that he had seen a flee or something like a flee jump out of the hairs and onto the old man's sleeve, and stared at the sleeve to try to see it again, while leaning away in case it decided to leap onto him. "He does not understand," the Druid insisted, straightening his beard now that the itch had been dealt with. "If he were here now, do you know what he would see?"

Galfall applied himself to the question, then realised that he was not supposed to give an answer, but shake his head and wait for the Druid to offer his own. "He'd see a castle that has defied him, and feel nothing but hatred for it, and a longing to tear it down. Don't blame him for that, Galfall, for he does not understand." He leaned closer. "You understand, though. You know what Bosscastle is, and of its beginnings."

"I'm just a farmer's boy from the Threeshire. How could I know of such things…?"

"Because you can feel them swirling in your blood. Stirrings of destiny, I'd say, that have brought you here this morning when you should be at sleep, to look upon the stones and see them as blocks of gold set against the glowing dawn. Tell me, then, that you do not look upon Bosscastle and see what I see, and hear ancient words on the breeze as I hear them."

"I see nothing but the Governor's fortress, and wait for the day when it is flattened," Galfall replied defiantly. Badad was not convinced by the youngster's stubbornness.

"No, Galfall, you must open your eyes and your mind and see what is before you, and marvel at it. Bosscastle is before you, and it is drawing you in."

Galfall rose from the log and stepped away from the fire. He seemed troubled. "I do see it. The Governor has no right to it."

"The Governor is a thief, then…?"

"Yes, he is that."

"And the castle enslaved, as we were?"

"We have tried so many times to take it back," the youngster replied, so eager to speak that his words stumbled from his mouth.

"We have failed every time."

Badad smiled. It seemed a strange time to smile, but then the Druid was anything but a conformist to the etiquette of war and troubled times.

"Fillian did well to chose our Bosscastle as his stronghold, for her walls and turrets are not so easily breached, and it takes a stronger army than Fogle's to do it." His smile turned quickly to a titter and then a chuckle, as though he was almost proud that Bosscastle had withstood the blockade and any attempt to bring her down thereafter. "Oh, how many armies have I seen encamped on the edge of this venerable forest! Too many to recollect, I think. Hordes of Shiremen, with every king new to his throne." He laughed again. "Forest kings looked down upon them all and mocked their sieges and waited for them to slacken and recede towards the northern road whence they came. Frustration and depression did befall those of old, as it does our own Fogle now."

With these words, Galfall examined the Druid again, and saw that his face was ragged and wrinkled. He wondered how old he was, for the times he talked of were of generations long gone and almost forgotten. Suddenly, it occurred to him that this might be a phantom of those days. A wraith come to torment him and cause him distress. He had, after all, seen one ghost whilst in this forest, and having looked at him the more he convinced himself that the old man was long dead. His skin was entirely without colour; strangely pallid and clinging to the bones as though it had been stretched over them like a mask.

"You are not real," he muttered to himself, and backed further away. "Be gone, you foul thing, and leave me in peace." To himself:

"I am not seeing you," and covered his eyes with his cold hands to make him disappear.

Badad was puzzled by Galfall's behaviour, and stood himself up to step closer to him. "What is it you see?"

Galfall uncovered his eyes. "I see you!" he blasted. "I don't want to see you!"

"Be calm, boy." Badad took hold of him and held him tightly in his arms. Galfall screamed and convulsed his body to be free of him, but Badad was the stronger. Exhausted, he stopped wriggling, and simply slid from the Druid's grip to lay upon the damp ground. "What has this war done to you, I wonder?" the old man asked, looking upon the youth. Then he helped him back to his feet and walked him to the fire.

"I am touching you."

"Of course you are. I am helping you."

Galfall paused to think. "Then you are not a spirit?"

"No, I am not a spirit," the Druid replied. "I may look like one, but I am as solid and real as you are, my boy." He sat him on the ground against the log and brought the fire to his feet to warm him through. "But you will be a ghostly sight unless you rest."

He drifted quickly to sleep. An easy sleep brought on by exhaustion and cold. Badad stayed with him and sat beside him by the fire, and breathed happily now that he was resting at last, and had reassured him that he would still be there when he woke. Now was the old man's turn to study the youngster; to look at him thoroughly and take him in; and survey his frame and his features to determine whether he was strong and bold. He had a slight, willowy physique, the Druid noticed, but strength also, in his legs and arms. The agility and speed of a spring hare, he thought, rather than the robustness of a forest boar. His face was tense and restrained and nothing exceptional, and his hair was disarranged and down to his shoulders. But the eyes, that were now closed, had been scrutinised earlier, and had revealed a spirit and intensity that only youthful eyes possess.

"Good, then," said Badad quietly, and took his gaze away.

He looked then across the valley towards the castle, and beyond to the Bodmiffel coast winding into the distance. The sun was rising from behind wooded hills that the Druid took to be in the region of Bossiney; that cast its streaks of flame across the tops of the trees to enchant them and thaw them from their nightly frost. And across the sea, too, to form a golden tarn within the icy, grey waters; a haven of tenderness in an unforgiving sea. A cheery and peaceful morning, then, but he knew that the early sun was weak and defenceless against the cruel winter, and would not last for long before it was lost again to the dismal clouds.

For now, though, Bosscastle was resplendent, and wallowing in the dawn. There could be nothing corrupt and sinful about it in this light. Badad looked upon it and smiled fondly and remembered all the times he had seen it, in all the seasons, but never looking so beguiling as it did now. He marvelled again at the high, unbreakable walls and her towers, higher still. Birds, that were black against the pale blue sky, disappeared when they flew beside the Keep, as though it possessed a mouth and had devoured them. He watched to see them fly away from the black Keep to be seen again, but they were not.

The youngster was sleeping so soundly that his head had tilted to one side and was resting against the log; one leg was stretched out against the fire while the other was folded underneath and dropped to the side. His eyes were flickering and every now and again his arm jolted and his hand was thumped against the ground. His dream disturbed him. Badad's attention was drawn away from the view, and he looked upon him and wondered what or where or whom his visions were showing him.

"Many a troubled thing that hover about men when awake, while in sleep are a thousand fold and move themselves to haunt and bring sorrow and fear." He edged closer. Galfall was mumbling something now, but he could not fathom what. "Murmurs of fear, I think," he said. Then he stretched out his hand to hover above the fire, without burning it. "Come nigh and show us where foot of man comes not, and lay bare your rule for men to see, to bring forth shape to fearful brows, and in your realm honesty is beholden to thy." Then he pulled back his hand and waited. Suddenly, the greyish-black smoke turned denser and seemed to be compressed in the air so that it spread out away from its source, and separated into dozens of parts so that it looked like a tree stump with branches coming from it. Except that this was smoke and behaved accordingly, twisting and contorting constantly, not by the breeze but something more powerful, that commanded it and moulded it into shapes. And the more tangled and elaborate it became, the more Galfall became restless and called out in his sleep and his body shook as though someone, or something was moving it.

Badad rose and stepped back to observe the smoke, taking his eyes off it only to check on the youngster. The view, the lovely dawn sunshine, was gone. In any case, it was not important now. So he watched, entranced as each individual plume twisted and wrenched ever more until a figure of a man was formed within them; and so exquisitely moulded that each man was given a face and a frame to make them almost real and recognisable. There were about a dozen of these shapes at first, six appearing from either side of the fire. Badad concentrated all of his attention on to them, and saw that these were, indeed, real men, and could easily see that Fogle was amongst them, and Toggett and Marrock, Gonosor, Gringell and Galfall himself, whose dream this was.

The other six were not familiar but wore armour, so the Druid took them to be Repecians. Then the twelve swirls swept down upon each other and clashed violently and fought a battle for the Druid to see. He glanced briefly at Galfall, who was twisting and turning and lashing at the air with his hand as though he was wielding a sword. In his dream, of course, that is exactly what he was doing. The smoke merged to form one, dense plume, and Badad wondered if this was the end of it. It was not, for it segmented itself again, this time to form two parts: one was Gringell laying upon the ground, and the other showed Galfall, watching from a distance; looking on helplessly at his father writhing in agony and torment, his throat slashed and his life ebbing away. Gringell's body fell still, Galfall slipped away and suddenly the vision ended and the smoke swooned back to its fire.

Galfall woke with a start as his head shook his eyes awake, and it took him a little while to remember where he was, why he was here. Realising that he was a little too close to the fire to be comfortable, he edged away.

"You're still here then?" he said, looking at the Druid through his fingers as he rubbed his face, and in a tone that suggested that he wished he was not. Badad, though, knew that he was.

"I told you I would be."

"How long have I been asleep?"

"Long enough to drift into dream. Not a restful sleep, my boy. I have watched you all the while. You were agitated. You were mumbling." Slightly cautious, the youngster asked:

"What was I saying?"

"Your father's name, over and over." The Druid approached him carefully, for he knew that he was haunted still by his dream, and was upset by it. "Wilfren, that was your father's name, yes? I never met him, but have seen him … fleetingly. They tell me he was a great man. A man of his people."

Galfall rose to stretch his aching legs. "He was a farmer. A man best used to beasts then people."

"Last night Fogle told me how much he'd missed him since his death on the outskirts of Tangelwitt."

"Yes, he was a man of his people. It's just his sons that he struggled with," Galfall retorted, running his fingers through his hair and hoping that the Druid did not pursue the matter.

"He must have been proud to have had a son like you."

Now Galfall tittered, more with sadness than genuine amusement. "If he was, he never told me."

"You are the youngest here, Galfall, and the bravest, I'd wager."

The youngster turned sharply. "Then you don't know what you're talking about, old man," he snapped. "I am not brave. I am a fool. A fool to have ever come here."

"Then why did you?"

He did not have to think very hard to find the reason. "Because he told me that I shouldn't! Couldn't!" A pause. "That if I did, he'd see to it that I wished that I hadn't."

"You came to this place of death to defy him, then?"

"I did. But if he'd told me to come then I would not have."

Badad stepped closer to him so that their shoulders almost touched. "A fateful day that brought you to this war." So close that when he spoke Galfall could feel his foul breath sweep over him. "A war that has brought you here."

"Why shouldn't I have come? I am old enough to fight."

"But not old enough to die, Galfall. Perhaps, then, your father was merely protecting you by forbidding you to follow him. Wars should not be fought by men with lives to live, and death should befall those who are prepared for it and have accepted it."

"I am prepared for it," Galfall protested angrily, assuming that the Druid was in some way disapproving of him being here. He was not. "I would die for this cause."

"Cause, you say?"

"Geramond ... liberty. And I would fight any man that opposed that cause."

"But would you?" the Druid quizzed. "You say you came here to defy your father ... which has nothing to do with the purpose of this war."

Galfall replied immediately. "And to fight Repecians. I loathe them as much as any man."

The Druid stepped away. After a pause, he turned.

"Why then did you keep yourself hidden?" The youngster was shamefaced. "And cower in the shadows to screen yourself from harm. For that was the way of it, was it not? You followed the rebels from safe distances, and played no part in the war until Tangelwitt, and only when the battle was won did you reveal your presence, when death was done and danger gave way to the giddiness of victory."

"NO!"

"You're right to say that you're not brave, Galfall." The old man's voice was risen in anger. "Coward, then, is a word best given to you! You say that you came here to defy your father, and yet he died without knowing that you had done so...!"

Galfall, too, was burning with rage, for he knew that the old man was wrong. "He did know!" he blasted, throwing his arms into the air. "He saw me."

"When?"

He paused, unsure of whether to give his answer. He decided to give it anyway, but spoke quietly, half in shame and half gloatingly, and decided that he did not care for the Druid's opinions of him after all.

"While he lay dying. Fogle was holding him. I had been watching him fight. He fought bravely, like he was fearless. I asked myself, what must he be thinking, and if he was thinking of me at all. Thinking of my brother, more than likely, and my mother, but not of me."

"You were his son, too. His first son at that."

The siege of the castle, that had gone on for two harsh, winter months, had been so relentless and pivotal that Galfall had almost forgotten about the earlier parts of the war. He had grown close to Fogle and Toggett, and had therefore been privy to the more significant decisions. Fogle had told him of his idea to attack the gatehouse before anyone else, and had even demanded an opinion out of him. But now, the Druid had cruelly reminded him of the reality, and shattered with one brief statement all of the delusions he had about himself. He was not privileged or important at all. Men did not admire him or adhere to his word. He was a child in their eyes, who needed their protection, and to be shielded from the most vile aspects of the war. And his closeness to Fogle was due to the fact that he was Wilfren's son, and had, in a strange way, replaced his father and had become his stand-in in his absence.

Very quickly, like sand through an hour-glass, he began to realise this, and his shame turned to self-pity and he wished that he had never come here. He brought to his mind how he had come to be here, and consequently his remorse deepened and tears welled in his eyes as his memory took him home.

"After Fogle's Field," he began, "my father returned home briefly to tell my mother that he was coming south with the others to start the war. She pleaded with him to stay, but she knew in her heart that he was leaving and he kissed her as though he was never coming back," he turned to look at the Druid. "As though he'd seen his own fate." And the Druid nodded to acknowledge the comment and the existence of such visions. "Then he brought my brother close to him and held him tightly and told him to keep watch on the farm and to fend for my mother, for she was slight of build and not strong enough to fend for herself. He said … 'I am depending on you to keep things as they are and should always be,' … then touched his head and left the house."

"And what did he say to you?"

"I was standing in the doorway and as he passed he took hold of my arm and pulled me out with him. He looked at me, and I noticed that his face had hardened and his eyes were like stones ..."

"What did he say, Galfall?"

The youngster's reply, though on the tip of his tongue, was stubbornly refusing to be uttered. Taking a sharp intake of cold, morning air, he forced it out, and spoke with a crack in his voice.

"He said ... 'don't be a burden to them.' And that's all he said, and then he set off towards the lane."

"And he hurt you with his words?"

"I shouted after him 'I'm coming with you!' As he turned, I grew afraid, but did not move. He told me that war was for men and that I was far from being one of those." A pause. "If he'd said that I was needed at home, to tend to the farm and if he'd said to me what he had said to my brother, then I would have stayed at home and done those things, and done them well. But he did not and had not intended to." He paused again to rub his eye, in a way to suggest that it was irritable rather than weeping. His face was red; flushed with rage and a certain level of awkwardness. The Druid felt sorry for him, for it had not been his intention to embarrass him or make him upset, and he certainly was not expecting him to have tears. He moved away from him and went back to the log, leaving the youngster alone to dwell on his memories.

Galfall lowered himself to the ground so that he was crouched like a frog, with his arms resting on his knees and his clenched hands supporting his head. "I wanted to prove to him that he was wrong," he continued. "That I was a man, and old enough to fight in the war, and show him how brave I could be .... and that I no longer feared him. I wanted to show him that more than anything else. So I set off from the farm the following day, and went to Woldark ... I figured that the rebels would meet there and come south on the old road, through Windell. By the time I got there they'd left, so I followed them, and finally caught up with them at the Ribble Bridge."

"A great victory was had there," the Druid mused, listening attentively and frowned angrily when he realised that he had interrupted.

"I watched the battle from the top of a hill. I hid behind a rock. I can remember that day so well. It was cold, but bright, like today. The rebels seemed so inadequate compared to the Repecians ... disorganised ... more like a protest than an army. And so disorganised that I couldn't tell whether they had more soldiers than the Repecians." He stopped and started to chuckle, and looked at Badad to see if he was amused too. He was not.

"Soldiers! They were hardly that. Poor, lost fellows, who had no idea what they were doing, or why they were there at all."

"They all had their own reasons for being there," Badad replied, slightly affronted by the youngster's apparent ignorance. "Fogle had lost his son ... others, who had not paid their taxes feared the same, terrible fate as Callarn." He leant forwards to emphasise his point. "All of them with a burning in their bellies that nagged at them to change what they thought could never be changed." He leaned back again. "A man will stay suppressed for only so long before he strikes a blow."

"I remember the noise," said Galfall. "Men screaming at the top of their voices, but I had no idea what they were saying, and I don't suppose they knew themselves. The Repecians just stood there and waited quietly. Yes, I remember that." Closing his eyes tightly, it was like he was transported back to Ribble Bridge, such was the clarity of his recollections. "Then it started. The noise dimmed. Strange that. You'd have thought that it would have got louder. A clatter of metal, though. And screams. Lots of screams. I watched my father fight, and saw him kill at least six of them, without getting wounded himself." He scrunched his eyes shut even tighter, and his face became contorted. "Take a blow. Take a blow."

He collapsed onto his backside, held his head in his hands and scraped at his hair as though Badad's fleas had infested it. Harder and harder he tore at his scalp with his fingers, all the while with his eyes shut and his body rocking forwards then back.

"Take a blow," he repeated, then louder: "Die!" Badad was bewildered by the youngster's behaviour, and by what he was saying.

"Galfall," he said, quite calmly. "Galfall." When he looked at him the Druid saw that his eyes were as red as berries and tears were rolling down his face. "You must not relive old battles or be haunted by what's gone. It is to things yet to pass that you must turn your mind." But that was not going to be straight forward, the old man realised, for what he saw before him was not the strong and solid youth he had taken him to be, but a quivering child, chilled to his core by the sight and sounds of the war. "Many victims," Badad muttered, ensuring the youth could not hear. "And in many ways. None so cruel as the wound inflicted on you."

"Don't you see? I wanted my father to be killed. And I should not have thought like that, should I?"

"Days such as these affect us all in different ways," Badad replied, trying his hardest to offer him comfort

"But I wanted him to die!" Galfall repeated. It was as though he wanted to be punished for allowing such thoughts to infiltrate his mind. The Druid could not punish him more than he was now punishing himself. "I was sitting there, behind my rock on my safe hill, and I was willing him to be struck by a sword or run through with a spear ... anything would have done. How could I have wished for such terrible things?"

"But he did not die."

"No, not there anyway. I was disappointed. If he had ... died ... then I would have gone down from my hill and joined them then. How could I now, with my mind filled with such hatred? So I followed them as they travelled further south, over the mountains into Bodmiffel. I had always wanted to see Bodmiffel. I'd heard so much about it. Oh, I'd seen trees, of course ... our lovely woods and spinneys .... but I'd never seen forests as vast as Tangelwitt or Ingelwitt." He dried his tears. "They turned out to be not such magical places. Dark, wicked places, I'd say. I watched the battle of Tangelwitt from a tree. I watched my father fight as I had done at Ribble. I thought, if he survives, then I will reveal myself and perhaps he will be pleased that I had come after all."

"And he did not survive."

"He nearly did. Towards the end of the battle, almost as the Repecians were retreating, he was stabbed in the throat. I suppose I should have been pleased to see it. But I was not. I swear I was not." Old tears were dried, but new ones were coming. "But I did want him to see that I was here. Fogle was holding him and comforting him. He looked at me, and tried to say something. He couldn't of course, so I never knew what it was." He had been staring intently at the ground, but he raised his head to look at the Druid. "What do you think it could have been that he wanted to say?"

It was impossible for Badad to give an answer, so he simply shook his head and said, "Whatever you wanted it to be."

Galfall smiled and dried away his tears on his sleeve so that they could not return. "He'd have been pleased that I was here."

"Well then, leave it at that, my boy. And on your feet, for the dawn is done and day has come at last." When he finally bothered to notice, day had indeed broken and the thicket was awash with sunlight. The fire seemed less comforting but a bitter breeze sweeping inland from the sea meant that it was not altogether redundant. Badad was stoking it with a stick, a purposeless undertaking for a fire conjurer, the youngster thought, as he came towards it himself to warm his backside after sitting on the damp ground. "I suppose we'd better be heading back to camp," he said, in a gloomy way, but he was not entirely sorry that his time here was done, for his dream and recollections had upset him and now he felt foolish for having wept in front of the Druid.

"Give them time to wake, Galfall, for there are things that must be discussed still."

Galfall was puzzled. Surely everything had been said, and he was tired with talking about himself; about anything.

What things?" he asked.

Badad tossed his stick into the undergrowth. "I must confess … I did not stumble across you this morning, but watched you leave the camp and followed you here."

"Why?"

"You have given your reasons for coming to the war, and I don't doubt that you believe them to be true. But I would say that fate has played a part, too, my young friend. Fate has a role for you to take in all of this business of rebellion and freedom fighting. A very important role at that. Which is why you have been sheltered from harm thus far, for your time has come, Galfall."

"Time for what?"

"To break Bosscastle."

At this Galfall chortled. These, surely, were the rants of a deranged old man. And after he had stopped chortling, he was saddened to think of Badad in such a way, and had hoped for better from him. He remembered how happy Fogle had been to see him and how his arrival at the camp had had the effect of calming them all after the turbulence of his initial appearance. Now, though, he was talking nonsense. Bosscastle was unbreakable, and by his tears and outbursts, Galfall had proven himself to be nothing more than what people thought of him: a boy that ought not to be here; lost in their ugly world. Badad, though, was not laughing, and looked perfectly earnest.

"We have tried so many times, and every one has failed."

"But if I told you that it can be done," Badad replied. "And how to do it ... would you...? Or has fate presented me with a fake and artificial champion...?"

Galfall, realising that the old fool was serious, addressed his mind to the question. He gave an honest answer. "I don't know if I could. Strong enough, I mean ... brave enough to do it."

"I would not expect you to do it alone, of course," Badad told him, and twisted his aged body to look into the trees behind him.

Out of the darkness of the forest, emerged Gonosor. Galfall, fearful of him still, backed away. "Do not be alarmed, my boy. He is quite harmless now. Docile you might say. But his strength has not left him." The Bodmifflian looked to be in surprisingly good health, despite his ordeal at the hands of the Druid only the night before. And, like Badad had said, he looked as mighty and fearsome as ever, and when he stopped next to the old man, it was like a pillar of stone set against a twig.

"He is bewitched," Galfall protested.

"He is subdued," Badad retorted snappily. "A servant of Geramond at last."

"Your servant, you mean," said the youngster.

"The servant of whomever possesses this." Badad's hand delved into his gown. When it emerged it was clutching the Bodmiflian's tongue; torn from his head the previous night. He offered it to Galfall, but he resisted it. "If you have it, he will follow you wherever you venture and do everything he can to protect you. But be careful with it, for should he ever get it back then the Gonosor whom you fear will return."

Galfall was disgusted, and turned his head away from the sight of the bloody organ in the Druid's hand. Blood, still fresh, was dripping from it and settling in a pool upon the ground.

"I don't want it. Put it away. Get rid of it."

"He can be your strength, Galfall. He can take you where you need to go. Once there, a deed will be done that will bring about an end to this war."

"I'm going back to the camp," insisted the youth, turning with the intention of leaving.

"Gonosor can take you into Bosscastle. But you must first learn to trust him, and not tremble in his presence." Curiosity compelled Galfall to stay.

"How?"

"I shall tell you how. Gonosor can show you."

"It's impossible."

Badad placed his bony hand on his shoulder. "But if it were possible ... would you go?" A pause for thought. He looked at Gonosor and his eyes in particular and saw that they were colourless and idle. Then he looked across the valley towards the fortress, and wondered if it was possible to breach it after all. If it was, then was he the one that was going to do it? "Hold out your hand," said Badad. Galfall, lost in contemplation, did as he was instructed. The tongue was placed in his hand, but instead of being repulsed, he held it confidently, like it was nothing more than a rock.

"If I am to do it, then I must leave now, for if I see Fogle and the others they will surely persuade me to stay, and then it will never be done."

The Druid sighed happily and a smile spread across his wrinkled face, that turned quickly to a laugh. He grabbed hold of the youngster's wrist, then Gonosor's with his other hand, and the three of them were linked.

"Son of Threeshire," he said, looking at the youth. He turned to look at Gonosor. "Prince of Bodmiffel." Looking forward, across the valley, he said calmly: "Well then. Let it be done."

Four

Kanance's Cove

At his own request, Galfall did not return to the camp that day. Instead, at noon, he and Gonosor embarked on their journey, with the Druid's assurance that he would explain to Fogle and Toggett where he had gone and for what purpose. They travelled along the coast road for about a mile, then left to follow the dirt lane that rimmed the far side of the valley; went down into the valley once they were past the castle, and up the other side to rejoin the coast road as it meandered and dipped towards the harbour at Bossiney.

Galfall was uneasy about taking this route, and argued that it would have been much wiser to stay amidst the trees of Ingelwitt until they were clear of the citadel's lookout towers. As it was they were like startled deer abandoning the safety of the forest to put themselves at the hunter's mercy. He had asked Gonosor where they were going and if there was another way to get there. Then he realised that he was asking questions of a man whose tongue he held in the leather pouch hanging from his belt, and spoke no more. The Bodmifflian certainly seemed to know where he was going and walked with mighty strides and a hearty desire to get there before dusk. Galfall, somewhat powerless, had no option but to follow him and hope to be safe. It took two of his strides to Gonosor's one just to keep up, so that he was almost running.

Five miles up the coast from Bosscastle, so its towers were barely visible, the drop towards the great harbour marked the final section of the old road. From here, there were no more roads, no tracks or lanes, for they were no use here. Just water; a huge expanse of water enclosed within hills that rolled to mountains in the distance. The opening to the sea was narrow; the tips of the land almost touched, to defy it so that it had to force itself in and send waves crashing over the rocks. However, Bossiney was a peaceful place, where the water calmed as it encroached on the land further in, to gently kiss the shingle beach. There was no activity in the harbour at all. Not like it used to be. There was a time, not too long ago to be forgotten, when boats and ships were seen here. Gonosor could remember. As a child he used to sit on the slopes of the Howe Hill and watch them come and go. Vessels bringing goods from the west, but mostly fishing boats, coming back with a haul and trailing clouds of scavengers behind them. He closed his eyes and he could almost hear the gulls again. They were still here, of course, floating about the cliffs and bobbing on the water, but it had all changed, and what Bossiney once was it was no more. Cottages once nestled in the hills, perhaps a dozen or more, but they had gone completely and had left no trace at all, like they were never there. And the hills, that once held livestock, were empty and barren, windswept and bleak; where purple heather, once complimented by dots of life, was a foreboding sight to two weary travellers.

Yet, it had only been sixteen years since the day when the Repecians first landed here. How speedily things are lost when those that have them care not. Fishing boats were smashed beneath the hulls of warships and cottages were pillaged and burnt to the ground. So cruel was the invasion, and so swiftly did death befall those who dwelled here, that when news of it reached Baladorn in the south, Lord Gonosor, as he was, flew into a rage and fell to his knees to weep.

"Miseries greater yet will come, for Bossiney has begun it, and until men stand planted on firm feet, they will wander homeless, destitute and facing their end." Now, no longer a lord and chief of men, he recalled his words and looked down upon the great harbour and would have wept again but for his heart telling him that those that had not stood firm, now had sprung up from off their backs to bring to an end what had started here. He looked at the youth standing beside him, and would have told him all about his wondrous harbour, but for the absence of the means with which to do it.

For Galfall, though, Bossiney meant nothing. He had never been here and although he had heard of the place, knew not that this was it, for there was no-one to tell him. Observing the Bodmifflian, he suspected that this was somewhere of significance by the forlorn look on his haggard face, but not why, and concluded that it was a personal thing concerning memories of lost days. This harbour, to Gonosor, was what the Shire River would be to him had he returned to see it again after so long an absence.

"We need to rest a while and eat something," Galfall said.

The meal, rabbit and bread, was brought by Gonosor and prepared by him on a small fire. He had brought it with him to save time. Time was crucial to the success of this undertaking, and they could not afford too much of it to the task of eating what the Bodmifflian had prepared. In any case, it was ravaged as though neither of them had eaten for days. What strange times these were.

Once the carcass had been stripped, Gonosor got to his feet and stamped out the fire, and waited patiently for Galfall to finish his mouth full.

"This is it then?" the youngster said, and wished that the meal was just beginning, for that would have given him more time to contemplate what was to come. Before they had left Ingelwitt, Badad had gone to great lengths to explain what the mission was about, but had neglected to mention the dangers that would surely be involved. Yet, had he talked of them, Galfall would still have agreed to go, for he was wise enough to know that any such undertaking would be perilous, if not self-destructing. Badad, then, had underestimated the Gringell boy, suspecting that had he known the truth about what was to come, he would have shied away from it and refused to do it.

As he swigged water from a flask, he recalled the Druid's explanation. It was necessary for him to do this to adapt his mind to the task ahead. He held himself back, therefore, as Gonosor took himself off and trotted down the hill towards the harbour, without glancing back to make sure Galfall was behind him.

"Let him go," he told himself, knowing fine well that Gonosor would not embark without him. He had, after all, his tongue in his hip bag, and he would not stray too far away from that.

"Fogle's folly," Badad had told him, "was to assume that Bosscastle was supplied via the coast road. It was not, and never had been." And it was true. While the Western Gate was the most potent symbol of the fortress's impregnability, it was not, however, the only way to get in. The secret of Bosscastle, known only to a few, lay in the sea. Galfall, then, recalled the old man drawing a mark in the sand. Just a loop, the youngster thought when he was shown it, until it was explained that it was a map of this coast. A very crude map, they agreed, but a map all the same. "Kanance's Cove," the Druid said, then made a square shape on top of it with the same stick: "Bosscastle."

The ancient fortress, he was told, was built around and above a natural cove in the Bodmiffel coastline.

"Kanance was the name of the very first King of Geramond, who began the construction of the castle we see today. He landed, with his army, in the cove and moved inland to do battle with the giants." Then he recited a poem not heard or spoken for a dozen generations.

"Nearer and fast doth the red beard come;
And louder still and more loud,
From underneath that swirling cloud.
The trampling and the thrum,

And plainly and more plainly,
Now through the gloom he come,
Far from top and far from bottom,
Corbilo of whom time forgotten.

'Now welcome, welcome Kanance,
And to my home come thy.
Why dost thou stay, nay turn away?
Here lies the road, for your folk will surely die.'"

"A battle raged for seven days." Badad continued. "And Kanance lost all of his men and Corbilo lost all of his, so that only the two of them remained … the little man and the giant. And where one was strong the other was swift, and so one could not defeat the other. So instead of fighting they began to talk, but Corbilo was so huge he could not see his new friend's face, and Kanance would not be lifted up because he did not trust the giant, so when he spoke he had to shout to be heard. 'I'll build for thee a tower,' the giant said, 'so that mere men can be as tall as a mountain, and look into the calm clouds.' He did, and Kanance climbed to the top of it and looked at Corbilo's face and was amazed at the size of it. 'Never to have seen it was best,' he said, and plunged his spear into the giants eye. Corbilo collapsed to the ground, caught the tower with his hand, and both fell into the cove. The giant was dead, but even now Kanance did not trust him, and weighed him down with stones."

"We'll need a boat if we're to get to the cove," Galfall shouted. Gonosor turned and gestured for him to follow. He did. A boat, of course, was waiting in the harbour. A neglected old thing that barely looked capable of taking them anywhere. Quite big, but with only two oars to propel them, it would take all of the Bodmifflian's strength to do it. He gestured again, this time for the youngster to get into the vessel, and then pushed it off the beach and leapt in himself when it was clear of land and floating on the sea.

All of this was a new experience for Galfall. He had seen the ocean before, on trips with his father to the sheep market at Dormlark, but had never touched it or felt its force, or the slipping sands beneath his feet that threatened to pull him down. He realised that he had never swam, and wondered if he was capable of it should the boat fail them. Thinking back to the time his brother swam across the Shire River and urged him to achieve the same feat, he rued the fact that he had not attempted it. At least now he would not be so afraid of the sea and his impending journey. What would it be like to drown, he wondered, and looked out to the vast, grey ocean appearing between the aperture in the land that formed the exit from Bossiney.

Gonosor demonstrated that his remarkable strength had not deserted him after his encounter with the Druid, and impelled the boat to move forwards with long, weighty thrusts and pulls. Now they were on the ocean proper, with the harbour disappearing into the distance. Then they passed the point in the land when it vanished altogether, and with it the end to any sense that this mission was not beginning now and here, and would not end until it was done. It was late afternoon, and the sky was trapped somewhere between the last vestiges of the glorious midwinter sun and the impending gloom of a winter's dusk. Although they stayed within sight of land, they were far enough out to feel the force of the wind and its dominance over the surface of the sea, and if Galfall was uneasy at the outset of the voyage, he was terror-stricken now and riveted to his seat with his hands clinging to both sides of the boat in a vain attempt to steady it. The Bodmifflian was his one source of comfort. He was unruffled and utterly absorbed in his task, pulling and shoving the oars regardless of the best attempts of the sea to stop him; unheeding as waves crashed against the boat from all directions, spilling over the edge to form a pool in the bottom, that swilled and washed against their feet and soaked their legs.

As dusk descended so the sea became crueller, raising the boat up and tossing it down. Galfall was lifted out of his seat and screamed in horror. He looked at Gonosor and could just about see him through the fret; saw that he had stopped rowing and had brought the oars into the boat. There were no expressions of exhaustion on his face, and his chest was behaving normally.

"I could have a go if you're tired," said Galfall. "I don't think we ought to stop trying, that's all. We should wait until we get there." He paused to think about what he had suggested, and quickly realised that he was talking nonsense, for there would be no safe haven where they were going; no time to rest and sleep or even recover from the journey. "I can see the castle ahead, Gonosor. I can see a light, so we cannot be far away now. Just a little further and we'll be there. Take the oars again." His voice was vibrating with panic. "We can't just give in."

Gonosor held his finger to his lips to quieten him. Water was pouring into the boat and the pair of them were soaked to the skin and as cold as they could be. Galfall lifted off the seat and took hold of one of the oars, and as he did a wave came across the boat so powerful that it swept him overboard. Gonosor leapt forward to grab hold of him but was helpless and could do nothing but observe as the youngster disappeared beneath the surface of the vicious sea.

Galfall was taken down by the current. He could see the boat above and stretched out his hand to touch it, but it was out of reach, and was there just to tantalise him; make him seem safe when in fact he was not. He tried to swim, like he had seen his brother as he had crossed the Shire River, but the water was too turbulent and after a while he gave up trying. It was like he was floating on air. He thought of his brother, and his mother, then his father; dear old Toggett, Fogle too, and the Druid in despair. And he could see them so clearly that it was as though they were in the water with him. Of all of them, it was his mother that he tried to touch. She was smiling at him, like she used to, and holding out her arms to invite him back to the protection of her bosom. He tried so hard to get there, but could not. Then she vanished. They all did, and he was alone again. He could hear her though, as she sang.

'Old song I will not sing,
Now better songs are sung.
Galfall is here, and is young,
And sweetness of love will bring.'

He thought to himself: "I am dying now." But he did not want to, and fought to fend it off. This was not how it was supposed to end. He had told the Druid that he was prepared to die, and he was, but not like this. This was not a hero's death. He told himself to be strong, but had no strength left in him. "This is it," he said in his mind. "Let it come now." And it went dark.

On the surface, Gonosor was dangling the oar into the sea, but when he realised that Galfall was not going to grab hold of it, he leapt in himself to fetch him back. Another savage wave came to destroy the boat altogether, and scattered it all around. It was of no more use to them now.

"I saw his eyes flicker." The voice was unfamiliar; a strange, unknown accent. "I did. Look, his eyes are opening. Ah, at last he is with us." When Galfall did open his eyes the face to accompany the voice was just as strange. In fact, the man standing next to him had had his face so close to him that it was the sense of his breath on his face that had brought him out of his deep slumber, so that when he woke his heart jumped and his whole body jerked instinctively away from him. Galfall looked at the stranger. Perhaps he did know him after all but had forgotten him. Then he concluded that he had never seen him before, for if he had he would surely have remembered. The man had a beard the likes of which Galfall had never seen; groomed and styled to form a thin point that was like water dropping off the end of his chin, but the rest of his face was clean shaven. His hair was as black as coal and although he was an elderly man his face was smooth and pampered. Add to that his colourful attire – a red, satin gown and leg wear to match, fingers that were filled with gold, and his ears and neck bristling with jewels – and Galfall realised very quickly that he had never seen such a man before. Then he looked about the room. The walls were richly decorated with pictures and fine tapestries, and the bed he was in was huge and covered in thick, luscious furs.

"Where am I?" he asked, slightly subdued.

"Welcome to the Buca Lapis," the stranger replied, rather excitedly. Galfall looked even more puzzled. "My ship," replied the man, affronted by the youngster's apparent ignorance at the mention of his ship's name. "The pride of the Trade Fleet. As sturdy as a leg of wood. My joy."

"And who are you?"

"Forgive me, my young friend, for introducing my ship before myself. It's just that I love her so. I am the Merchant Budogis." He lowered his head. "But you may call me Bucenta Budogis, for you are not my crew, but my treasured guest. Nay, patient, if I may be so bold." His voice rose excitedly. "But now you are awake and thriving."

Galfall turned to look to the other side of the bed and saw that Gonosor was standing next to him. "He has not left your side all evening," said Bucenta, then quieter: "I think the shock of your ordeal has made him mute."

"He has no tongue," Galfall replied, pulling himself upright and resting his head against the wall.

"That would explain it. Men with no tongues usually are mute, are they not...?"

Beneath the covers, Galfall moved his hand down to the side of his leg and felt for the leather pouch, then sighed with relief when he knew that it was still there with its contents intact. Bucenta put his hand behind the youngster's neck, pulled his head away from the wall before gently lowering it back onto a plump, feather pillow.

"You are kind," said Galfall appreciatively.

"You are my honoured guest. Both of you are my guests."

He rushed around the bed, took hold of Gonosor's arm and urged him to be seated on the chair behind him. Gonosor happily obliged his host, and Galfall smiled.

"Ah, your joy pours into the wide hollows of my heart," he said. "You are most welcome here, and precious to me. My lovely ship is yours."

"You are not from these parts," Galfall insisted. Bucenta shuddered and rubbed his arms briskly. "I am from warmer climes." He wrapped a shawl around his shoulders. "My homeland is a place where clothes such as these are not needed."

"Where exactly?"

"A place called Eliad, in the southern seas. You won't have heard of it. Lovely it is. Lovely and warm."

"What brings you to Geramond?"

"The Buca Lapis does," Bucenta replied, looking at the youth strangely. Galfall smiled at him, and made him smile too. "Your smile pours into the wide …"

"Why are you here?" said Galfall, interrupting.

Bucenta laughed boisterously. His laughter ended abruptly when he intended to reply. "Forgive me. You must think I'm a fool. Now I understand the question. Trade brings me here. My lovely ship is full of lovely things. I am called the Merchant Budogis for that is what I am, you see … a merchant…!"

"Who do you trade with?"

"Enough of me. You must be hungry after your ordeal. I have food for you and wine warmed with spices. You must eat, my treasured guests. And regain your strength after your ordeal." Bucenta hurried towards the door and opened it preparatory to leaving.

"Ordeal?" said Galfall. "Where were we when you found us? How were we, I mean."

"Oh, clinging to the remnants of your little fishing boat," the merchant replied. "And clinging to life itself, I'd say. A sorry sight indeed, even for a professional sailor such as me. In all my years, I have never seen anything like it, nor wish to again. But here you both are, with breath in your lungs. Breath means life, and the Merchant Budogis is thankful for that." Then he left the room, chuckling to himself, happily.

Galfall looked at Gonosor then loosened the pouch from his belt and held it in his hand. "I wish this were yours again, so that you could tell me what is going on. If you ask me, Gonosor, I will gladly give it back to you."

Gonosor stepped forward. His eyes were fixed on the article in the youngsters hand. And how he desired it back. He allowed his hand to hover over it, even to touch it. Galfall prepared himself for the pouch to be taken from him and held his head back and closed his eyes. He then heard a voice in his mind: Gonosor's voice, as he remembered it, gruff and forthright. 'Do not tempt me, young one, for it is mine to take.' The pouch was not taken. Instead, he felt his fingers being closed around it, but not by his doing. 'Offer it to me again when this is done and finished. If you give it to me now, it will never be finished.'

They took their time over this meal. Time here seemed to pass slowly. They were given chicken and an assortment of vegetables, accompanied by the warm wine finished with spices, with as much fruit as they could possibly eat awaiting them on the table next to the bed. Bucenta did not partake in the feast, but gained great comfort by merely watching them, as though he was tasting every mouthful. Gonosor finished every last scrap on his plate, then leaned over the bed to delve his rough hand into the fruit. His lack of finesse made the merchant giggle with glee. Galfall, though, filled easier, and he rejected the fruit.

"We thank you, Bucenta," he said. "You are kind."

"An Eliadian is nothing if not a gracious host to his guests. You do me a great honour, sir, by eating what I have given to you. I get little chance to entertain these days. The life of a humble slave merchant is not what it once was in these days of empire."

Slave merchant. The comment brought Galfall upright in the bed, and he cast aside his covers to be free of them. The expression on his face suggested that he was neither impressed nor pleased by the merchant's statement.

"You trade in slaves?" he asked, indignant at the mention of the word.

"Indeed he does." This new voice belonged to the man standing in the doorway looking into the room. He was a tall, sturdy man with a harsh face and an authoritarian tone to his voice. Certainly, when he came into the room, Bucenta changed and became agitated and uneasy in his presence. "There is a great demand in the southern colonies for the more exotic type of slave. The Merchant Budogis is one of the empire's foremost traders and the only one to come this far north in order to satisfy that demand and make himself incredibly rich in the process."

Bucenta smiled and bowed his head gracefully, taking no notice of his guests' discomfort with such talk of slaves and empire, and only interested, it seemed, in wallowing in the newcomer's praise of him and accepting his compliment without any humbleness at all.

"Allow me to introduce my other beloved guest, Ambassador Corsula, from Repecia no less. Corsula Corbissa, representative of the Imperial Senate, and here on their business." His voice was trembling as he spoke, half enraptured by this important man and half weary of him, and his eyes rolled upwards as he hoped beyond hope that he had said the correct thing and not too much, as he usually did. Corsula stepped towards the bed to fully take in its invalid incumbent. He looked at Gonosor too.

"Now you know my name, but have not told me yours."

"Nor me," said Bucenta, quite rudely, shifting his allegiance swiftly away from his two new guests to his original one. To demonstrate this he picked up the bowl of fruit and took it to the far side of the room and placed it on a table that was well out of their reach, then turned and looked at them sternly. "Who are you and why are you here?" Galfall was bemused.

"You saved us and brought us here."

"Yes, of course." He looked at Corsula. "They were in trouble, you see. Forgive me, Ambassador, but I couldn't let them drown."

"You should have consulted me before bringing anyone onto this ship," Corsula replied angrily. "Now what are your names?"

"Galfall Gringell, and this is my ...." he paused to think. "My father ...." another of Gonosor's thoughts passed through the youngster's mind .... "Bowen Gringell," he said. "We were fishing and got caught by the storm. We'd surely be dead if it hadn't been for the merchant."

Corsula chuckled and turned to leave.

"How fortunate you are to have been saved by a slave trader." He took the merchant to one side to tell him: "Prepare your men, the portcullis is about to be opened and we must be ready." Then he left.

The Repecian had spoke quietly but Galfall had heard him nevertheless.

"Bucenta ..." The merchant turned. "Where are we exactly? I know we're on your ship, but where is your ship...?"

Bucenta hurried excitedly towards the door, turning, he replied: "At the end of its long, horrid journey, on spiteful seas far from home. A chance to walk on ground that does not move with the ocean's temper." He turned the handle and opened the thick, wooden door. "We've been here all afternoon, but only now have they decided to let us in. Like we bring them harm! Trade does no-one any harm. The citadel of Ardala, meaning cliffs. I believe the locals here call it Bosscastle." Then he bowed his head and left the room and closed the door behind him. They heard the key turn in the lock and realised that they were no longer the Merchant Budogis's guests but his captives.

Bucenta and Corsula rushed to the deck of the Buca Lapis, along with most of the crew. The sky was dark and clear, dotted with stars and dominated by the moon, that shone defiantly to cast its light against the walls of Bosscastle. Walls that extended as high as the eye could see, to almost touch the moon so that it was more like a torch hanging from them, to guide them safely into the cove. There was a collective gasp of breath when the portcullis began its ascent to the top of its gatehouse, like an entrance to another world, a magical world, was opening up before them. Even the Repecian, who had seen many marvels, was captivated by the event, and stood back and lurked behind the Merchant, in awe of it and fearful that the huge, iron structure might fail and fall on them. This was Geramond, after all. He had heard so many tales of the place, wicked things, and now he was entering into it, where empire ended and myth began.

The ship sailed beneath the portcullis and into a tunnel, high enough to allow the masts through unhindered and wide enough for the oars, a dozen on either side, to function adequately and propel the vessel forwards. It was dark. The bright moon had no impact here and torches were relied upon to guide the Buca Lapis safely through to its destination. And quiet, so all that could be heard was the sound of a drum beating slowly in the keel, the oars then splashing into the water and the water lapping against the stone walls. "This is the worst part," Bucenta whispered. "We'll be out the other side soon." But his words, the grovelling way that they were uttered, were more an irritation than a comfort.

The ship emerged from the tunnel into the cove itself. What was once a natural harbour was now anything but and resembled nothing more than a dock, enclosed within a ring of walls and towers that extended high into the night sky. At least the moon and the stars were visible again. Men were standing along the tops of the walls and peering out from windows in the towers; each man was holding a torch and together they presented the Ambassador and the Merchant with a feverish welcome, clapping and cheering as the Buca Lapis was pulled along side. Bucenta reciprocated their warm greetings by waving back with heartfelt joy, with both hands for one was not enough. Corsula, however, was not so enthusiastic and leaned towards the merchant and mumbled:

"Perhaps they are not applauding the ship and its owner." To which Bucenta retorted snappily: "These people know me of old. They know that the Merchant Budogis on his beautiful ship brings with him food and wine aplenty. I am a dignitary ... a big wheel. Whereas you, Ambassador, are not known to them at all." He rested one of his arms. "Stick close to me and you cannot go wrong," and winked proudly.

The gangplank was extended from the deck of the ship to the dock, where a small group of Repecian soldiers were waiting to greet the luminaries as they disembarked. Corsula was affronted by the lack of a proper welcome committee, and his facial cast was gloomy and disapproving. The most senior of the four soldiers was a mere tribune by the name of Madius, who offered his arm to the ambassador as he faltered along the gangplank. Corsula accepted the gesture, then withdrew his hand once safely on the dock. Bucenta, more used to the ways of the sea, almost skipped down it, then leapt onto the dock and smiled with glee.

"Where is the Governor?" asked Corsula miserably.

"He does not come down to the cove," replied Madius. "It holds memories for him, bad memories. His wife perished here. A long time ago, but she haunts him still." As he gave the explanation, he was becoming more aware that this man that had accompanied the merchant was a man of significance. His clothes were dull and plain but cut from a fine piece of cloth, not accessible to just anyone. Madius paid more attention and saw that his boots were made from the finest leather, and his hands were covered with velvet gloves with a huge, gold ring on his right index finger. He had seen such a ring before, on his uncle's finger, and remembered what it was for, what it signified. A man of significance indeed: a man of the Senate.

"The Governor was not expecting such an exalted visitor," he said nervously.

"He should have been," Corsula retorted. "The mess he's made of his position here. Take me to him."

"Indeed, sir. He is waiting in the main square." Madius extended his arm. "Please, follow me. I will take you there." The young soldier set off up the steps that led to the main part of this castle complex, taking his time so as to accommodate the Ambassador's slower pace. Bucenta followed and the three remaining soldiers took up the rear.

From a small porthole in the top of the wall, standing on a table to be able to see through it, Galfall watched as the merchant and the ambassador were led out of the cove. Much of the place was blocked by a poor view, but enough could be seen to give an indication to the size and scale of it.

"This must be it," the youngster said, his excitement tapered by his captivity in the cabin. "Kanance's Cove … like the Druid said." His face was enraptured by the thought of being here. He remembered the Druid's account of the castle's beginnings. The truth, however, was lost in myth. Badad believed those myths to be the truth. "The place where Corbilo fell." He leapt off the table and took hold of Gonosor's arm. "Come and look, Gonosor. You must see it." Gonosor pulled his arm away angrily. "But this is the place we set out to reach. We're here at last. I don't know how and why, but we're here. It is Badad's doing."

It was true that they had reached their intended destination, but what good was it when they were confined to this one room on a ship built to accommodate slaves? Would such a man as a slave be filled with joy and hope at the sight of a sea-lashed, wind-swept cove. They had arrived at Bosscastle, but were kept from it by their own enslavement. Gonosor did not go to the window, but to the door, and pulled on the handle; placed his foot on the wall and tugged at the blockage with all of his might. It did not open or give an indication that it would. And the youngster realised now that the cove meant nothing to them, and he sat on the bed to sigh and mumble to himself despondently.

"Perhaps this is how it is meant to be." He was suddenly filled with renewed optimism. "Badad meant for us to be picked up by the Buca Lapis. So that must mean that there must be a way of getting off this damn ship after all." He sank into the bed again. "But what if he didn't and there isn't? Then we have failed, haven't we? May as well have drowned than be here."

The events of the day had taken their toll on the other rebels, too, and the mood in the camp was as gloomy and melancholic as at any stage of their uprising. It had been a grim day for the men of Woldark, Fogle and Toggett in particular. Toggett had slept well and Fogle had had to wake him. The old man grumbled and objected to the disturbance.

"Galfall has disappeared," Fogle said to him, and the Took brought his head off his pillow. "I've been looking for him all morning."

"But you ain't found him, eh? That's why you've woke me?"

Fogle shook his head. "I haven't found him, but men are still out looking. Gonosor and the Druid have gone too." And Toggett instantly panicked and cast off his blanket. Fogle placed his hand on the old man's chest to calm him. "No, my friend. That's not why I woke you. While I was in the forest looking for the boy, I found someone else instead … someone who went missing, that we tried to find but couldn't. Someone on the list." Toggett knew to whom he was referring. He rubbed the sleep from his eyes.

"Miggel?" he said, then looked at Fogle and waited for him to confirm it. "Well, we knew that he must be dead, didn't we? You don't go missing for three days then stumble back to camp whistling, do you?" He chuckled fondly. "Not even old Miggel Thrull."

"At least we've found him," said Fogle. "And can put him to rest at last."

He was buried in the afternoon in the traditional Shire manner. No pyres or smoke, songs or hysteria. Just a shallow hole in the ground, covered with stones to mark this part of the earth as a grave. And just a word or two from Toggett, the man who knew him best of all, and who recited his name and those of his family, his profession and his deeds. Finally, they toasted him with a jug of warm ale and Toggett smoked a pipe in honour of his old friend and drinking partner. Then the storm came in from the sea, and they retreated to their shelters.

Fogle's shelter was the cosiest and his fire was usually the warmest, so Toggett and the Druid joined him there. It was raining heavily and the roof was leaking, so pans and pots were carefully placed to catch the drips.

"How many more?" asked Fogle. "How many more must fall before this is done?"

"Do not seek a quick solution, my friend," the Druid warned. "For in that way lies failure. We can only hope to win freedom after countless pains."

"But we have all suffered, and can take no more." Then Badad grew angry. "Do not blame misfortune for what you have all brought on yourselves. Wars are not started by a course of events, but by a want of good sense or by necessity."

"Death's a means to liberty, so it is," Toggett added, as he tossed a pan of water out of the opening and then replaced it beneath a particularly heavy dribble.

"Then never to have lived is best?" Badad said. "Never to have drawn the breath of life? Never to have looked into the eye of day? Never to have laughed or sang?"

"The second best's a strong pipe," Toggett replied. "And a quick goodbye." Then he covered his head with his jacket and left Fogle's shelter to return to his own.

"He won't admit to it, but he loved old Miggel like he was his own brother," said Fogle, as he watched the old man trot back to his bed, skipping and jumping to avoid the puddles.

"And will you admit to loving old Toggett as a father?"

Fogle chortled, and thought for a moment. "I will. And I begin every day by willing him to survive this war. And young Galfall, too, for I owe it to his father to keep him safe, as I vowed I would. But now he has gone and I can't help him anymore."

"Only destiny can decide his fate now, my friend. We will soon know what destiny has in store for us all, for we are all entwined by the same cord."

Fogle, then, went quiet, preoccupied with his own thoughts, of himself and his own failings. Had the Druid offered him the chance to break Bosscastle he would surely have refused, dismissing the plan as being impossible and fraught with danger.

"You say he accepted the venture of his own free will? Or was your magic at work, Badad?" he asked carefully.

"Do not take me for a mind meddler!" Badad replied. "And do not underestimate the Gringell boy. I simply told him what his undertaking would involve, he thought about it for a moment, then decided that he wanted to do it. He needed no persuading from me."

And Fogle found that remarkable. In the past he had noticed that there was something different about Galfall, but had never taken him to be heroic or braver than himself. He thought about his own son; stubborn and childlike at times, but when faced with danger and threat, reacted just like a man and fought with the strength and mind of a warrior. The exhilaration of youth; an ignorance of the world that annulled all thoughts of risk and death.

"Have you noticed, Badad, that there is something weighty about Gringell's son...?"

"Oh, yes," replied Badad. "It is safe to say that he is capable of doing remarkable things."

Fogle smiled to himself. Another private moment, until he decided to share it with his companion. "The other evening, when it was clear that the attack on the castle gate had failed, I told Galfall that I was tired of it all and wanted to return home." He spoke in a tone that suggested he was ashamed of himself. "I will never forget the look of disgust on his face. He protested, of course, and told me that we couldn't leave until we'd finished what we'd started here. Isn't that amazing? Anyone else would have agreed with me, and we'd be halfway back to the Threeshire by now. But not him. And it was like he was chastising me for thinking in such a way. I'd let him down, hadn't I…?"

"The course of a man's life is filled with doubts, Fogle." Badad reassured him. "Galfall's too, if you did but know it. There is an old, Tragaran proverb: 'Let him without flaw be master of his house; but let the flawed one be king of us all.' I'm sure that we have all had our doubts and regrets during the course of this shabby war, my friend. The trick is to listen to them and then shun them like an old foe. That way lies courage and enterprise."

"This new king," said Fogle, tentatively. "Will have no finer servant than you, Badad." He was right to be hesitant, for Badad seemed troubled by the remark, and stepped away from the fire to stand and look out of the door.

"I cannot serve him, when he comes," said the Druid, sadly. "My time as council to kings is done." Not wanting to pursue the subject any further, he concluded simply: "Perhaps Galfall will offer wise council to him?"

"What if the boy fails?" Fogle asked.

"Make no mistake, Fogle. It will end in the only way it can, one way or another. For the time being we must preoccupy ourselves with recovering from battles fought, to the one still to come. If Galfall's mission succeeds, then we must all be ready. Strong in arm, heart and head."

Five
A Message from Palmatine

The popular perception of the Governor of Geramond, in the markets and taverns of Ramrah and especially in the Repecian Senate, was that he was a stunted and feeble man; of negligible intellect and renowned only as being the first Governor to lose his province. Disobedience was not uncommon. Uprisings happened regularly and just about every region of the Empire had experienced a rumble of discontentment and restlessness at one point or another. But in every instance, the mechanics of empire, its politicians but mostly its army, had combined to suppress them and bring order where there had been chaos. Most of the empire, most of the time, was peaceful and prosperous. Whenever that peace was threatened, whether it be a riot or a revolt, it was dispelled with a ruthless efficiency; its perpetrators were made an example of and the locals calmed and subdued. Geramond, though, was different. Here the rebellion had managed to grow from its source to envelope the whole territory, and had been so successful that the province had almost been lost. Almost. The Repecians still had a foothold, and while they had that there was always hope. Geography had played its part: Geramond was their northern most possession and the furthest away from the hub of empire. But there was another significant factor, or so the senate thought. It's Governor was not a Repecian but a local man, and that was unusual. And how could a local man react as swiftly and mercilessly as a Repecian? It was a compelling argument, but quite wrong, for they did not know this particular governor as well as they thought.

There was nothing puny or feeble about him. The opposite, in fact. He was a tall, sturdily built man with a long face with prominent features, especially the chin, which jutted out from the jaw like a beard. He was to have received the ambassador and the Merchant Budogis in the Great Square at the top of the cove steps, but it was now raining so heavily that he had long retreated into his own, private quarters. Nevertheless, the roads leading into the square, and the square itself, were packed with the people of Bosscastle, come to watch as the party of the Buca Lapis made their way to the Great Hall. Bucenta waved at them as though he was their conquering king, but no-one waved back or smiled at him, for they all knew his business, why he was here. Indeed, a line of soldiers had to form a pathway through the crowd, fully aware of public hostility towards him, and held their arms apart to form a barrier. When they climbed the steps to the Great Hall, there was a murmur of unrest and the crowd began to jeer and hiss.

Delabole was sitting in his seat at the far end of this vast, stone hall. Next to him, his servant – an old man – was in attendance, and filled his cup with wine and then stepped away to stand behind the high, wooden chair. Corsula looked about him, and saw that this was a fine, old building, impressive in size and splendour. He looked up to the high, vaulted ceiling, from where three huge, branched candelabra descended to hover just above their heads and shed light on them as they made their ascent towards the Governor. If the perception of Delabole was wrong, then so too was the thought that this province was in some way primitive and unsophisticated; a place where the people lived in huts and caves, where there were no stone buildings or grand and ancient monuments. Corsula, therefore, was surprised to find that this building, and others that he had seen in his short time here, were as elaborate and sturdy as any public building in any provincial capital. He was impressed with the vastness of the place; the intricate buildings on their streets and alleys, enclosed within and protected by those massive walls. Bosscastle, in fact, was like nowhere he had ever seen, and primitive only in the sense that it belonged now to his people and not the sons of those that had built it.

Bucenta held out his arms and smiled. "My dear friend," he said, looking at the Governor. Delabole, however, did not reciprocate the gesture, and looked into his cup instead, then held it out for the servant to refill.

"You have arrived safely, then?" he asked, in a dull, gravely voice, in a way that suggested that he did not care either way.

"Indeed, sir," said Bucenta. "And with a ship filled with wondrous things for your excellency to indulge himself."

Delabole looked up. "Have you brought the wine I like?"

Bucenta chuckled awkwardly. "Alas, sir, no. You see, we have been plagued by locusts in Eliad this summer, and our lovely vines have been decimated." Sensing that the Governor did not believe him, he babbled on. "I have substituted the wine with a beverage of equal potency, excellency." He clapped his hands loudly and almost straight away two of his lackeys came in carrying a barrel of the aforementioned beverage, and placed it in front of him. "A mead from Urm."

"A what from where?" snapped Delabole.

"Fermented honey and water," Bucenta stuttered. "Very fermented indeed." He scrunched up his face to form a kind of gleeful cringe. "It'll blow your head off."

Delabole came down the steps from his seat and smashed the hilt of his sword through the top of the barrel to get access to its contents; scooped some into his cup and slurped at it. He was not impressed.

"It's an acquired taste," Bucenta assured him.

"Then I shall acquire it," said Delabole, taking another cup full and returning to his seat.

It quickly became apparent to the ambassador that the Governor of Geramond was drunk. Not a giddy, flighty form of the condition, but so intoxicated that he could barely speak or hold his head straight. He stood by and observed as the merchant helped himself to a cup of mead and raised his arm to toast his new, wine-soaked host, harbouring no intentions of joining them himself, intent only on watching and scrutinising them. He had, however, formed his opinion of the Governor already, even though he had not yet exchanged words with him. His weakness, the scourge of his governorship, was plain to see.

The more Bucenta drank the more he giggled and the more annoying he became, both to Corsula and Delabole.

"Lovely, lovely things, my friend," he said giddily. "Spices from Tega and all sort of edibles from all over the place." He winked at the Governor. "And plenty more mead, eh…?"

"I shall inspect your goods in the morning," Delabole replied.

Bucenta climbed one step closer to him. "And what, I wonder, do you intend to offer the Merchant Budogis in exchange for all his cargo?" He rubbed his hands together in anticipation.

"What would you like?" Delabole was teasing him.

"You know what's precious to me, excellency."

"I don't know if I can spare any more."

Bucenta huffed. "But they're valueless here! Worth a small fortune in the slave markets of Ramrah."

"Very well," said Delabole. "I have selected fifty for you to take away."

Bucenta, foremost a businessman, quickly calculated how much he could expect to make from fifty slaves, and was delighted with his conclusion.

"Fifty good ones?" he asked. The Governor did not care to answer. "Plus the two I already have, makes one for every week of the year!" Then he laughed boisterously; completely unwarranted for such a humdrum remark. He stopped abruptly with the realisation that no-one else found him amusing; a severe glare from the ambassador was enough.

Delabole realised that he had not noticed the stranger in his midst. He had seen Corsula, of course, but had not paused to question who he was or why he was deemed important enough to be standing in his presence. The drink, seemingly, had numbed his brain, and he briefly wondered if he had already asked, to be told the answer, only for him to have forgotten about it. He also asked himself if he had seen him before on any of the merchant's other visits, and concluded that he would have remembered such a miserable face. Delabole, had, however, seen the look Corsula had given the merchant to quieten him, and quickly grasped the fact that this was no ordinary visitor. So, finally, he asked:

"Who's your friend?" whilst looking at Bucenta.

Bucenta momentarily forgot himself. "He's no friend of mine," he said. Realising his error, he choked nervously, and offered the ambassador a smile. "What I mean to say is, I am not worthy of your affection, sir."

"Just tell the Governor who I am," Corsula replied, tiredly.

"This is his excellency Corsula Corbissa, emissary of the Imperial Senate, and here on their business …"

Corsula was enraged.

"No!" he blasted, reserving his venom for the hapless merchant. "I serve but one master! The same master whom he will serve, when he is done with serving himself…!"

"And who is that?" asked Delabole, as he came forward in his seat, his cup hanging precariously by the tips of his fingers.

"The Great One himself. Lord Gauin Lucial Fillian, Imperial Dictator and Protector." He returned his gaze to Bucenta. "I am here on his business and no-one else's!"

The cup fell from the governor's hand and crashed onto the stone floor. He made no attempt to retrieve it. That name had not been uttered in this hall for many a year, and the sound of it spoken again was like a bolt of lightening striking his body to render it useless and paralyse his face. He remembered that he was drunk, but tried not to look drunk. The mead had been sweet, that belied its potency, and now he wished that he had not drank it so enthusiastically, for he knew that he needed to be sober. His eyes were glazed and his face was motionless; he was aware that the newcomer was awaiting his reaction and staring intently at him until he gave one. If only the cup had not fallen from his loose grasp. Corsula picked it up and placed it on the table.

The pause seemed to last an eternity. Then, rubbing his face with his hands briskly in an attempt to sober himself up, Delabole seemed to spark back to life.

"Then you are most welcome, sir." He tried to make his words sound as though he meant them, but fooled no-one. He even bowed his head, but instead of being gracious he appeared to be weak. Suddenly, his drunken condition overcame him again, and he leant forwards and placed his head in his hands and scratched his scalp with his fingers.

Corsula, with his hands held behind his back, casually stepped away to examine a tapestry on the wall. It depicted a woman, the fairest, wisest most generous woman in the world; a shining vision in gold, set against the bleak backdrop of a window, with a view of the cold, grey castle; and a man, of Delabole's likeness, looking in, half hidden behind a pillar.

"Is this your wife?" he asked, and looked back to see the Governor confirm that it was. "She is very beautiful. But now she has gone?"

"Yes," Delabole replied, sadly. "She has."

"I will need rooms," said Corsula. "I want to be comfortable while I am here."

"Of course. I have set aside some rooms for the merchant, but you must have them." Bucenta opened his mouth to oppose the suggestion, then realised that any such resistance would be pointless, so closed it again.

"I will retire for the night," Corsula said. He left the great hall happy in the knowledge that the Governor had been humbled. The cause of Delabole's discomfort was clear for him to see. Following the final and ultimate conquest of Geramond, an age ago now, it seemed, General Fillian withdrew from this land to return to Repecia, taking his army with him. A new army arrived: the Sixth Legion. Delabole, having allied himself with the conqueror, was given the Governorship of this newly formed province, and the command of the army. His tasks were simple: impose Repecian rule on the people, collect their taxes and maintain order. The trouble was, however, that Delabole pursued these tasks with a relentless and ruthless fervour, until the people rebelled against him. They branded him a traitor and a collaborator, which, of course, he was. 'The hateful governor' they called him.

For fifteen years Delabole ruled Geramond like he was a king, divorced from Imperial laws and influence. For fifteen years Delabole behaved like a tyrant, and fully deserved the name given to him by his countrymen. And while men starved he lived lavishly; while they toiled to pay their taxes he creamed a little off the top for himself. As his province splintered and eroded he eased his pain with drink until eventually he became Bosscastle's hostage. Corsula's arrival indicated the end of his Governorship, and he knew it. Things, it seemed, were about to change.

Rooms were provided for the ambassador in the East Wing of the castle. The tribune took him there, via a back door from the

Great Hall to avoid the mob, and led the way with a torch. A servant girl, a pretty thing, went with them. Corsula watched her from behind and admired her walk. She sensed that his eyes were scrolling up and down and was uncomfortable to be walking in front of him. At the end of the corridor, Madius unlocked the door to the room and went in first to light the candles. The girl began to turn back the bed as quickly as she could, built up the fire that had been struggling in the hearth, then bowed her head courteously and vanished quickly. Corsula was amused by her rapid, panicky exit. He removed his long, black overcoat and placed it over a chair near the fire to dry. His room was nothing extraordinary but it was comfortable and warm enough.

Madius lit the last remaining candle.

"Not the luxury you'd be used to, ambassador?" he quipped. "This is, after all, Geramond."

"You're very young to be a tribune," Corsula observed, as he sat in the chair beside the fire. "Your family must be of a high order. What is your family name?"

Madius, at first, was reluctant to give it. "Junus," he replied, with trepidation. "My uncle is a member of the Senate, though not a respected one. Madrill Junus, of whom, no doubt, you know."

"A family of high order indeed," Corsula mused. "Or, at least, it used to be, until Madrill brought shame on it. No doubt why you were posted to this forsaken backwater. How long have you been here?"

"Two years," replied the tribune. He chuckled, as though to suggest that two years was too long a time to spend in this place, and that he must be unsound of mind to have done so. "When we came here they said it would be for six months, and then another legion would come to relieve us. It never did." He seemed to be full of regret and self-pity. "In any case, even if it had, the uprising happened, didn't it, and we would still be here, fighting this battle that we cannot win. For the past two months we have been confined to this damn castle. Can't go out. Can't go anywhere anymore. Always on the lookout for infiltrators."

He placed his torch in the fire hearth. Now that the candles were lit it was no longer useful. "I have walked every inch of the castle walls. Climbed every step in every tower. And every night I have watched their camp fires burning on the edge of the forest, and wished them all to hell. They tried to attack us the other day, and I was glad they did. It was starting, you see, and anything that starts must have an end. I wasn't bothered what the end was, so long as it came to pass and was over with. I would have gladly died that day, if it meant that I was out of this damn castle at last!"

"The attack failed?" asked Corsula.

"It was a close run thing, but it failed. They have not gone away, and will try again soon."

"We must not allow them to succeed," Corsula stated. "If Geramond is lost then what hope is there for our empire? None, tribune, none. And while we hold this castle we hold the entire province. That's why they want it so badly. It is the key to everything." He sensed the tribune's despair and feeling of abandon but also his sense of duty and the courage that had been indicative of his great family, for as long as his family had lived and walked. For a soldier or legislator, of any rank, a posting to this province was like being sent to another world, a wicked place from where soldiers or legislators seldom returned. Geramond was at the end of the earth; of spell-working and untold wickedness; and daylight was minimal so darkness prevailed; from where a man's home seemed gone forever. Fillian, when he returned from such a place as this, was not the same man: just as strong as before he had gone, and as sparkling as ever he was, but somehow possessed by the encounters of his journey.

Madius looked out of the window over the rooftops and smoking chimneys of Bosscastle.

"I often think of home," he said. "Of the farm I'm promised when I've done with this job. The sun on my back as I toil in a field. Fields of golden corn. The sound of birds in the trees ... crows, on an autumn morning. And of my children laughing at me, for I will be a clueless farmer ..."

"You are a Repecian, my friend," said Corsula. "And such things are yours by right of birth."

"Then why am I here?"

Corsula leant forward. "To do a job and do it well." He began to wag his finger. His senatorial ring glinted with the reflection off the fire. "Make no mistake, tribune. This province will not be lost. Oh, there are those in the senate that would gladly give it away. They say it is too remote, too brutal a place to be governed. But the senate is waning. The days of the old Republic are over, and the age of kings has returned. Soon we will have an emperor. It is the Great One himself who has decreed that the rebellion must be crushed. It is he who sent me here."

The tribune was surprised, not only by the ambassador's announcement, but by his willingness to talk candidly to someone as lowly as him. He felt honoured, and not a little puzzled. Corsula wore the ring of the senate, yet condemned it openly with talk of its demise. But talk of kings made him uneasy, not because of any strongly held convictions or his loyalty to the republic, but because Corsula knew who he was, who his ancestors were, and he had realised that he was being roused to give a reaction. He had no intention of involving himself in such matters. They were for others to debate, and did not seem relevant here. Corsula was looking at his ring and twisting it as it sat on his finger.

"A circlet of treachery and pretence," he said, but did not take it off.

"I'm pleased you're here," said Madius. "I thought that we'd been abandoned to perish in this cursed castle."

"You must be patient, tribune," Corsula replied. "I have come with a message for the Governor, and will give it to him when he is sober enough to listen and I am not too tired to speak."

"Forgive me, sir." The tribune turned to leave.

"Always on the lookout for infiltrators, you say?"

"It is our primary concern," replied Madius. "In some ways, it's all we can do. And when we find someone we don't recognise, we kill them."

Corsula smiled. "That's the first sensible thing I've heard since I've been here. You will find two people you won't recognise aboard the Buca Lapis. The Merchant Budogis rescued them from the sea. They claim to be fishermen, but I'm not sure. They're locked in the main cabin. Do you understand, tribune?"

"I understand, sir," the tribune replied, then left.

Galfall was lying on the bed with his hands behind his head and his legs crossed at the bottom. Gonosor was still trying to prise the door open.

"You're wasting your time, my friend," Galfall told him. "It won't open. We'll have to wait until the Merchant returns to let us out." Then, filled with a dangerous mix of energy and frustration, Gonosor began to ram the door with his shoulder. "No, Gonosor," Galfall said, leaping off the bed to stand between the Bodmifflian and the door. And Gonosor looked at him in a way that reminded him of the man he used to be: a face filled with rage and cold, heartless eyes; that powerful body that trembled with an uncontrollable, silent raving. The Gonosor familiar to Fogle. For the first time since embarking on this mission, Galfall was fearful of his companion and that must have shown on his face, for the big man suddenly remembered himself and withdrew from the door.

The footsteps of several men could be heard beyond, coming down the passageway towards their room. Galfall was half afraid and half relieved that something was finally happening at last. Perhaps it was the Merchant Budogis returning to release them. The youngster asked himself who it could be that was with him, and stepped away from the door himself. Gonosor, too, had heard them approaching and grabbed hold of Galfall's arm and pulled him behind him. "It's the merchant," Galfall muttered, reassuring himself. "Who else could it be?" He remembered that he'd told the ambassador that they were just fishermen, stranded at sea. He tried to remember the name he had given to Gonosor in case anyone needed to know.

The key turned in the lock, the handle lowered and the door opened slowly. There were six of them, the same six that had been standing on the dock when the Buca Lapis had arrived. Six Repecian soldiers to confirm Galfall's fears. "Where is Bucenta?" he asked. Madius came in first. He was evidently the most senior of them because his uniform differed slightly: a red cloak and plume instead of blue. "We are fishermen. Bucenta rescued us." But it was clear that they did not believe him.

Madius drew his sword from its scabbard and the others did the same. Galfall, babbling with fear, tried a different tact. "We are the property of the Merchant Budogis. You cannot harm us." But he had over-estimated the importance of his rescuer, for that was precisely what they intended to do. A legionary plunged at Gonosor with his sword, but failed to land a blow, for the Bodmifflian reacted swiftly and grabbed hold of the blade. Galfall escaped to the far side of the room, behind the bed, and armed himself with a stool. Madius and another legionary went after him. The blade of the sword cut deep into Gonosor's hand and blood dripped from the wound to spill down his arm and drip off the tip of his elbow. He kicked the legionary in the gut with his knee, and smashed his head into his face as he buckled; the sword was released from the gaping wound and Gonosor got hold of it by its hilt. Another legionary sped towards him but his face was slashed from one ear to the other and he screamed and collapsed to the floor. Gonosor wished that he, too, was able to scream, for he knew that he would have been twice as formidable had that been the case.

Galfall was preparing to defend himself with his stool, but Madius and the three remaining legionaries turned their attentions to the Bodmifflian, for unless they tackled him, he would destroy them all. Galfall, after all, was just a boy in their eyes, and no threat. The four of them approached him slowly. Gonosor was holding his sword aloft and willed them to come closer. How he longed for his tongue and to be able to roar like a bear, for that alone would have been enough. Why had Badad taken away such a fearsome weapon? What use he could make of it now.

'Go, Galfall, go. Be gone from here. BE GONE.' And that is what he did: ran from the room as swiftly as a hare from a trap, and did not care to look back, for the sight of his friend's demise would have haunted him forever. His friend. Was he really that? Gonosor of Baladorn, who had tried to kill Fogle and had tormented the rebellion from the start. Yes, he was truly his friend, and a true servant of Geramond.

He ran down the corridor without looking to see if any of the soldiers were pursuing him. If he had, he would have seen that one of them was. Nevertheless, he guided himself through the narrow corridors of the Buca Lapis as though he had designed the ship himself; knew at what point to turn, what steps to climb, until he found himself on the deck. He paused to catch his breath, and saw the legionary emerge from the ship's bowels, so leapt onto the dock bellow.

"Stop him," yelled the legionary, giving up the chase, and watched as the youngster scuttled up the steps that lead away from the cove. Suddenly, two further legionaries appeared in the gateway, forcing him to turn back from whence he'd come. "Get him," the legionary shouted. "He must not escape."

And so he was trapped on the dock with the first legionary coming down the gang plank from the ship and the other two hurrying down the steps. He looked all around him and saw nothing but water and an impregnable wall. Then an archer appeared on top of the wall and started to fire arrows down upon him. He stepped back towards the water's edge. It looked cold and dark in the pale moonlight, but was his only escape. He remembered that he could not swim and what had happened the last time he had tried, but the arrows were getting closer and one scuffed the side of his leg, so he had no choice but to step back further until he toppled in. The legionaries pursued him no longer, and merely peered over the edge to ensure that he had gone, and were glad to see that the surface was still.

The following day came quickly. Druim Square in the centre of Bosscastle was bustling with activity, as Bucenta inspected his fifty new slaves. They were organised into five rows of ten, one shackled to the other at the ankles and the neck; forty men and ten women. The merchant was scrutinising them closely; Delabole accompanied him down one row then another. It was snowing again and settling on the slaves so that it had to be cleared off their heads to reveal their hair. A good head of hair was seen as a sign of good health. And Bucenta forced open each and every mouth to look at the teeth for the same reason. One old man, nearly bald and with only a mouth full of gums, was rejected and pulled out of the line.

"A blind man would not buy this," said Bucenta scornfully. "And neither will I. You know what I like, my friend ... brawn or beauty." And the governor gestured for a soldier to unshackle him and remove him from the line, which was done. He was killed on the spot and carried away.

Bucenta continued until all of them had been looked at. Particular praise was reserved for a young woman, to whom Bucenta had taken a liking. "If she didn't command such a fine price I'd be tempted to keep this one for my own use," he snarled, unconcerned that the girl recoiled from him as much as her confinement allowed her to.

"You'll take them?" asked the Governor.

Bucenta stepped back to look at them again, and paused for thought. "I've seen better. I suppose I shall be able to sell them on cut-price."

"I know that slaves from Geramond are much sought after," Delabole replied, with as much craft as the merchant. "You'll sell them." With that said, forty nine pairs of eyes turned on him. Delabole could feel their loathing for him like it was stroking his skin, and he momentarily lowered his head, not with shame, but indifference.

"Take them away," he told Bucenta. "And send for me when your ship is unloaded. I want to see if I've got a fair deal."

"You will be pleased, excellency," Bucenta grovelled.

Corsula was standing on the balcony at the top of the East Tower, or the Cora. He was wearing a heavy cloak with a hood to protect him from the icy wind, and looked down upon the events in the square below, watching with interest as the slaves were lead away to the cove, the Buca Lapis and their new lives as workers and scullions. He knew that some of them would be fortunate and be purchased by a benevolent master who would care for them and treat them well. Most, though, would be subjected to cruelty and savage beatings like they were no better than street dogs. First, they had to survive the journey, and that was the hardest and most vicious part of the ordeal. The hull of the Buca Lapis was designed for boxes and vessels, not humans; a dark place where the air was foul and minimal. Yet, slavery was as old as the empire; an unquestioned necessity: indeed, the rock bed of Repecian society. Corsula, himself, had eight working in his household, a sign of his wealth and importance. Survill Cina, the leader of the senate, had eighteen. The supply of slaves came through conquest, shipped in from all over the world. The sale of slaves was a Governor's perk.

However, this was the first time Corsula had witnessed a man sell his own people into slavery, and had he not seen it with his own eyes he would not have believed that it was possible.

Delabole's gaze was drawn to the Cora. He saw the ambassador standing on the balcony looking down, and went to him. Corsula watched him disappear into the tower and waited for him to emerge.

"What would they have done, Governor, had they not been shackled?" he asked. Delabole was taken aback by the question, and concentrated on catching his breath rather than risk an answer. "Tear your head off, and peer into your body to search for your conscience?"

"I have no conscience," replied Delabole. "That is my strength. Why they fear me."

"Not so much that they dare not rebel. Perhaps it is not you they fear, but the walls of Bosscastle, and its dungeons."

From the top of this tower, the whole of the castle sprawled below them, and the sea beyond the east Wall, and the valley and the vast forest to the west. Smoke was emerging from the canopy of trees, just a mile or so away.

"That is how much they fear you, Governor," said Corsula, pointing westwards. "So much that they sent an army of peasants to seek you out."

"They will not break Bosscastle."

"No, they will not. I am here now." He stepped away from the edge and smelt Delabole's breath as he brushed past him.

"I am pleased to find you sober this morning. Before you indulge yourself with more of the merchant's mead, I will tell you why I am here!"

At midday, the remaining soldiers of the Garrison of Geramond were summoned to the Druim Square and instructed to stand in order of rank. At the front, the tribune Madius, a lone figure; his seniority indicated by that dark, ruby-coloured cloak and gold body armour. Behind him, five centurions, with grey cloaks and silver breast plates; then hundreds of legionaries, with short blue cloaks, plain bronze helmets and just leather tunics to protect them. The snow was still falling but not as heavily as at the break of day. The wind brought with it a chill, and got caught in their banners to rustle them like leaves. The soldiers held their banners proudly, but they were tattered and torn, as they were. Around the periphery of the Garrison the idle folk of Bosscastle gathered to see what was going on, and chattered amongst themselves like birds.

The snow was drifting and clinging to the rugged stone wall of the Great Hall, and to the steps that came down from the balcony in front of its entrance. The ambassador and the governor emerged and the chattering stopped. Delabole was puzzled as to why the army had gathered in the square, as much as they were puzzled as to who this newcomer was and why he had come. Corsula surveyed them all and then simply shook his head in disbelief. He gestured for the tribune to join them.

"I asked for the entire garrison so be summonsed."

"Yes, sir," replied Madius, and looked out over the square.

"Then this is all that remains of the mighty Sixth Legion?"

"It is."

Corsula turned his fearsome gaze on Delabole. "Tell me, Governor, how it is that the finest unit in the Imperial Army could be reduced to this by a band of peasants and serfs...?"

Delabole paused to think of his reply. He was shame-faced and his mind was frantically searching for a reason. "Do not underestimate the rebels, ambassador," he said. "For what they lack in military prowess, they more than make up for in numbers and enthusiasm." He realised instantly that he had said the wrong thing, and strained to think of something else that would have better explained what he was trying to say.

Corsula's face contorted with rage. "You are telling me that your legion has been annihilated because it was less enthusiastic for a fight than a butcher or baker or candle maker...?!" His voice was raised so that it could be heard as far away as the far side of the square. "Where is General Macara? Why isn't he here?" Delabole turned away and refused to answer at first. Corsula looked to the tribune to provide an explanation.

"He was killed," said the Governor urgently, glaring intently at Madius to quieten him. "He fell in the forest of Tangelwitt." He thought some more. "Took his own life when he realised that the battle, and the war, was lost. Tangelwitt was our last hope. The rebels had come from the north and were encamped there. Macara planned to rout them to stop them from coming to Bosscastle, but I warned him that the forest was no ally to a Repecian army."

All the while he had been talking he had been looking mainly at the tribune as though he was telling him, and Corsula detected that there was something not quite right about the Governor's version of events. Madius knew the truth, it seemed, but said nothing and appeared to be flushed and harassed, and looked at the ground. "After Tangelwitt we were forced to retreat into the castle and have been here ever since," Delabole continued. Yet if the General had listened to me and heeded my warning then we would have kept our army and strength and finally defeated them here. It would have been over and done with, and you would not have needed to come. You could have stayed away." He smiled, for he suspected that the ambassador believed him, or even if he did not, that the tribune had remained loyal.

"How different things would have been had the calibre of the general matched the quality of his soldiers." He stepped to the front of the balcony and stretched out his arm. He was swelling with confidence, now, and revelling in his performance. "So here is your precious legion. Barely able to stand let alone defend a castle. When the rebels attacked the gate we were able to fend them off. We may not be so fortunate next time. The fall of Bosscastle is close, and we must make arrangements for our escape."

Corsula came forward, reached into his deep pocket and produced a sealed envelope. Delabole was puzzled and wondered what he was up to.

"Stand to the back of me, Governor," he said, and broke open the seal. Delabole moved away. Corsula unravelled his piece of paper but when he spoke he was looking out to the crowd and not reading from it. "Friends … soldiers of Repecia," he began, in a loud, clear voice. "I come to you as the mighty tide is turning! I come to you just in time. My name is Corsula Corbissa, envoy of Palmatine, and I bring with me a message of hope from the Great One." He had their attention. "I will begin by telling you how things were in the homeland, how they are now and how they will be. Four months ago the Imperial Senate in Ramrah decreed that no army would be sent to Geramond to relieve you of your burden. They said it was too distant, too remote and too barbaric a land to be governable. And with that judgement all of you were condemned to suffer and die here; forsaken to the savages that would murder and massacre you all. They had betrayed you. We who were present had witnessed the first step on a road that would lead ultimately to the destruction and ruin of the Empire! Certainly the ending of the old Republic. There is a man, however, that will not abandon you or this province. A great man, sent by the Gods to save us all from the evils of corruption and decay." He held his arms aloft and managed, somehow, to raise his voice even further. "A new age is upon us. A golden age. The age of kings! And men will obey him and all will be well. The savages of Geramond may revolt against the will of a hundred old men, but will yield before the might and power of an Emperor! You know of whom I speak. The Great One himself. Lord of us all and master of the world." He held up the hand that was holding the letter.

"This is his message that I have been sent to deliver unto you. The word of Lord Fillian of Palmatine!"

There was a collective gasp of disbelief and all eyes were raised to the plain piece of paper in the air. To ordinary people standing around the edges of the gathering, the paper and the message within meant nothing: just another example of the strange and oppressive Repecian culture at work. The ambassador was another harsh and cruel figure sent to replace the missing General Macara and Delabole was there, as he always was, simply to make up the numbers and reveal himself to be the traitor and colluder that they knew him to be. Of all of them he was the most reviled, and a question frequently asked was asked again beneath their breaths. They looked at him and were amazed at his ability to look more imperious and alien than any of their conquerors; like a foreign general and their one real tormentor. He was dressed in his thick, black coat of office; the one with red fur around the hood and sleeves, while they were huddled together to keep warm and fend off the icy wind. The hood concealed his face and none of them could recall the last time they had been close enough to him to remember what he looked like. A man now so distanced and removed from them that they could hardly believe that he was once one of their own. But there was something different about him today: he seemed to be less significant than he usually was, and on edge, fidgeting as he stood and waited for the ambassador to reveal his message.

It was true. Delabole wanted to snatch the paper from Corsula's hand so that the message was never delivered, as though he sensed that it was in his interests that it was not. It was certainly a significant development and the Governor was anxious to know what it was before the rest of those present were told. He leant towards the ambassador and quietly suggested that he should be shown the paper, and reminded Corsula that he was, after all, Fillian's chosen representative of this province. The fact that Corsula refused his request and stepped further away from him was an ominous sign, and it prompted Delabole to withdraw even further into the background. He wished not to be here to listen.

Corsula, in that high, clear voice, read directly from the paper, without stumbling over the words or looking up. "I will not turn my face from the task of saving you, or be deterred from the road that the Gods have set down before me, at the end of which lies the destiny they have given me in order that all of us may be saved. This time of confusion and lawlessness must be done with, and order must be restored in the Empire, in all parts of Empire. We are the heirs of customs and traditions hallowed by age and handed back to us by these divine hands. No squabbling can topple them, whatever logic this age of the Republic can invent. And we must embrace a new age like an old friend, come to save us from extinction. The age of kingship, for only one man can rule now, and care for your suffering and deliver you to salvation. I am the Lord of Empire now, and all will serve me and yield to my demands. My good servant has been sent to you to give you hope so that you may remain strong and resolute, for only then will victory come. The conquest of Geramond and the fall of the Kings of Ardala began the ending of the old ways, and so it will be re-conquered to bring about the fall of the Republic once and for all time. Then we will prosper and rule the world as the Gods intended it to be ruled. I have in my house a prince of Geramond. A strong man whose name is Vagor, but whose strength belongs to me alone. A prince no more, but a servant of his one, true king, and who is caught in the glare of my majesty, so that those that would do me harm must harm him first, which they know they cannot do. Soon all men will be mesmerised by that blinding glare, and like Vagor, obey just one master. Be patient, noble soldiers, and wait for the ships carrying my army to arrive in those cold, northern seas. The war you have fought alone will soon be joined, and the tide will turn, for then it will be Fillian's war again. Be braver still until that day, and resist the death the rebels would bestow upon you, so that you can bestow upon them a worse one. Keep Ardala secure and its mighty walls strong, for that is the key to the entire land. Lose Ardala and lose the war. Be patient and brave and I will not turn my face from the task of saving you!"

Corsula, having finished the message, folded the paper and placed it securely in his pocket, then looked up. Suddenly, a ripple of applause from the back of the square, soon to be accompanied by a cheer that turned quickly into a tumultuous roar of approval. And hands were slapped on backs and their torn and tattered banners were waved in defiance. Corsula, a semblance of a smile on his face, acknowledged their thankfulness by holding up the back of his hand, as was customary for a man of the aristocratic order, then turned to withdraw into the Great Hall.

A roaring fire warmed the place. Corsula was sitting at the head of the long, broad table, with the tribune sitting at one side and the Governor at the other. A dog roamed about the floor until it settled in front of the fireplace.

"I will take some of the Merchant's tipple, now," Corsula said to the servant. "For all of us, for I wish to propose a toast." Their cups were duly filled with mead that had been warmed against the fire. "To empire. To the return to the rule of law."

"He means to return, then?" Delabole pondered.

"Yes," Corsula replied. "To finish what you could not."

"Then I wish him better luck. May he not make the same mistake as his chosen general, by assuming that the rebels are nothing more than farmers and peasants. He should know better than anyone that the people of Geramond are as hardened to the ways of war than any of his legions. They have been at war, in one way or another, for sixteen years." He gulped at his drink and held on to an expression that suggested he regretted that the ambassador had ever come here or the message was ever uttered or heard. His servant refilled his cup to put him one ahead of the other two. Corsula merely sipped at his and cringed at its sweet, sickly taste.

"Be assured, Governor, that when the Great One returns he will bring with him an army the likes of which has never been seen, in these parts or any other. The rebellion will be quickly dispersed. His retribution thereafter will be even quicker." He smiled to himself wickedly. "Those that survive will be transported, not to the slave markets of the south, but to the salt mines of Tega. You know not of where I speak. Why should you? But the tribune here will tell you that such a punishment is worse than any slow, painful death. While Geramond is cold, Tega is hot. So hot that a man's skin will blister and his blood will boil. Then, as the salt burns at his wounds, it is like a thousand arrows piercing his skin in a thousand places, until he dies and is cast in to the great salt pit within which he has toiled."

Delabole fidgeted. "And when the province is retaken, will Fillian return to Repecia?"

"And leave you in charge to lose it all over again?" Corsula chuckled. "I think it is safe to say that things will change. The Great One will want answers, like how his legion was annihilated and his favourite province almost lost."

"He will blame me," said Delabole, panicking. "But I have already told you that it was the General's incompetence that lost us this war!" His voice was quivering with frustration and anguish and his hands, used to rub his face and flatten his hair, were shaking. "I told him that Tangelwitt would ensnare him and so it did. I told him that the rebels would enter Bodmiffel over the Mor Pass, and that if we defended that route they would be forced to turn back or be stranded in the mountains where the snow and the wind would destroy them for us. But he did not listen and chose to let them come down into the forest lands." He stood up and pushed his chair away with the heel of his boot. "So I will not be blamed!"

"You are the Governor!" Corsula blasted. "You should have made Macara listen!" Delabole stepped away from the table and went to stand beside the fire. "Or was it the case that he did not trust your judgement? It's hard to heed the ramblings of a drunkard, after all. Besides, the rebellion should have been crushed the very day it began. Were you so intoxicated by the grape that you failed to even notice it, I wonder?"

Delabole stamped his foot on the ground and thumped his fist against the wall, opened his mouth wide and gave out a mighty scream of despair. "Damn them all!" he raged. "Damn them for ruining what I had." His hands encased his head. "Why couldn't they just pay their taxes. We all have to pay our taxes, don't we? They used to give their money freely to the kings of old. Why not to me? Am I so loathed? It is the Druid's work, all of this. He has filled them all with hatred and drove them to war to fulfil his vision." His face contorted with his own detestation. "He lives constantly in a dream, for what he believes will happen will not. They will not unite. They will not. The land of which he talks is gone forever. I am the future. The Druid must die." He had been rambling to himself for the most part, but now came back to the table and leaned his hands upon it next to Corsula, and told him emphatically: "The Druid must die!"

"You're drunk again, Delabole...!"

"No, no, I am not drunk. Listen to me and I will tell you how to finish this war so that it is done with forever."

"It will be done with when Lord Fillian returns," said Corsula.

"No. There is magic at work here." Corsula scoffed and looked at the Governor as though he was looking into the eyes of a mad man. Perhaps he was. "I thought magic and sorcery had gone from the world, but it is what drives this war, and your great Lord will not succeed unless he contends with him first...!"

"With whom? Of whom do you speak?"

Delabole, suddenly consumed with an irrational inclination to giggle, brought his face close to Corsula's.

"Badad the Wanderer, that's who."

"I have never head him speak of this name before," Madius said to Corsula, but with words that lacked conviction, and looking at the Governor out of the corner of his eye as he uttered them. The young tribune had a manner that was so sly and diffident that Corsula was inclined not to believe him and suspect at once that something was not quite right. Madius turned his face away from the Governor, lowered his mouth to the rim of his cup and sipped at his mead, hoping that the matter would be neglected and forgotten. But something was stirring within Delabole; he seemed to be possessed by a demon that compelled him to stride the length of the hall; the heels of his black boots clipping on the stone floor as his steps became broader and speedier.

"Liar!!" The word boomed and travelled the length of the place and seemed to reverberate off the walls and slap the tribune in the face. Delabole, who had said it, rushed to the table and pulled Madius out of his seat by grabbing hold of his upper arm. The cup was spilt and its contents oozed towards Corsula. "The name has been uttered before, by you as well as by me. And now we must speak of him again, for his work is afoot in the forest beyond the castle walls." He moved his head to look at Corsula.

"When your Lord asks me those questions, I will tell him that his legion was lost to magic, defeated by a sorcerer, for that is the truth. And when he calls me a fool and accuses me of falsehoods, it is when he sees it with his own eyes that he will know that I am not the man to blame!"

He released the tribune and let him collapse over the table. "I can control many things with an army, but not the craft of the Druid." Corsula was puzzled. He knew that the tribune was loyal to his homeland and the workings of empire, but he sensed that he was also loyal to the Governor, for they seemed to share a secret. And he regarded such loyalty as wasted and misplaced for the Governor, to his mind, was a drunken halfwit. More than that, now it seemed that he was bordering on madness with all his talk of magic and Druids. Corsula had heard the stories connected with Geramond but believed none of them. A Druidic culture once thrived here in the same way that the old Repecian Gods once held sway over those people, but not now. This was the age of men, not magic. And men of war changed the world, not sorcerers. Even here, in these times of hardship and conflict, such talk of witchcraft and spell-working was unsound and unacceptable.

He concentrated on the question nagging at his mind. Just what was their secret? He had suspected that they had one all morning, and now he was determined to find it out, even though he had already concluded that it was something totally incredulous and highly unlikely.

Six
A Face from the Past

Madius had settled, and swigged at his drink to encourage himself. Delabole resumed his position next to the fire, his own cup refilled, emptied and filled again. The servant had been so harassed that in the end he decided that it would be easier on his old legs to stand behind the Governor with a full jug.

"We have not been truthful with you, Ambassador," said Madius, shamefaced. "I am sorry." Then he paused, for although he knew what he wanted to say, had no idea how to say it. Normally very correct and eloquent, now he was struck with dumbness. He quickly glanced at the Governor. His loyalties, it seemed, were torn in two.

"Tell him," Delabole instructed. "Tell him and be done with it."

"General Macara was not killed at the battle of Tangelwitt Forest," the tribune continued. "Oh, that's where the war was lost, but he was lost long before that." Corsula was intrigued, and leaned in to the table to hear more. Madius cleared his throat. "When the rebellion started, in the Middle Lands, the Governor believed it to be the work of the aforementioned Druid."

"I knew him of old," Delabole added, rather unhelpfully. "And long had I waited for him to stir again in the Middle Lands. It had been quiet for a long time, but I knew that he had not gone away. The revolt in Woldshire was his doing, I was quite certain of that."

"The General was sent north to seek out this trouble-causer. Five others, of high rank, went with him. The Governor seemed to know where he could be found. A lake in the far north, where the mountains rise. He even drew him a map. The task was straightforward, or so we thought."

Corsula was inclined not to believe them. Why should he, after the lies and deceit they had already spun.

"It seems to me a very strange decision to send a general on an errand that could have just as easily been done by a lesser, more dispensable rank, like a centurion say, or a tribune." He was directing his remarks towards the Governor. Then his eyes moved to look upon Madius. "I'm sure that had you charged the tribune here with this assignment he would have welcomed the opportunity to make a name for himself. He is an ambitious young man. What better way to impress his Governor than to accept a mission that would rid him of his tormentor...?" Madius was uncomfortable, and every now and again glanced across the room at the Governor. Corsula, sensing that something was amiss, noticed everything: every look, every twitch of a hand or finger. "Very ambitious indeed, I would say. A yearning, perhaps, to emulate the great members of his noble family." He was talking to no-one in particular now and was merely offering his opinions to the air. "Distant ancestors, but fresh in his mind, and better men than his men-folk are nowadays. With the general safely out of the way, a tribune would be the highest ranking soldier here ..."

"You're wrong," the tribune protested, and surprised himself, and the others, with his forthrightness. "It's true to say that I was ambitious when I came here, but only to prove that the men of my family were not all as feeble and as purposeless as Madrill. But the one thing that Geramond does is to strip all such notions from a man's mind, to leave nothing but an instinct to survive. The only thing I desire now is to escape from here with my life and my honour, if possible."

"The tribune is not responsible," said Delabole. Whereas Madius had surprised himself with his frankness, the Governor now surpassed that with his righteousness. "I sent the General into the frozen north and no-one else. The rebellion had barely started and was nothing more than a tax protest at that point. As the tribune said, it was an undemanding task, but to be certain of its success, I insisted that he should be the one to do it."

"But your little tax protest spread, didn't it?" Corsula demanded. "From one town to the next, until finally the entire province was up in arms. And all the while the one man with the knowledge and expertise to be able to crush them was searching through the mountains for a harmless, old Druid! And for what...? To calm your jitters on a whim that a tax protest could have been the work of a sorcerer...!" He rose to his feet, his face was flushed with rage. "Tax protests, Governor, occur in every province several times in a year! If they are all the work of magicians then there are more of them than we thought...!"

Delabole, though, was unconcerned by Corsula's sneering and scorn, and remained steadfast to what he believed to be the truth. He came back to the table. His servant, jug in hand, went with him.

"You have been here barely a day, Ambassador," he said. Now it was his turn to be lordly and the master of the conversation. "You know not the workings or the power of the Druids. You come from the south, where things are not the same as they are here. Where men are masters of their destinies and fashion themselves to be masters of each other." He scoffed as he drank again. "Your country has no soul ... no perception of unworldly things. Therefore, anything that is done that is not done by earthly hands, is not seen, or if it is, it is not believed. You may not have magic in the south, but we certainly have it here. And it is all-powerful and men are slaves to it for they believe and know that it exists. The Druids were once numerous, and as mighty in their own right as the kings they served. There are few left these days. One that I know about. The last of the Wanderers, the most potent kind. He is Badad, and long has he sought to restore the kingdom of Geramond, and will destroy anyone who dares to defy him. Even your Lord Fillian, if he does, as you say, return here."

"Make no mistake about it, Governor," replied Corsula. "The Great One will return."

"Then when he does," said Delabole, firmly. "Mention the Druid's name to him, and watch him cower and coil, for he has met him before, on his last visit."

Corsula, frustrated and enraged by the Governor's insolence and his insistence on the subject of the Druid, stretched out his arm and with one rigid swipe knocked the cup out of Delabole's hand, to send it flying through the air. As though slowed by the thick, befuddled atmosphere, it went towards the tapestry and crashed against it, covering the image of the woman in steaming, red liquid. Delabole, shaken, stepped back to look upon the lady. Her face was covered, like her head was bleeding; her eyes peered through the fluid to look down upon him; to cut through his chest and stab him once more in the heart. He stepped back further and further, toppling his chair, until he was flat against the wall and could see her no more.

The Ambassador observed him closely as he slid down the wall to finish on his backside. As he placed his head between his knees and began to sob.

"He is drunker than I thought," he said quietly to Madius. Not so quiet that Delabole did not hear him. "I will have no more talk of Druids," Corsula said, louder. "I demand to know the truth. Where is Macara…?"

"We have told you the truth, sir," the tribune replied.

Corsula sighed deeply and his face sagged with sadness. "I fear that you have been here for too long, my friend, for you are as mad as the Governor!"

"I barely believed it myself," Madius insisted. "Until …" he paused, seemingly reluctant to say anything more.

"Until what?" probed Corsula, filled with intrigue. Delabole's sobbing was replaced by that strange, hysterical laugh of his.

"Until he saw him with his own eyes!"

Puzzled, the Ambassador asked: "Saw the Druid?"

"Saw the General," replied Madius, sadly, for the truth had been uttered at last. Delabole rose, scraping his back against the wall until he was on his feet again, laughing all the while.

"He came back. The General is alive still. That is to say, he was alive the last time I saw him." He paused for thought. "Alive might not be the correct word to describe him now. Breathing! That's what he does. He breathes…!"

Corsula was disturbed to discover that the General had been placed in a cell within the castle's dungeon, deep beneath the central keep, the Bossmilliad.

"Why have you put him amongst the thieves and traitors?" he demanded.

"You will see," replied the Governor, leaving the Great Hall and going down the steps onto the Square. "I can't wait for you to see."

With an urgency and eagerness that suggested that he had a point or two to prove, Delabole led the way across the square towards the Bossmilliad. Corsula and Madius followed, and those soldiers that had not dispersed with the others from earlier in the day, applauded and cheered as the Ambassador passed them, but he had no time to respond and barely looked at them. There was other business to attend to now.

The entrance to the dungeons was via a small door at the far end of the ground floor, now being used as a stable and saddlery. The place stunk, not of horses in particular, but of leather and dung combined into a pungent combination. Those whose job it was to tend to the animals abandoned their work temporarily to look on with interest as the three of them strode by and disappeared through the door. And down they went, deeper and deeper into the earth. The staircase was dark and narrow, lit only by the torch Delabole was holding at the front. As they descended into the pits of the fortress, groans and yelps of madness became louder and louder.

They were met at the bottom by the jailor; a vile, decrepit man whose smell was worse than the beasts above them. Delabole told him who they had come to see, he checked his records, then ushered them down the corridor to where they needed to be. The corridor was lined with cells – small, iron doors with only a small, grated opening. No windows here, and no daylight at all. Just darkness, infiltrated by flame. Now the groans became loud enough for them to hear. And those words and curses of madness were audible and recognisable and alarmingly real. Jailors shouted and whips cracked; final mummers of death resonated from the damp, algae-covered walls. The air was thickened by the mortal breaths of those that had died, to form a haze against the flickering torch. In all his years, Corsula had never seen such a foul place, and wished not to be here. And although his people were wicked and cruel, this was an ancient place built by the hands of the men that did not know they even existed, to punish and imprison their own people. Nowhere like this existed anywhere in the empire. It was unique, and their own perception of viciousness.

The cell containing the General was at the very end of the long corridor. The jailor unlocked the door and pushed it open with his foot. They entered; Delabole first, then Madius and finally the Ambassador, who promptly covered his nose and mouth with his sleeve to fend off the stench. The jailor scoured the room with his light, until Macara was found, cowering on his bench in the corner opposite the door. Rats screeched at the intrusion and when Delabole lowered his torch to the ground it revealed dozens of them, scurrying in all directions.

"We give 'im food," said the old jailor. "But the rats eat it! He eats the rats...!" And then he left them alone and disappeared into the blackness.

Corsula took the light from Delabole's hand and held it against the General. What he saw prompted him to step back towards the open door, and his breath to fall from his mouth to leave him aghast. He had known Macara before he had come here: both were regular visitors to Palmatine in the summer. He could barely recognise him now. Hair that was once black and neatly groomed was white and wild; skin that once was red and healthy was now grey and hanging from his face like wax from the tip of a candle. His eyes, though, were covered by a rag tied around his head, and he dare not give thought to what it was concealing.

"This is a man in his forties, yet he looks twice that age ..." he gasped, looking at Delabole for an explanation.

"He was the only one of the six to return," said Delabole.

"He came back clinging to a horse ... almost dead ... aged beyond recognition." He approached him and loosened the blindfold. Only now did the General realise that he was no longer alone, and began to fidget and panic. "He is cursed." The rag was pulled away to reveal eyes as red as blood, filled with pain.

"Who is it?" asked Macara, in a weak, strained voice. Corsula edged towards him. "It is your old friend ... Corsula."

Suddenly, Macara took hold of him by the shoulders and drew him towards his face, with strength that belied his frailty. Madius drew his sword but was stopped from using it by the Governor. Corsula cringed as foul, decaying breath swept across him. And the eyes, those damnable eyes, glared at him like he was a stranger. He realised that that is what he was: a stranger that would do him harm, come to mock and be repulsed. The name meant nothing to the

General. His old life, his old self, was lost. This miserable body and diseased mind, existing in a dark, wet cell, was the only life he knew now. When his lips parted to speak they revealed teeth so yellow that they almost shone as brightly as the flame torch. Red eyes, yellow teeth, set in a white face.

"Go back," he said, so meekly that he could hardly be heard. "Go back. There is nothing here for you. Nothing but death and despair!" He paused to recall Corsula's words. "Old friend...? Friend of mine...? You are mistaken, surely...? Who would be a friend of mine?" He wrapped his spindly arms around him. "Then if you are my friend, you will not leave me. Do not leave me alone in the dark. I am afraid of the dark. I am afraid of the rats...! They bite me and gnaw my feet...!"

Corsula levered his gripping hands from his arms so that he was free of him, and he withdrew to his corner again. Was a great general gone to be replaced by such a creature?

"Who did this to you?" asked Corsula.

Macara came forward; his eyes were wide open and sought the Governor. "He did," he hissed, once he had found him.

Corsula was satisfied by the answer, for it seemed to confirm what he had suspected: Delabole had imprisoned him to gain control of the war to move it on to his own agenda. Delabole, then, had turned a worthy general into this meagre figure writhing with sickness of mind in the corner of the cell. Nothing but the darkness and his solitude had warped him, and that was the Governor's doing, not an unknown and unseen Druid in the far north. Corsula, satisfied that this particular chore was done, for he could do nothing to help Macara now, took hold of the torch and turned towards the door. His eye caught Delabole's and it accused him of betrayal and treason, in a way that only his eye could.

Then: "He sent me there!"

Corsula, horrified, turned to look upon the General again. This time, as the torch turned with him, he caught sight of Delabole smirking.

"He sent me there," said Macara, sobbing and trembling. "And he knew what would happen to me! So I hate him for it. I hate him! I wish I'd never come here." He came forward on his bench and took hold of Corsula's arm again. "The other five died! Died horribly. I saw them perish." He whispered: "Tore their guts out, he did. Then he made me eat them." His eyes widened with horror and sadness, and he stuck his tongue out to try and clean it with his hair. "I wish I'd died too. No life have I now. Haunted, am I! Kill me!" He snatched hold of the tribune's sword, and cared not that it cut his hand. "I can see that you want to. Pity me. Kill me! Do it any way you like, but don't leave me alone in the darkness with the rats...!"

Madius did pity him and would have killed him there and then but for the Governor constraining his arm. And Corsula would have let him and would have taken the sword and done it himself, but for his curiosity nagging his mind. Macara let go of the blade and scurried back into his corner, held his head in his hands and closed his eyes tightly.

"He is coming!" His voice was shaky and full of terror. "Don't let him come." Instinctively, Corsula held the torch against the door and looked out along the passageway, before realising that this was a mind rambling with madness, and brought the light back into the room. "He's here!" Suddenly, a howling wind came along the passageway and entered the cell to extinguish the light and plunge them all into blackness. They panicked, and in their panic bumped into each other, and knew that nothing could ever be as terrifying as this: total darkness, and a chilling wind howling around the cell.

"Jailor!" yelled Delabole. They waited, and when they realised that nothing was happening, called out as one, fearful voice. And then they heard footsteps coming along the passageway, getting louder as they approached the cell. "It's him!" Macara panted.

The cell door swung shut but whatever was coming down the passageway was now in the cell with them. They could hear themselves breathing and the rats scurrying under foot, but were too afraid to talk. Suddenly, the torch in Corsula's hand was ignited again, to reveal Macara standing directly in front of it. He stepped back until he was against the stone wall, and gasped with fear. Something was different about the General. He seemed calmer, like his scraggy body was possessed by something that did not care for flesh and bones. His eyes were still shut tight, and his hand took the torch that gave light to the cell. Here, where light fails to come, he who has it will control all who fear the dark. Delabole and Madius had stepped away so that they could no longer be seen in the dimness. Corsula's heart was beating fast and faster as he waited for those grey eyelids to open. When they did, eyes as white as snow peered at him; to indicate that Macara had gone and had been replaced by something else.

Corsula cringed and recoiled as its bony fingers brushed against his face. The light was brought closer so that its flames almost singed his hair.

"Fillian, whoever he is, if this be his name, I will call him." The voice was not Macara's. Not filled with pain and torment in any way, but clearer and firmer. "He is strong, but I shall wear him down. The blood that is still wet on his hands, is the blood of a nation, that waits for vengeance. It will be his folly to return here, for I will finish what was started when last he came, and send him to ruin. Remember then my warning, messenger of Palmatine. When you are all trapped by ruin, don't blame fortune, for his want of power will tangle you all in this net of despair, past hope of rescue."

Delabole was found cowering in the corner of the cell where Macara had been, as though he was now the prisoner and the cell his own, private enclosure. He was cowering for he knew, had always known, that this moment would come, and was fearful for he also knew what it was that sought him. Corsula had been touched by an entity unknown to him; Delabole, now, was all too aware of what was standing before him, holding the light. He had been face to face with such a thing before. The head and the face was the General's, but the eyes within belonged to someone else, and they shone as brightly as clear ice.

The Governor shook visibly, and when it opened its mouth to speak he shrunk into himself. "It is you who must take the brunt of a nation's anger," it said, almost whispering so that only Delabole could hear. "Lord Governor ... betrayer of his kin ... murderer and tyrant. No longer feared, ne'er pitied, ever more reviled. Think, now, of what will happen when they find you. Think, now, of the pain that you will feel as they kill you. Like all the pain you have inflicted, my Lord, manifested into your own death. A death by your own hands is your only escape from such an end. But you must do it quickly, and tell no-one of your intentions. No glorious end for you." Momentarily, it glanced at the others and found it amusing to see their faces straining to hear the words that he was whispering. Then it brought all of its attention back to the Governor.

"Glorious endings are the proper covenant for righteous kings, like Vercingoral, your brother, or his son, the one, true king of Geramond."

"What ending did he have?" asked Delabole, bravely. "He was murdered, remember?"

"I remember." Its face turned sad, almost as though Macara had returned. "Fearful of the boy, to keep him from his course, your servant was sent to destroy him, like poor Macara was sent to destroy me."

"Servant? I sent no servant to kill the child. It was Gonosor of Baladorn that did the deed, and he was no attendant of mine…! Do you remember him? More your enemy than I ever was."

"You never saw him again, did you…?"

"How could I? Enraged by his actions you pursued him to Baladorn to destroy him."

"A courier came to you to report on the boy's demise."

"A glorious day." Delabole was recovering from his initial fear to be quite strong and stubborn again.

"The Union is broken, he said to you."

The Governor's face contorted with anger.

"There never was a union. It was only ever a misguided notion of a forgotten Druid. Geramond is an ancient land, corrupted by time, and will never rise to be a country again."

"Then why send Gonosor to kill the boy?"

"The same reason you killed Gonosor for doing it," was Delabole's instantaneous reply. "Those were giddy times when a man's mind was ruled by thoughts of his own needs."

"How foolish you were to place your trust in a stranger, for his words have deceived you, Lord Governor. What you thought was done was not done." The torch was thrust into Delabole's face, but the flames did not burn him or hurt him physically in any way. They wrapped themselves around his face; curled around his ears and covered his head.

"Look into the fire," it said. "And the truth you will see."

Within the yellow flames a vision came to Delabole; of a boy, nearly a man, toiling in a field to round up his wayward sheep. Recognising the face, Delabole tried to pull his face away from the flames, but where he went they went with him, forcing him to look. "He did not perish, but lives in the middle lands. Can you see him? Do you know who he is? He is your kith and kin. Your nephew, the king. Soon he will come south to claim his throne and fulfil the destiny of his men folk. He is Carthrall of Kaw, king of all Geramond. Untouched and unscathed despite your assertions to do him harm."

The vision ended as quickly as it had come and the flames returned to the tip of the torch. It stepped back into the middle of the cell, giving Delabole space to catch his breath and compose himself. Suddenly, the light disappeared and the three of them were plunged once again into darkness and turmoil. They panicked as they had before, and called out again for the jailor, without any hope of him coming to their aid. Corsula took hold of Madius's arm and held him close. Delabole remained in his corner. Then, from out of the door, further along the passageway, the light returned and lured them towards it.

Perhaps the jailor had heard them after all. Carefully, feeling their way along the damp walls, they moved towards the light, and as they got closer to it, walked freely. It was coming from a cell two doors from where they were. Madius was pushed to the front; he drew his sword and held it in front of him as he stepped into the doorway. Delabole and Corsula moved behind him, and saw that it was still with them, standing just inside the cell.

It chuckled to itself. "Where light was all forbidden, my prying flicker shone; all that men lay hidden, it dark my shining shone...!" It was interested, specifically, in Delabole, for whom his words were intended. Strangely, Macara seemed to have returned, for it was that low, agonising voice again. "Men that were forsaken, and in forest graves they lay; disturbed the leaves and rose again, to see the light of day." It held out its puny arm to shed light against the wall of this new cell.

Delabole's eyes spread open as wide as they would go, his mouth was agape, for what he saw now shook him to his core. The other two were puzzled, but not too discomposed, for what was now being shown to them had no significance other than what it was: a prisoner shackled to the wall. Delabole, though, was disturbed and stepped back and could barely look at him, for he knew who it was, had not thought of him for years and had hoped never to see him again. It was Gonosor of Baladorn, and he was alive still, which meant that the vision he saw in the flames was true and that the boy was also alive.

Governor Delabole was known to suffer fits of rage when he was not given what he desired. He was suddenly overcome with rage now, grabbed hold of the torch and pushed Macara to the ground. The General collapsed into a heap and scurried away from the rats. Delabole held the light against the prisoner's face to confirm his fears, then turned and fled the dungeons. The other two hurried to keep up with him, afraid of being forsaken to the dark. The door was not closed and locked.

They returned immediately to the Great Hall, leaving the Bossmilliad with such eagerness that they were almost running, drawing attention to themselves. The fire was still burning in the hearth and the servant, who had seen them trotting across the square, was standing aside it holding the jug of mead in his hand preparatory to filling his master's cup, as though it was his only duty, and that the Governor required no other service but this.

"His name is Gonosor, Lord of Baladorn." Delabole found great comfort from the fact that his hand was gripping a cup. "Prince of Bodmiffel ... and one time heir to that throne ..." He glanced momentarily at the tapestry. "Until he was usurped by his sister. From what I know of him he is a troublesome, vicious man. So cunning and scheming that his own father banished him to the southern forests and hoped never to see him again. So did I, but it seems that the Druid spared his life to serve his own purposes. And now he is here, in my own fortress. How? How can it be?"

The Merchant Budogis burst into the room, in something of a panic and dilemma.

"He has gone. My beautiful slave has gone." He came towards where Corsula and Madius were sitting. "My cabin door was open and my lovely guests nowhere to be seen. I had such high hopes for the big one."

Delabole, at first, was annoyed by the Merchant's sudden and unwanted interruption, but was drawn to his words and looked at Corsula, not Budogis, for an explanation. He had now regained his authority and had placed himself firmly in charge of events, for he had proved that strange things were afoot in this province that were beyond Corsula's comprehension. The Ambassador had gone quiet again, like he was when he had first arrived. Like Madius, all he wanted now was to escape this ghastly place with his life and his sanity. To be in a land where magic and sorcery thrived was to be in a land where a mortal man was helpless; a mere pawn in a game that would be won by only the one who possessed such trickery. He was quiet when he had arrived whilst he observed his new surroundings and acquaintances; he was quiet now because he had nothing to say. It was left to Madius, therefore, to offer the explanation.

"The Merchant Budogis rescued him from the ocean, with one other, a youngster who claimed to be his son. He told him that they were fisherman, stranded by the storm." Delabole laughed at the thought of the mighty Gonosor pretending to be such a lowly man. "They were given food and comfort, little knowing that they were to become slaves."

"The youngster ... what became of him...? Is he too in my dungeons...?"

"He is dead," Madius replied.

"How do you know?" Delabole came to the table and rested his hands along its top edge. "Did you run him through yourself? Put your own hands around his slender neck to throttle the life out of him?"

"He escaped from the Buca Lapis ... we gave chase and trapped him on the dock. Rather than give up he chose his own death by stepping back into the water."

Not satisfied, the Governor slumped into his seat. "He is still alive then," he said, sadly.

"No-one that has ever fallen into the cove has survived the

current," Madius protested, then realised what he had said and immediately regretted his choice of words. Delabole glared at him angrily, for he of all people did not need reminding of that particular, grim statistic.

"He did. They were sent here by the Druid." He would have sounded paranoid and dazed had he been talking to any other men but these. "And the Buca Lapis was meant to rescue them from the sea and bring them into Bosscastle. Do you think that he would let this youngster drown in the cove after going to such lengths to get him here…?" He rubbed his face with his hand. "He is still alive, and is hiding in this fortress. Find him. Use however many men you need, but find him quickly." The servant, seeing the cup neglected on the table, came forward to fill it. Strangely, Delabole gestured for him to leave it.

"This is folly." Corsula's voice was nervy and his manner less confident. "Every man must be employed along the walls to ward off an attack. The castle must not fall. The Great One will return to the harbour at Bossiney. If the castle falls then the road from the harbour will be blocked." He uttered his statement more because he knew that it was his duty to, than the fact that he believed it.

"The rebels tried to attack us once before, and failed miserably," said Delabole. "Their leader is not so bold as to try it again." He was talking specifically to Corsula. "But hear this. Gonosor of Baladorn and his young stooge were brought into Bosscastle for one purpose alone … to open the Western Gate! The rebels of Ingelwitt are waiting in readiness for that undertaking to be accomplished. What we must do is make sure it never is. Now, the Bodmifflian is no threat so long as we have him bound and chained to a dungeon wall, but make no mistake, the youngster is at large within this fortress … wandering the streets … lurking in shadow, waiting for his moment to come…!" He turned his attention to the tribune. "Find him. Keep twenty men on the gate and instruct the rest to scour every inch of this castle … every room in every house, every tower, every sewer. And when you find him bring him to me … alive if possible but dead if necessary."

Madius acknowledged the demand and stood up and left the Great Hall with an urgency in his stride. The Merchant made quick use of the vacant chair. "I'm not quite sure what is going on, nor that I care to be involved," he said, sheepishly. "But I gather that my guest has made himself a nuisance to you, Governor, and I feel that I must take part responsibility for that." He bowed his head and held his arms apart. "I am sorry, my Lord. All I can say is that I will take him back and lock him away with the other slaves in the bowels of my ship. I can assure you that he won't escape from the Buca Lapis so readily next time, my lord."

"There will be no next time," Delabole replied.

Bucenta's eye twitched.

"I would respectfully remind your Excellency that the slave belongs to me. What a man scoops off the surface of the sea surely then belongs to him, to do with what he wishes. The young one is no great loss to me, he was too white-faced and his arms were as narrow at the top as they were at the bottom. But I have great hopes for the big one whom you currently hold in your nasty dungeon...."

"To sell him at auction to the highest bidder...?"

"Yes, Excellency. That is what I do. How I make my living."

"I have no doubt that you are very good at it, Merchant. But you would be well advised to leave Gonosor where he is ... where he can do no more harm."

Bucenta was suddenly enraged and abandoned his courteous approach.

"Have you any idea how much a man like him could fetch at auction...? A hundred, a thousand demari...! More if enough people covet him, and they will."

"Then they covet death," Delabole said, firmly. "And whoever bought him would be dead before they could get him home."

"I shall take my chances," the Merchant protested

Impulsively, Delabole picked up his neglected cup and hurled it at the hapless Merchant to shut him up once and for all. "You don't know him like I know him!" He was angry again. "You have no idea what he is capable of ... how violent he can be and how swiftly he dispels those that would try to control him. In a rage, he is as strong as an ogre and as vicious as he cares to be." He spoke with genuine concern, as though he had himself experienced the wrath of the man. "And when he is like that, no-one can contend with him. Make an enemy of him and his wickedness knows no bounds. Those that would stand in the way of what he desires shall see it for themselves. Only now he is ever more dangerous, for he has allied himself with the Druid and yearns to please him."

"What will become of him?" asked Corsula, timidly, almost afraid of the answer. Delabole thought for a moment.

"There can be only one solution to the Gonosor problem. We must kill him. And quickly."

"Such a waste…!" slammed Bucenta.

"The Governor is right," said Corsula. "We will hang him tomorrow … and let the others see us hang him … then we will tell them that such a fate will befall all that rebel against the rule of law…!" He rose to his feet, invigorated again. "We must build the scaffold strong and make the noose tight so that he does not linger too long." He stopped talking when he noticed that the Governor was lost in thought. "What is it…?"

He emerged from his trance, and smiled cunningly.

"I wish to see him before he is gone. There are some things that cannot remain unsaid. And there is something I wish to show him."

Corsula did not hide his disapproval.

"I must protest…!"

"Rig up the scaffold on the balcony beyond that door!" The Governor was insistent. "This room shall be his death chamber."

"You said yourself that he is dangerous."

"Then bring him to me bound in chains." His tone was serious and forthright. "But bring him to me."

The fact that there were soldiers everywhere, separating into small groups of five, spreading out across the Druim and disappearing with speed and urgency into the narrow streets and alleyways, suggested to the people of Bosscastle that something was afoot, and they began to chortle and chatter amongst themselves as to what it could be. Under normal circumstances these type of gatherings were strictly forbidden and quickly dispersed, but these were not normal times, and gossip thrived in the absence of control. One particular rumour was the strongest, and overcame all others until it was known to all of them, to thrill them and fill them with hope.

"I tell you I saw him with me own eyes," said Crispill Crull, a short usually bad-tempered man who worked on the dock. "It was him all right. As mean-looking as ever he was. I watched as they brought him off of that ship … and it took all of the strength of four men just to pull him up the steps. Oh, it was that very man. The Lord of Baladorn, come back to save us, just when we need him most."

The very mention of the name brought about a collective gasp of astonishment and excitement. It was a name from the past, that ought not to be uttered now, and once it had been said they all looked around to see who else might have heard, for this was a time when talk of days and people long gone was to disobey the Governor and therefore risk life for it. No-one who should not have had heard, and they were glad of that at least. They mumbled the name to themselves under their breaths and could barely believe that they were doing it. Each member of this small group knew precisely what the other was thinking for their faces, one and all, carried a grin of hope. But when the giddiness of the thought subsided, they began to question the validity of the rumour and the accuracy of Crull's observations. Could it really be true that Gonosor had returned to Bosscastle after so long in exile? And if it was, had he truly returned to save them? Each of them was inclined to doubt it. Then they noticed another band of soldiers emerge from the Bossmilliad only to disperse into the streets beyond the square, they began to allow themselves to hope that it was true after all.

Seven

The Tapestry

Crispill continued with his revelations and said more than it was wise to. Listening on the back edge of the gathering was the young servant girl, Salissa; and with a keen ear and a sharp interest in what was being discussed that belied her status and her presence beside these tall, burley men. She left before the talking was done and disappeared quickly into the narrow street that led to her house, before any of them had even noticed that she had even been there.

What had always been just a routine journey down this dark street, past the bakers and the now closed-down Forester Inn, was suddenly a formidable undertaking now, for the soldiers were everywhere; knocking on doors, and when they were not opened promptly kicking them down with their thick, heavy boots. So that this was a girl who had spent her whole life longing to be noticed, now wanting nothing more than to be invisible. She stayed close to the old, dilapidated houses on one side of the street but crossed quickly to the other side when she approached a house that was currently being paid a visit.

"Open up in the name of the Governor!" she heard them say, but dared not linger for too long in case one of them noticed her and followed her home.

Turning left into her alley, where the houses were so close they almost touched at the top, she breathed a sigh of relief at last, for this part of the citadel, her own part, was seldom visited by anyone let alone the Governor's soldiers.

Her own dwelling was more a shack than a proper house, built not of stone but made entirely of wood, with one narrow window beside the small door, and a roof that looked ready to slide onto her head as she knocked quietly on the door, lifted the latch and slipped inside.

This was just a one-roomed shack and dark because of the solitary window. Galfall was sitting on the bed at the far side clutching a thin candle for warmth as much as it's light. Salissa closed the door and pushed her mother's old dresser in front of it to keep it closed. Not a word was spoken. She lit the three candles on top of the dresser, the one on the table beside her bed and finally the one on the shelf above the wash basin. Galfall had already sensed that she was uneasy and agitated.

"I slept a little while on your bed," he said, carefully. "I hope you don't mind."

"The streets are full of soldiers," she replied, snappily. "They're looking for someone and won't stop until they've found him."

This moment was bound to come from the moment Galfall had accepted this girl's kindness, and the guilt-ridden expression on his face confirmed her fears.

"They're looking for you, aren't they?"

He nodded.

"I never meant for you to become involved." He got onto his feet and walked to the door. "I will leave now and no-one will ever know that I was here."

"And go where?" she demanded. Her tone suggested that she was on the lookout for answers to the new questions in her mind. "To the Western Gate and hope that the guards will stand by as you open it and let the others in? For that is your purpose here, isn't it?"

"What do you know about me?" he demanded, shocked that she knew as much as she did.

"I only know what is being said in the streets," Salissa replied. "That you came here on the Buca Lapis with Gonosor. The Governor has him where he wants him but somehow you managed to escape." She momentarily turned away from him and lost herself in her own thoughts. "I've been sheltering you. I've given you food and warmth." She turned sharply. She was angry. "Have you any idea what they'll do to me if they find out you were here?" She was panicking and wished that she had never seen him laying in that gutter, much less picked him up and brought him back to her home.

"They will not find out," he assured her. "I will go now and no-one will see me leave." Galfall turned to go but hoped that she would stop him. She did.

"What does it matter anyway?" she pondered. Then she noticed a new patch of damp on the wall but cared not to be troubled by it now. And she noticed how dark and cold this place was, how the ceiling dipped in the middle; a crack in the door that was not there when she had last looked. Still, she was not troubled by any of it.

"Look at it." Her tone was one of embarrassment. "This room is the sum total of my life. It's cold and wet and only mine because no-one has ever wanted it for themselves. I've always hated it. So what does it matter that they find out that I've been helping you? What can the Governor do to me that's worse than living here? Alone, night after night, listening to every noise and every footstep past the door and longing for them not to stop."

Now it was Galfall's turn to ponder questions in his mind about her. Who was she? For he did not know anything about her at all. Why was such a pretty girl living alone in this depressing place? He assumed that she was about the same age as he was, but he had a mother at home and friends in the forest, who were willing him to succeed and return safely. Who did she have? For the first time since he had arrived in her home, he paused to look closely at her. Her clothes were tatty and worn and her hair, although full and long, was dirty; her face, although beautiful, was troubled and filled with sadness. He realised, suddenly, that for the first time in his life he pitied someone more than he pitied himself.

"You don't have to go," she said, and took his hand away from the door. "Soldiers are everywhere. They will see you … interrogate you if they don't recognise your face. They will take you away!"

He was pleased, of course, to be stopped from leaving, but was not convinced he should stay. He was hesitant and thought for a moment about what he ought now to do, and told himself that he must be bold and step onto the street, for his task was not going to do itself. Badad, Fogle and the others were waiting for him to succeed, even though the Governor knew that he was within his castle walls and had dispatched his entire garrison to find him. The time to venture out and fulfill his errand was surely now, just when everyone was least expecting it.

Hesitating for a further minute of so, he remembered that he had not done something he had meant to, and walked briskly towards the fireplace. It was laid out with kindling and straw and required only a flame to set it off.

"I was going to light it earlier," he said. "But this is your home and it didn't feel right that I should be warm while you were working."

It struck her as a very generous and gallant gesture and she removed her shawl and placed it on the bed then handed Galfall the candle to light the fire.

"Wait!" she said, filled with panic. "They will see the smoke from the chimney and know we're here! The entrance to the alley is narrow and it's always dark. With luck they won't come down unless we give them reason to."

Galfall took the candle off her and held the flame against the straw.

"They will come regardless," he said, as though it was inevitable.

"Doesn't that worry you?" she asked, surprised at how calm and measured he seemed. "They'll ask for your identity and expect you to prove it there and then. If they don't believe you, and they won't, they'll take you to the Bossmilliad!"

The fire began to roar up the back of the chimney.

"So be it."

"People who are taken to the Bossmilliad are never seen again!" she stuttered. "I've heard men talk of the things that go on there. Wicked, evil things!"

Galfall, still calm, turned to look at her. "There is nothing anyone can do to me that can keep me from my course," he said, bristling with confidence that was close to arrogance. And he was going to say something else but decided not to. He was going to tell her that he was invincible, but realised that she might scoff at the remark, which she would have. In fact, she could not understand his attitude at all, and wondered how he could be so still and serine when the entire Repecian garrison was looking for him.

Galfall stepped away from the fire and came and sat next to her on the bed. She edged away, not fearful of him but annoyed at his indifference to the danger he had placed them both in. He sensed her mood but was not bothered.

"Remember where you found me?"

"Lying in the gutter, exhausted and barely alive," she said.

"Well, I shouldn't have been alive. I should have been dead." Salissa was confused. "What do you mean?" she asked. "You were alive. Had I not found you when I did then it might have been different. But you were alive."

He thought of the correct words to use to properly express what he was trying to say.

"It took the strength of three Repecian soldiers to suppress Gonosor," he began. His train of thought took him back to the Buca Lapis. "I have never seen such strength in just one man. Like a giant, he is. And while they wrestled with him I made a run for it and got off that ship…! Didn't get much further, though. One soldier behind me and two more coming down the steps. Have you ever been in the cove?" She replied that she had not. "One way in and one way out … up those steps or down them. They had me trapped on the dock side, them in front of me and nothing behind me but water. As I stepped back I knew one thing was for certain … I was done for … and I had failed. The Druid had given me an impossible task, I thought. And it was bound to have ended like this from the moment I had agreed to do it. So I stepped back into the water because I thought that it would be the easier way to die!"

"Down I went, and further and further, until the light at the surface was gone. It was cold … I have never been so cold. I held my breath for as long as I could, but what was the point of that if I was going to die anyway? A strange thing, preparing yourself to die. I was not afraid at all. The Druid once told me to fear only fear itself, for it is the enemy of valour and courage. Nor did I pity myself, for it would have served no purpose but to make me miserable my final moments. Pity and fear are one and the same, I think. And so down I went, until my final breath was spent and it all went black. Then I heard a voice …a woman's voice, but no woman I knew … definitely not my mother's.

"So a watery end for Galfall after all," she said. Her voice was soft and it soothed me to think that I was not alone. "He has brought you here with promises of greatness. And blinded by the wisdom of his tongue you did choose to obey him. Foolish is this son of Gringell, for his faith is his undoing. Wise is the man who only has faith in himself." Then, just when thought was about to abandon me, I was saved.

"I was caught in a mighty breath, that carried me upwards towards the light at the surface, and propelled me into the air on a column of water. I opened my eyes and saw the Buca Lapis down below, resting in the dock, and I knew that I had been spared again. The column of water I was sitting on was as firm as solid ice, and it changed to form a hand ...like a giants hand ... that cast me down onto the dockside before withdrawing into the middle of the cove. Turning, I saw ten soldiers running towards me, but I did not fear them now. And I was right not to. The column of water collapsed back into the cove with such force that it gave rise to a great wave, that crashed against the dock with such force that the soldiers were washed away to their deaths, while it merely lapped against my feet and barely touched me at all. It was the Druid's wonderful work again."

"And I found you at the top of the cove steps," said Salissa.

"Yes," he replied. "Soon after that in fact. Although, in truth I don't know how long I had been lying there." Sitting on the bed, he leant back and rested on his elbows. Salissa walked to the window next to the door and carefully peeled back the curtain to look out into the alley. "Let them come, if they will," Galfall told her. "Let them take me away, for the Druid will not allow them to harm me. I am protected by him now for I am here to do his bidding. Wherever they put me he will find me and rescue me so that I can fulfil the task appointed to me."

"So you are invincible?" Galfall paused to think, then agreed that he was. "This Druid can save you from all things?" The tone of her voice and the edgy way she lowered the curtain suggested that she was not entirely convinced. Looking at him lying casually on the bed she quickly deduced that he was either quite mad or did actually believe that what he had told her was the truth. The truth in his mind only, she pondered and concluded that his mind was troubled, which went some way to explaining his detached and nonchalant way of behaving, that was beginning to annoy her so.

She had heard mention of Druids before, mostly as a child listening to her father talk of olden days, before the conquest of his land. Secret talk whispered behind closed doors. Suddenly, her recollection of such times brought back memories of her father too, which in turn brought her mother to mind. Private thoughts and not for her guest's use, as she had no desire to lay them on the air as easily as he seemed to manage. Her memories were happy ones for the better part. She recalled how lovely her mother was; not beautiful to the eye at all: a short, podgy woman, but one that bristled with goodness and love for her. As did her father, who worked as a cook in the Governor's kitchens: a forthright and proud man so loathing of his oppressors that his hatred consumed him totally, yet whose loyalty to the bricks and stones of Bosscastle meant that he would never have left it, even if he had been permitted to. Yes, they were happy memories for the better part, but so distant as to seem unreal to her now.

Finally, as she placed a log on to the fledgling fire to give it sustenance, she recalled how and when they perished, so that her final memory of them for now was the saddest of them all. An event that had made her an orphan and condemned her to this miserable life. Had hardened her and taken away all her womanliness to leave instead a bitter void. She seldom laughed and had cared for no-one, had no-one care for her, since that day when they were taken from her. She was, however, her mother's daughter and was also filled with goodness; had once thought herself capable of loving someone and having someone love her; someone to talk to and to fret about, someone like her father, who would be strong so that she need never be afraid; and her life would be less ordinary.

She had deliberately chosen the one log in the pile that should have been avoided: the dampest, mossiest one. As it began to smoulder in the hearth, with just one paltry flame clinging to the embers of the kindling wood, thick grey smoke began to bellow up the chimney. Galfall had noticed and was waiting for her to become panicky, but she did not.

"Do you know the way to the Western Gate?" she asked him.

He shamefully shook his head for he felt foolish to have to admit that he did not. The truth was that he had become disorientated amidst the maze of narrow streets and alleyways that had brought him to this particular dwelling. Salissa went to the window beside the door and peered out again. Then she turned to take another look at her guest. His hair was ruffled and his face was soiled with soot from the fire; slim but with broad shoulders, and his eyes sparkled. She knew that she was capable of loving someone and asked herself if she could fall in love with him, before deciding that, for now, she could not.

"I will take you there," she said.

Galfall was taken aback by her sudden courage and interest.

"I cannot ask you to do that," he replied.

"I am volunteering," Salissa insisted.

Galfall rose from the bed. "I am protected by the powers of the Druid, and no harm can come to me, but his powers will offer you no such protection. It's too dangerous and I cannot allow you to do it. I will find my own way." He gently pulled her away from the door. "You have been very kind, and when Bosscastle is liberated I will come and find you and thank you properly. I am leaving now." He pushed the dresser away from the door.

"Do you have any idea what my life is like?" When Galfall turned he saw that Salissa was fastening a belt around her waist to gather in her gown; then she put her shawl around her shoulders and fastened it tight against her neck. "I have waited years for something like this to happen to me."

"But it's too dangerous," Galfall insisted.

"If the gate is opened will the rebels be waiting?"

"The Druid is waiting," he replied, sadly, for he knew now that she was not going to heed is warnings.

"And will he free us? Will the Governor be finished?"

"Yes."

"The Governor killed my father." As she passed him and went out of the door, she concluded: "I will take you to the Western Gate!"

On the Governor's orders, a scaffold was erected on the balcony of the Great Hall. A wooden structure simple in design but adequate enough to hang a man and take his strength for as long as it took him to die. The day of the execution started out cold and blustery with occasional flurries of snow. Gonosor was brought from the Bossmilliad to the Great Hall before sunrise so that he was safely inside before people had began to gather in the Druim Square. The Governor had been waiting all night for him, snatching only a little sleep from the clutches of his drunkenness, in his chair at the far end of the room.

He had been calm for most of the night and very spirited at times, sharing his precious tipple with Corsula and even offering a cup to his poor, over-worked man-servant, who politely declined; had told stories and jokes and laughed at them himself even though the ambassador did not find them amusing, largely because most of them were about his own people and he did not understand, nor want to, the strange ways of this strangest of lands. Then, after stepping outside to take the air, to discover that dawn was approaching, the Governor suddenly became agitated and anxious again. And as Gonosor was brought across the square to the Great Hall, he was an utter wreck and recoiled in his seat and slipped into a rage, cursed his servant and threw his cup at him.

Delabole caught his breath and brought his body forward to rest his hands on his knees; took several further intakes of breath and began to settle himself down again. Gonosor had arrived; standing in the doorway, just a silhouette against the deep blue of the early morning sky, but whose bulk and broadness was unmistakable. Corsula was intrigued to witness the prisoner's arrival and the Governor's strange, trans-like reaction to it; like a lion had wandered into the room and he was frozen with fear and dread. And the fact that the lion was secured on a leash made no difference whatsoever.

Gonosor was brought further into the room, or rather pushed and prodded into the centre of the room by the three soldiers who controlled him. Only when Delabole saw how gaunt and feckless the Bodmifflian looked did he begin to relax and thaw into his old, dogmatic self, to regain control of the Great Hall and those within its walls. And when Corsula realised how feeble the prisoner was – his hair had been hacked by his jailor and his beard cut badly so that in places his face had been slashed and in others thick hair remained

– he began to wonder what all of the fuss was about, for this man was no threat and much less a prince.

Delabole's resurgent confidence was manifest in the devious and gleeful smirk across his face.

"Leave me alone with him."

"There is no time for your games," Corsula protested. "We should hang him before the mob assembles in the square. If he is who you say then his execution might rattle them and cause us problems we cannot cope with. Our only charge is to keep the fortress secure." Although the Ambassador was tired after a long night spent in Delabole's company, he was nevertheless forthright and spoke firmly. "We cannot allow ourselves to indulge in personal grievances and fantasies. If this man is a threat to the security of the castle and the province then he should be executed without delay and without a fuss, for his death, if witnessed by the mob, could be turned against our advantage and stir feelings that are best left suppressed."

The Governor chose not to hear. "Is he bound securely?" he asked the soldiers. They all nodded at the same time. "Then leave me with him. I will call you when I am done." Corsula rose from his seat at the table and stepped from behind it.

"What business is more important than the business of defending Ardala...?" he demanded. Delabole grudgingly turned his attention away from the prisoner to look at the Ambassador. His eyes were still and firmly set in a resolute face.

"If only you knew," he said. "I wish that I had the time to tell you. But time, as you rightly say, is limited. Please, leave me alone with him. What I have to show him will not take long ..."

His request was granted. Corsula walked towards the exit, pausing only to look at the prisoner one last time, and went out, shaking his head in disbelief, for he still did not know who he was or why he was deemed so important to be granted one last audience with the Governor before his execution. He decided that some things were best left to those who were bothered by them, and left.

The servant scampered out next and the Governor gestured for the soldiers to leave too. Before they did, however, Gonosor was pushed further into the room, and because his ankles were bound together, he stumbled and fell to the ground. Then the two of them were alone at last. Delabole did not move from his seat and Gonosor seemed reluctant to get to his feet.

"Do you know what Ardala is?" asked the Governor as he reclined in his chair. "It is what the Repecians call Bosscastle. It means ... servant ... or obedient servant to be more precise. You see, that is all it is now ... a servant of the Empire, just like any other building in any other province." Gonosor did now attempt to get up, but Delabole knew that he was listening. "Long gone are the days when this place echoed to the roar of the High Kings of Bodmiffel ... or the Forest Horns ... or the gentle laughter of the fair lady Henwen." His final statement was said in a low, sadder voice as though he regretted that laughter was no longer heard within this vast and venerable room.

As Gonosor scrambled to his knees and just as he was about to get back onto his feet, Delabole, preferring him on the ground, rushed from his seat to where he was and kicked him back down, and took great pleasure from the discomfort he had caused him.

"Now there's a sight I thought I'd never see," the Governor chortled. "The mighty Gonosor writhing on the ground like the dog that he is." He paused to revel in the moment. "My, the Druid has done a job on you, hasn't he? Not only has he made you mute but he has taken from you the one thing that others have feared, even coveted ... your strength and power, your courage. To leave what...? A slave where once was a prince." He stepped over and around him. "As much a slave of your master as I am to mine. The only difference is that I have had the good fortune to be a thousand miles away from my masters, while you are forever watched and dominated by yours." Delabole stepped back to lean against the table, and looked down upon his captive with glee and contempt.

"I was shocked when I saw you hanging on that dungeon wall, and a little unnerved, I admit. At first, I thought that I had seen a ghost. Do you believe in ghosts? I do. That's what you are, for you have been long dead, my old friend. Oh, Badad may have spared your body, even your mind, but has destroyed your spirit, Gonosor. You are here and alive, but your legend, your soul, has gone forever. The Gonosor of myth, of legend would have broken off the chains that bound him.

The first sign of daylight was beginning to shine through the two huge, stained-glass windows in the far wall of the Great Hall. It promised to be another fine, mid-winters day for the execution of the Lord of Baladorn. The fire cracked in the hearth at the end of the hall to draw the Governor's attention away from his hostage, to see that the fire was all but out and in need of urgent attention if it was to survive. Instinctively, as a force of habit, Delabole looked around the room for his servant, before remembering that he had sent him out. However, rather than restock the fire himself he decided to let it fade and die. Then his attention was pulled to the other end of the hall, to the doorway, when he noticed that a soldier had stepped in front of the opening and had peered inside. He therefore walked briskly to the door and pushed it closed for what he desired now, more than anything else, was to feel totally alone with his guest, as though they were the only two men left within this vast citadel.

In a remarkable and unexpected act of benevolence, Delabole placed his hand under Gonosor's arm and helped him to his feet. A strange thing to do considering it was his boot that had forced him back down in the first place. Perhaps that was just a gesture of his power over the prisoner, and this a sign of his nobleness. In any case he walked him to the table and sat him down in a chair, poured him a drink and held the cup as it was drank.

"Strange how things have turned out for the both of us," he mused, as he prematurely removed the cup from Gonosor's lips and placed it on the table, before stepping away. Gonosor, sad that the drink had been taken away, looked at the cup longingly for he knew that there was still some precious liquid left in it and he wanted it so badly. As things were, it was crueler to have had tasted the warm, sweet mead, and to be denied it all, than to have been given any in the first place.

"Neither of us have got what we wanted," said Delabole, turning slightly without looking directly at Gonosor. "Our scheming and deceit, our lies and betrayals, have amounted to nothing when all is said and done. We are both lost. We have both wasted so much time, for what we craved turned out to be beyond our reach after all." He chuckled. "And we are both so despised by our people that had we not the protection of our masters they would have torn out our vile, feckless hearts long ago."

Gonosor was becoming restless and his wrists and ankles began to writhe at the ropes that bound them. His gaze was fixed firmly on the Governor and he watched as he sat down on the steps that came away from what seemed to be his throne.

"As you came across the square you will have noticed a scaffold," said Delabole. "Do you know what it is for? Of course you do. You've seen enough of them in your time. It is for you, my friend. I told them to make the cross-beam that bit stronger to take your bulk. And whenever I decide, you will be hung on that scaffold until all of your legendary spirit and strength has been spent and you stop struggling. The end of Gonosor Lord of Baladorn will pass with a whimper and you will be forgotten without lament, save for the Druid perhaps, who needs you still. Therefore you could say that I have fared better in my task than you have in yours, and that I have achieved something with my life if not all that I set out to. The boy, too, will be found and brought to account for his actions." It was as though he was speaking to Badad and not Gonosor of Baladorn after all, for he knew that Gonosor was his servant. "And then I will have won, won't I? Bosscastle will remain safe and in my control until such a time when my master will return and all will be well again."

Delabole caught his breath and suddenly his triumph turned to despair.

"My master!?" he whispered to himself. "Then I am a slave, too. And a prisoner of Bosscastle, for I can never leave. Which makes me the same as you, doesn't it?" He got back to his feet and stumbled towards the door, then stopped. "It has been fifteen years since I set a foot in my homeland. Oh, I have all this luxury and greatness, but it is not where I should be at all. I am lost, Gonosor. I DO NOT WANT TO BE HERE!" He placed his hands on his head and dug his nails into his scalp until his elbows clashed. "How I have longed for the green hills and meadows of the Middle Lands. The gentle Woldark, where I used to go with my brother. The little inns … the Shireman Inn, where I used to drink with my brother when we were young, disguised as woodcutters so no-one would realise who we were. I was just a boy. An innocent boy. Who grew into a man that became a monster…!" He turned. "But I am not the monster they think I am. I am a man of simple needs. I AM NOT THE MAN THEY THINK I AM!!"

When Delabole caught sight of Gonosor he realised that he had not been listening. Instead, his attention had been consumed by the tapestry hanging from the wall above the table: the tapestry that depicted the beautiful woman dressed in gold. His eyes had filled with tears, for he had recognised the woman that looked down upon him, and felt a pain in his heart such as he had not felt for a very long time. Rather than being affronted by the prisoner's ignorance, Delabole was pleased, for he had intended to show him the tapestry all along.

"Do you know who it is? Of course you do. The likeness is remarkable and such beauty is unforgettable, isn't it? The most beautiful woman that has ever lived. She is more than a queen … almost like a goddess." He came back to the table and looked at Gonosor's face to comprehend his reaction to seeing the woman again. The reaction, although rather surprising for a man with Gonosor's reputation, was understandable, for all the men who had ever known this woman were silenced and stirred when they saw this depiction of her, the only one known to exist.

"You hoped never to see her again," Delabole continued. He was revelling in Gonosor's unease and deep sense of regret and shame. "You have spent all these years trying to forget about her, and sure enough the years have annulled what memories you had. In your mind she never even existed, save for a few glimpses of her face when you closed your eyes in the dead of night. Such is the depth of your shame and the regret for what you did all those years ago." He was walking around his seat taunting him all the more with his footsteps. "Have you forgotten how you betrayed her, Gonosor? Is your memory now so selective that you deny ever betraying her … your own sister!? You hated her, didn't you? She had what was rightfully yours … the throne of Bodmiffel. And yet she made a much better queen than you would have a king! But you hated the wrong person. It was your father that disowned you and stripped you of your birthright, not Henwen."

Gonosor turned his face from the tapestry and began to writhe at his ropes again; filling with anger like it was being poured into him. "Of course, it is all the Druid's fault really. He was counsel to both kings ... Vercingoral and Sodric. He persuaded them to pursue a course to peace. You opposed it as much as I did, only I went about demonstrating my dissatisfaction in a more discreet, dignified manner than trying to usurp a king. You desired the crown of Bodmiffel and tried to take it prematurely. Had your little coup succeeded you would have undone your father's work and defied the treaty by declaring war on the Shire Lands." He paused before continuing, almost ashamed of what he was about to say. "I hoped that you would be successful, for the thought of a union between our two lands repulsed me. But you weren't. You hadn't bargained on the power of the old Druid, who was not about to let his life's work be undone by someone so disreputable and vulgar as you. And Badad would have killed you had he been given his way. The fact that he didn't was his greatest mistake. Instead, Sodric disowned you and banished you to the forest town of Baladorn and forbid you ever to return to Bosscastle ... to the life you knew and craved. Henwen, beautiful, true and fair was named as your father's successor, and the people rejoiced at the news."

Gonosor's angry eyes momentarily glanced at the image of the said lady. So did Delabole's, for as he had talked so his memories of her and those distant days had been refreshed.

"She would rule her people the way Sodric had ruled them, and persist with the treaty with the Threeshire. More than that, she would relent to the demands of the Druid and give both her body and crown to Vercingoral, thus unifying the two lands of the realm of Bodmiffel forever."

The Governor picked up the cup and upon seeing that it still contained a drink, drank it with one gulp.

"Geramond would be resurrected and the true king would sit on the Boss Throne once more." He chuckled. "The sacred land. Where goodness prevails and men are happy and contented." He was scoffing at the idea that such a place could ever exist or have existed. "Where there are no wars or disputes and men sing and dance around their fires and hug each other and drink to their combined happiness and good health." His chuckle turned to a laugh, made more frenzied with the combination of his fatigue and drunkenness.

"I have heard enough." The words came from Gonosor's mouth but they were not his. Delabole knew who they belonged to and sighed with sadness and disappointment.

"Would it not be easier for you to put in an appearance yourself rather than speak with the tongues of those you have possessed?" His tone was impudent for he was reassured by the fact that Gonosor's hands and feet were bound together and that Badad could do him no harm but to speak and shout at him.

"I have no desire to look upon something so contemptible and depraved with my own eyes," Badad replied.

"Whatever I am, don't forget that I've kept you in work for the past fifteen years!" the Governor retorted. "The people will only ever need the services of a Druid while his sorcery is set against a common enemy ... someone they fear and dread. So without me, they would not revere you half as much as they do."

"The people have no feelings for you but hatred and pity," said Badad, snarling and contorting Gonosor's face into an angry frown. "They hate you because you betrayed them and pity you in equal measure for ever being capable of such a thing in the first place. Betrayal is a cowardly friend and a fleeting one. The advantage gained from a treacherous act is quickly captured back but the traitor lives long in the memory and is scarcely forgiven."

"I seek no-one's forgiveness," Delabole croaked.

"That's just as well for you would never get it. You speak of a return to your homeland ... to the Shire of the Wold. You ache to lay your eyes upon those golden valleys again ... yearn to dip your toes in the Shire River ... drink warm ale in the inns and lodges of Woldark ....!"

"I should have guessed you were listening...!"

You know that you can never go back there. Can you imagine what they would do to you if you did? An army ten thousand strong could not protect you, Lord Governor, from the retribution of the people you deceived and bound in tyranny."

The Governor paused to contemplate what the Druid had just said to him, and did try to imagine what would happen to him if he did one day return to the Threeshire. It was a question he had asked himself on numerous occasions, partly because of his lack of concern about his peoples' opinion of him, and partly due to those agonising bouts of homesickness he suffered from every now and again. Even after all his time at Bosscastle as Governor of the new province, he felt that it was not his home; not really, not like Old Lampas Hall at Woldark, his birthplace and the traditional home of the Shire Kings. Bosscastle, compared to the Lampas, was sprawling and unfathomable; not intimate in any way and certainly not homely.

He was lost in his thoughts but quickly brought himself back to the here and now. It was vital, he told himself, to stay calm and resolute and not let the Druid see that he was currently suffering from a bout of homesickness, brought on by the idea that he may never return to the Middle Lands. He stepped away from the table, taking time to make sure that Gonosor's body, therefore the wrath of Badad, was still securely bound at both the wrists and ankles.

"Words, old man," he said, not turning around. "That's all you have. And you think that if you speak to me with enough disdain and contempt they will hurt me, but you are wrong. I have heard them all before, spoken by men with a greater distaste in their throats then you can manage. Words can harm me no more, and have not since the day I realised that the only way I was going to be noticed and listened to was by talking loudest. Louder than my brother at least. When I was fifteen years old my father told me that I was not his son. Oh, I knew that I was and that he said it to hurt me .... we'd argued about something or other. The point is, by the time I'd turned sixteen I did not care whether I was or not. Words, you see. Words are as good a weapon as a sword or a spear, and a man must guard against them in his mind like his armour would protect his body. Fortunate is the man who cares not what others think of him, for then he is free to be what he truly is, be it servant or tyrant."

The door creaked open and a gust of wind came through it and caused the curtains against the windows to dance and twist together. The iron frame of the tapestry rattled against the walls. Delabole turned and looked at it. Because of the iron bars along its bottom and top the material in between began to ripple, an effect that made the woman appear to move. Momentarily, Delabole lost control of his breath and his poise. Then, the tapestry was undone by the wind and came towards him, unravelled as though the lady herself was coming. He caught it in his arms and brought it to the ground and sank to his knees with her face looking up at his.

"There was one whose favour you cared to win and whose opinion ... affection ... you yearned for." Badad was speaking calmly, almost with pity in his voice as he looked upon the shrunken Governor clutching the tapestry. He looked at the door and it suddenly swung shut with a clatter that reverberated around the room. "And you would have forsaken everything you had ... your wealth and your power ... just for one moment with her when she was truly yours."

"Upon my heart she lies still," replied Delabole, full of remorse and sadness as he gazed at the image of the woman.

"Upon your conscience perhaps...?"

"I did not bring her to her end," Delabole snarled. "She brought it upon herself. I offered her everything. More than all the jewels and gold, I gave her the chance to govern at my side. She was once a queen. She could have been again."

His mind was cast back to the night she died. A balmy midsummer's evening. At dusk he had gone to her bed chamber and let himself in with his key to find her asleep upon the rugs that covered her bed. A gentle breeze was blowing in from the window and filled the room with scent from the garden beyond. He sat upon the bed and touched her face with the back of his hand, thus waking her. She was alarmed at the sight of him and recoiled away to the far side of the bed. He went with her.

"You may have my body," she said to him, her voice quivering with fear. "For you are stronger than I am and I cannot stop you. So I will lay beneath you but I will feel nothing. And when it is over my heart will still belong to Vercingoral."

"I tried to force her to love me." Delabole was touching the tapestry on the woven gold that made her gown. "But her heart was

Vercingoral's. After that first night we spent together, I knew that she would never succumb to me. And so I began to detest my brother more than I ever imagined was possible. The first thing she asked after the deed was done was what had become of him. I told her that he was dead, hoping that after she'd mourned him for long enough she would finally fall in love with me."

"Instead, she climbed upon the castle wall and threw herself into the icy water of Kanance's Cove." Badad was still speaking gently. "Did she do that to be reunited with her true love or to escape from your clutches…?"

"I am not a bad man, Badad," Delabole sobbed. "And if you would dare to admit it, you do not loathe me as much as you know you ought to."

"I pity you, Delabole Bubinda," replied the Druid. "You have sought everything yet ended up with nothing at all."

Eight
The Hour of the Wanderer

It was the first time Delabole had been called by his proper name, his birth name, since he had ascended to the provincial governorship, and it had the effect of stripping away the veneer of authority that covered him; to leave but a man, and a sorry sight indeed, rocking back and forth on his knees, clinging to the tapestry as though the lady upon it was actually with him still. An hour had passed and he had not moved. Nor had Badad said anything else and for that time at least the Great Hall was a peaceful place.

Badad, though, had not gone away and still possessed the Bodmifflian's body and used it to serve his own needs.

"What you said earlier," the Druid muttered, breaking the silence. "You said that I would be nothing had you not been the man you are." The temperate tone in the old man's voice brought Delabole out of his trance-like state. "In a way, you were right to say it. You are responsible for all that has happened ... and for what is yet to pass." Delabole shifted from his knees onto his backside and shuffled back until he was resting against the wall. He was interested in what the Druid was about to say for he did not understand.

"After the great battle of High Cleugh, when the combined armies of Vercingoral and Henwen were defeated and Fillian went on to conquer the Shire Lands ..." He looked directly at Delabole. "After your great betrayal, when all was lost, it seemed to me that my life's work was lost also. All that I had achieved, the union between Vercingoral and Henwen, the conception of their child ... that was the legitimate king of both lands ... had all been in vain. The undertaking given to me had failed, and I began to lose my belief that it could ever have succeeded." Badad was speaking ever so quietly with a tinge of sadness so that Delabole had to strain his ears. "My powers diminished and I retreated to Kaw in the foothills of the Tragaran mountains, and hid myself from the chaos that held sway over the land of Geramond ..."

So engrossed was the old man that his recollections took his mind back to those dark days. He thought of how pitiful he must have appeared to a watching eye. A desolate time when he grew old and older still through self-doubt and an overbearing sense of shame. When his hair and beard grew and changed into what it was now. He survived on scraps of food, caught in the woodlands that surrounded the lake: hares and squirrels, nuts and berries. Walked upon the wooded hills for days on end, returning only to sleep soundly in his bed.

Badad was the last of the Druids. A cult that once had thrived had been reduced to just one solitary man, whose task seemed impossible to fulfil. So impossible that he had stopped trying, and reconciled himself to the life of a recluse rather than as counsel to a king and the chief of good judgment. What purpose had his long life served when everything he had ever advocated and recommended been cast aside like scraps? Common sense, he had concluded, could not be conditioned into the mind of a mortal man. Therefore he was alone. The wisdom of his words were not understood, or if they were, not heeded. His kind had vanished except for him and while men progressed ever further and advanced into turmoil and madness, they would do so without the respect and veneration that once surrounded men like Badad. The fact was that he was no longer associated with wisdom and knowledge but looked down upon as an oddity; a remnant of a lost age, an age that men doubted ever existed. He was not needed nor tolerated, therefore he was nothing; lost and bewildered in a place and time he did not belong.

Ten years passed quickly since he returned to his birthplace: the cave in the hill atop the lake at Kaw. Quicker than he could have hoped, and a time when agony and rejection gave way to a gentler, more humdrum existence. Badad the Wanderer, counsel to kings, had turned into a hermit, neither longing for nor anticipating any association with the world of men ever again. Then, at the dawn of a balmy, mid-summers day, something happened that would turn his life again towards a life of servitude and to be burdened by the troubles of the very men that had spurned him.

He was awoken by the sense that someone was in the cave with him. A whiff of fragrance in the air and a light weight at the bottom of his bed. He opened his eyes to a sight that he thought he would never see, and although the spectre meant him no harm, he was nevertheless fearful, and pulled his covers all the way over his head. It was the Lady Pannona of Fa-Noodar, mistress of Druids and ruler of the unexplained, sitting at the end of the bed like a watchful mother above a sickly child. She was dressed in a flowing, brilliant white gown that shone so brightly that it was like sunlight had filled the dark cave; her hair was like gold weaved into plats that adorned a face of such ashen beauty that any man, Druidic or otherwise, could never have resisted or denied her.

She stretched out her hand and gently pulled the cover from Badad's face.

"My old friend," she said, softly. The old man brought himself upright and propped himself against the scabrous cavern wall; suddenly overcome with a warm fondness for the lady, and although he had never seen her before, he knew exactly who she was.

"Where were you ten years ago when I called for you…?" he asked, his tone sad rather than angry. "Things went wrong, but together we could have overcome the problems of the time, and my task would now be complete."

Pannona smiled. "Patience was never your greatest virtue, Badad. And yet, when you were first given your task, you knew that it would not be done in a year, and would take many labours before it was accomplished." She brushed a wisp of hair away from his tired eyes. "A life that is not yet spent."

Badad got out of bed and stepped to the other side of the cramped cave before moving towards the light at the narrow exit.

"It's too late now," he said, his voice strained and weak. "I am tired." He turned his head briefly to face her. "I have accepted that my undertaking has failed. I am happy to live this simple life … my little cave and my fire … to walk in the hills and feel the wind in my hair … to watch the moon dance across the surface of the lake in the dead of night."

Pannona rose to her feet, a movement that seemed not to happen; one moment sitting and the next she was standing next to him, as though she had drifted across the cave like smoke in the wind. "You have lived such a life for ten years," she said. "You must ask yourself whether you could live it for a thousand more." Badad turned his head sharply to look into her face, prompted by the harsh even threatening tone in her voice. "For that is the fate that awaits any Druid who abandons his course altogether. You will be cursed to spend time without end living in this world of mortal men. Bare witness to a thousand wars, and the pain and suffering that war brings. Observe love in all its wonder and its soreness, without ever knowing love yourself. Your body will fail and die but your mind will stay as sharp and bright as the day you were born. Real pain, Badad, awaits you should you choose to discard the undertaking that was given to you. But should you see it through to the end … its natural end and not one you have given to it … then your path will lead you to the gates of the afterlife. Where the water is sweet and the air scented with blossom and joy."

"Fa-Noodar?" Badad said, for he knew that was the place to which Lady Pannona was referring. He had heard talk of this place but never truly understood what it was. All Druids, it was said, went there upon completion of each one's individual task, and lived a joyous and contented existence in a place where time mattered not and men could not tread. Even when faced with such a choice, the old man was not fully convinced that he should listen to the lady.

"I wish this task had never come to me."

She lost her firm disposition to adopt the gentler more temperate tone that best suited her. "You are the last of the Druids because the task given to you has been the hardest to accomplish. The minds of men are not so easily turned in this age of war and bitterness. You have achieved much since you started, my friend, but much is still to do. Soon, all that you have done will come together, and from seed a mighty oak will grow. You have spent ten years doubting your skill, even questioning the aspirations of Fa-Noodar. It is all right that you pass through such a phase, so long as you realise in the end that what you are trying to do is for the common good of all men."

"Why?" Badad asked prickly. "What difference does it make

that the Shiremen fight the forest dwellers? In the end, they will do what comes naturally to them. Men are brutal creatures and nothing we can do will change them."

The lady seemed disappointed with her old friend.

"But there was a time when Geramond was at peace … the first age. The age of understanding and when kings cultivated goodwill and wisdom. There was but one war in the first age, that split Geramond into three pieces thus bringing in the second age. The age of warfare, loathing and fear." Now she fell silent, before resuming in a quieter, sadder voice. "And the third age has been a time when myth and magic has receded and the Druids have all vanished. Except for you. Mortal men have learned to live without guidance but in the absence of insight and a distrust of all things that are not of their world, they have become ignorant and irrational."

"When I am gone men will be alone?"

"Yes, Badad. They will have to find wisdom within themselves and in each other. The forth age will be such a time. Geramond, unified under the one, true king, he who has sat upon the Boss Throne in the old fortress, it will be as it once was, and people will rejoice and find the way to live without us."

"What must I do to bring in this new age?" asked the Druid.

"I trust necessary arrangements have been made?"

Badad nodded happily. He seemed willing to oblige his lady at last.

"The union between Henwen and Vercingoral bore fruit. A child was conceived … a boy …"

"And he will sit upon the Boss Throne?"

"The son of the King of Threeshire and the Queen of Bodmiffel, conjured in Tragara…?! Surely a legitimate king of all Geramond?"

Pannona was happy and laughed aloud.

"You have exceeded my expectations, Badad."

"What must happen now? What should I do?"

"Nothing for the time being," she replied. "Stay here at Kaw until you know the time is right to move south, back into the Shire Lands."

"And with that she was gone."

Delabole looked again at the tapestry, this time with a more furious glint in his eye.

"Then it is true what Henwen told me before she died … she really did have a son." He had not moved off his backside all the time Badad had been recalling his time at Kaw following the conquest.

"I never saw Pannona of Fa-Noodar again. A further five years passed and I began to doubt that anything would happen. Then, one afternoon mid-winter, six riders arrived at Kaw."

"Macara?" Delabole uttered sadly.

"An uprising had occurred in Woldshire. Thinking that I was responsible for it, you sent the General north to finally rid yourself of the troublesome Druid. And that was your great mistake, Lord Governor. The fact was, I had nothing to do with it. The uprising was genuine. You had taxed the people of the Shires too highly. No doubt to sustain your lavish lifestyle whilst keeping your master contented at the same time. But a humble blacksmith by the name of Fogle Winnersh refused to pay, so your collectors ordered that his lands be taken in lieu of the back-tax he owed. In the struggle that ensued, Fogle's son was killed, and so the end of the conquest of Geramond had begun."

"What did you do to Macara that turned him so insane?" Delabole was beginning to fidget nervously.

Gonosor's face contorted into a grin and his mouth opened to reveal the black void. "I took out their guts and made him eat them…!" Badad replied.

Delabole scrambled to his feet and hurried towards the door. "You are mad yourself, old man," he roared. "But whatever you do, you can never win this war." He was agitated, almost hysterical, and spoke with a squeak in his voice. "My master intends to return. As we speak he is on his way back and will land at Bossiney within weeks … with tens of thousands of soldiers. What hope does your little rebellion have then, eh?" He scurried back to Gonosor, took hold of his face and squeezed it as tightly as he could. "What hope for you all then?"

"It will be his folly to return, for I shall finish what was started when last he came, and send him to ruin."

Delabole stepped away, and smirked as though to mock the old man whilst at the same time trying not to believe him. "And ten thousand men? No, admit it, Badad, the rebellion will be crushed and you will be sent to ruin." Now he chose to swipe the back of his hand across Gonosor's face. "And this slave of yours will be hung within minutes of me giving the order...! The boy, the one who seeks to open the Western Gate ... he will be found and hung on the same gallows!"

The Governor strode across the floor of the Great Hall towards the door and called out for the guards outside to come in.

"When Fillian returns to Bossiney," Badad continued. The door opened slightly and a nervous young soldier poked his head inside but Delabole pushed him back out and turned to listen to the Druid's closing statement. "He will bring with him his loyal and trusted servant, Vagor."

"So? What of it?"

"He has been his trusted servant ever since he took him away from his homeland. Vagor is the Repecian word for strength, and he certainly possesses that. His real name is, of course .... Vercingoral. King of the Shire Lands! Your own brother....!"

Delabole closed the door. Strange as it was, the thought that one day his brother might return to Geramond had never occurred to him. However, it was difficult for the Druid to estimate the extent of his shock and horror as he was already hugely agitated and harried. "He will surely be dead by now."

"If he is not," replied Badad, "then you should pray to which ever god you serve that he has forgotten what you did, or at least forgiven you for it."

"And was what I did so bad?" asked Delabole.

Badad began to laugh, a booming sound that echoed around the vastness of the Great Hall. Then he settled. "You sold your brother into slavery so that you could steal his wife. A trend that you continued. I trust that the Merchant Budogis is still a regular visitor to Bosscastle...?"

"I did what I did because I was in love," the Governor insisted.

"Ah, yes ... love! That wonderful thing that makes anything acceptable. A man cannot be so vile if he is capable of love, can he...?"

"Am I so reviled that I can never be forgiven?"

Badad did not answer. Gonosor's body flopped forward and it seemed as though the Druid had vacated it and returned it to its owner. Then Gonosor pulled his head upright and looked at the Governor and Delabole wondered whether he had been a party to all that had been said.

A strange quiet descended over the Great Hall and Delabole, at last, had time to collect his thoughts; to secretly curse the old Druid for ruining the time he had set aside to torment Gonosor prior to his execution. This was to have been his moment of revenge against an old adversary. To demonstrate his own prominence and command of the land of Geramond; yet sabotaged by an even older, more cunning opponent, who had not the courage or style to appear in person.

The quiet nurtured the noise: the sound of men screaming collectively, not in agony or despair but in rage and aggression, and as persuasive a row as any beast could muster. It was like the great giant Corbilo had risen to wreak havoc again, and the windows of the Great Hall echoed to the sound. The young legionary poked his head through the door "The Ambassador is asking for you," he said.

Delabole sped down the steps from the balcony of the Great Hall, skimmed the crowd that had gathered in the Druim Square to watch the expected execution, and entered the West Tower, or 'Slim Bomo', and raced to the very top, where Corsula was waiting for him. The two men did not speak. They did not need to. Delabole's eyes followed the Ambassador's; over the valley towards Ingelwitt, where, on the edge of the forest, the whole rebel army had gathered to roar their insolence and boldness as one voice, and were waving their arms to show their weapons. A sight that sent the feckless Governor recoiling to the centre of the tower. He had disappeared from view, but the din did not stop.

At the front of the rebel army, and shouting as loud as a man twenty years younger, was old Toggett Took; next to Fogle, waving his axe with one hand and punching the air with the other. Toggett turned around and pushed down his trousers to reveal his bare backside. "Feast thee eyes on that, Lord Swine-skin...!" he bellowed. How the others laughed, including Fogle. Delabole did not see the old man's gesture but Corsula did, and pursed his lips in disgust, for a naked backside was not a traditional weapon of war in the southern colonies.

The rebels seemed to split in two to form a narrow lane between the two sides. Delabole came to the edge of the tower just in time to watch Badad ride to the front of his army, resplendent in a flowing white robe, on the back of a horse as black as coal. The horse reared onto its hind legs and Badad held his old staff aloft, and the rest of the rebels cheered twice as loudly.

"What's he up to?" the Governor mumbled to himself.

"They're getting ready to attack the Western Gate," replied Corsula, his voice shaky and panic-ridden.

"It it secure?" asked Delabole, just as agitated. "Has the boy been found...?"

"He is still at large," Corsula replied.

Delabole held his hands against his face and lowered his face slowly onto the stone turret at the centre of the tower. He uttered something but the Ambassador could not comprehend what it was, so decided that it did not matter. Then, the Governor pushed himself upright and turned to look out at the scene across the valley. The rebels had begun to walk down into the gully at the bottom of their side, Badad the Wanderer at the front. At the top of the slope, men were still emerging from the trees, even though the front of the column had begun to rise towards the castle, ten or more abreast. The rebel army had recovered, it seemed, and had grown.

Nine
At the Western Gate

Toggett sang as he walked:

> "To the Great Gate come thronging,
> Fathers and men, by night or day;
> To trace footsteps back to freedom,
> The prize, their hands reach longing."

Badad replied:

> "Glory then to men come knocking,
> For they seek nought but thee.
> Pray take them in and set them down,
> Or throw them out a key."

Fogle rushed to catch up with the Druid and trotted alongside the horse. "What if ..." he began.

"Fogle Winnersh, master of men," Badad said, turning to look at his little friend. "What if the sun does not set!? What if the tide will not turn...?"

Fogle was annoyed at his interuption.

"We are being too hasty, Badad. What if Galfall does not open the gate? Soon we will be within range of their archers."

"The sun will set and the tide will turn, for all things will pass and go on to an end."

Not totally satisfied, but realising that the Druid was determined to press on, and he usually knew what was best, Fogle dropped back into line.

"He's a funy little chap, that Druid," Toggett whispered. "Too much hair for such a little chap."

"I hope he knows what he's doing," Fogle replied, bothered by the fact that the front of the rebel column was straying too close to the castle for comfort, and that any further step would be crucial if their archers decided to fire out from the perimeter wall. A strain on his mind brought on by the outcome of his army's last venture to the gates of Bosscastle.

The Druid seemed unconcerned and his horse dashed ahead. Then, the one word they all dreaded. The weapon they were unable to defend against. "Arrows!" someone shouted, prompting them all to look skywards. Sure enough, a black cloud of them slicing through the air with that horrifying sound to accompany them, turning downwards onto them. "Stand firm!" Badad instructed. Some did but others bolted backwards. The arrows came down, nearly all at the same time, just in front of the Druid's horse, thumping into the ground close enough for the old man to feel the draft on his face. He turned on his horse to face the others.

"We will wait here," he smiled. "Not a step further shall we go."

"The lucky old blodger," Toggett murmured.

Fogle was deep in thought. "I think you should move further to the back, Toggett."

"Why?" snapped the old Took. "Too old, am I? War is for young snappers, is it?" He seemed affronted. "Well, you're no spring chicken yerself, Fogle Winnersh, and if I should be at the back then so should you...?!"

Fogle's determined, severe exterior, gave way to a smile. The old Took, it seemed, had a surprise or two left in him, and was as full of keenness and daring as the day Fogle had first met him, and that was too long ago to be retained in his mind.

"War ..." the old man concluded ... "is for men old and wise enough to know when to pack in and stop. Men like old Toggett and fat Fogle...!" And they shared a laugh.

The Western Gate was ahead of them. Galfall and Salissa had concealed themselves in an alleyway off the main thoroughfare from the road that came across the valley. Close enough to have reached their destination, but far enough away to be able to poke their heads around the wall every now and again to see what was happening; who was guarding the gate, how many and how well armed they were. It seemed to the youth that Repecian soldiers went around in groups of six. Six had come after him on the Buca Lapis and six were guarding the gate now. He recognised one of them from the ship. The leader, the one in the red cloak. The other five, as before, were just ordinary soldiers.

"Now what do we do?" Salissa sighed, rubbing a speck of dirt off her face but actually smudging it deeper and further instead. Galfall felt obliged to answer, but sounded unconvincing and unsure.

"There're only six of them ... we can handle that...!"

"Don't be stupid," she replied, and paused for thought. "I know ... we need to distract them. I will distract them and take off down the road. With any luck they'll give chase, and you can go to the gate and open it."

"Now you're being stupid," he replied. "It won't work. They won't all follow you. None of them will follow you. They're on the look out for me. Not a slip of a girl."

She scoffed. "If it wasn't for me you'd still be wandering the streets aimlessly. I got you here, Galfall."

"Now we're here, there must be a way," he pondered.

He poked his head around the wall. The soldiers were sharing a joke. Except the leader, who was looking all around him, and looked in his direction, but did not see him. The two huge oak doors encased within the huge, stone gatehouse, were secured by a beam across the middle. The top of the gatehouse was adorned with battlements for archers, accessible via a staircase from the road, but no-one was up there.

"If we got on top," he whispered, raising his eyes for Salissa to follow, "we could see the others in the valley...." She did not understand what difference that would make.

"They would see us! Then they would attack the gate and those soldiers would flee. You see, there aren't enough of them to defend it so they would need to go and raise the alarm. By the time they returned we would have opened the gate and the rebels would be inside the castle!"

She thought for a moment and despite her initial reaction to dismiss the plan outright, realised that it might just work.

"It's risky," she murmured. "What will we do if, when we get to the top, they aren't in the valley at all? What then, Galfall? We will be stuck up there by ourselves. Easy targets for their archers." Her attention was brought down from the gatehouse to one of the soldiers, who seemed to be coming towards them. Fleetingly, she took notice of his uniform, particularly his headwear, for it disguised the man beneath. "I've a better idea," she said, pulling Galfall back into the alley.

They held themselves flat against the wall and tried not to make a sound. Salissa grasped the bottom of her tatty gown to stop it floating on the wind that was whirling around the alleyway. Galfall moved his head ever so slightly to his right, and saw that the legionary had stopped on the road outside the narrow entrance to their hideout. As the soldier turned to go back towards the gate, Galfall slipped as quietly as he could further down the passageway, to leave Salissa alone.

"I am lost, soldier," she said.

The legionnaire turned abruptly. "Come out of there!" he insisted.

"Why don't you come and get me out!" Salissa replied.

And that is what he did. As soon as the soldier was off the road, Galfall jumped out from where he had been lurking and grabbed his head in his arms to punch him in the face as many times as he could. Once the legionary had been subdued, Galfall took out a dagger and held it to the throat.

The young lady noticed that the sense of infallibility and fearlessness that Galfall had earlier shown had all but gone from him, to leave but a vulnerable, frightened young man that ought never to have been given this impossible task. The blade was held against the legionary's throat for what seemed like an age when set against the scheme of things.

Galfall looked at her. "If I kill him now, blood will spill onto the clothes I am bound to wear," he said, quietly.

"Then leave it as it is," she said to him, in a kind voice, for she understood what he was really saying: that he had not the nerve nor the will to do it. "Take off the uniform and I will bind his arms and feet."

Another age passed while the youth removed the uniform and then fumbled his own, puny body into it. The iron-mail tunic was a snug enough fit and the cloak hung around his shoulders just as it should have, but the helmet was too large for his head and had to be padded at the top with the socks off his feet; his bare feet then covered by the thick, leather boots.

"Right," Salissa puffed as she straightened the tunic. "Take me out there …" Galfall looked at her in puzzlement. "Let them see that you've captured me…!"

"No," he protested. "It's too dangerous. And it's not what the Druid intended."

"Sometimes you have to take things on yourself. It will need at least two of them to take me to the Governor, which will leave just three and you at the gate."

"Then what do I do?"

"Follow your instincts, Galfall. Now take me by the arm and do it as though you mean to."

Galfall promptly took a firm grip of Salissa's arm. "What do I do if they speak to me…?" he asked, gulping nervously.

She was beginning to lose patience with him. "I will have to live on my wits when the Governor asks me what I was doing at the Western Gate, so you will when they speak to you."

"With any luck that fellow down there wasn't too popular!" said Galfall, then pushed Salissa out onto the street.

"Well, then, look at you," said Madius when he saw his legionary coming towards him pulling the slip of a girl along side. "What would a pretty young thing like you be doing so far away from where you ought to be…?" He looked at Galfall. "Where did you find her?" Galfall, not really knowing what to do, pointed back down the road at the entrance to the alley.

"I lost my way," Salissa insisted.

Two of the other four soldiers came strolling towards the scene, amused by the capture of a girl.

"You lost your way, did you?" Madius put his hand on her face and pushed her head back. "I have seen you before." He paused to think where. "You are a serving girl, aren't you? You were attending to the Ambassador's room the night he arrived. So why should you be lost now…?"

Salissa, taken aback, was at a loss for an answer. Then, opening her mouth to offer a reply, she stuttered and stumbled over her words. "I was walking with my dog …."

"Lies!" Madius snarled, squeezing her face harder and harder to force the truth out of her. "All lies. You are an accomplice to the boy we seek. He who would open the gate. You are a rebel and a traitor…!" He put the flat of his hand on her face and pushed her back so that she fell against the wall. "Where is the boy? You can't protect him now." Then the Tribune looked at the legionary and noticed something strange, almost craven about him: he did not stand like a soldier and Madius had noticed that his hand had moved onto the hilt of his sword. "Yes, of course. Very cunning." He gestured for the three legionaries to come closer.

Galfall had known from the start that the plan was doomed to failure and had only agreed to do it with a lack of any credible alternative. He had no option now but to stand and fight, and hope that the Druid's trickery was at work in the air. He drew the sword, momentarily held it aloft, then plunged at the Tribune, but missed markedly. So ineffective was he, so utterly incapable of landing a blow, that the Repecians began to ridicule him and taunt him as he became encircled by the points of their swords. Madius, whilst holding the girl with one hand, swiped the helmet from off his head, thus revealing the interloper within it. The fact that he was so young and naïve-looking only served to add to their great amusement. For the Tribune, however, his amusement was improved in the knowledge that he had finally ensnared the prowler who had sought to bring down Bosscastle.

It was midday now and the early morning promise of winter sunshine had gone to leave a sky burdened with murk and cloud. Druim Square was packed with the combustible residents of Bosscastle, and the side streets that fed into the square were full too, such was the level of interest in the impending execution on the balcony of the Great Hall. More than interest: the morbid sense of the end of an era; a collective fervour to lay eyes once again upon their old Prince, the Lord of Baladorn.

The front of the crowd were pushed back from the balcony steps by a thin line of Repecian legionaries, struggling to maintain order and calm. Delabole and Corsula were standing next to the scaffold. Then, the murmur of the huge crowd stilled so that a quiet descended over Bosscastle, and from out of the darkness of the Great Hall, Gonosor was brought out to face his end.

"Lets get this over and done with," Corsula snarled, mindful of the rebel army waiting in the valley beyond the curtain wall, just a little way behind him.

"Some things must be savoured," Delabole replied. "Regardless of what may happen elsewhere." The Governor was serene and full of abhorrence again. "Long have I awaited this moment."

The crowd, even after the jolt of seeing Gonosor again, did not stir or rant, and the silence prevailed as the big man was pulled towards the scaffold. Their hearts and heads were full of regret that such an end should come to one of their own kind. And full of revulsion that it should be dealt out by the hands of Delabole the Traitor, their common enemy, even more than the young soldiers that were fated to carry out the act. However, their recollection of Gonosor was that of a raucous, disreputable man, with the strength of a bull and the mind to match. Why then, did he seem so subdued and meek now, at the one point when it really would have been appropriate to be aggressive and unwieldy? Gonosor never had been a man of the moment.

A commotion at last at the back of the crowd spread forwards like a wave until Madius emerged at the front with the youngster in tow. Delabole saw him first, and was at once filled with excitement and frenzy, for he knew now that the castle was secure and that the Druid had failed. Then he did something rather peculiar: came down the steps at speed, ran towards the West Tower and disappeared inside, to leave everyone else rather baffled.

He appeared atop of the tower to look down upon the rebels in the valley below. The Druid saw him, then Fogle, Toggett and the others. A quiet descended over them too.

"I have him, Badad...!" Delabole cried, as loud as his excitable voice would allow. "I have your boy! So you see, you have failed, Badad ... your great enterprise has failed...! The gate of Bosscastle will remain shut, until such a time when it will please my master for it to be opened...!"

The energy and zeal drained from Fogle's face. "Then it has all been in vain," he sighed. "And the young Gringell condemned to die a failure's death."

"Many a pitiless word uttered in the rush of battle," Badad replied, and looked away from the tower.

Delabole did not return to the square. Instead, he intended to observe the execution from atop of the tower. Galfall was taken to the scaffold and forced to stand and watch as Gonosor's head was threaded through the noose. Even now, he retained hope in his heart, for he knew that Salissa had not been brought back from the Western Gate. All hope was gone, however, when he caught sight of her at the bottom of the steps, and he knew that his fate was sealed and that the noose would be for him too.

Gonosor stepped onto the box and the noose was tightened. Slipping his hand down his side, Galfall felt that the little, leather pouch was still in his trousers. As furtive as a fox, he pulled out the pouch and gradually inched himself towards the scaffold.

"I merely wish to return to him something that is his by right," he said to the legionary that tried to stop him. He was allowed to proceed.

'This, surely, is what the Druid has intended all along,' he told himself as he positioned the pouch in Gonosor's hand. It fell to the ground, but when he picked it up he was pleased to find that its contents were back where they ought to be. Suddenly, Gonosor began to twist and writhe on the rope; he opened his mouth and let out the most thunderous roar imaginable.

"I will not die here!" he cried. "This will not end now...!!" He wriggled like an eel, and sought the Governor with his eyes until they'd found him, then roared his defiance all the louder. The huge crowd, so long merely passive onlookers, suddenly cheered with joy, for this was the true Gonosor of Baladorn. The wild man they remembered and had for so long feared, had returned. They took up a chant and as one voice said: Hail Gonosor, son of Sodric, brother of Henwen. Hail Gonosor! Hail Gonosor! And with that, they pushed forwards.

Delabole drew back from the edge of the tower. His face as grey as cold ash; his mind racing with fear and rage in equal measure.

"Kill him!" he shouted, returning to the edge. "Kill him now...!!" He saw that the crowd had broken though the line of soldiers and had engulfed the scaffold. He could not see Gonosor, and his heart stopped momentarily with the realisation that the Bodmifflian had been cut loose.

"Call back all soldiers," Corsula gasped, pulling Madius towards him. "Wherever they are ... bring them here ... order must be restored...!!" And with that said, he scuttled away to the safety of the Great Hall.

The exuberance of the crowd could be heard in the valley. Badad turned to face his men, looking first at Fogle and then at them all.

"Man's life is a day. And what a day this will be. Will you follow me again to the gate of Bosscastle ... precious sons of Geramond...? Will you follow me there ....?" They responded with a resounding "Aye!"

Like in his dreams they came up the hill towards the castle; strident and proud. Arrows came down and some were felled. Delabole glanced towards the Western Gate, though in his heart he knew what he would see. The two huge doors were open, and on top of the gatehouse, almost at his eyelevel, he looked upon the one who had opened them. Like in his dreams Macara smiled at him, and opened his mouth to shout across the chasm that separated them: 'Where light was all forbidden, my prying flicker shone. All that men lay hidden, in dark my shining shone...!'

Badad was first to pass through the gate. His ebony horse galloped along the brick road and deep into the fortress courtyard. Soon after, the rebel army swarmed through. Delabole, from his lofty viewpoint, could see everything as it unfolded below him. This, he was sure, was the end of his Governorship. He sped down the tower as quickly as he had climbed it. He had time enough to escape, he thought, and cast off his thick, black cloak for fear that it burdened him.

An arrow was fired from a turret on the courtyard wall, a chance shot that came down like lightening. Old Toggett was at the end of its flight, and was hit in the shoulder. A blow that floored him. Fogle was up ahead but realised quickly that his old accomplice was no longer at his side, turned to see where he was and then rushed back through the chaotic advance to tend to him. Arrows were still being fired down, and one of them missed Fogle by inches, so he dragged the old man to the comparative safety of the alleyway near the gatehouse.

Toggett's breathing was laboured. His chest was covered in blood and his eyes were rolling in his shrivelled head. He steadied his eyes just enough to know that Fogle was with him.

"You were right," he muttered, grimacing as though every word caused a bolt of pain to shoot through his body. "I should have stayed at the back. Toggett does as Toggett does."

"You never do listen to anything I say," Fogle replied, trying to be jolly but not succeeding.

"You're missing all the fun. Leave me here, Fogle. You've waited so long for this …"

"Hush. Be still, my old friend." He cushioned his head with his hand, and moved his other hand to the arrow.

"Leave it where it is," Toggett demanded. "It will do no more good out than in." He closed his eyes. Fogle shook him and he opened them again. "Where are we?" he asked.

"Bosscastle," Fogle affirmed, his words uttered in such a way as to suggest that Toggett, and the others, had reached the end of their great adventure.

"I know we're in Bosscastle, you great lummock!!" the old man snorted. "But where is this place?" He found the energy to raise his head and look around his new surroundings. "Trust old Miggel Thrull to die in the heat of battle, while I depart from a filthy, dark alley…!"

"You are not going yet. The Druid! I'll get the Druid."

"His magic will not work on me." Toggett steadied Fogle's hand and would not let him move it from beneath his head. "I'm too strong-willed. Stubborn as a wife." He groaned and took a deep intake of breath.

"Badad can take the pain away," Fogle pleaded.

"The pain I can take. I've just realised … I'll be seeing the wife again soon, won't I? Nag, Nag, she will. What did you have to go and get yourself shot for, you old fool…!" He managed to chortle, and made Fogle smile at last.

Archers lined the walls and rooftops around the Druim Square. It was every man for himself. Arrows came down from the top of the Bossmilliad to fell a rebel or two as they entered the centre of the fortress. Badad, on horseback, was a prized target, but was missed time after time, and rode boldly through the crowd towards the Great Hall. There, a hundred or so Repecian soldiers were trying to hold back the horde of people that had swelled to the front of the square following the arrival of the rebel army. Indeed, amidst the confusion, this rebel army was lost and scattered.

Gonosor was at the forefront of the fighting, and was so high and strong that his mighty hands were his only weapons as he swiped at the soldiers whilst keeping their short swords at bay. They plunged and prodded at him as though they were fending off a lion or a wolf. The distraction allowed Badad to arrive at the front unharmed by arrow or sword. In his wake, a path had opened up through the crowd and the rebels came along it. They were all rebels now, but those with weapons, those that were adapted to battle, moved rapidly to the front to engage the posse of Repecians.

The skirmish went on for some time. Repecian soldiers were as sturdy as they were cruel, and they only turned and fled up the steps to the Great Hall with the realisation that this fight could not be won. All the while, arrows were being fired from the Bossmilliad. Galfall could see the damage just a dozen or so archers were inflicting on the people all around him. Not just mortal wounds but causing a panic that was becoming a stampede, which itself cut down more people, men and women, than the archers could manage. He called those standing close enough to hear him to arms, and led them off towards the great Keep, wherein another clash would occur and go on until the Bossmilliad was taken.

Madius called all soldiers to form a phalanx on the balcony. Swords were drawn and ready and the soldiers at the front, Madius amongst them, formed a hedge of spears to meet the advancing rebel hordes. Corsula dared to peer out between a crack in the doors, and gasped at the fear-filled air when he saw the scene beyond. A rattling at one of the windows brought him back into the room. The window was smashed and as he turned his head to find what had come in, he heard footsteps, scuttling across the floor and stopping behind Delabole's old seat.

"What is it?" he screeched. "Come out, I say...!" It did come out, and Corsula recoiled in horror. Macara, once his acquaintance but now just a puny, foul ghoul, was in the room with him. "How did you get out....? What do you want?"

In spite of the tumultuous din in the square, Madius could actually hear Corsula's screams.

"That's the end of him, then," he thought aloud, then readied himself and his men to defend themselves against the thousands of slaves and rebels that would do them harm. The hope that Corsula had brought with him had gone and Bossiney seemed a thousand miles away.

Badad, having presented Gonosor with his sword, sped off towards the cove. Once there, he dismounted and ran down the steps onto the dockside. The Buca Lapis was already well on its way towards the tunnel that would lead it to the open sea. Its oars on either side at full speed. Delabole appeared on the rear-deck, and held up his hand to signal his defiance.

In return, Badad held aloft his old staff, tilted back his head and muttered: "Rise again, Corbilo, from watery depths. Badad the Wanderer doth call. Whenever I might be minded to pull on you, I drag you up, earth and sea all with you...! Rise, then Corbilo, far from top and far from bottom. Giant of old, of whom men hath forgotten...!" He breathed out and lowered his gaze to the water. It began to swell and waves crashed violently against the sides of the cove. Badad himself moved back up the steps where the water could not harm him. Then, the surface of the water broke and from the depths a hand emerged. A giant's hand; as large as the largest ship, followed by the whole of the arm, and as it rose so the water became more troubled.

"Faster...!!" Delabole bellowed. The Merchant Budogis was not listening. Instead, his mouth was agape and his wide eyes fixed firmly on the giant hand that pursued them. "Faster...!" Delabole repeated, his words echoing all around so that his instruction was repeated several times. Suddenly, just as one finger touched the back of the ship, enough to tip it up slightly and certainly slow it down, the hand slid back into the water, and the water calmed again. Delabole and Budogis looked at one another, but did not utter a single word, and just breathed.

The Druid watched in dismay as the Buca Lapis disappeared into the tunnel. He searched the cove for a sign of Corbilo, but none were to be found. 'Once the giant is risen he will never go back whence he came.' Badad looked behind him, and saw a vision of the Lady Pannona of Fa-Noodar. 'A great ally will he be, but not here and now. Not to suit your own needs, Master Druid. Other battles are yet to be fought. Call on him then.'

"Delabole is escaping, my lady," Badad spluttered.

"Let him go, my friend. A part to play yet has he. You will meet him again, and you will have your hour with him." A horn sounded. That precious, golden sound of old. Pannona smiled at the little Druid and touched his face with the back of her hand, then faded away to leave him all alone in the cove.

Ten
The Going Away of Toggett Took

Fogle and Toggett heard the horn. That sound was followed by the clamour of men and women rejoicing in the square.

"Can you hear it, Toggett? It's everything we've waited for. The Sacred Horn. It means the war is over." Old Took's breathing was becoming slower and he could barely keep his eyes open. Fogle's delight was tapered with a tremendous sense of anger and loss, and he wondered how it was possible to feel all things at the same time. "We've done it, old friend," he continued. "We can go home, again." He was sure that Toggett could hear him and understand. "Back to the Threeshire. Home to Woldark. Your little cottage is waiting for you to return." A tear appeared in his eye but he made no effort to wipe it away. "The Shireman Inn is still there. The chance stones. You used to enjoy playing them with old Miggel." More tears welled in his eye and finally spilled over to run down his cheek. "Everything will be as it once was. How it was in the good days. I will take you there, Toggett. I will take you back to Woldshire ...."

With one final bout of energy, Toggett fully opened his eyes and replied:

"I am already there...!" Then he died.

A fire had been started in the centre of the Druim Square and the bodies of dead Repecian soldiers were being tossed on to it like logs into an inglenook. All around it men and women were rejoicing at the end of their enslavement. The glorious Shire Horn sounded and was met by a tremendous roar of approval. Then, from nowhere, a drum began to beat, and that too was greeted with a cheer and a ripple of applause. The two went together: the Shire Horn and the Miffell Drum, as though it was meant to be.

Galfall cut a swathe through the joyous crowd, his eyes searching all around. He was looking for several people, Fogle, Toggett, the Druid, but one person in particular. He finally found her towards the back of the square. Salissa was amongst her usual group, those that she was most familiar with.

"I've been worried about you," he said, smiling at her. "Isn't it all wonderful…?"

"It is," she replied, offering a smile in return.

Galfall paused, his face flushed. "I must go back to the Threeshire," he stuttered. "My mother will be expecting me to go home. Will you come with me?"

The question took her aback. She thought about what answer she would give. Again, she asked herself if she could ever find it in her heart to love this boy, even like him moderately. She decided that she could not.

"My place is here, Galfall." She smiled politely, and then turned away.

Badad did not go back to the square. Instead, he searched everywhere for Fogle, and found him in the alleyway, holding Toggett in his arms, stricken with grief.

"So many lives lost," he said sadly. "So many good friends."

"You may yet see them again, Fogle," Badad replied. "One day you yourself will travel to the Valley. Toggett will be waiting to greet you, and Wilfren …"

Fogle's face mellowed. "And Callarn?"

"Yes, of course Callarn."

"I promised Toggett that I would take him back to Woldark. He cannot be buried here, in a strange land."

"Bodmiffel is no longer a strange land, Fogle," Badad replied, slightly annoyed, but he understood. "But you are right. I will come with you, for I must return to Aldshire myself. We will rest tonight and leave at first light tomorrow."

It was a night of great celebration. The fire raged in the centre of the Druim Square well into the darkness, and illuminated the unfathomable winter sky to shed light over Bosscastle. Fogle and Galfall observed the scene from the balcony of the Great Hall. Drums and horns sounded still, and pipes and fiddles were played at speed to give off a jolly, exultant sound to which men and women danced and skipped around the fire. And as some danced others brought forward banners and decorations of empire to give fuel to the flames. Bosscastle was being rapidly cleansed, and the people rejoiced as they did it, for song and laughter, at last, filled the square.

Galfall seemed to be possessed by a silent rage within, that showed in his face. He could hear the music and was watching the dancing, but it did nothing to change his mood.

"Don't be sad about Toggett," Fogle told him, even though he was as sad as anyone. Grief, he thought, should be the preserve of those that had lived a life, not a youngster like Galfall. "He died having played his part to the full. He is at peace."

"It's not that," Galfall replied. "Oh, I am sad, Fogle. It's just that …" he struggled to find the correct words. "Nothing's like I imagined it would be. The war is over, and it's like it never was. The Druid told me that I would be the hero, but I am not."

"You did what was asked of you. No man can do more than that. I know that the Druid is pleased with you."

"But I was just a decoy, Fogle." The youngster was genuinely infuriated. "He told me that I should bring down Bosscastle … that it was my destiny. And all the while he had the man in place that was destined to do it. I was just a distraction."

"Badad's means, whether you like them or not, have brought us to this end. A glorious end," said Fogle. "Stop all this, Galfall. Enjoy the moment. Just think, in a few days time we will be home. Your mother will be pleased to see you, I'm sure."

Galfall looked out onto the square and saw Salissa dancing with the others, close to the fire. She looked quite beautiful and he could not take his eyes off her. Fogle searched to find what had suddenly taken hold of the young man's attention, and followed his gaze to the dancing girl. He smiled to himself. It all seemed so normal and refreshing, and just the kind of thing a boy of Galfall's age should be gripped by, instead of battles and wars, even old Druids. However, he was yet taken aback by the boy's next statement.

"I am not coming with you," he said, and seemed quite determined about it. "I intend to stay here, at Bosscastle. Tell my mother that I am safe and well. Tell her about my father."

"Shall I tell her to expect you some time soon?" asked Fogle.

"Tell her to expect me sometime," replied Galfall, then took off down the steps. "Farewell, Fogle," he said, without turning. Suddenly he was lost in the throng of the revelry.

Salissa was the best dancer of them all, and held her arms above her head as she twisted and turned to the music, and was the centre of attention of her small group. Galfall moved carefully towards her like a cat stalking a bird. The girl had seen him coming and turned her back. Undeterred, he moved to stand in front of her, and began to sway with the tune of the jolly music.

"I've told Fogle all about you," he panted. "How you saved me, took me in …. helped me to find the Western Gate. Even though we didn't manage to open it." Salissa was embarrassed and not a little annoyed. She recognised the arrogance and conceit in him again, that brash attitude that had initially nauseated her. At first he was a distraction from her sad and hum-drum life. His talk of the Druid and the rebellion, of adventure and destiny had initially excited her. Now, though, all that was done with and finished, and he could offer her nothing that she craved.

"It all turned out for the best," she replied, dancing still.

"Fogle said that you are a brave woman, and you should be rewarded when everything settles down." His words were desperate and his tone one of yearning.

She chortled. "I am not so brave, Galfall."

"Then why did you save me? What drove you to do it?"

Salissa knew full well why she did it, and thought whether she should tell him or to spare his feelings. Rather cruelly, she said: "Because I felt sorry for you."

He had been dealt the blow, but it was not her words that hurt him so much as the fact that she had said them with a grin on her face and while she danced. She turned away from him again but he pulled her back and close to him, kissed her and then pushed her away. "I've decided to stay here, in Bodmiffel," he said, then simply walked away to leave her to ponder his statement.

Very early the following day Fogle and Badad set off on their long journey back to the Threeshire. Toggett's body had been swathed in a wool blanket and placed on the back of their small, rickety hay cart. Daylight had barely broken and Bosscastle was quiet and still. No-one, save the rooks in the Bossmilliad, saw them leave. Rather than risk the demanding trek across the Border Mountains, they travelled along the coast road, passed the harbour at Bossiney and turned inland along the course of the Shire River. As they travelled they passed others making the journey home, and it occurred to Fogle that his army of rebels was disbanded and no more. He was pleased that it was over and they were going home, but sad also that he may never see some of them again.

"I hope they're content with their lives in the Threeshire, after so long on the road," he said, rather wistfully.

"What about you, Fogle?" asked Badad. "Will you be content?"

Fogle thought for a moment. "Woldshire is my home."

"But had you not promised to take Toggett Took back, would you long to return there…?"

It seemed an impossible question to answer, yet it should have been so easily settled. The fact was that Fogle Winnersh had been changed by the war. He was no longer the man he once was, and he was pleased that he wasn't. Whereas once he was angry and discontented, now he was at peace with himself, as was the land of Geramond.

At dusk that same day, they rested by the river. The following morning they crossed the Rustic Bridge and into the Threeshire. Two days further travelling ensued, and then they reached the outskirts of Woldark. The place seemed much the same as before he had left. A golden town, set amidst naked trees, against the rolling hills beyond.

"I think here is as good a place as any," said Badad, and pointed his nose to a sign at the side of the road. It said: 'The Shiremen Inn … warm food and warmer ale … not far to go now'. Fogle agreed.

Together the grave was dug out and Toggett's delicate body was placed into it, then covered with earth and stones.

"Travel swiftly, travel safe;
And cast out mortal thought.

One promise you have heard will be true:
The land of men long gone, of friends and sons,
Will open their arms for you."

When it was over the two men stepped away from the grave.

"I wish to go home, but I know that I must travel to Aldshire, to the Gringell farm."

"Go home for a little while, Fogle," Badad replied. "I will go to Aldwark myself. Madam Gringell shall be expecting me, for there is business there that I must attend to. She has something that belongs to me and I wish to have it back." His statement was vague and baffling, but Fogle knew that to probe any further would be a hopeless task. "When you are rested, have drunk your fill in the Shiremen Inn, go back to Bosscastle and wait for me there." He climbed back onto the cart. "Find the room that holds the Boss Throne, for it was bricked up and lost centuries ago."

"Then you intend to return with the king?" Fogle asked.

"Find the Boss Throne, Fogle. Dust it down. The king will wish to sit upon it when I bring him to Bosscastle. And keep a keen eye on Gonosor, for he will be true to himself and no-one else." Then he smiled. "My dear Fogle. Until we meet again."

"Goodbye, Badad," said Fogle, and watched as the cart rolled away and disappeared beyond the bend in the road. "Goodbye, Toggett Took," he said, looking upon the grave. He drew a deep intake of breath, then set off down the hill towards Woldark.

Eleven
The High Moor

The Gringell farm lay three miles north of Aldwark, the northernmost of the three Shire towns. While the countryside around Woldark consisted of serene and gentle hills and meandering rivers through valleys; and Dormlark tripped and slipped until it fell into the vast grey ocean beyond, Aldshire was altogether different. Wilder, somehow. Not pretty in a conventional way; nothing easy on a traveller's eye here, just vast expanses of barren uplands and bleak moors; but not without a certain appeal all of its own. And twice as high as the other two Shires for the mighty mountains of Tragara were not far away, and poked and prodded the sky to churn the clouds, away in the distance.

Badad had rode here straight from his parting from Fogle. However, the rickety hay-cart had been dispensed with shortly after the fork in the road, to allow the old man a swifter and more comfortable journey. He had stopped at Aldwark to rest and eat at the local hostelry, 'The Moorman' and found the townsfolk in good spirits for news had only just reached them of the rebel victory in the south. In such high spirits, in fact, that the pub was full to bursting and had run dry of ale hours before he had arrived. They had been placated with strange coloured beverages from dusty bottles, that were far stronger than the customary tipple and had gone straight to their heads. Badad did not linger long for he had been mystified enough by sober men to try to fathom a drunk one.

He knew precisely where he needed to go for he had been to the Gringell farm once before. A road went north from the main square, that would have taken him back to Tragara had he stayed on it for long enough, but instead he turned off soon after embarking, onto a dirt track that led onto the High Moor. It was a track seldom trod and of no great importance to anyone who was not a hill farmer.

The High Moor was a desolate and uninviting place; regularly battered by storms and with nothing to look at but clumps of gorse and grazing sheep, with only the odd farm dwelling glowing in the mist. Thankfully, the dwelling he needed was the first calling along the track, and not too far onto the Moor to have made it an utterly miserable journey. The farm itself consisted of a large, rundown house, a barn built onto the side of the house and several smaller buildings to form a courtyard. A light was on and smoke came out of the chimney, but he did not knock. Instead, he took himself off into one of the fields and sheltered from the weather in a hay-shed, lit himself a small fire and from there watched the house.

A week passed. Badad scrutinised the daily routine of the boy, Carthrall, the youngest of the Gringell boys. His day started at first light and went on until dusk, with little rest in between, not even to eat, it seemed. And most of the day was given up to the dreary and onerous task of feeding the animals. First those around the yard and next the beasts in the field, which meant that he needed to come into the hay-shed several times a day. The Druid concealed himself sufficiently so that the youngster had no idea he was being watched. Badad had tried on several occasions to see the boy's face more clearly for what he looked like intrigued him, but the late winter light was insufficient and so only his frame had become familiar. There was plenty of time, the old man told himself, to discover more about this youngest Gringell boy.

At the end of the week, before dusk, Carthrall left the farm and disappeared down the lane, so Badad afforded himself a little time to rest. He split open a bale of hay and scattered it to make a comfortable bed and lay back and allowed himself to drift into sleep. And just as his busy mind was beginning to settle for the night he was brought upright by the sound of the shed door creaking open, and he scrambled to his knees. Peering over the stacked bales he saw a face that was familiar to him, that of Madam Gringell: Mirrial, mother and wife.

She entered the shed tentatively, as though she knew that someone, something was lurking inside. Then she stumbled across the remnants of the Druid's fire, and her fears were confirmed. And

Badad realised that his lair had been found and thought about coming out from behind the bails, but not just yet. Mirrial came further inside, holding a flame torch in front of her to light her way, taking care not to ignite the straw as she passed through the shed towards the frail ladder that went to the upper level. She held out the torch and glanced upwards but saw nothing but the dark recesses. The farm had been troubled of late with burglars and rustlers, ever since the end of Repecian rule, and she told herself that this shed had been used as a base or hideout, not thinking that anyone was still there. Then another quick thought hurried through her worried mind that Galfall might have returned and been too afraid to show his face at the house, until she remembered that Galfall would never be too ashamed of anything and was, in any case, too selfish to come home when she needed him most. Satisfied that whoever was using this shed was not here now, she turned to leave.

"It's been a long time, Mirrial, my dear."

She turned sharply and when she saw the little Druid standing atop of the ladders she stumbled backwards and had to catch her breath for the sight of him was worse than a thief or a vagabond. Badad came down the ladders and stepped towards her but she backed away, half inside the shed and half out.

"I might have guessed it was you lurking in my shed," she said, angrily. "You have been stalking us!"

"I have been watching, yes," Badad replied, softly for he could detect her deep unease at being in his company again. "You look well, Madam, if I may say so. I am pleased to find you in good health. It has indeed been a long time since our last meeting. Sixteen years to be precise."

"You don't need to tell me how long it's been, Druid!" she snarled. "There hasn't been a day go by in all of those sixteen years when I haven't waited for this moment to come."

Badad took hold of her arm and brought her fully inside the shed, and closed the door. "And yet you hoped never to see me again, didn't you?"

"Of course I did," she replied. "For you have come to take my son away! And then I will have no-one, for my husband is dead and

Galfall ...." She scoffed. "He is not dead, I know that much. But where is he, eh? Trying to be someone he's not and will never be. Getting in people's way as he always does...!"

"Galfall joined the rebel cause after the battle of Tangelwitt, and played his part in the struggle to the full thereafter," Badad told her, but she did not seem bothered that he had been with her son and would know of his welfare. Badad continued regardless. "He has decided to stay at Bosscastle, for a certain young lady has caught his eye."

She chuckled. Not in a nice way, for there seemed to be nothing nice about her anymore. "Typical of him. Never mind about me or whether I'm managing this farm. His father told him not to go to the war, that he was needed here, but did he listen? Of course he didn't listen. Galfall has always done as he pleased. Not like his brother." Now she smiled fondly. "I don't know what I would have done without Carthrall. And now you've come to take him away too."

"I told you when I gave him to you that one day I would come back to retrieve him."

Mirrial turned angry again.

"You told me to rear him as my own, and to love him as my own. And that I have done, so that he is as much my son as the other one is...!"

"He is not your son, Madam," Badad replied sharply. In fact he was very sharp for he needed to extenuate that particular fact so that she understood, no matter how painful it was for her.

"Then what is he?" she snapped. "And what have I been doing for the past sixteen years if not bringing up and loving a son of my own...?" With the corner of her woven shawl she covered her eyes as she wept. "I wish you'd never brought him here, Badad. I wish I'd never met him."

"What did you expect?" the Druid asked, gently, for he could see how sorry for herself she was and felt deep sorrow for her himself. Mixed with a little remorse, for all of it was his doing.

"What I didn't expect was to have my heart broken," Mirrial sobbed.

Badad placed a comforting hand on her forearm.

"It is true that I have come back to take Carthrall. The time is right, you see. In fact, time is something we have very little of. And he will discover his true identity and his world will be changed forever. But that doesn't mean that he will forget about you and the love and kindness you have given him." She was still sobbing, and it seemed that the Druid could not find any words of comfort. "You have always known that this day would come. Who did you think he was? Why do you think I brought him to you?"

"I thought that he was an orphan," she said, between sobs. "That you knew his parents and took him in, then brought him to us for a chance of a better life."

"I brought him to you because I knew that no-one would come looking for him amidst these dark hills."

Madam Gringell was intrigued, and took her shawl away from her face. Her tears had dried. "Who would be looking for him? Who would do harm to a child?"

"Believe me," Badad replied, sadly, "there were those who would have killed him. A child is only blessed if it is wanted. There were plenty who did not want him."

"Who is he, Badad?" she pleaded, prepared, at last, to listen.

"Where is he now?"

"He's gone to Aldwark. There is a feast and dance in the square to celebrate the end of the war. The fifth such gathering this week. He won't be back until late. Why?"

"I feel as though I owe you an explanation, Madam," the Druid replied. "When I gave you the boy I told you to keep him safe. Now I am going to tell you why."

Twelve
A Second Meeting

"I had a start. I had made Vercingoral and Henwen fall in love with each other. And then Fillian invaded Bodmiffel and my great venture was in ruins. Henwen brought her people north, across the mountains. That, at least, was a glimmer of hope ...."

Gonosor, also at the front, brought his horse along the first column until he was next to the Queen. The morning was bright and the air was clean and fresh. Behind them, thousands of men and women best suited to dark forests than this wide open countryside; ahead of them, high on the hill, an army of Shiremen who had been their common enemy for as long as anyone could remember.
"I urge you, My Lady," he said. "Stop this now. It is folly. It is treason, no less." His tone was threatening.
Henwen smiled without turning to look at her brother. She removed her helmet and her golden hair spilled over her shoulders and cascaded down her back.
"What would you have me do, Gonosor? Our lands have fallen. Bosscastle is conquered. If we had stayed then our people would have been butchered or enslaved."
"We should never have left," he insisted, grunting his assertion. "We should have stayed in Bodmiffel and fought the invaders. But it's not too late. We can turn back."
"You saw what happened when we tried to fight them, Gonosor. With your own eyes you saw women and children cut down in their villages like corn in a field. We have never known an enemy like Fillian."
"It makes my stomach ache with shame when I think of him sitting in the Great Hall at Bosscastle," he replied. "But not as

ashamed as when I think of asking the Shire Lord for refuge." He leant towards her and said quietly: "Turn back, Henwen. Or this will be a sin for which you will pay the punishment. You know what punishment will befall a traitor. You know of the chamber beneath the Bossmilliad. So turn back now, before you set in motion a chain of events that will have you betray your race."

Henwen looked at her brother in disgust, then behind at her people. And a thousand faces at once looked at her.

"We cannot fight someone who is willing to unleash a total war. We cannot fight Fillian on our own, Gonosor. I would have been a traitor to my people if I had been so foolish as to try."

Gonosor hacked at his throat and spat out the contents of his mouth onto the ground below; a thick, green cocktail of bile and hatred that landed next to his horse's hoof like a heavy stone.

"Then what are you expecting here, sister, if not total war?" he asked. "Do you think Vercingoral will welcome you in the Middle Lands with open arms? He has, after all, brought with him his finest."

The Queen looked out across the plain, to the men atop the hill. "He will welcome us," she replied.

Delabole brought his horse closer to the King's. "Send them into the abyss, my Lord," he hissed. "Destroy the forest wretches once and for all, and then march on Bosscastle to claim what is rightfully yours...!"

Vercingoral surveyed the scene that was evolving below him, on the edge of his village of Celwig.

"I don't know what I shall do yet," he said.

"What is your heart telling you to do, Vercingoral, King...?" Badad came to the fore and stopped next to him. "Well?"

"This is not an army," Vercingoral replied.

"No," replied Badad, "It is a plea for help. Henwen has brought her people into your lands because her heart is telling her that you will not turn them away, or destroy them altogether. But help them..."

"What shall I do, Badad?" asked Vercingoral, genuinely confused and puzzled. Delabole brought his horse along side the king and leant inwards so that only his brother could hear him.

"Does your Mistress have such a hold over you that you would be dishonoured…? You are an intelligent man. So send this vile whore who has desecrated the reputation of the Shire kings into hell …"

Vercingoral looked at his brother with scorn. Then he checked his sword and tightened his helmet.

"I will ride out to meet her," he said. "To hear what she has to say for herself."

"Good, then," replied Badad. "Wisdom has not forsaken you altogether, Vercingoral." And then as a whisper in his ear: "Fortunate is the man who walks this earth having known what true love is, and of the great things it can achieve …"

Henwen watched as the King rode down from the hill alone, and was pleased to see it.

"I will accompany you," said Gonosor.

"No," Henwen replied. "I shall go alone."

"You cannot trust him, my Lady. I insist."

Now the Queen was forthright and resolute.

"I am Henwen, daughter and Queen, and I command you to stay where you are…!" And she rode out to meet Vercingoral alone.

Slowly they approached each other in the middle ground between their two peoples, until they were close enough to speak.

"My Lady," said Vercingoral, bowing his head courteously.

"My Lord," she replied, performing the same motion. And then, carefully, for neither of them were sure if they were far enough to be out of earshot, they smiled at each other. Vercingoral chuckled, and Henwen accompanied him.

"I had hoped to see you again," he said, "but never imagined that it would be like this. Here and now, at my village of Celwig."

"Fate has decreed that it shall be like this, my Lord," she replied.

Vercingoral looked at her. He had not forgotten how handsome she was or how her face cut through his heart and mellowed him thus, but he had forgotten how much she had bewitched him and just how deeply he had fallen in love with her the last time they had met, at Bosscastle. She was just a daughter then. Now she was a Queen.

"What would you have me do, my Lady?"

"Help us, my Lord."

"My brother thinks I should exterminate you all while I have the chance."

She smiled. "And my brother thinks that we should turn back and return to Bodmiffel to defend our lands until none of us are left."

"My brother is a fool," said he.

And now she laughed.

"Then we have more in common than we thought."

He stretched out his hand and touched the back of hers, gently and secretly.

"You are welcome here."

Delabole was watching and saw the final gesture, then broke from the front line and turned his horse to face his own people. He was enraged.

"Your King has abandoned reason," he proclaimed. "For all our great ancestors he has no care! The forest witch has a control over him that would see him throw away the value of the Shire people...! He has pushed aside hundreds of years of our history so that she will come to his bedside and do his bidding! So ride out, proud Shiremen, and let him know that you will not be subdued...! Ride to me, Delabole ... ! I will fulfil the promise of the Shire Kings."

Some did. Badad, though, sped in front of them for his black horse was the swifter. And with the haft of his thick sword he dealt Delabole a blow so strong that it toppled him and sent him crashing to the ground.

"For the life of me," he said, disgusted and ashamed. "When will you learn, Delabole Bubinda?" And to them all: "How poorly you look, Shiremen, in the eyes of those that come to ask for your help." He pointed his sword at Vercingoral in the hollow. "He would not betray you now. He seeks to make a whole of this race of Geramond. For we have been invaded in the south ... by an enemy common to us all! Do not oppose him. Do not seek to be masters of Geramond. Seek to be a part of it."

Those that had broke free to join Delabole skulked back into the ranks. Vercingoral and Henwen had observed the scene and quietly Vercingoral was pleased to see that his brother had come across the brawny wrath of the little Druid.

"Come north, to Woldark," he told Henwen. "You shall find refuge there." He looked over her shoulder at her people. "Even Gonosor, I'm sure, would welcome a rest and some good food."

By the King's orders the people of the city of Woldark, and the villages surrounding it, opened their homes, their kitchens and their fields to the refugees from Bodmiffel. An uneasy situation but by-and-large a peaceable one. Henwen and her associates were brought to the Lampas Hall, the home of the King and the centre of his government. And a great feast was held in her honour and to the memory of her father, Sodric, king. Looking around him, at the humble backdrop of the old Lampas, Gonosor commented, "little wonder that the Shire Kings have long desired our mighty Bosscastle."

Henwen sat at the top table next to Vercingoral. Her brother sat beside her and the Druid beside him; Delabole, quiet now, sat next to Vercingoral, and on the other tables sat the personage of both the Middle Lands and Bodmiffel. In the centre of the feast, a group of musicians played and a troubadour danced to their tune. And the food was devoured, the ale was supped and the pipes were smoked. The air was filled with jollity but Gonosor choked on the swirling fog of the Shire's weed.

He hammered his fist onto the tabletop and it shuddered beneath it, then he rose to his feet.

"My men and women are being killed while we make merry!" he blasted, so that the entire Lampas could hear him.

"You are weary, sir," said Vercingoral.

"I am appalled, sir," replied Gonosor. "For my heart is bleeding. My country has been conquered and yet my Queen has nothing on her mind but the body and countenance of a foreign king…!"

There were those that urged the Bodmifflian to take his seat again. But not the Druid. He rose to his feet, but no-one knew that he had so he got on top of his chair to make himself seen.

"Gonosor, Lord of Baladorn, is quite right. It is correct that we celebrate the arrival of the Queen of Bodmiffel, for that in itself signifies an end to the old ways. But she has not come here without just cause and reason. It is time, gentlemen of the courts of

Threeshire and Bodmiffel, to turn our thoughts to the plight of our predicament."

Henwen, having giggled and flirted for most of the evening, stood up, and everyone went quiet, including her brother and even the Druid.

"I must tell you that Bodmiffel has been invaded. Not by Shiremen or a familiar enemy, but by Fillian. And he is someone quite different. Never have I encountered an opponent such as him. His army is strong. I don't mean proud and tenacious, but organised and ruthless. And it is his gratification that my people have suffered. And I don't mean just my soldiers, but women-folk and children."

Vercingoral and the others present were listening with a great interest and fear. Gonosor was pleased to hear his sister, his queen, speaking in this style at last.

"The great forests have been burnt to the ground and the land of Bodmiffel cleansed to make way for his redoubts and camps. Anyone caught in his way has been killed. Women have been violated then butchered, children eradicated."

"And he will not be satisfied with Bodmiffel," Badad added. "He knows that further conquests await him beyond the high Border Mountains."

"Let him come," said Vercingoral, tossing his food back onto his plate. "He will find an altogether different opponent here."

"What's that supposed to mean?" Gonosor demanded, angrily. And as he spoke he leant towards the King, over his sister, and pushed him in the chest. And as he pushed him the Shiremen present rose to their feet and protested strongly at his conduct, and Henwen urged him to be still and quiet, while knowing that Gonosor was never such a man. Delabole, all the while, smiled and shrunk in his seat.

"Only by uniting as one nation can we hope to defeat the invader," Badad called out. But no-one could hear him for the din of the scuffle was too loud.

"I despaired of my wretched task. Even now, on the eve of their destruction, the people of Geramond bickered and spoiled each other. And I knew then that to seek the fulfilment of my commission through these men and women was stupidity. Then, later that night, the King came to me in my chamber and asked: "I would have the Lady Henwen to myself, but too many of her kind and mine are opposed to it. Will you help me, Master Druid?"

"Bring her into Tragara, my homeland," I told him. "But bring her only if you're certain of the contents of her heart, for you will not return from Kaw the same man, nor her the same woman."

Thirteen

Kaw

A good day's ride saw the three of them cross into Tragara. A hard ride for the further they went the more steep and rock-strewn the land became. Vercingoral wore plain clothes; a long, brown article of clothing down to his knees, and a reddish robe with a hood that almost covered him. Henwen wore a grey gown and a black robe trimmed with fur around the hood and the sleeves. Badad was his usual dishevelled self, and his hair seemed to be detached from his head with a life of its own the faster his horse went into the wind.

Through the high countryside of lower Tragara and up into the mountains. It was fairly late in the day, that time when dusk surrenders to night proper, when they arrived at Kaw. Badad led the way through the woods, along a narrow path that seemed to open up before him, and after him a gentle breeze that prompted the trees to crunch and crackle, a familiar and comforting sound to the Lady Henwen. And then they emerged from the woods and their eyes opened in wonder and delight, for below them, in the hollow, was Kaw; the silver lake and its wooded hills.

The late evening sky was the deepest blue and stars had just begun to appear to accompany the full moon, that cast itself down to be scattered across the surface of the still water.

"Where is this place?" asked Vercingoral, looking all around and not quite ready to take it all in. "You have been in my service, Master Druid, for as long as I have been king, and yet you have never mentioned it before." He looked towards the lake below, then up at the mountains, closer now than at any time throughout the day as they had approached, and high and mighty enough to impose themselves upon him and cast doubt over his significance.

"It is truly an astonishing place," Henwen added.

Badad was pleased. "I'm glad you both think so. Welcome, my friends, to Kaw, my home and birthplace. Travel any further north and the mountains will trap you … beyond them, no-one knows because no-one has ever ventured there. A magical place, they say, and no place for a mere man to tread. Come now, you are both travel-weary. Follow me." And his horse cantered down the hill towards the lake. Vercingoral and Henwen did follow him.

He took them to a small thatched house on the edge of the lake, where inside a fire was burning in the hearth and a pot of stew was bubbling above it. Vercingoral entered behind the Druid, removed his hood and was at once puzzled.

"How is this possible when no-one knew we were coming?" he quizzed.

The Lady laughed. That short, cheerful chuckle that had so endeared her to him. "For a king you can be quite dim sometimes," she said. "Badad knew we were coming, and he can do wondrous things."

Vercingoral returned a smile that suggested he was pleased to have been corrected like this. And Badad was pleased because it confirmed one thing to him, that they were indeed deeply in love, for only lovers would behave like this. Although he knew little about the ways of the heart, he knew that much.

They settled down and warmed themselves by the fire and ate the stew. Badad could do wondrous things, yes, but his cooking was appalling and they ate it in silence and with a struggle and a sweat on their brows. Then, when the Druid had finished his and had placed his bowl on the floor, he said:

"I shall marry you here."

Both of them were taken aback and when Badad saw their mouths agape he wondered if he had spoken too soon.

"What's the matter? You both love each other. That much is clear. From the moment you met you have been in love."

"You have no authority in Forest Law to marry us," said Henwen.

"Or the Shire Law," said Vercingoral.

Badad was infuriated. "You are in Tragara now, and I have all the authority I need here!" he exclaimed. "Besides, what's the alternative? To conduct a secretive and iniquitous affair? To chance a look across a crowded hall? A clandestine smile when you're sure your brothers are not watching? Would you conduct such a condition? A king and a queen who dare not do as they please? And what is the good of Forest Law when the forests are fettered by the tyrant, Fillian? Or the old Shire Law when it forbids its king to love and marry a foreign woman, when that is precisely what is needed now?"

Vercingoral was baffled. "What do you mean?"

Badad answered immediately. "Storm clouds are gathering in the south. Fillian will invade the Middle Lands now that he knows they exist. You can only hope to defeat him if the two great peoples of Geramond are united."

Henwen smiled. "Of course," she said. "And it takes a little Tragaran to tell us that."

"But marriage?" asked Vercingoral. "Here and now?"

"Do you fear it, my Lord?" replied Badad.

"No."

"Could you imagine your life without the love of the lady Henwen...?"

"No."

"Then there can be no other way. Threeshire and Bodmiffel must be reunited now, while the chance is there."

"Our courts will not accept it," said Henwen, sad and seemingly reconciled to the fact that it could never happen.

"What does it matter what Delabole Bubinda or Gonosor of Baladorn think of it?" the Druid said. "They oppose the union not because of pride or principle but jealously and resentment. Both would take what you have now ... power and love and devotion. If Delabole were the king in this event he would have wedded the Lady long before now...!"

"She may not wish to be wedded to me," Vercingoral murmured, looking at the half-eaten food in his bowl.

"Then ask her!" blasted the Druid.

The King looked at the Lady Henwen. He saw in her such beauty and grace.

"Could you see yourself married to me?" he asked, embarrassed and bashful. "Harnessed to me for the rest of your life?" Henwen was embarrassed too, not for herself but for Vercingoral because the Druid had forced him to ask.

"Answer, please," Badad urged her.

She looked into his face and saw kindness and shrewdness beneath that cut-jaw and pronounced attractiveness.

"I can see it, but more, I long for it," she replied, and Vercingoral sighed happily. "But you realise that our firstborn will be heir to Geramond, and Threeshire and Bodmiffel will fade and welter…?"

"I do," he said. "And will accept that for our firstborn will come about through love. So our two lands will unite."

The little Druid heaved a sigh so deep and loud that the house shook. A mere mention of the word Geramond from the lips of a King and a Queen was all he had ever wanted to hear. And he laughed, nay danced on the tips of his toes when Vercingoral leant in and took the lady Henwen in his arms.

On the shores of the lake, at midnight, they were joined together.

Fourteen

The Battle of High Cleugh

"And that, I thought, was that. As a star raced across the dark sky I knew that the deed that been done. The seed had been sown. I was convinced that my undertaking was complete at last, and I waited for the Lady Pannona to come and fetch me. I waited and waited but she did not come, and I knew that fate had twisted against me once again. I looked into the still water of the lake and saw a terrible vision of wanton death and ruin ... that we had all expected and dreaded in equal measure. I waited until first light the following day before I broke the news to Vercingoral and Henwen..."

Badad, knocking first, entered the hut. Vercingoral and Henwen were sleeping still, naked save for the blanket that covered their midpoints, their legs entwined and their arms holding the other one close. The King woke first, and brought his head off his pillow, that woke the Lady, who brought the blanket over her chest, though was not embarrassed.

"What is it, Badad?" he asked.

Badad did not come into the hut but stayed in the doorway to deliver his news.

"Threeshire has been attacked," he said. "Fillian invaded your lands late yesterday afternoon. The township of Celwig has been taken, all its inhabitants have been slaughtered."

Vercingoral pulled himself fully upright. A look of shock had descended over his face. "All of them?"

"Every one," Badad replied.

"What kind of evil is this...?" asked Henwen.

"An evil that has been thus far unchecked," Badad said. "It is the nature of your enemy. It is the way Fillian wages war...!"

They left Kaw soon after waking and made with haste to Woldark. As Vercingoral entered the city he removed his hood to let his people see that their king had returned, and they cheered as his horse sped through the streets towards the Lampas, even though Henwen was with him.

The Lampas Hall was full and bristling with a tense and prickly bout of activity. They were all present: the court of Vercingoral, Gonosor and other noblemen from Bodmiffel.

"Nearly two days have passed since our country was attacked, the people are troubled and some are making for the mountains, the Court is at a loss ... and finally our king appears...!" Delabole's tone was sardonic, his words uttered with a gleeful glint.

"I am here now," said Vercingoral. "What news?"

A map was spread out across the tabletop and all gathered around it.

"Celwig is lost," said an equerry, pointing at the town. "We think Fillian has set up camp there," said another, older man. "He won't come any further north yet. His men will be weary after their trek across the Mor Pass."

Those words, at least, were a comfort to the King. Until Badad stepped forward. They did not know he was even there until they felt him brush against them, and he could just about make out the map on the table top.

"He will have already made further advances into the Shirelands," he mumbled.

"How do you know?" Delabole insisted, scornfully, agitated further by the little man's presence.

"He is here to conquer everything he surveys," the Druid replied, with equal scorn. "And he wants that business over and done with as quickly as possible. He knows that he must meet the Shire army before his task here is complete. And he knows that the Queen of Bodmiffel, with some of her army, has passed into the Middle Lands, and will want her hour with him."

"Then he will be on his way here," Vercingoral mused.

"Yes," said Badad. "He will know that if he takes this city he will have completed his task."

"How many are there?" the King asked him.

"From my discussions with the Lady Henwen, I would say that Fillian has brought two of his legions with him ..."

"How many?" Vercingoral demanded.

"Ten thousand men!" replied the Druid.

Delabole was suddenly overcome by a coughing fit, that seemed to choke him. "Ten thousand!!" he repeated. And to his brother: "We cannot fight that many men!"

"You have no choice," said Badad. He looked at them all in turn: the King, his feckless brother, Henwen and Gonosor, then the others. "But you only have a chance if your two armies are joined together."

Delabole snorted and scoffed. "The noblemen of the Threeshire do not fight alongside the peasants of the forest!"

"Then you will surely fail," Badad replied.

Vercingoral looked at Henwen, then stretched out his hand and pulled her close to him. "We will be joined. We shall be united again." And Badad was pleased.

"We will not be a part of this," ranted Gonosor, turning to leave, taking hold of his sister's arm and pulling her with him. Vercingoral tried to hold her back but it was Gonosor who was the strongest, and Henwen was dragged into the middle of the floor as her brother made for the exit. And the King went to assist her but was held back by the Druid.

Then, as strong as he was, Henwen pulled herself free of him and stood stock still. Gonosor stepped towards her.

"What have you done?" he asked.

"Nothing that I am ashamed of," she replied.

"What exactly!?" His voice was risen in fury. "Have you defiled your race? WELL?"

Vercingoral came to stand beside her. "We are now one and the same," he said, quietly. Then, louder and to them all: "Henwen is my wife! My love!"

They recoiled in horror, every one of them. Gonosor sped towards the door and had to gasp at the evening air. Delabole twisted and sneered like a snake, banging his fists onto the tabletop.

"Betrayer of your kin!" he blasted. "And the House of Bubinda is destroyed with one night of passion! Much more, a nation is rubbed out and is no more!"

All of the men present in the Lampas gave a voice to their repulsion and loathing. And Henwen and Vercingoral, like villains, were surrounded. Then the disgust that was initially aimed at the two of them spilled over into the more general, familiar hostility of Shiremen versus the Bodmifflians. Badad lowered his head, then raised it sharply to look at the ceiling.

"What more can I do?" he muttered, sadly.

Vercingoral, king, broke free of the mob and ran towards the exit and out onto the balcony of the Lampas Hall. Outside, in the bright evening light, he looked down upon the people waiting in the square. Forest folk as well as Shire folk listened as he spoke to them.

"There is no other love for me than Henwen, Queen. When I look into her eyes I see the forests ... when she looks into mine she sees the Shires ... and yet when I look into the eyes of my own people I see the sadness that it presents." He twisted and veered his body towards the bricks of the Lampas. "This place blazed with trophies, but within a scandal. And the household of Bubinda I have shamed with my illicit affair. So to rid this roof of the stain, I will stand aside, and Henwen will stand aside."

Badad crept out of the door to stand behind the King, for he knew that something was occurring. Then Henwen came out for she had heard her name mentioned; then Gonosor to see where his sister had gone; then Delabole. Vercingoral, aware that he was no longer alone, continued.

"Delabole Bubinda shall be king of Threeshire. And it is he who must steer you through these troubled times. Gonosor will be king of Bodmiffel...!" And as he spoke he surveyed his audience, who were beginning to mutter and stir anxiously. The Druid also observed them with great interest. He mumbled to himself:

"I hope you're watching, my lady. I chose well."

"Vercingoral and Henwen will withdraw from public life. And as simple folk will live and die...!" the King concluded.

Delabole stepped to the front of the balcony so that he was standing aside his brother. He held out his arm to the crowd and was smiling happily. Then, the crowd, as one voice, started to boo and jeer him, and Delabole moved to the back again. Vercingoral was smiling now.

"All hail Delabole, king of the Middle Lands! Hail Gonosor, king of Bodmiffel!"

The mob was growing restless and swelled from the back of the square to the front, and three men, two old and one younger, were tossed onto the steps of the Lampas. And once there, the bolder of the three, having caught the eye of the luminaries on the balcony, felt obliged to say something.

"We don't need no other king but thou." Vercingoral went down the steps and picked him up off his scrawny knees. Caught by excitement and with a renewed swagger in his aged legs, Toggett Took held aloft his free arm so that the crowd could see him and be suitably impressed. They cheered and applauded him but his friend, Miggel Thrull, was not as tickled as he knew he should be, and the other one of the three, Fogle, shook his head with embarrassment.

"Then I have your affection and support still?" Vercingoral asked the old man, but loud enough for everyone else to hear.

"Aye, lad," replied Toggett, audaciously. "So long as thee gets us out of the mess we're in...!" Then, turning to the huge crowd, but with Fogle and Miggel in his eye, he shouted: "We would prefer 'im to his brother, wouldn't we?" as though he had every right to ask the question. Perhaps he had. They responded with a resounding 'Aye!' and 'Too right we would!', then sincere and clamorous applause.

The old man was handed back to his friends, who immediately told him off. Then Vercingoral went back up the steps to the balcony and gestured for the cheering and applause to stop.

"With every fibre of my body I shall endeavour to serve you, my people. And, with Henwen, shall be your champion. Our country is in peril, and the danger comes ever closer to this, the heartland of Threeshire. The land of Bodmiffel has already fallen, and so shall we unless strength is our bond." The Queen came to stand beside him. "Only by uniting, and fighting as one race, can we expect to win." The crowd was silent and hanging on his every word, waiting to hear anything that would give them hope. "Be under no illusions, my good people. A great battle must now be fought in our Shirelands! And if we lose, this decent, gracious country shall be forsaken forever. So we must be strong, determined and unyielding!" Finally, the King surveyed his audience. "We are the heirs of these ancient lands. We are the protectors of traditions and customs that stretch back to the dawn of time. No invader can destroy what we have, whatever this clever General brings …!"

And he held his arms aloft and tilted his head back to immerse himself in the ovation. Delabole, sulking, slipped back into the Lampas.

Badad approached Vercingoral. "You shall be the King until the day you die," he said, smiling.

"Yes. It would seem so."

"I hope that is a very long time," the Druid said.

"Believe me, my little friend, so do I," the King replied. And then he noticed that Badad seemed gloomy and preoccupied. "What is it?" he asked. "Are you annoyed about what I did a moment ago? I was only teasing. I knew that the people would recoil from the notion of having Delabole as their king. He is my brother, yes, but I know as well as anyone what he's really like."

"Of course you do," Badad replied. "I have taught you well during the course of our association. So you are a shrewd and dexterous man where your forebears were fools or despots!"

"Then what is it?" asked Henwen, stepping away from her brother to stand beside the King. Badad thought carefully for a moment. Glumly, he replied: "Vercingoral, I have helped you many times and in many ways, but I cannot help you now. This new battlefield will be no place for an old Druid's magic and sorcery. You and the lady Henwen must face this peril alone. If you rely on me I fear you may fail."

Vercingoral was saddened to think that the little Druid would not be by his side in the battle. He had been by his side for as long as he had been the king. He glanced at his wife, who was smiling and seemed to bear no regrets or doubts. And he quickly consoled himself with the thought of having her with him instead of Badad.

"You have not strayed far from my thoughts from the day I met you, fair lady," said Badad, smiling fondly and not gloomy at all now that she was smiling down upon him.

"And you have been a true and faithful companion, Master Druid," she replied.

Vercingoral laughed. A nervous chuckle.

"You are speaking as though we may never see him again," he said to his wife.

Badad looked at the King. He was fond of him, yes, but silently hoped that it would be so. If he never saw either of them again, or any of the others, it would mean that the battle had been won despite the improbability of it happening. And then Geramond would be restored and he could finally diminish and fade from their lives and the world of men.

"Where will you go?" Vercingoral asked him.

"I will wander," Badad replied, woollily.

Vercingoral placed his hefty hand on the little man's thin shoulder. And Badad placed his arm around the King's waist.

"We shall see you again," said Vercingoral.

Badad smiled. A strange, submissive smirk. "Yes, you probably will."

And then he walked away. As he passed the door of the Lampas he glanced inside and said to Delabole, quite firmly:

"Don't let your brother down!" And went down the steps and disappeared into the crowd. Delabole came to the doorway and watched him leave. Gonosor, too, who was silently pleased to be rid of him.

Men came down from the hills of Aldshire and joined the others outside Woldark, and as they moved further south so the able men of Dormshire mingled with them. In Dormshire, close to the village of Fingle, a scout came back and reported to the King and the Queen that Fillian's army was close by, so the battle sight was chosen. High Cleugh was the name of the hill that dominated the landscape: a vast and sweeping vale before the mountains rose again in the south. In total, four thousand Shireman had come to the battle, and two thousand forest folk. Vercingoral and his Shire army occupied the left of the hill and Henwen and Gonosor took the right. And there they waited. Until another scout returned to report that the Repecians were approaching, and they readied themselves for battle.

Vercingoral rode out from the mass of men that had surrounded him, and turned his horse to face them.

"Here it will be that the Shiremen and the men of the forests shall make war! Shall defend their country! Hold your backs straight and your heads high and proud, for the strength of this land is in its men folk! Be obedient. Bear your portion of what this day will offer! Allocate a portion of your valiant hearts to acts of brutality and wickedness, for you will need to be merciless and the blood in your veins must this day run cold!"

He could see fear in their eyes, and would have had it glow in his had they not been looking at him. And then they looked beyond him and he knew that the enemy was at last in sight, so he turned to watch.

On the distant horizon, almost lost in the mists of a summer morning, Fillian's army appeared. And thousands of soldiers marched towards them, their armour gleaming in the faint sunlight, their standards fluttering on the breeze. And they marched to the slow beat of a drum, that made their approach even more menacing, like the beating heart of a dragon that got louder the closer it came.

The King studied them closely. He had taken part in many battles during the course of his life but mostly in Bodmiffel, and that place was covered in forests and the enemy was largely unseen. This new enemy stretched itself out below him to reveal the full extent of its weaponry and strength, and that was something that was totally new to him and his men. He was filled with a sense of foreboding and a longing for it to start. He had never waited to do battle before; never been delayed while the opposition positioned itself. A new experience for everyone, and he was distressed to watch as this thoroughly professional army came on to the field, in perfect formation and here merely to fulfil their instructions, no matter what they happened to be.

At the front but on the edge of his army, he could clearly see Fillian, whose red cloak and the high plume on his helmet clearly set him apart, and he asked himself what his army would look like to the commander down below, across the field.

"There lies your task!" he shouted, without turning back to look at his men, for he dare not. "There lies your toil for the day!"

Two rows from the front, Toggett Took leaned towards his friend Fogle and whispered: "I think old Toggett may 'av dropped a clanger by agrein' to come 'ere!"

"We didn't get a choice!" Fogle replied, looking out across the field, his fat body rigid and still. "Don't stray too far away from me, old man."

"Why? Is thee shitin' theself?" Toggett laughed.

"Aye, I am. But when you die it's down to me to take your body back home. I don't want to be spending all night looking for it…!"

Toggett laughed louder, loud enough for the King to hear him, who turned to see what was going on.

"The day will come when this old stick is snapped," said the old man. "But I'm telling yer this … it won't be snapped by them blighters down there! When Toggett Took dies it'll be cos he's sick of livin'! And that ain't today. Today the wife's not 'ere, and I intend to make the most of it…!"

A gleeful smile momentarily spread across Vercingoral's face, and the sound of his men laughing was very welcome indeed.

"There lies your task!" he repeated, but louder and looking at them directly. "Are you up to it? Well, are you…?" They responded the only way they could, with a loud 'Aye', accompanied by a bout of clamorous cheering.

Delabole brought his horse close enough to the King to speak.

"Are you up to it, my Lord?" he asked.

"Of course," replied Vercingoral. "Come on, brother," he ranted, "It'll be like the olden days! Me and you against the world…!" Delabole thought for a moment, for he could barely recall that such days had ever existed.

"What would you have me do?" snarled the King.

"Negotiate with Fillian," replied Delabole, quite seriously, not discouraged when his brother turned away and scoffed at the remark. "He already possesses Bodmiffel. Let him keep it. He may be content with that."

"And what would I be, and my heirs?" the King snapped. "His puppet king? And would our people live freely with his wicked empire on our border…?" He looked down upon the enemy. "Besides … does it look as though he needs to negotiate?"

Fillian stopped his horse and held up is hand to gesture that they had come far enough, and his army came to a halt and the beat of the drum stopped. Macara came by.

"The sun is shining at last, Great One," he said, looking at the sky. "Had I not seen it for myself, I never would have believed that the sun shone here at all."

"Wherever I am," said Fillian, "wherever I chose to make war, the sun will shine."

Macara bowed his head. "Quite, sir."

"Although, I am a little disappointed that Vercingoral has brought a wretched army of peasants and yokels to the battlefield."

Macara was confused. "Vercingoral, Great One?"

"Yes, the King of these Middle Lands," replied Fillian, his eyes fixed on the aforesaid ruler, and glazed with approval and desire. "They say he is a fine warrior. Sturdy in body and mind. What you would expect on an expedition like this. A bristling bear. A lion tawny-necked. And a man whose mind is ignorant of his fate, for he knows not what shall befall him when this day is done…!" Yes, his eyes were fixed on him, and it was as though Vercingoral was already caught in his net. "Whatever this battle brings," he told Macara. "However well he fights and no matter how many of our men he slays, no harm must come to him."

"Whatever he is," Macara snivelled, "he is not the man you are, Great One!"

Fillian laughed out loud.

"I like your style, Macara," he said. "You'll go a long way, my friend."

Fillian himself was a fine warrior; tall and robust, with a firm jaw line and with all the classic features of a great man. A general, like Macara, once, but whose endeavours had made him much more than a mere man. He was more like a god now. Revered as an unearthly being set down amidst mortals. And like the Druid, his virtuosity had bewitched his people, especially his soldiers, whom he had beguiled so that they would fight to the last drop of their blood had spilled onto the ground. So he was no longer a general but a deity and in total command of his people. After his great victories in the south that had so endeared him to this own race, the Repecian

Senate had reluctantly granted him the title of 'Dictator for Life'. He was sure that after his conquest of Geramond the Senate would need to bestow an even grander identity upon him, like 'Emperor'.

On the right side of the hill the Bodmifflians mustered, and stirred anxiously as they observed the enemy across the field. Henwen was at the front with her brother by her side and her people behind her.

"Remember what you are fighting for," she said to them. "You are fighting for your honour!"

"We are fighting for the Shirelands," Gonosor whispered despondently in her ear. "For your lover…!"

The Queen, with her golden hair in two tight plaits at the back of her head, was as fierce-looking as any of them, and wore a face set with fury, and glowered at her brother and opened her mouth to correct him, but her attention was diverted by a raucous noise coming from the far end of the hill – the Shire Horn, and thunderous cheering to accompany it, like the Shiremen were trying to intimidate the enemy with noise. Inherently, the Miffel Drum was pounded and so the forest folk realised that it was their turn to cheer and shout at the top of their voices. Fillian, in the dip, was faced not with a wall of iron or stone, but with noise, and it seemed sturdier and more enduring, for the noise came from the men he had come to conquer, but who had no inclination to be fettered by him or anyone else who would dare try to.

Amidst the din and the commotion Vercingoral glanced across to Henwen and offered her a smile. The Queen forced a smile and nodded to confirm that she was on form and ready for the events of the day, whatever they may be.

Fillian, rather than intimidated, was roused and thrilled by the booming clatter rolling down from the hill, and his face bore a wide, toothy grin and he actually took his hands off his reigns and clenched them together with delight, as though he was applauding their impudence and bravery. Then his smile disappeared and he leaned towards Macara and told him:

"Send them a volley. See if that won't quieten them down a bit."

Macara, turning to face his soldiers, called out, "Archers!" and several hundred of them stepped forward from the ranks, loaded their bows, stretched them back and fired their arrows high into the morning sky.

"Arrows!" shouted Vercingoral. "Hold steady!" But some of his men bolted back instinctively and caused turmoil as they ran into others. Then the cloud of arrows above their heads burst and came down upon them, killing many and wounding many more. The Shire Horn was quietened and the goading ceased. Vercingoral checked behind him to survey the damage but did not look too closely.

"Please, my Lord," said Delabole. "This is madness!"

"You can stay here and be struck down, brother," replied the King. "Or you can come with me...!" And with that said he held his mighty sword above his head, tightened the reigns of his horse, and called out: "It starts now!! The Shiremen join the battle!"

They came down from their hill with great speed. An urgent dash to render an arrow useless. But the Repecian archers loaded again and fired straight at the Shiremen as they sped towards them. Then, again and again. And men fell to the ground and were abandoned; dead before the battle had even begun.

"Send out the cavalry," Fillian shouted. Then, to himself: "Let's finish this as quickly as we can!"

The Shiremen were too close at last for their archers to pick them off, but out rode the Repecian horses, and they did as much damage themselves, and many more fell, slashed in their guts or bludgeoned on their heads or in their necks.

Vercingoral was the first to engage a Repecian soldier proper, and slashed his hefty sword down to slay a legionary, then another one. Delabole, on horseback, also ploughed into the enemy ranks, as did other mounted Shiremen. Then, after all the arrows and the attack from the cavalry, the foot soldiers of Vercingoral's army finally joined the fray. And with sword, axe and spear they did their best, with some success in the early stages as they cultivated a conduit through the Repecian ranks.

Henwen and the Bodmifflians had not yet come down from the hill, for their part in the battle was yet to come. So they watched from their lofty haven and waited for the signal. And listened, for this was a noisy battle, filled with screams of defiance and despair. All the while, the Queen did not take her eyes off Vercingoral for a second, and followed him wherever he went, supporting him and urging him to survive these early skirmishes.

Fillian was watching him as well, willing him to stay alive for very different reasons. All the things he had heard about this young, tribal king seemed to be true, for he fought with a ferociousness seldom seen against his mighty soldiers. His lone sword was achieving as much as the rest of his men put together, until a space opened up all around him. Now it was Fillian's turn to join the tussle, and he rode his stallion towards Vercingoral hurriedly. Repecian legionaries towards the back, who were swilling forwards but had not yet done any actual fighting, saw what their great general was doing and cheered him raucously.

Amidst the confusion and hysteria of the battle, the King and the General engaged each other. Vercingoral was fully aware of who it was he was now fighting. So was Henwen, and the sight of it was as painful as a dagger in her heart, and she was inclined to ride out herself, only to be held back by her brother.

One sword clashed against the other. One sword smashed against a shield, then defended against a blow. Two horses, one brown and one black, pressed their sweaty bodies against each other, and their necks clashed as though they were fighting their own, private battle. Vercingoral managed a few words, as he dealt another blow to Fillian's shield.

"You will not prevail in my lands...!" he panted.

"Not if they're all like you," Fillian replied, pushing his shield against the King's sword. "But they're not!"

A legionary emerged from the throng of the main brawl, and seeing that one man was just as strong and capable as the other, decided to help his commander, and pushed his short sword into Vercingoral's horse. It fell to the ground but the King managed to avoid being crushed. Fillian glowered at the legionary and drove his own horse towards the hapless soldier, sending him scuttling back into the crowd. With a mere plunge of his sword he could have finished it there and then. But he did nothing of the sort.

Instead he did something quite remarkable. An act of foolishness that took Vercingoral completely by surprise: he jumped off his own horse and sent it away, so that they were both on foot now, and equals again.

Henwen, herself watching intensely, decided that the time was right to bring her own army down from the hill. To ignore the arrangement that had been agreed and pre-empt the signal to offer up their lives to the cause.

"Now it's our turn!" she yelled. "The Forest Folk are coming!" She forcefully instructed her horse to charge down, kicked her heels and even pushed its head forwards, but it did not move, and because it did not move neither did her men. She screamed angrily then got off the beast and ran down from the hill on foot. Now her men did make a move, but Gonosor held out his arm as a gesture to stop them, that was obeyed.

The Queen looked behind her and was despondent. "If it has to be that your queen must fight alone, then so be it," she said to them, and turned to run towards the battle. In the distance, at the side of the field away from the fighting, a lone horseman appeared, and was coming towards Henwen.

"We can't just abandon her!" objected at least one Bodmifflian. Then, from another: "Look! It's the Druid!" It was true. At first Henwen was relieved to see him and actually sighed with relief, for now they at least had a chance. But Badad had not come here to fight. Instead, as his horse sped past the Queen, he gathered her in his arms and lifted her up, then sped off with her, away from the battlefield. Restraining her, he offered an apology.

"Forgive me, my Lady. We must flee, and you will see why soon." And the others were left with their mouths agape as they disappeared over the brow of the hill.

"Why have you come here?" Vercingoral grunted.
"We are the masters of the world!" replied Fillian, plunging towards the king then ducking as his opponent's sword struck back. "You cannot hold out against the might of Repecia...!"

A clash now as blade struck blade, so that at last it was a matter of which one was the stronger. Vercingoral was, and he took hold of Fillian's sword arm and pulled him close to him, then promptly inserted his knee into the General's groin, and when his head came down that same knee smashed against his chin, sending him toppling backwards into the mud. With his foot the King kicked away Fillian's sword, then towered above him with his blade pointing downwards. Fillian wriggled beneath his adversary but could not escape.

Vercingoral placed both hands on the hilt of his sword and looked directly into Fillian's eyes, but could see no fear. Instead, the Repecian had stopped writhing in panic for he had accepted his fate, and was now waiting for his death to come. The sword was raised so that it was level with Vercingoral's chest, preparatory to it being plunged down into Fillian's chest, and it seemed that this mighty contest had been won. And the battle too, perhaps, for every army must follow the fate of its commander. A pitiless frown moved onto Vercingoral's face, and his hands clenched the hilt of the sword ever tighter ...

Then, a scream. A solitary sound amidst a thousand other sounds. Vercingoral momentarily turned his head to see that Delabole, his brother, was pinned to the ground with a Repecian blade standing over him. A thought passed quickly through the King's mind, that would have been lengthy to say but flashed through his head like lightening: "I didn't even know he was there!" Another quick thought: should he slay Fillian or salvage his brother? He had not the time to do both. Nor did he have the time to ponder the quandary for too long. He decided to save his brother, and lunged at the legionary and slit his throat. Delabole got back onto his feet and scurried away. And in the absence of his assassin, Fillian also got back onto his feet, and was pleased to see that Vercingoral had already taken on another antagonist, so quickly withdrew from the battlefield.

In the thicket of trees beside the battlefield, as the land sunk further before it rose again, Fillian sought a reprieve from the fighting. In all his years as a soldier and a commander, and in all the battles he had fought, he had never come up against an adversary as strong and overawing as the young king, and as he leant against a tree to catch his breath he marvelled at the power of the man and pondered his own narrow release from his immense grasp. Then, quite suddenly, he had an urge to throw up, and did so at the foot of the tree, before straightening himself and preparing to rejoin the battle.

He heard a sound, the crack of a twig beneath a foot, and turned quickly to investigate, his sword poised. Delabole tried to stoop out of sight but it was too late, so he held his arms out wide to demonstrate that he did not desire a swordfight. Fillian remembered his face from the battlefield, and that Vercingoral had broken away to rescue him. Studying him closely he could see the resemblance and did not need to be told that this was the King's brother. Just as tall and sturdy, he thought, but nothing like Vercingoral, for he was cowering like a scalded dog. So Fillian lowered his sword, and grinned contentedly.

All the while, even in Fillian's absence, the battle continued. Vercingoral, between opponents, took stock of his army's condition, and was gladdened to see as many Repecian dead as his own men. He was, therefore, sure that the time was right for the Bodmifflians to join the fighting. The plan had been for the Shiremen to launch the initial attack, then for the Bodmifflians to strike at the enemy's flank, so that a second front was opened. Now it needed to happen, and the King searched amongst the deceased at his feet for a Shire Horn, and found one pressed against the chest of a young man, so took it away from him and blew into it, then looked to make sure his partners had heard.

Whether they had or not was extraneous. Vercingoral, amidst the battle, and fighting himself from time to time – when a legionary determined to make a name for himself, and daring enough, leaped at him – watched as the Bodmifflians on the ridge of the hill at first stayed still and then, to his dismay, turned their backs on him and headed off in the opposite direction. And suddenly his mind was consumed, not by anger or fret, but other emotions that were new to him. He had never felt so forlorn or utterly helpless; and disconsolate for his heart, at that precise moment, was breaking, and the pain was the worst he had ever known. He looked again and the last remnants of the Bodmifflian contingent had vanished. "Damn forest folk!" he mumbled to himself, then thought of Henwen, his wife and lover.

"Henwen would not do that!" he said, rejoining the battle proper and slicing his hefty sword across a Repecian throat. Then the point of that sword was thrust into a legionary's gut, then pulled just as quickly to be swept across another's face, and blood was discharged to soak his beard and cover his mouth.

"Henwen was not there!" he grunted. "That damn brother of hers!" Another legionary fell at his feet. Onto his feet, actually, and he had to kick him away so that he could get to the next one. "But where is she ....?" He had never felt so helpless. In pain and with his mind racing like a torrent of white water, he called out 'Henwen' over and over, killing Repecians like they were mere boars in a forest.

Watching from the thicket, with Delabole at his side, Fillian was smiling and was filled with envy and spite in equal measure.

"Magnificent," he said. "Simply magnificent!"

"What would you have me do?" asked Delabole.

"I want him!" replied Fillian.

"Then you shall have him, my lord," Delabole responded, almost immediately and without having to pause to ponder the statement.

Fifteen
The Scourging of Woldark

"I was not a fool. I knew that the battle was lost and that there was nothing Henwen could do to salvage it. Geramond was conquered, and Vercingoral soon realised that his cause was hopeless, and sounded the retreat on the old Shire Horn. Men returned to their homes ... their loved ones. Back to Woldark, Aldwark and Dormlark. As for Henwen, I took her to Kaw. Where else?"

Outside the hut beside the lake, looking out across the still water, Henwen fumed and her heart burnt like a hot loaf of bread.

"What did you think you were doing?" she demanded. Badad approached her. She thought that he should have been shamefaced and damned, but he was not. Instead, for the first time all the while she had known him, he appeared to be perfectly calm and still.

"There was nothing you could have done to help the King!" he replied. She panted with rage, and tore the plaits out of her hair so that it spilled down her back again, then scratched at her scalp to make a mess of those golden locks altogether.

"Then I would have died in the attempt!" she said.

"Precisely," said Badad. "You would have. But you cannot die. Not yet, at any rate."

Her reply was instantaneous.

"I would rather die than live a life of servitude," she said, blunt and assertively. "I will not be the mistress of my own misfortune. I am Queen of Bodmiffel, and I know what fate shall befall me when Fillian and his underlings track me down. A fate that is far worse than death. So I will return to the Shire Lands ...to the battlefield if I must ... but I will not be kept here against my will...!"

She folded her hair into her hood and brought it over her head, glanced contemptuously at the Druid then walked away. She was not sure of where it was she needed to go, just that she could not stay here any longer, so to walk away was to make a start, and more, to prove the point of how maddened she was.

"You must not leave now!" said Badad, though his tone was finally more subtle and diplomatic. But Henwen did not stop or acknowledge his statement in any way. "By the time you reach the road it will be dark…!"

She scoffed. "I am not afraid of dark forests, Badad."

"Of course you aren't," he replied. "You were brought up tracing the paths and tracks of Ingelwitt and know them better than anyone … but you do not know these parts at all." He had caught her attention at last, and concluded: "A traveller lost in dark, unknown places is lost for good."

The Lady came back towards the hut, removed her hood and unfastened her cape at the front to suggest that she was prepared to spend the night here at least.

"I just want to be with him, that's all," she said, very sombre and close to tears. "I don't understand why you devoted so much time to bringing the two of us together, only to try and keep us apart now!" She walked past Badad without looking at him and went inside the hut.

A fire burnt in the hearth and gave light as well as warmth, and moonshine spilled through the open door to illuminate those parts of the hut where the fire's glow did not care to venture. Henwen was sitting closest to the door leaning forwards to peer out across the glistening lake, enjoying the gentle breeze as it brushed against her face and through her thick hair. Badad was sitting beside the fire peering into the flames, almost motionless. Then the awkward silence was broken.

"When my story is written, people may think of me as a madman," said Badad. "For I do many strange things and no-one but myself knows why. And what people don't understand they mock and disapprove. But I have never done anything that was not required and you have to believe me when I say that I would not have taken you away from High Cleugh unless it was necessary to do so." He turned his head to look at her. "But you do not believe me, do you, for your heart is tender and throbbing with pain, and all you can think is that I have deprived you of your great love."

"Have you ever been in love, Badad?" she asked, returning his gaze at last. In fact, glaring at him quite intensely for she was very interested to hear his answer. The Druid was at first taken aback and secretly recoiled in horror at the notion of having to respond. This was the first time he had ever been asked a question relating to his personal life, about who he really was. Many enquiries and problems had been placed at his feet in his time, and answers and solutions had always been provided, but this was different altogether. The fact was, he had to think hard about how he ought to reply – whether to snigger and ignore it or to rebuke the Lady for having the nerve to ask such a thing. Then, quite remarkably, and without any hint of embarrassment, he replied: "Yes."

Henwen, utterly intrigued, craned her neck towards him. "Who was she...? Is she alive still...?"

Badad smiled fondly as he remembered her.

"She was my wife. A sound and fair woman. Not possessed of great beauty like you. Short and dumpy like me! But kindly and completely without malice. And no, she is not alive still. Long dead, in fact. So long that to think back on my time with her is like another lifetime. Back then I was a very different man...!"

Henwen would have asked him more questions, for she sensed that he was willing to talk about his past life, that had long been a mystery to everyone that had ever known him; but her own, current predicament was more pressing.

"Then you know how much it hurts to be separated from the person you love," she said, falling to her knees in front of him and placing her warm hand atop of his wrinkled one. "Like half of your body and soul is missing, and you cannot perform the task of living until you get it back...!"

"Yes," replied Badad. "I do know." He looked directly into the Lady's face, and saw great angst and pain, and he did feel sorry for her momentarily. "I am happy to tell you that it gets easier as the years roll by...!" She rose and stepped furiously towards the exit, then turned and would have killed him with the stare she gave him if it had been a normal weapon.

"How can you be so cruel?" she snapped. "You have been my friend for as long as I have known you. I am the woman I am now because of you. I am Queen of Bodmiffel because of you." A tear welled in her eye, even though she was ranting and wagging her finger at the little man. "I fell in love with the king of the Shirelands because of you...!"

Badad lowered his gaze for he could not look into her face for a moment longer. So he rose and turned his back to her and entertained himself by dragging the dirt and the straw on the ground beneath his foot.

"What is your agenda, master Druid?" she demanded. "What is your great plan...?"

Badad turned sharply.

"My plan, whatever it is, is in ruins ... thanks to those filthy, foreign hoards!" Then he stopped to think. "Well, not completely in ruins. Even amidst this dark storm there is a glimmer of hope."

"Hope has abandoned these lands," she replied.

"You're wrong," said Badad. She was interested again, and temporarily forgot her pain and suffering.

"What hope is there now...?"

He was able to detect the despair and resentment in the tone of her voice and the disparaging way in which she had asked her question. Yet Badad had a genuine reason to be optimistic and was confident that when he had shared his secret with her she would smile at last and be buoyant again. So he offered his reply, perfectly composed and unruffled, but with his eye fixed firmly on her.

"You are pregnant," he said, and waited for her response.

Her response was initially one of shock and she went quiet and still for a little while. Then her mood turned dark as her stunned face formed a disbelieving frown, then a smile to deride at his statement.

"If, when your story is written, people call you a madman," she hissed, "then they will be correct with that assessment, because you are mad!" She stepped outside momentarily, took a deep intake of the chilled night air, then came back inside. "It seems to me you will go to any lengths to keep me here ... but it won't work, old man. I intend to leave at first light tomorrow!" Then, she concluded, "I don't know who you are now! Certainly not kind and no ally of mine!"

Badad had not expected her to react like she did, and was a little disappointed, but was still unruffled.

"The night you consummated your union with Vercingoral, you conceived his child!" he said. "A boy, I believe. Well, I know it to be a fact actually."

During all the years she had known him, for he had been a regular visitor to her father's court during her childhood, Badad had been a kind and helpful acquaintance. She had never thought of him as anyone but the wise, if somewhat peculiar little man that always seemed to be somewhere and everywhere. And he had endeared himself to her with his kind-hearted smile and offers of good judgement, so that she had liked and trusted him and had always taken heed of his counsel. But now, and only for the past half-day, he had turned into someone she did not much care for; someone who was in control of the more private aspects of her life, as though it was his business and his duty to have power over her. For the first time she was wary of him. So wary, in fact, that she had not given much thought to his assertion that she was with child, nor intended to.

But the Druid was insistent. "So you can understand why I had to take you away from the battle at High Cleugh? I could not risk any harm coming to the boy! He alone is this country's great hope!"

"A king of Geramond...?" she mused, suspiciously glancing at the Druid but not for too long for she had no desire to engage him with a lengthy, antagonistic stare.

"Yes," he replied, becoming aware of her hostility towards him. "Finally, after hundreds of years we have someone who will be able to sit at ease upon the old throne in the fortress of Bosscastle."

"And that's what you've always wanted, isn't it?"

"It's what we've all been waiting for, is it not?" he asked, somewhat disappointed with her reaction.

Henwen went quiet. Badad rose from his seat by the fire and took a small, tentative step towards her. She recoiled slightly but not enough for the little man to sense that her hostility was brought about by her sudden fearfulness. That particular emotion was best left hidden for the time being, she thought, and to appease the Druid she touched her belly with the flat of her hand.

"So if no harm must come to the child, you intend to keep me here, at Kaw, with you, until my time is done…?" she said.

Badad, now, could indeed distinguish her fright from her stubbornness, and was saddened as she retreated towards the doorway as he went closer to her. Nevertheless, regardless of what she thought of him at that precise moment, or however much she disputed what he was telling her, for he was not a fool, Henwen had asked a question that required a direct answer. Badad was not at her side, nor the King's, to be popular and conciliatory, but to execute his mission.

"Oh, no, my Lady," he said, no longer concerned by politeness or allowances for a queen. "The situation is too perilous to wait that long!"

Henwen tittered nervously and backed further away from him.

"You are capable of many strange and extraordinary deeds, master Druid, but not even you can hustle the course of a woman's natural term." And then her smile disappeared and her heart thumped against her chest as she realised that he most probably was. Badad stepped closer and held out his hand to hold her back but her reaction to pull it away was the keener. "Definitely mad!" she mumbled as she sped out of the door. Then the sleeve of her gown got caught on a sliver of wood in the doorframe and although she tugged hard she could not break loose, and she was ensnared.

Badad took hold of her forearm and carefully brought her back inside the hut, and closed the door behind her so that the only light came off the fire.

"You have no need to fear me, dear friend," said Badad, quietly, gently pushing her towards the hearth.

"I implore you one last time, Badad," Henwen replied, her voice rickety with fear. "Let me go."

"I cannot. I wish I could, truly. But whether you like it or not you are caught up in the great events of your age …"

"What are you going to do to me?"

"Have I ever done you harm, my Lady?" he asked her. And she shook her head, though his comment did nothing to allay her trepidation.

He warmed his hand against the flames for a moment or two before moving them to her belly. Just as he was about to tear apart her gown, and sensing impending danger, Henwen pushed him away and sped towards the door. As she pulled and tugged at the bolt she dared to glance back, and was relieved to see that Badad had not come after her. But she was startled still for he had adopted that strange stance of his, the one that preceded one of his tricks and mysterious conjuring: his legs apart and his head tilted back with the eyes within it shut tightly.

He mumbled something but she could not fathom what, but she knew that something was about to happen. Just the usual, incoherent ranting of the last Druid, she told herself, and tried to listen more carefully.

"Now does he dwell in ignorance and bliss!" she heard. "And beloved and honoured is he within a mother's womb! Time is needed but none can be spared. So let me bring him from within that harbour and into the cold, dark air will he come, like fragrant smoke...!"

Suddenly she felt a twang of pain in her abdomen and jolted forwards and held the area with her hands.

"Do not do this, Badad!" she screamed, then fell to her knees and then back until she was flat against the cold, stone floor. She looked down and saw a belly that had been flat just moments before was now swelled and aching. The Druid stood over her and continued with his wizardry. Her belly swelled further and she screamed louder, but was in so much pain that she could not speak to plead with him to stop. In the space if minutes her body developed to a stage that would normally take months. But then, there was nothing normal about what was happening to her here and now.

News, in dreadful times, travels faster than in normal times. As the first stragglers of Vercingoral's routed army made it back to Woldark, the city-folk already knew of the defeat and the impending danger. Some made for the hills, but most remained to receive their injured husbands, sons, brothers and friends. And when they had and had bandaged them and somehow patched them up, all they could do was wait. They gathered together on the steps and balcony of the old Lampas Hall, for it was the loftiest position in the city, from where they could look beyond the rooftops to the plain beyond. In the early hours of the following morning, amidst the blackness of that time, they saw the approaching lights of Fillian's army.

Little knowing that their own prince, Delabole, was riding at the General's side. Macara was on the other; thousands of Repecian soldiers behind them, with every fifth legionary baring a flame torch, that formed a blanket of flame to the distant eye. Delabole, secretly, was pleased to be back at Woldark. Fillian was pleased to see the city, too, for he knew that it marked the end of his long campaign on this desolate island in the northern seas.

"Think of Ramrah, dear men," Fillian shouted out, for all his men to hear. "That city of marble and golden bricks! Then look upon these primitive dwellings with contempt!" And quieter, to Delabole, "I wouldn't let my cattle live in such conditions." Delabole chortled, not realising that the comment was intended as an insult. Then he stopped and looked towards Woldark with a troubled frown on his brow. Troubled not because he was unsure of Fillian's intentions regarding the city, but whether his brother had returned there, and if so if he was watching him from the steps of the Lampas and plotting his vengeance on his treacherous brother who had guided these trespassers here. Then he consoled himself with the thought that while everyone else, including Vercingoral, was being persecuted for their resistance, he would survive. In any case, if the King had returned to the city he would have surely come out to fight by now; one final bout of defiance before it was finally over. There were no other thoughts in his mind at this time other than his own survival, certainly not the predicament of the city folk. He was therefore impassive as a volley of fire was sent into the city by the Repecian archers, and watched obediently as the wooden structures burnt, and lit up the black sky.

"Secure the city," said Fillian to Macara. The general led a contingent of horsemen towards Woldark. Some time later, Fillian and Delabole followed him.

The few city folk that had not fled into the hills, mainly the elderly or those still awaiting the return of their kin, instead locked themselves in their houses, so when Fillian entered the city in a dominant mood there was no-one except his own men to see it. Delabole, riding by his side, was satisfied that his brother was not here so was able to take pleasure in his return. They rode along the narrow streets, three horses abreast, until they fanned out into the main square. By now the Repecians had overwhelmed Woldark so that legionaires were everywhere. The Lampas Hall was deserted, the flags of the Shiremen torn down and burnt and replaced by Fillian's own banners. Inside soldiers opened every door and searched every room, but there was no-one here.

"A far cry from Palmatine," said Fillian, for Macara's ears, looking around these new surroundings.

"Palmatine, sir?" asked Delabole, sneaking up behind the Great One as though he was now his personal attendant. Fillian, suffering a little from sudden homesickness, perhaps brought on by the quick end to his campaign, was obliging.

"My country residence outside Ramrah."

"A magnificent dwelling fitting for such a great man," Macara replied.

Fillian was not an idiotic man. Macara and Delabole seemed to be locked in a competition to determine which one could crawl to his feet fastest. Delabole seemed to be winning, not by his words but by his manner: hunched, almost doubled over in awe and worship, and without looking at him. Macara, at least, had a little dignity.

"You told me the King would be here," said Fillian with a slight smirk, as though he knew that his statement would panic Delabole. To make sure that it did he followed it by kicking a chair across the floor of the Great Hall. Delabole skulked away.

"I was sure that he would be," he replied.

The Great One noticed a legionary standing in the doorway with his back to them, assigned by Macara to keep out any unwanted visitors. He went over to him and tapped him on the shoulder. The young soldier was taken aback when he turned round.

"What is your name?" asked Fillian.

"Madius," the legionary replied.

"Well, young Madius ... I have a little task for you. Scour this city, if that's what you can call it. Make sure this king of theirs isn't hiding anywhere. If he is, bring him to me alive. He must be alive...!" The legionary acknowledged the command and made off down the steps, taking other soldiers with him.

Between gasping for breath, Henwen screamed. In a matter of minutes she had done her full term and was now in labour. Badad stood over her and encouraged her but the sight of him made her confused predicament worse. When she had the energy she cursed him, beneath her breath and above it. And then it was done with. Her physical pain eased. Badad scooped the child in his arms, swiftly cut the cord that fixed it to its mother, then enveloped it in his filthy cloak.

"I am truly sorry," he said. Henwen heard his apology but recoiled away.

With her back to him and her baby she said:

"If Fillian and all his men had taken me then I would not feel more violated than I do right now...!"

Badad, the baby boy in his arms, left the hut. Only when she heard his horse speed away did she turn and bring herself upright, covered her legs and then sobbed. A life that was once promising was now in ruins.

Madius searched the city of Woldark, every house, every hut and even beyond into the surrounding fields and farmsteads, but did not find Vercingoral. He reported back to Fillian and was fearful of the Great One's response. Then Delabole offered a suggestion.

Sixteen

The Hay Shed

The wind howled outside like a distant wolf, then came closer and blew the doors open. Mirrial went to close them again and looked outside to see that the rain was pouring down and the beasts in the field had huddled together at the bottom of the hill, a sure sign that another storm was about to sweep across the High Moor. It took all of her strength to force the doors closed.

"And that's when you brought him to us?" she said, turning and coming back towards the fire.

Badad was sitting on a bale of hay and looked tired, but was relieved to have reached the end of his long, sickening tale. And happy that Madam Gringell had understood it all and had seemed to reconcile herself to the truth.

"Yes. Actually, I had already decided that you Gringells were the ideal couple to rear the boy. Solid, decent people, and you farmed on the High Moor, where no-one would think to look for him. And Wilfren had joined Vercingoral's army at High Cleugh and so had proven himself to be a brave man who understood the necessity of defending his homeland. So I rode here directly from my parting from Henwen …"

Mirrial smiled. An ironic smile. "Straight from her womb and into my arms," she said. "Where he has been cherished ever since."

"Then I chose wisely," replied Badad. "You have done a better job then I could have hoped for."

She seemed upset by his comment. "How do you know?" she demanded. "You haven't met him yet. Well, not since that day. So how do you know I haven't ruined him? How do you know I haven't turned him into someone you would not much care for? Someone who does not live up to your expectations?"

"I don't," he replied. "So tell me, Madam, have you? Is he flawed? But tell me the truth for should you choose to lie I will know it."

Mirrial thought about her answer and she thought about her beloved son, and therefore had to conclude that he had no flaws, and lowered her head as she shook it.

"Good then," Badad muttered happily.

She looked up without raising her head. "He is just a child, Badad, and not ready to learn the truth."

"Sixteen winters have passed since I brought him here. And that's too many. He deserves to know who he really is."

"He deserves to be left alone!" she scowled.

Badad was beginning to get irritated by her constant resentment and prickliness. Deciding quickly that she listened most to his authoritative tone, he snarled at her: "Now that Geramond has been released from its shackles of the tyrannical empire, it needs its king! Carthrall must travel south with me!"

"When...?" she asked.

"As soon as possible," he answered. "Tomorrow, when the boy returns from his trip to Aldwark, I intend to tell him everything!"

Madam Gringell released a sharp, almost hysterical laugh. She had been pacing the floor but was now standing stock still.

"And you think he'll believe you, do you? He doesn't even know who you are. He'll think that you're a mad old tramp ... and he won't be far wrong!"

Badad was incensed. He had not travelled here from Bosscastle, the very place he was most needed at this time; or suffered his task for so long, to do battle with the Gringell widow now, in a cold, damp hay-shed on the stormy High Moor.

Nevertheless, he tried to answer as calmly as he could, for he was mindful of her contribution in the story so far; more than that, he knew that he would need her help if he was to convince the boy that he was indeed the correct and endorsed heir to the throne of Geramond.

"He will be disbelieving at first, I'm sure," muttered the old man. "But he will come to the idea quickly, for he will already know, deep in his heart, that there is something different about him.

He will believe me enough to accompany me to Bosscastle. Once I get him there I shall prove to him that he is the son of Vercingoral and Henwen."

Mirrial was careful not to speak too quickly. When she did, it was in a quiet, almost trepid manner. "If I tell him that you're words are the ravings of a man whose mind is lost to lunacy, who has returned from the war disturbed by the terrible things he has seen, and that he should not give any thought to what you tell him, and certainly not do as you ask ... who do you think he will take notice of ... you, or the woman he loves and thinks of as his natural mother...?"

"You would do that?" Badad asked, annoyed and a little anxious. "You would keep him from his course, just so that you could keep him here, with you on this desolate farm, with no hope of a decent life...? If so, then you do not love the boy as much as you profess to."

Mirrial's manner turned angry again. "I would do it for his own sake ... to stop you from ruining his life ... meddling with his mind so that he would do your bidding, just like ...." And then she stopped talking and turned her face away from him.

Badad seized his chance. "What were you going to say, Mirrial?" he demanded, rising from the bale of hay and stepping towards her. "Like I did his father? His natural father! Or his mother ...?"

She was calm and sad again. "I am not a fool. I know that I am not his real mother. You don't have to keep repeating it over and over. And I know that there is nothing that I can do to stop you from taking him to Bodmiffel. It's just that I worry for him. I worry for myself too." She walked to the door and peered out of the gap, into the storm. "What will become of me, I wonder? I can't stay here on my own. But this place is all I know. I shall have to move to Aldwark and become the window-woman I am, and hope that they take pity on me and throw me a coin or two to buy a stick of bread."

If it had become her new tactic to harass the Druid with her own, wretched predicament, and therefore gain his sympathy, it did not work, for Badad already had the solution and he hoped that it would raise her spirits.

"When all is said and done and the crown rests upon the boy's head, he will wish to be surrounded by the people he knows best.

Galfall will be no less his brother and I am sure that he will not forget all that love you have shown him during his upbringing. Bosscastle is an extensive residence, even for a king. He will set aside rooms for the woman who has cared for him as though she was his real mother even if she wasn't."

She thought for a moment or two, whilst looking down the hill towards the farmstead. Quieter and more composed, perhaps finally reconciled to the reason Badad was here, perhaps submissive and dutiful at last, she said: "Do one thing for me before the boy returns from Aldwark…?" She looked at him and he gestured that he was prepared to do anything. "Finish your story."

"My story…?" He was puzzled.

"Tell me what happened to the king and the queen."

Badad walked away and began to busy himself as though he did not want to finish the story. "What happened to them is not important," he mumbled.

"Or is it that you don't know what became of them? Did you take what you needed and then abandon them?"

"It's true that I never saw Vercingoral or Henwen again, but even now they are with me, in the deep recesses of my mind. And in any case, there was nothing more I could do to help them once the battle of High Cleugh was lost." He steadied himself and lowered his backside onto the closest bale, seemingly happy to talk again. And Mirrial was happy to listen.

"Soon after, the Shirelands, like Bodmiffel before them, were under Repecian control, and subject to Fillian's cruelty and his desire to tyrannise anyone who would resist his will. Woldark suffered first and worst. Delabole had assured his new master that the King would not have abandoned his city, and so every inch of it was searched. Men, old and young, who had been associated with Vercingoral, were arrested and interrogated and then executed in the main square when they were of no further use. It was Delabole who had pointed them out."

"Did they find him … Vercingoral…?" Mirrial asked.

"Not there and then. The King had fled the city and arrived at Kaw shortly after I had left."

"... And was reunited with Henwen...?" She seemed pleased.

"They comforted each other, and the Lady told him what I had done. Told him that he had a son." He smiled. A cheerless grin. "I think it is a safe assumption that from that moment I slipped from being the King's faithful counsel and friend and turned into the man he despised most of all. Just another sinister, reckless old Druid!"

"And that saddens you?"

He did not need to answer. His smile, through his pain, was more decipherable than any words.

"I was very fond of him," he said. "and had grown to admire the Lady just as much. I would not have hurt them like I did if I thought for a moment there was another way. But there was not. Henwen would not have been permitted to carry her child for her natural term. Or if she had been, it would have been murdered soon after it had been born. And then you would never have known your beloved Carthrall, would you...?" She understood. "I did what I did through necessity. I may have broken her heart at the same time, but there was no other way."

"What happened to them?"

"Delabole suggested that he knew where his brother had gone. He assumed that he had gone looking for me, in Tragara, and so Fillian sent his soldiers into the mountains. Delabole went with them, and they scoured the forests, burning them down when they became too dense to pass."

"Why would they bother?" asked Mirrial. "I mean, what threat were they now?"

"A man with a claim to what you possess is always a threat, Madam. That's why I brought the boy to you. Delabole would have seized him within minutes of his birth. But Fillian wanted Vercingoral capturing for different reasons. They had fought each other at the battle, and the King, remember, had come within seconds of slaying that vile general, and would have had it not been for his feckless brother!"

"So Fillian wanted revenge...?"

"Not really. Revenge would have been too quick and simple. Fillian coveted the King. Like a wild beast in a hunt, he wanted to restrain him, have power over him. Above all else, it was his desire to take him back to Repecia ... a trophy of his conquest ... that spurred this frenzied search through the mountains and forests of Tragara. It was Delabole who spotted the smoke rising through the trees, and went down the narrow track that took him to Kaw ... alone. He entered the hut and found them sleeping next to the fire ... and crept back out to signal for the soldiers to come closer.

"And so the King and the Queen were brought back to Woldark in shackles, and as they passed through the crowded streets any residue of hope in the hearts of the people was extinguished once and for all."

Mirrial, perhaps for her own, personal reasons asked: "Were they killed ... in the end...?"

"Again, that would have been too simple," Badad replied. "Six months passed before Fillian announced that he intended to return to Repecia, and take his 'prize' with him. So, on the beach at Bossiney, Vercingoral was finally wrenched away from his homeland ... his people and the woman he loved." As Badad spoke so the tone of his voice became more agitated with anger. "Henwen was brought along and was forced to watch as the King was loaded onto Fillian's galley like a piece of cargo. She knew that she would never see him again. And that was the cruellest thing." He looked at Mirrial with a sharp, furious frown on his brow. "So if you think you're hard done by, Madam, think of her...! She had lost every-thing. Her agony was absolute. A life, once so promising, was in ruins!"

"I can't imagine," Mirrial replied, staring forlornly into the flames of the old Druid's fire, and at the same time pondering her own, cheerless life. Then a thought occurred to her, and her face was animated again. "But he may still be alive ... the King! We don't know what happened to him after all...! Carthrall may yet meet his father."

Badad chortled.

"He may. But Vercingoral, if he is still alive, will be much changed from the man who left these shores all those years ago. He will be a servant of the Empire. He will care not for the troubles of our people, and he will not know his son or care for his safety."

She seemed clandestinely pleased, but struggled to disguise the smirk on her lips. "Henwen, then...? What happened to her? Will

Carthrall ever meet his mother...?" she asked, then turned her face away as though she hardly dared to listen to the answer.

"This story does not have a happy ending," the Druid continued.

"For his efforts, Delabole was made Governor of the newly formed province of Geramond, with Macara and his soldiers garrisoned here to defend it from insurgents and out-and-out revolt. Fillian, at least, had the sense to realise that the people had honour and pride. Delabole's first deed after taking over power was to bring Henwen to Bosscastle, his new stronghold and her ancestral home. Remember, Madam, that he had always been resentful of his brother the King, and had always coveted what he possessed ... his position ... his courage and wisdom ... and his lovers! So Henwen was forced to share his bed...!"

"I bet she would rather have died," Mirrial commented, not smirking anymore and genuinely bothered.

"Yes," Badad replied. "Delabole disgusted her, as he did, and still does, the people of this island. Eventually, her heart utterly broken and her world in disarray, she decided that she no longer had a will to live."

"I don't blame her," she said.

"You say that ... but think for a moment about what her state of mind must have been at that time. What I mean is ... you have not had an easy life yourself, Madam ... up here on this bleak moor; and Wilfren was not an easy man to love but you did, with your full heart ... and now he is gone, lost to the war. But even with all the suffering and distress you have encountered, I don't imagine that you have ever considered ending your own life ahead of time...?"

She knew that the thought had never crossed her mind, but lingered for a while before giving an answer, as though she wanted the Druid to be unsure whether she had or not.

"I am a strong woman," she said.

"So was Henwen," Badad snapped, angrily. "But that did not stop her from climbing up and into the tower at Bosscastle and throwing herself into the icy waters of the cove below!"

"I suppose, after all that she had been through, she had had enough. And I also think that each of us would have come to the same conclusion."

"Yes, and a lot sooner."

"So that was the end of Henwen," Mirrial pondered. She seemed saddened.

"Yes," said Badad. "But not the end of the story. As a final act of revenge against the Governor, and her final words to him ... to anybody ... she told him all about her son ... Vercingoral's heir... Geramond's heir. Delabole was enraged, and not a little unnerved, for all that his scheming, treacherous ways had achieved seemed threatened." He stopped to think. "Carthrall would have been about three at that time."

"What did the Governor do?"

"Nothing at first. He knew that I had something to do with the child's disappearance, and he still feared me more than anything else in the world. Then, in the spring of the following year, a group of insurgents were captured in Tangelwitt Forest. Only fifty or so, but canny enough to have caused a great deal of damage to the Repecian patrols ... more of a nuisance than a real threat. Their leader was Gonosor. Remember him? He was brought before the Governor, who told him all about the child, and that if he could find him, then his life would be spared."

"Yes ... Gonosor was just as unhappy about the marriage of Henwen and Vercingoral as any of them, wasn't he?" said Mirrial. "But he did not look very hard, because he never came here."

"That's why I brought the boy to you, Madam. No-one ever comes onto the High Moor." Badad seemed pleased with himself. "Besides ... although my power was diminished, I was still around. I followed Gonosor and his henchmen from afar, but closely enough to watch wherever they went. They did actually come to Aldwark, and set off on the Moor road. Then a snowstorm blew down from the mountains and the road became impassible."

"And that was your doing?"

Badad smiled. "Alas, no," he replied. "As much as I would like to take the credit for that, it was merely a coincidence. A timely snap of a Tragaran winter. But it worked. They turned back and decided to look somewhere else. It wasn't long after when they gave up the hunt altogether, and disappeared into the wilderness again, out of the Governor's reach. Once I was satisfied that the boy was safe and secure I returned to Kaw, content to be away from the court of kings and isolated from the world of men."

"Poor Henwen," said Mirrial, glumly. "Poor Vercingoral."

"Like I said ... no happy endings," Badad replied. And then a happy thought occurred to him. "Except, now the rebellion is over and the people are free again, hope and joy has been rekindled in their hearts. Joy because they are unbound and hope because they know their King will soon be with them. They know that I have come to fetch him. They are awaiting his return. Madam, it is time for Carthrall to enter the story."

Mirrial went quiet. Her face dropped and she turned unfriendly and remote again. She walked to the door and opened it slightly, though mindful not to let the wind in too much. "The storm is set in for the night," she mumbled. "The weather can be spiteful on top of this moor ...!"

Badad was disappointed. "You should return to the house, Madam. Your fire must be struggling by now. I shall wait here and call on the boy when he returns from Aldwark."

She closed the door and looked at him. "There has to be another way," she said.

"There isn't."

She stepped towards him. "He is happy here. His life is here. He has friends here. And he has me."

Badad sighed with great sorrow and weariness. "I thought you understood. Why have I wasted the last two hours explaining evything to you ...?"

"I understand," she replied, assertively and cross. "I understand that you want to destroy my family. Yes, I have listened to what you have told me. And I have heard a great deal about kings and queens, generals and their battles. But I don't care about any of it. All I care about is my son."

"For the last time, Madam, he is not your son!"

Mirrial's face turned sour and her eye began to twitch angrily. Badad, thoroughly drained and glum, stood up and stepped away from his antagonist, walked towards the door and would have left there and then had it not been for the wretched weather outside, and the warm fire within.

She glanced to her side, reached for the pitch-fork that was propped against the wall, and screamed: "Yes he is!" and threw herself upon the little man, who had no time to react or defend himself. The fork pinned him against the door but she did not possess enough strength in her arms to push it into his stocky body. He put his hand on one of the prongs and tried to push the fork away, but she did at least have sufficient strength to prevent him.

"You shall not have him," she sobbed, aware that what she was actually doing was wrong but convinced in her own mind that it was utterly necessary, and therefore she pushed all the harder. The fork pricked his skin and was about to enter his flesh proper.

He mumbled to himself beneath his breath. Then the building began to tremble. Mirrial looked up to the roof, that seemed about to blow off at any moment, so abandoned her endeavour and stepped back into the middle of the floor, dropping the weapon as she retreated.

With one mighty gust the wind took the roof off the hay shed and shards of wood and a mass of soil dropped in and covered Mirrial, but did not kill her. She was injured, however, but had sufficient strength left to try to dig her way out.

"Please ..." she looked at the Druid and held out her arm. "Please help me." Then, meekly: "Do not do this."

Suddenly what remained of the roof caved in and buried her completely until she disappeared from his sight. He was pleased that she had gone for he no longer wished to look at the pain in her face for a moment longer. And then the thought occurred to him that he had at last ruined the whole of the Gringell family, and yet they had done him no harm during all the years he had known them. Had, indeed, aided him greatly. Simply because of their association with him, through his own prying and intrusive manner, both Wilfren and Mirrial were dead, Galfall was lost to the war and Carthrall, the lady's son in his mind as well as hers, was about to suffer a great loss and pain when finally he returned from Aldwark. He had said the same to her husband in the forest and now said it to her, as he stood over the pile of wood and earth: "Rest peacefully. Your work is done."

Seventeen

Gonosor's Tongue

The journey back to Bosscastle seemed much longer and more gruelling than the one home to Woldark, even though Fogle had followed the same route along the Shire River and across the Rustic Bridge into Bodmiffel. Perhaps it was due to his sense of urgency and a longing to be back in the midst of the action that made his ride seem twice as long. When a man knows that he ought to be in one place but is in another, then his passage is never even, but laden with toil and aggravation, and the horse upon which he depends never seems quite swift enough.

Fogle had returned home to Woldark with every intention of staying there and if he had never gone south again it would have been just fine by him. But something strange happened to the man as soon as he had entered the old city. He realised very quickly that he no longer belonged there. At once he felt like a stranger in his home town. The people welcomed him home eagerly enough and cheered him as he passed through the streets. And he did indeed feel a warm glow in his heart as the occupants of the Shireman Inn abandoned their ale and spilled out into the street to greet him and beckon him inside. He had thought about it momentarily; a jug of warm ale would have been most welcome. But then he remembered that the Shireman Inn would be a very different place without Toggett or Miggel sitting in there arguing or tossing those Chance Stones. Their seats would still be by the fireplace but taken by other, less familiar men. And because of that, the ale would have a bitter taste.

When he saw his house in the hollow beside the hazel thicket his heart quickened, but not in a joyful way. This was the first time he had returned since the day of the fracas and the air was tainted and the land spoiled even though the dead had long since been removed. Memories could not so easily be erased from his mind, and as he looked down he could hear the events of that day as though they were occurring right there and then. Nevertheless, he pushed on down the lane, keeping a steady course and holding his back straight. This was, after all, his own dwelling, that he had toiled to build, and would therefore have it back now, even if he no longer wanted it.

Firstly he went into his old workshop and was startled to find everything exactly as it was left. Embers in the forge with the wheel rim of Toggett's cart sticking out, half finished; his hammer on the ground where he had dropped it; but most disturbing of all, their two mugs on top of the table, half drunk and with a thick layer of mould to cover them. He realised that the last time he had been in here was that dreadful day way back when the Governor's tax collector called. If only Callarn had stayed to finish his drink instead of running out to see who was approaching.

The memories inside the house were just as painful. Gone were those happy thoughts of the years he had spent here with his wife and son; replaced by that one, overpowering recollection. A vile, bleak memory that dominated his mind as he looked around the room. So there and then he asked himself where he would rather be; here or back at Bosscastle. And after concluding that he did not wish to spend even one more night under this roof, he knew that it was time to return to Bodmiffel, regardless of who or what may be waiting for him there.

Barely a month after he had left with Toggett's body, Fogle arrived back at Bosscastle. A contented grin spread across his lips as he passed through that great gate that had for so long defied him; its doors flung wide open like welcoming arms. Only, the sight within was not so easy on his eyes. Six men were hanging from ropes. Three either side of the road. And they had been there for some time judging by the state of their bodies. Weightless now, and the ropes had no work to do to keep them dangling. Sullen faces with black skin that had shrunk to fit the sharp bones beneath; open eyes that even now described the horror of their deaths; straight fingers. And Fogle covered his mouth with his sleeve as he rode past them.

The first person he saw upon his return was young Galfall, and as he dismounted he beckoned him over. The youngster was at once filled with delight. "When did you get back?" he asked.

"Just this minute," Fogle replied. "And just in time. Who are they...?"

Galfall chanced a brief look. "They were collaborators!" he said. "Gonosor said they had succumbed to the temptations of treachery and had them arrested and tried for treason. You don't need me to tell you that they were found guilty."

"A fair and just trial?" Fogle mused. "Or was Gonosor chief judge and hangman rolled into one?"

Galfall withdrew. "Be careful, Fogle. He has reverted to the man he was before the Druid got hold of him." He was shamefaced. Fogle had never seen such an expression on his youthful face. And he seemed troubled. "I gave it back to him," he said. "His tongue, I mean. And he has been wicked again ever since."

So this Gringell boy did have some meekness after all. All semblance of that secure and confident youth seemed to have vanished, but Fogle hoped not forever. "I should have kept hold of it," he continued. "He was a good and spirited friend whilst I had his tongue in the pouch by my side."

"Where will I find him?"

"Where else? The Great Hall."

"Then that's where I'll go." The little man set off walking, then stopped and turned. "Get someone to help you and cut those poor souls down. Then bury them or burn them, or whatever it is they do in these parts."

"I'm glad you're back," said Galfall.

Fogle thought for a moment, then smiled. "Do you know what," he said, "so am I, lad. So am I." And he surprised himself with his announcement more than he did Galfall.

Looking around him Fogle observed a happy sight. Men and women, some with faces that were familiar to him, others strangers, going about their business seemingly without a care in the world. Then he heard someone laugh and turned to watch as two old friends shared a joke as they passed him. Life seemed to be more normal now; eventless and ordinary. Old women huddled into groups to gossip and when mordant laughter got caught on the breeze it echoed around the Druim Square.

As he climbed the steps to the balcony of the Great Hall, Fogle looked upwards and saw the old Bodmifflian banner hanging down from the roof, flapping and flickering in the wind. A green tree above a wolf set against a white background. He heard laughter coming from the Hall. Not the jolly sort that he had heard just a moment before, but that menacing, bullying boom that was unmistakably Gonosor. He took a deep intake of breath, straightened his back and ventured inside. Was he fearful? He did not care to ask himself whether he was or was not. He just happened to be there and there was nowhere else to go.

No-one noticed his presence at first. The place was bustling with activity; groups of very tall, hard-looking men, chattering quite nonchalantly. Gonosor and his group were closest to the fire, so Fogle pushed his way through, and as he passed the chattering stopped for everyone was more interested to see what Gonosor's reaction would be. When he eventually got to the front all eyes were on him and he was sure that he was not among friends here.

Gonosor was just as he remembered him: broad, bearded and boisterous. He had listened as Galfall and the Druid had talked almost with fondness of the docile, muted Gonosor, but could not imagine that there ever was such a man. Fogle had not seen him during that time. In fact, the last time he had seen Gonosor was in the forest on the night of the Druid's arrival, and he was reminded of the events of that night now, as he stood before the Bodmifflian once again. Only, he was not as tense and edgy this time, and stood there quite calm, for in the back of his mind was the little Druid, who had saved him in the forest and would not abandon him now.

Gonosor's reaction was predictable. He pointed at Fogle and released a shriek of laughter and fright in equal measure, then scratched his hefty beard as though he did not know what to do with his hands, then rested them on his knees and leaned forwards in his seat.

'Look who it is! The Rebel Master! Well, you've got some guts, I'll say that much for you!'

Crispill Crull, just a lowly dock-hand during the occupation, had somehow endeared himself to Gonosor, and was standing by his side. Fogle wondered who he was. He had not seen him before and was not with Gonosor in the forest, before the castle fell. An ordinary-looking, scraggy man, and he seemed a bit dim-witted. Not at all the type that were usually permitted to keep Gonosor company, and certainly not allowed close to him. And even though Crispill wore fine clothes – a thick, woolen shirt and a good-quality fur over his shoulders – his face was dirty and the flat grin on his face suggested that he was not used to keeping such good company and could barely believe his own fortune. After a moments thought Fogle realised why he was here. If this stranger had not been one of his rebels then he must be an inhabitant of Bosscastle, and was therefore a witness to what had gone on here during the Repecian occupation. Fogle was so confident that he had worked it out correctly that he even dared to pass a comment. "Is this your sneak, Gonosor?" he said, then waited for a reply.

Everyone present, except Crispill, had seen what had happened to little Fogle the last time he had provoked Gonosor, and they were sure that the same would happen now. Fogle, though, was not so certain, and he was relieved to see that the Bodmifflian had remained perfectly still and calm. As he sighed he said to himself; "Definitely not the man he used to be." And he was right. Gonosor was irritated by the question but apart from his eye twitching he barely responded at all.

Crispill, however, was irritated by the question, and rolled his eyes. "If you're referring to those six hanging in Gate Street, then they merely got what traitors deserve...!" he said. "Better than they deserved if you ask me. Their deaths were a lot quicker than if the mob had got hold of them!"

"Traitors?" Fogle mused. "Why were they traitors?"

Gonosor tittered, and Crispill chortled because Gonosor had.

Fogle smiled too. "Forgive me, but I haven't been around lately," he said.

"The one on the end, nearest the gate ... the short, fat one ..." Gonosor began.

"Yes, yes," giggled Crispill, excitedly. "Let's start with him!"

Gonosor glared at his sidekick furiously, and Crispill was at once reminded of his proper position.

"What about the short, fat one?" Fogle probed. "What did he do that was so terrible?"

"He was the chief jailor in the Bossmilliad," replied the Bodmifflian. "I experienced the full extent of his betrayal at first hand! And the one next to him ... the skinny one ... had been the Governor's personal attendant for as long as he'd been at Bosscastle, and had therefore ignored many an opportunity to finish him off once and for all."

"And the other four?"

"Their crimes were the worst of all," said Gonosor. "You are aware of the Governor's lucrative trade with the Merchant Budogis?"

Fogle nodded, then shook his head, half in sorrow and half in disbelief. "Slaves in return for wine and gold. It was his greatest felony, and one that will stain the lives of many for years to come, perhaps forever."

Gonosor was pleased to hear Fogle speak in such terms, for it made what he was about to say all the more compelling.

"Those other four were involved in that foul scheme, for it was in the name of the Governor that they fettered those poor folk ... bound them with chains at their ankles, their wrists and at their necks! Then they used to help the Repecian soldiers take them down to the dock and load them onto the ship!" Now his voice did boom again in anger. "Forest men, mind you! Who deceived their own kind and did not care for the pain and torment of their countrymen!"

"They lived a fine life in the Bossmilliad," Crispill added. "And were paid handsomely. They never associated with anyone but themselves ... and occasionally the Governor...!"

Fogle, whose initial instinct had been to be suspicious of Gonosor's actions, and still was in a small part, was nevertheless subdued and willing to go along with them for now. And as he spoke he almost spluttered out his words.

"Well, from what I've heard you did the right thing bringing them to justice, and showed remarkable control in the way you did it. What I mean is … the good people they betrayed might not have been so merciful if they'd got their own hands on them."

"I'm glad our actions meet with your approval, Rebel Master," Gonosor replied, mordantly.

But Fogle was not satisfied so easily. "It's just that …" he paused. "I worry about how far it will all go. How many more people do you intend to pursue?"

"Oh, make no mistake, Shireman," snarled the Bodmifflian. "There are plenty more out there, walking the streets, keeping quiet and hoping that their wrongdoings have been forgotten … their slate's wiped clean with the passing of the old administration."

"And you intend to find them?" It was more of a statement than a question, for Fogle knew full well that Gonosor was a man with a mission. "But how do you know who they are?"

"We have a list," said Crispill, producing the said object in the form of a long, grubby piece of parchment. "And if a man's name is on this list then we will find them, won't we, sir…?"

Fogle persevered. "Then tell me … how does a name get onto that list of yours?"

Gonosor leaned back in his seat. His whole method seemed to be calmer and quieter, Fogle had observed, and not at all like the Gonosor of old, from the forest. Even as he spoke the tone of his voice was low and subdued. It was all, Fogle was quite sure, as a result of his encounter with the Druid.

"People come to us and tell us things."

"What kind of things?"

"Things that once would not have been listened to. But we listen."

"You mean people snitch on each other?" Fogle said.

"People are anxious for the wrongdoers to be punished," replied Gonosor. "By wrongdoers I mean traitors! Men … and women … who cooperated with the enemy, and benefited from their association with those that trespassed here. Good people will not let such acts of betrayal occur in front of their noses without silently longing for vengeance. And so they come here and they tell us all about who did what and who with. We listen, then decide which names shall go onto the list."

Fogle held out his hand and touched the parchment. "Perhaps

you might let me look at it?"

Crispill looked at Gonosor, who agreed, so he released the document and Fogle took hold of it, unraveled it until it was flat and began to read. The list contained about thirty or so names, mostly men, but with women on it also, although the women seemed to be guilty of only one transgression, that of an association or liaison with a Repecian legionary, and the fact of whether that encounter was voluntary or otherwise did not get mentioned and did not seem to matter. The men on the list seemed to be just as unfairly treated. One, by the name of Marvitt, was guilty of treason because he had cooked for the garrison for many years, despite the fact that that is how he made his living. Another had worked in the dock and unloaded the trade vessels that had visited Bosscastle during the occupation, who had no doubt lead a guiltless life until he was seen to be sharing a joke with the merchant and even accepted a gift of a parcel of food. And on it went, name after name, and none of them seemed to have done anything to deserve a mention.

Fogle's gaze rose from the parchment and his eye met Gonosor's, who was waiting for the little man's response.

"Well?" he growled.

"None of the people on this list have done that much wrong," said Fogle. "There are no traitors here ... no crimes committed. Just normal folk trying to live their lives as best they may. The way you were talking I was expecting to see murderers and robbers on here. He flicked the paper with his finger. "But there aren't any. Just people. Ordinary people ... like me."

Gonosor forced a smile. "That's a response I would expect to hear from a Shireman," he groaned. "That's a Shireman's logic all right." But that was all. The thought quickly crossed his mind that Delabole, the greatest traitor of them all, was from the Shirelands, and would have normally forced the point to win the argument, but not now. He said nothing further, just twisted his face and sat back in his high seat.

Fogle, and the others, could barely believe it, and if the rebel master had had any lingering doubts about the effectiveness of the Druid's hold over the Bodmifflian, they were dispelled now. Galfall had told Fogle that Gonosor was docile and obedient whilst he was muted, but any concerns that with his tongue back he had reverted to the man he used to be seemed quite unfounded. His eyes were dull and his great strength and doggedness were gone. Yet, in some strange, inexplicable way, it seemed a shame that they had.

"That's just the way it is!" Fogle replied. "None of the people on this list deserve to be pursued or hunted down."

"The people on that list are spineless cowards!" Gonosor snarled.

"That maybe so. But you can't hang a man for being a coward!"

"Why not?" The Bodmifflian was arguing but he did not seem eager to engage the Shireman in a deep, forceful debate.

"Because there'd be no-one left," said Fogle. "Not everyone's as bold or as boisterous as you, Gonosor. And not every man says or does the things he knows he should. Most of the time, in times like these, just the things he knows will keep him alive…!"

Gonosor leant forward and with one swoop he grasped the list out of Fogle's hand and placed it by his side.

"That's your point of view," he snarled. "A very 'Shireman' point of view." He seemed to be getting more irritated and his face, at last, was flushed and heated. "But you're in Bodmiffel now, and we look at things differently here. Loyalty among the forest folk is everything, and a betrayal, no matter how small or irrelevant it may seem to you, is still a crime to us! And crimes must be punished! That way lies harmony and obedience. The people now look to me to bring the wrongdoers to justice. It is my burden. And I will not shy away from my obligations because a …" he tried an insult but his tongue would not utter one. "… blacksmith from the Threeshire does not approve!"

Murmurs of agreement fluttered through the room. A large grin spread across Crispill's face, and on other faces too. They, at least, did approve.

"In fact, I don't know why you've come back, Fogle," Gonosor continued, his tone menacing and resembling the Gonosor Fogle knew from the forest. "You are the leader of a rebellion that no longer exists. There is nothing here for you now. Take my advice, little man, and go back to wherever it is you come from and try to rebuild whatever life you had before the rebellion started, for the life you have here is that of an intruder and worse, one that does not understand his host."

If Fogle was supposed to feel intimidated, he did not. In fact, he was emboldened by Gonosor's affirmation for he knew that he was quite wrong.

"Badad instructed me to come back," he said.

A lurid laugh came out of Gonosor's mouth. "Ah, the little Druid. I was wondering how long it would be before his name was mentioned again. Sent you back to keep an eye on me, did he? Afraid that I might try to undo all his good work, is he…?"

Fogle's reply was instantaneous. "Oh, no. I think that the Druid knows that you're not the disruptive influence you used to be, don't you? Or have you forgotten that night in the forest when he appeared, and what happened thereafter…?" The Bodmifflian went quiet. A little embarrassed but more in fury that Fogle dare speak of that night so openly.

"Have you all forgotten what happened that night?" the Shireman asked them all. "When the Druid emerged from the forest…?"

"He had changed himself into a wolf," was one comment that Fogle overheard from someone in the throng, obviously explaining to someone who was not there what exactly had happened. "Then remember the promise Badad made to us all," continued Fogle, undeterred by Gonosor's incensed fidgeting. "Remember what he said?"

Gonosor recoiled in horror as the Druid's words passed through his mind once again. 'No more will this tongue speak of the kings of Bodmiffel, or any tongue of the kings of Threeshire!' Then he straightened himself and shook off his demon. "So he has told you that he intends to return with the King?" he snarled.

"Yes," replied Fogle. "And has instructed me to find the room that contains the Boss Throne, for the King will need it."

"A waste of time," Gonosor retorted. "Not only is that room long lost, but the Druid will not return with anyone who would be able to sit upon it even if it were found…! I had heard it rumored that my sister and her lover had spawned a son long before that night in the forest. Remember, Fogle, that while you were banging away at your forge I was privy to the great events of our age!"

Agitatedly, he rose from his seat and began to pace the floor, brushing past Fogle with his shoulder to unsettle him on his feet. "After the Repecians had finally conquered Geramond I began to look for the boy. I searched everywhere ... every inch of your Shirelands and even went into Tragara, but found nothing. Delabole, when he was first made governor, decreed that anyone sheltering the boy would be killed and that if anyone knew of his whereabouts they should inform us and claim a great reward...!" Then he went quiet, for he realised that he had associated his actions with the reviled governor, but hoped that no-one had noticed.

A voice, again, nagged his mind. Not the Druid's this time but his sister's and his gaze was drawn to her image in the tapestry on the wall. The voice asked: 'Did you search the High Moor?' And then he knew that the rumor was true after all.

Fogle broke the silence. "I don't doubt that you know more about these things than me," he said. "All I'm saying is that if the Druid says that he is bringing the King to Bosscastle, then I for one am happy to believe him." There was a slight mumble of agreement but not a very convincing one, for people were still wary of Gonosor. But to Fogle's ears it was a heartening sound nevertheless. "And if Badad has asked me ... us ... to find the Boss Throne, then that's how we should be filling our days! And we should be more concerned with doing that then messing about with that there list!"

Gonosor was lost in thought. He pulled his attention away from the tapestry and placed it back onto Fogle. "You go and do whatever you need to do, but leave us to do the same."

"But I need your help, Gonosor," Fogle pleaded. "You know the secrets of this old castle better than anyone here."

"Certainly better than a Shireman," Gonosor snapped. "But I cannot help you. The Boss Throne was lost centuries ago. No-one knows where it is or whether it still exists or has ever existed. Perhaps it is purely myth. If you want to spend weeks looking for an imaginary object then be my guest, but don't expect me to have any part of it."

Fogle remained defiant. "Then I will find it by myself," he said, and turned to leave. Gonosor walked back to his seat, took the scroll off the cushion and sat down.

"There is a name that needs to be added to this list," he said to Crispill. "Indeed, placed at the top of the list."

The late morning air had a feel of spring in it. The long winter was at last behind them and although the breeze off the sea was chilly, the sky was bright and the cloud broken in places to reveal its blue canvass beneath. Fogle emerged from the Great Hall and took a deep intake of breath. Galfall, at the bottom of the steps, was surprised and pleased to see him emerge at all, and caught his attention by holding his arm aloft.

"How was he?" the youngster asked.

"Just as stubborn as I remembered," Fogle replied, coming down the steps.

"At least he didn't try to kill you this time."

"He wouldn't dare," Fogle chortled. "I'm on a mission. I'm here to do the Druid's work." Galfall was intrigued. "I'll tell you all about it later. But now I need to eat. Where have you been staying, young friend ... with that girl of yours, eh...?"

Galfall smiled.

"She is not mine yet. But yes, with her. I'll take you there. She lives quite a way away. I hope your short, fat legs are up to the walk."

"Oh, indeed they are," Fogle replied. And he followed Galfall across the square with quite a spring in his step, for he was certain that these were better times, despite Gonosor and his wretched list.

Eighteen
Lamorak the Chronicler

The house was small, just a single room with an off-shoot as a kitchen, but warm and far enough off the main hub of Bosscastle to be safe, which was its best feature as far as Fogle was concerned. He watched as Salissa prepared his meal and saw in her great grace and beauty, and congratulated his young friend for having such a fine taste in women. And as Galfall built up the fire it seemed to Fogle that this was a very cosy, domestic arrangement between the two of them and realized why Galfall had no inclination to return to Aldshire after the end of the war. Why would he want to return to his humdrum life on the family farm after meeting and falling in love with such a charming girl as this? And his thoughts naturally turned to his own wife and how it was between them when they were young and free. That was the thing; what had been missing all these years: freedom. It made all the difference.

"The best life is a free life," Fogle muttered to himself beneath his breath. He looked at Galfall again and saw in him the same youthful endeavor that his own son, Callarn, had possessed. That flush and activity that everyone has at some point but only ever in their early, formative years. Galfall was the same age as Callarn would have been had he lived. Thinner, for the blacksmith's son was a chubby lad, but the same height and with the same content in his heart. Wilfren would have been very proud, Fogle was sure, as he was proud, of Galfall as he had been of Callarn.

Salissa handed the plate to Fogle, who gratefully accepted it and was at once shocked and delighted to see four fish waiting to be eaten. Just mackerels but cooked over a hot fire and even though he knew they would not fill him for very long he was sure they would be a rare treat, and intended to enjoy them.

"I've never heard of it," Salissa said as she sat down on the bed next to Fogle, and smiled as she watched him devour the first of the four little fish.

"But it must be true," Galfall replied, quite firmly. "Or else the Druid would not have us look for it."

With his mouth full and being very careful not to lose even the smallest morsel of food from his lips, Fogle added: "I don't doubt that it's true. The problem is ... where is the blasted thing? This castle is so vast I really don't have the first clue where to look."

"It's a throne we're looking for, right...?" asked Salissa. They nodded so she continued. "Well, that's the seat of a king ... so it'll be in one of the grand buildings in the centre ..."

"The Great Hall," insisted Galfall.

"No ... if it was there then everyone would know all about it," replied Fogle.

"The Bossmilliad then," the youngster affirmed. "That place is huge ... I've been in it remember ... and it goes down into the ground as much as it goes into the sky...!"

Fogle paused to finish his mouthful, all the while making his mind work hard. "Think, Fogle ... think...!" he demanded of himself. "Where would it be?"

"It's a pity Marrock isn't here. He'd know." Galfall muttered, sadly, for he missed his friend still.

Fogle raised his head.

"Yes. I'm sure he would." Then a thought occurred to him. "The Boss Throne was used by the early kings of Geramond," he pondered. "So it'll be in the oldest part of the castle. Only, I don't know where that is!" He was beginning to let the puzzle spoil his lunch, but could not help it.

Galfall rose from in front of the fire and leapt into the middle of the room like a spring hare. "That's it! I remember."

"What ... what...?" pleaded Fogle.

"Something Badad told me before I set out for Bosscastle with Gonosor. Something of the origins of this place." He turned his head to Salissa. "What's the name of the cove where you found me?"

"Kanance's Cove," she replied, but was puzzled.

"That's him," Galfall blasted. "Kanance. He was one of the early kings. In fact I think he was the very first."

Fogle, having finished his meal too quickly for his liking, placed the plate on the floor. "What about him...?"

He did battle with a giant and where the giant fell he decided to build his castle. To weigh him down with stones."

"The cove...?" Fogle mused. Now it was his turn to ask a question of Salissa. "Can we get access to the cove?"

For a brief moment she was sad to reply.

"While the Repecians were here the only people who ever got to see the cove were those that had been sold as slaves," she said.

"And now?"

"The fishermen use it to go and come back again."

Fogle beamed with delight and relief in equal measure.

Later that day, in the last of the evening light, the three of them went to the cove. The entrance, that had been guarded during the occupation, for the Governor did not want anyone to see what happened there, was unmanned now and wide open to allow access to anyone who wished to go down. Galfall lead the way down the steps and onto the dock side. And once there a shiver of fear spread up his back and all he could do was stand there and remember the last time he had been in this cold, austere place. For Fogle, however, this was a new sight for his eyes and he marveled at it. He had thought that Bosscastle could no longer fill him with awe, that he had seen the best of it, but he knew now that he had not. Nowhere like this existed in the Shirelands. The blocks of stone in the walls were themselves as big as a Shire house, and when together formed a colossal frame to the harbour. Not for the first time he wondered how anything so big could be built by human hands. Surely a place like this was the work of other, unworldly things. Galfall had mentioned a giant. Just a story, he thought, but now he was not so sure. Only a giant could lift and lay stones the size of houses.

Nevertheless, once he had had time to take it all in, and he had got his breath back, he began to look around with inquiring eyes. And what he saw, the thick walls crowned with high towers; the sheer scale of the place and the ancient feel of it convinced him that they were looking in the right location.

"Now what?" said Salissa. It was a good question, for there seemed to be nowhere for them to go; behind them was the way they came in, all around were those immeasurable walls, and directly in front of them was the icy water of the cove itself. Then they heard a sound from below and looked down to discover a boat bobbing on the water.

"Oh, no," Galfall stuttered. "I'm not getting in that." His remark annoyed Fogle, who thought the youth was more courageous than that. But Fogle did not know anything about Galfall's previous experience in a similar size boat. Salissa did, and she offered him a reassuring smile. Reinforced by that, he agreed to go with them, and they clambered down from the dockside into the vessel.

The youngster took up the oars and slowly they moved out into the cove, without really knowing where they wanted to be. Fogle pointed to the tunnel, for although he knew that it was the way out into the open sea beyond, the tower above it was the largest and most imposing of all the towers that topped the walls, and therefore more likely to be the one that contained the old throne. As they got closer to it the more daunting it became, and the remaining daylight seemed to fade with every stroke of the oars, like the tower was the giant, and it gobbled the light up to leave just a faint trace of daytime; a warning not to come too close and to turn back now while they still had the wherewithal to do so.

Galfall gave Fogle a glare that suggested they should do just that, but the little man was so intrigued that he offered a look in return that told him to keep rowing and get closer to it. The waters of the cove were spirited and the boat rose and sank with the ebb and flow, but the sounds of the cove were more unsettling than anything; a groaning noise that seemed to come from the deep; a whistle that was like the wind but without the feel of the wind, more like a breath or a wheeze; and their own creaking boat as it strained to stay afloat. Then they entered the tunnel and the last of the light was left behind.

"This is far enough," Galfall insisted, almost panicking. "Any further and we'll be on the ocean proper...!"

Fogle stumbled to his feet and the boat rocked from side to side under his weight. "There must be a way in," he mumbled, looking closely at the tunnel wall. Then, just as he was about to instruct the youngster to take them back, he spotted what looked like a small, wooden door a bit further down, so instructed him to take them there instead.

"You go first," he said to Galfall, realising that the first one to climb from the boat onto the narrow path would have the most difficult task, and could then pull the others up. So Galfall pulled himself out of the boat while Fogle and Salissa pushed him. Then the youngster pulled Salissa out of the boat and finally Fogle.

It was Fogle, however, who pushed the door. It was not locked, had probably never needed to be, but was stiff which suggested that it had not been opened in a very long while, and as it opened dust and dirt fell from the frame and covered the little man's hair and beard. Blackness was all there was at first, but then, as their eyes adjusted, a glimmer of light appeared at the top of the stairs, so they ascended to follow it. But the stairs seemed to go on forever and with every step they took the light got further away.

They finally emerged into a room, that from the view from the window must have been the very top of the tower. The light that came in from the window was from the rapidly setting sun on the horizon of the sea, to give this place a bright orange glow. It was obvious to all three of them that no one had been in this room for many years. Cluttered with furniture, that was covered in a thick film of dust, and with a pungent stench of damp stone, it was a strange place to be. On top of the numerous desks and tables, yet beneath the prevailing grime, were scrolls of paper. Yards of them, hardened and tainted by the years. What was this place? And how long had it been abandoned? Fogle searched all around but could not see a throne of any sort. Plenty of chairs and stools, but nothing that could be considered a seat of kings. Then the thought occurred to him that the Boss Throne would be a very old thing, and basic in design, so he began to look at one chair with more discerning eyes, and stepped closer to it.

"What are you doing?" Galfall asked.

"I think this is it," Fogle replied, his voice soft but unmistakably excited.

"It's just a chair …" Galfall scoffed.

"It may look like a chair to you … but I'm almost certain."

"How can you be certain what the Boss Throne looks like when you haven't seen it…?"

"There's something about it."

"It's just a chair!"

"You'd better come and have a look at this," said Salissa, from the far side of the room. Galfall and Fogle walked over to where she was, in front of a large desk, piled high with papers. So high that at first they could not see what she was directing them to, but when they did they both gasped with fright. Behind the desk, dropped forwards into the mass of papers, was a skeleton, and it held a quill in one hand and a sheet of paper in the other.

"He must have died writing," said the girl.

Galfall, having recovered, was the keener of the three of them to discover just who this was and what he had been working on. He carefully pulled the paper from its hand then stepped back. Having been moved after so many years, as though it was a relief to have its work taken off it, the skeleton finally relaxed and let its arm slip off the desk, away from the body altogether and crash onto the floor. This made Fogle leap further away, which amused Galfall a great deal.

"What is it?" Fogle pried.

Galfall held up his free hand in a gesture that told them both to wait a while. He began to read, but the ink was faint and he struggled to make sense of it.

"It's some sort of diary, I think," he said, though he was not totally convinced. He read the beginning out loud to demonstrate what he meant. "Here follows the final account of Lamorak the Chronicler. I am the last of my line and the last of the 'white knuckle scribblers'. Reader, this is the final account in the 'Annals of the Kings of Geramond in the first age and the Kings and Queen of Bodmiffel in the second age' …" Then the youngster lowered the piece of paper. "There's more. Should I read on?" Fogle nodded, leaned against the wall beside the window that looked out over the cove, and prepared himself to listen. Galfall read a little of the text to himself first before continuing where he had left off.

"I don't know what to write. My mind is numb. Accept for that one thought that keeps occurring to me: what would my forbears, those witnesses to the great events of their days, make of this land now…? Would they think it a desolate and debatable place; ruined and decaying? A place riddled in strife and trampled beneath the feet of the invaders? And if they looked out of my window now would they see that infinite, great sea crashing upon the shores of the old country that the first kings built, or an unnamed wilderness; a distant province of a foreign empire? They would not know this land anymore. It is filled with evil and terror, where men speak not of wisdom and justice, but are inspired by fury and war. Where people are not ruled by kings with pure blood, but by an imposter who would be their king save for the fact that he is really just a servant of his distant master"

"That's enough, Galfall," Fogle said. "We haven't got time for anymore."

Galfall, though, had continued reading.

"Wait. Listen to this," he said, quite insistently. "My mind is drawn to Iblin, who chronicled the days of the first two kings of Geramond, and I think how fortunate he was …"

Fogle's attention was captured again. "Go on," he instructed.

…. "to have lived in days of such hope and insight, and written the accounts of the very foundation of the country. I wonder, now, what I have done to deserve such misfortune as to bear witness to the ending of it. I was told as a child that a scribbler cannot in any way influence the course of events set out before his eyes, and can only observe and record them as accurately as he may. How I wish that was not true. With a heavy heart, a tear on my cheek, I set down in black ink, for the record, that I have seen the event that denotes the end of Geramond and all that it once stood for. The fact that this day will be forgotten in time, that people will have other concerns above this, is testament to that. Queen Henwen is dead. I have seen her demise with my own eyes. She climbed upon the 'red beard' at dusk yesterday and threw herself into the waters of the cove below, and was taken down by the current. The Governor is left with a stain on his heart and on his conscience too. That's all I have to say. My arm is too weak to continue. The door is unlocked but I will not pass through it again. My life has been my service to the Queen and her father before her. Now she has gone there is nothing left to live for ...."

"That's all there is," Galfall concluded.

"Poor man," said Salissa, staring intently at the skeleton. "He mustn't have moved from that seat from the moment he'd written his last word."

Fogle gazed out over the cove and imagined the sight of the fair lady falling from the tower, then brought his attention back into the here and now. He seemed to be enlightened with a sudden bolt of thought.

"Somewhere in this room there is a book that contains the whereabouts of that blasted throne!"

"It will be the oldest of all the books" Salissa added, equally excited. "The very first one, written by ..." she picked up Lamorak's paper and quickly glanced. ... "Iblin, who chronicled the days of Kanance ... who set down the foundations of this castle...!"

Fogle was filled with excitement and started to do a little jig on the spot where he stood. Salissa, who found the sight of the little, fat man hopping and skipping highly amusing, took hold of his hands and danced with him. Galfall looked on. As the girl's long, unadorned gown puffed-out the faster Fogle spun her around, he caught sight of her legs. Her laughter, that quaint, sharp chortle that seemed to last but a few seconds at a time, filled the room and was like a melodic tease to the young man's ears. He asked himself why she had never allowed herself to behave so freely and impulsively with him. Not even at the end of the rebellion, after all their efforts at the Western Gate, all they had been through together, had she opened herself up to him in the same way she danced and laughed with Fogle now. In fact, he had never made her laugh like this, and although he was heartened to see it, wished above all else that it was him she was dancing with.

As Fogle spun the girl around to face the window that looked out over the ocean, she suddenly stopped and glared into the distance, over the darkening sea.

"What's that?" she mused.

"What's what?" asked Galfall, coming to stand by her side.

"Lights ... a ship ... on the horizon ..." She was sure that she had seen them, but when she looked again they had vanished.

"Never mind that," Fogle bellowed. "Find a lamp or some candles, we have books to read...!"

Matches were found and candles were lit all over the room and the shadows of eventide began to prevail. Fogle, candle in hand, began to search through the hundreds of books that lined the walls. Galfall joined him but Salissa's attention remained on the horizon of the sea, seeking a second sighting of those lights.

They were the lights of the Buca Lapis. The ship drifted on the surface of the spring sea, for the oars down below had stopped for the night. In any case, when the vessel was fully propelled it had nowhere to go. Bucenta had insisted that they sail south, to the warmer waters of Eliad, but Delabole refused to leave these cold, northern waters just yet, and would stand on the stern of the old ship each evening and look across to the black outline of the Geramond coast, and the sparkling lights of Bosscastle. This night was particularly chilly and he wore a heavy cloak over his hunched shoulders.

"Come down below," said Bucenta. "Where be warm food, my friend ..."

"I will have it back," Delabole mumbled to himself, shivering in the breeze, and looking at the castle. "It would be mine still if it wasn't for that blasted Druid...!"

Bucenta took hold of Delabole's arm and gripped it tightly.

"You say the same thing each night. It is sad for me to look upon my old friend and see his pain, and yet there is nothing I can do to ease it. There is no drink left but water. No food but bread."

Delabole, once pristine and faultless in his appearance, was disheveled and hollow-looking now; with sullen eyes and a drawn, exhausted face at the tip of which hung a dirty, brown, unkempt beard. His degeneration from provincial governor to a mere guest on a merchant ship had taken its toll on him. So had the lack of wine or mead or anything alcoholic. Then, strangely, he started to weep into his hands. Bucenta, bemused and discomfited, withdrew his arm and turned to walk away, but Delabole grabbed hold of his sleeve and pulled him back.

"I know you're anxious to leave these waters and return to your homeland. But I cannot depart this place."

Bucenta, puzzled, replied: "I don't understand you. Every night it's the same. You come here and look out at the land and always with a longing in your eye to return. But if you ever did return they would kill you. And it would not be an easy death, but the worst ... slow, painful and public! That's how much they despise you."

Delabole wiped his eyes. He responded groggily to the remark. "They are wrong to despise me," he said. "I have only ever tried to help them. My whole life has been dedicated to their welfare!" Budogis started to chortle so Delabole continued in a louder, more forthright tone. "I accepted the burden of the governorship just to stop a foreigner from getting it, who would not understand their ways...!"

"Who are you trying to convince, my friend...?" the merchant laughed.

"It's true," Delabole affirmed.

"Then you have surpassed yourself for you persecuted them far worse than any foreign governor would have."

"I never persecuted any of them!"

Budogis's chortle now turned into a loud, crude cackle, and he actually had to hold his fat belly to stop it from aching. Then he calmed down.

"There are fifty people in the hull of my ship that you sold to me in exchange for strong drink and fine foods! Fifty poor souls that will now be subjected to a life of misery and turmoil just so you could fuel your little habit! And what's more, you abandoned them to their wicked fate without turning an eye!" His tone moved from jovial to critical in an instant. "Do you know how many people you have sold into slavery during your governorship?" Delabole had turned his face away to look out at the land, so did not acknowledge Budogis's question. "No less than five hundred...! Little wonder they loathe you so." He turned to go back below deck. "By the way … I should get a refund on the last lot on account that half of them have starved to death since we left Bosscastle, and the other half aren't fit to piss for a fuller…!"

With that said Budogis walked away, but just as he was about to go below he caught sight of something out of the corner of his eye, and quickly ran to the front of the Buca Lapis. Delabole, realising that the merchant had seen something, abandoned his self-pity and followed him.

"I can't believe my eyes," Budogis said, his mouth agape in wonder and incomprehension. Delabole suddenly turned nervous and began to shake from his head to his feet.

Fogle, Galfall and Salissa had been searching through Lamorak's books for what seemed like an age. What little light they had now came from the candles dotted all around the room. Fogle and Galfall were weary and struggled to concentrate on the book they had in their hands. Salissa was rummaging through the books and papers on the shelves against the wall. It was a thankless task.

"There are no books by anyone called Iblin on these shelves," said the girl. "Nor any mention of a King Kanance…!"

"There's got to be," Fogle insisted. "Look again."

"I've looked three times already," she retorted sharply. "I'm telling you there's nothing here!"

Fogle sighed with despair, and placed the book he had in his hands on the floor between his feet. Then he looked at Galfall, who was straining his eyes to read the book he possessed.

"What is it, Galfall? Is it Iblin?"

"No," the youngster replied.

"Then who is it?"

Without raising his head Galfall replied: "Boso of Bossiney."

"Is it relevant, lad…?"

"I think so. It's hard to read. The writing's so small and this Boso must have been short of ink. Listen. This bit's written more clearly than the rest of it, like it's more important. 'Everything has changed. As I write the land and the people upon it are at the threshold of a new age, for everything that was once is no more, and that fair, heroic country once called Geramond is gone, lost forever, squashed like a ripened fruit under foot. It is three months since the death of Calamthor, the childless king, and the squabbling between the northern folk and the forest folk over the issue of who should succeed him has intensified. No-one can seem to agree on anything anymore. I think there is going to be a civil war. And all the while the Old Throne stays empty and of no use'."

The mere mention of the throne, however inconsequentially it appeared in Boso's text, was enough to make Fogle spring to his feet, take the book out of Galfall's hands and read it for himself. He had to hold the candle so that the flame was almost touching the paper for him to be able to read the words. The rest of that page, and the following three pages were just about impossible to read, but then he came across something of great significance to their quest. As before, it had been written with more care for it was important to Boso that these particular words were clear on the page. Fogle read it to himself; twice, for he barely believed it the first time.

"Tell us, Fogle," said Salissa.

"There were two men who claimed to be Calamthor's proper heir ... Maldorc, his stepson and chosen successor, and Lampas. Lord of Woldark, his nephew and only living blood relative. After weeks of skirmishing, the elders of Bosscastle have decided that the only way to settle the dispute once and for all is to let the Old Throne decide who is the rightful king. Lampas has arrived at Bosscastle and the air is filled with excitement and trepidation, for it has been many hundreds of years, since the Boss Throne has selected the true and lawful king of Geramond. The Druim Square is packed with people but they can't actually see anything and all they can do is wait for the news to reach them. The walls that line the cove are crowded too and the cove itself is full of boats. It seems that the whole of Geramond has come to Bosscastle this day. I can't recall anything like this ever happening before, and I am privileged to be recording these great events in the Annuls of the Kings. Above all else, the Elders have invited me into the very room where the ritual will take place. A scribbler longs for days like these.

"Maldorc, being the younger man, approached the Throne first. Although he was a man of mighty proportions, he bore a fretful look on his face as he lowered himself into the seat of kings. Those present, namely the five Elders, Lampas and myself, actually gasped with anticipation as Maldorc fidgeted until he was sitting comfortably. He needed to remain seated until the sands of the hour glass passed through to fill a quarter. It actually seemed to take a lot longer than that, and the longer it went on the more agitated Lampas became. Finally, the Elders instructed him to rise. I was sure that at that precise moment, as Maldorc's backside rose from the Throne, I had witnessed the instigation of the next King. Nevertheless, it was requested by Lampas that he also should be given the opportunity to sit upon the throne. There followed a debate among the Elders about whether this was necessary, indeed lawful at all. Then, Maldorc let out a howl of distress and all our eyes turned once again onto him.

"He was holding his head tightly in between his hands, and it was clear to all of us that the process had started. And what started as a pain his head quickly spread to his whole body and poor Maldorc did not know what to do to stop it. Neither did the Elders, Lampas or myself. Not one of us tried to help him for we knew that he was beyond that. Then his face began to contort in pain, and his eyes, that before looked to us to help him, gave up and turned blood-red. He opened his mouth, not to say something but to let out another mighty roar, and with it came a gust of foul breath that formed a cloud of green gas that lingered in front of him before being sucked back into the mouth whence it came.

"The room began to shake and we thought that the tower was going to collapse, so we each of us sped out of the door, down the steps and out onto the cove. Even from down there we could hear poor Maldorc's screams, and looked upwards to the top of the tower. Then he emerged from the window, swallowed up in red flames, and plummeted into the waters of the cove. At that precise moment I realised that Maldorc had not been selected to be the next King of Geramond after all ..."

Fogle took his nose out of Boso's book, seemingly quite taken aback by the power of the object they sought.

"This new king ... whoever he is ... would be well advised to stay well clear of that throne...!" said Galfall.

"Yes, what if the Druid's got it wrong? The poor man will suffer the same fate as Maldorc," Salissa added.

Fogle put the book down and went towards the window and again looked down upon the black waters of the cove. It occurred to him that this small square of water had claimed so many lives; Henwen and Maldorc to name but two. Then he was revived again and allowed his thoughts to turn to more pressing matters.

"Badad will not have got it wrong," he stated. "And he instructed me to find the Boss Throne so that is what I intend to do." He began to pace the floor, candle in hand to light his way. "Now, let's think about what Boso wrote. A tower, he said. And a tower overlooking this cove, because he said that Maldorc plunged into the water ...."

Galfall moved swiftly to Lamorak's table and snatched hold of the first page they had read, the last one written. His eyes moved swifter over the text, then he lowered his arm and sighed with relief and enlightenment. He rushed to the window.

"Lamorak wrote that Queen Henwen threw herself off the 'red beard' tower, which must be that one over there, on the far side of the cove." Fogle and Salissa joined him at the window. There was indeed a tower that rose from the top of the wall higher than any of the others.

"There're so many," Fogle groaned. "How do we know that is the one called 'red beard'?"

"Nearer and fast doth the red beard come, and louder still and more loud. From beneath that swirling cloud, the thunder and the thrum...!"

"What crap are you talking now, lad...?" Fogle asked, utterly bemused and getting more tired and frantic by the second.

"Corbilo had a red beard!"

"And who's he?" said Salissa.

"Just what I was going to ask," said Fogle.

"Corbilo was the giant Kanance slayed and then weighed him down with stones!" He pointed out of the window. 'That is the tallest of all the towers, and from where Henwen and Maldorc plunged to their deaths! That is the 'red beard' tower, I'm sure of it, Fogle. That's the oldest part of the castle."

Fogle concentrated his eyes on that one tower. "Then that is where we'll find the Boss Throne," he mused, then laughed out loud and began to dance again.

Delabole and Bucenta did not move from the front of the Buca Lapis all night. The following morning, at first light, they leapt to their feet to look out once again at the sight that had struck them down with dread and awe. And in the clear, clean light of daybreak, the sight was even more impressive and terrifying. A flotilla of ships, and so many, so tightly packed, and so close to them that the sea and the sky seemed to have vanished completely, to be replaced by wood and sails, that fluttered in the early morning breeze and when combined sounded like thunder. And not ordinary ships, but war galleys, twice the size of the Buca Lapis and many more times stronger. They were more like floating cities than wooden boats, and as Bucenta's craft drifted closer towards them it quickly occurred to him that unless he made himself known it would be rammed and boarded. "Run up my banner," he shouted. His crew had gathered behind him to watch the spectacle themselves and one of them took up Bucenta's commandment and raised the flag that announced that this ship carried no threat and was just a trading vessel.

Delabole stepped back, away from the front of the Buca Lapis. "Are they Repecian ships?" he asked, his voice croaky with fear.

"Oh, yes," replied Bucenta, quite jolly now that his banner had been raised and his ship was safe.

"Trading ships…?" Delabole said, although really he knew that they were much more than that.

"War ships!" sneered the merchant. "Aren't they magnificent?" He inspected the fleet more closely. "Oh, and demolition ships … and fire ships as well! The Great One has brought with him his full arsenal! It seems to me that he intends to take no chances this time."

"The Great One?"

"Don't you remember, Delabole? Corbissa said that the Great One intended to return to Geramond." He clapped his hands together with excitement.

"Fillian?" Delabole muttered to himself. "I didn't believe him."

"That's why the Ambassador was sent ahead, with me, to inform the garrison that Lord Fillian was on his way, and to hold out until he got here. To keep the fortress safe and secure so that he could land safely. Don't you remember? That's what your instructions were. Only, you failed. The fortress is lost and here you are, on my ship instead of in your castle where you should be...!"

Delabole wrapped his cloak higher around his shoulders and nipped it at the neck. Suddenly the extent of his failure occurred to him. Suddenly his master was no longer thousands of miles away. He was here now, in northern waters, just yards away on one of those ships. And then another thought entered his already clotted mind: that his brother may be here too! And that, more than anything else, caused his heart to race and his head to ache. So he pulled his black cloak over his whole head to conceal his identity. Bucenta, giggling, said: "This is a typical Repecian military tactic. Put on such an awesome display of power that your enemy crumbles and gives in without even striking a blow. And to think that those foul villains back on that island have no idea what's coming their way...!"

"But ... but they won't give in," Delabole spluttered. "So what will he do then...?"

Bucenta stopped giggling and his face turned quite stern and pitiless. "Then he'll unleash hell upon them!"

The Buca Lapis was pulled alongside one of the ships in the font column, ladders were thrown down and Bucenta and Delabole climbed up to the lower deck of this mighty craft. The captain, a gangly man called Punil, came towards them.

"How honored I am to be your guest," Bucenta snivelled. "And I trust that my own ship shall be safe in the midst of this great fleet, for I should hate to lose my livelihood."

"We saw that you're a merchant," said Punil. "I was quite surprised to find a merchant ship in these treacherous waters, then I realized that you must be the Merchant Budogis ..."

Bucenta beamed with delight and pride. "I told you that I am renowned for my do-daring and my enterprising spirit," he said.

"It's not so much that," Punil replied. "You're the only

merchant dim-witted or greedy enough, perhaps both, to trade with these heathens!" And the captain laughed smugly as Bucenta's conceited look was withdrawn from his face. Then he noticed the man standing by the merchant's side.

"Who's your hooded friend?" he asked.

Bucenta leant inwards and whispered to Delabole: "You are the Governor of this province, a rank that outstrips that of a lowly ship's captain. Tell him who you are and he will treat us with the respect we deserve."

But Delabole, not wanting to be identified, walked away. "He is Lord Delabole Bubinda, Governor of Geramond," Bucenta announced haughtily.

"The Governor?" Punil mused, realising that if the provincial governor was here then the province must have been lost after all. "Then you're on the wrong ship, my friends. You will need to brief the Emperor...!" He pointed at another ship, in the second row; much larger than any of the others and with a huge, purple sail hanging from the central mast. A ship befitting an emperor.

They were taken to that ship by rowing boat. Punil accompanied them. Bucenta seemed rather excited, but Delabole, still with the hood of his cloak concealing his face, was fidgety and wary.

"By 'emperor' you mean General Fillian?" asked Bucenta.

"General?" replied Punil. "You've been away from the south for too long, merchant. A lot has happened since the Great One was just a general."

And as the small boat got closer to the Great One's ship, Delabole fidgeted all the more, for he knew that he was about to come face to face with his master at last.

Nineteen

Vagor

"Everything in the Great City has changed," Punil said to them. "And some people don't think that it's a change for the better." It was mid morning and they were standing on the lower deck of the Emperor's ship. Although the sun was in the sky and the morning had a warm feel to it, Delabole's head was still concealed beneath its hood, as though a storm was raging past him. Bucenta, however, was pleased to be aboard, and pleased that his extravagant garment stood out on a ship full of drab soldiers and seamen, as though his finely embroidered silk costume pronounced that someone of great significance had just arrived. However, everyone knew that he was a mere merchant and therefore his presumption was for his own benefit.

There was no doubt that this was the flagship of the fleet. The size of it was impressive enough, at least four times the size of the Buca Lapis, but it was also ladened with weaponry. Not just legionaries in full armour, but machines and contraptions of war. At the front of the ship there was what looked to be some sort of ballista, only larger than anything that had been used before, and capable of hurling more than just boulders. Several of the ship's crew attended to it, cleaning its metalwork and testing its cables and lines. One man was even chiselling around what was obviously the projectile: a huge, shaped sphere of rock that was the size of a horse. And when Delabole finally lifted his head and looked around him he saw that all of the ships were equipped with such a weapon, but on a smaller scale. As he withdrew back into his hood he thought to himself: 'They're going to destroy the castle, everyone will perish'. It was a thought that gave him great satisfaction.

They were taken below deck to the stern of the ship, through the soldiers' quarters and past the kitchens, until they were in the Emperor's private chambers. An usher, elderly but solid, came out of a side room. Punil spoke privately to him and then left. The usher disappeared through the large door at the end of the corridor then emerged a few minutes later and gestured for them to come towards him.

"Listen to me," said the old man, quite curtly as was the Repecian way. "When you go in drop to your knees and bow your heads! When he asks you a question you must answer quickly and concisely. If you start to ramble on he will lose patience with you, and you do not want that to happen, believe me …"

"Certainly not," Bucenta replied, politely. "How do we address him, sir…?"

"Call him 'your excellency' or 'your majesty'! Do not call him general!" He turned to open the door. "Oh, and don't mention the Senate! All you need to know is that he's the Emperor now!"

"Fine by me," said Bucenta. "I always liked him anyway."

The usher, an impatient man, blinked slowly and pointed his head towards the door. "I'm pleased it meets with your approval," he said.

"Before we go in," nagged Bucenta, for he was quite nervous. "Is the Great One expecting us…?"

The usher looked directly at Delabole. "He's expecting him!" he said.

They went in. The room was long and the walls were covered with panels of oak which made it very dark. At the far end of the room, in front of the window and therefore veiled in what little sunlight there was, sat the Emperor. Bucenta remembered what the usher had told them and promptly fell to his knees, only he did so with a little too much gusto and his knees almost shattered, so as he bowed his head he drew a deep intake of breath to suppress his groans of pain. Delabole was less enthusiastic, but performed the gesture nonetheless, though only on one knee. As he rose he noticed that the room was lined with legionaries, who, in their shining armour, were like trophies hanging from the walls.

"The sight of the Governor would lead me to believe that my Ambassador had not come here, but for the sight of the merchant standing by his side," said Fillian, his voice strained and his breath short. "Where is Corsulla Corbissa?"

Bucenta looked at Delabole, and whispered: "You tell him."

"No!" Fillian blasted. "You tell me, Budogis! You were the one charged with his safe passage!"

Bucenta gulped with fright. "And so his passage was safe, your Excellency," he stuttered. "We arrived, safely, months ago!"

"And the message that he brought with him?"

"Safely delivered, my Lord," Bucenta quickly replied.

"Then where is he?" repeated Fillian.

"He's dead," replied Delabole, at last removing his hood for he realised that it no longer served his interests to be hidden and silent. The Emperor went quiet for a moment, genuinely saddened to hear of Corsula's demise, for they had been friends.

"What about General Macara?"

Delabole was quite bold with his reply. "He's dead too!"

Fillian, strangely, began to roar with laughter. "They're all dead! All of my friends are dead!" His laughter petered to an end. "And yet the Governor has survived! The merchant that supplies the Governor with drink has survived...!"

Bucenta, trying to distance himself from Delabole, stepped forwards, then realised that he had not been told to move. "May I?" he snivelled.

"Yes, yes, come to me, little man," replied the Emperor.

The merchant quickened his pace until he was standing beside Fillian, who had remained seated. It was then that he noticed how old the Great One looked. He had lost weight from the last time he had seen him, his face was withered and ashen and his eyes, once so virile and lively were now discoloured and tired; his arms were uncovered and were spindly and scrawny. He was wearing a purple toga, the colour of kings, and a wreath on his head to conceal his thinning, white hair. Not the man of legend at all, and less threatening close up than from the far side of the room.

Bucenta allowed himself a moment to wonder just how and why Fillian had aged so much in such a short span of time. Then he remembered what he was going to say. "I've seen so many strange things since I've been here," he said.

"It must have been dreadful for you," replied Fillian.

"Oh, I've had a hell of a time. What with the Druid ... who cursed the general, by the way...! And those rebels! Not to mention the giant arm...!"

"Giant arm?"

"Came out of the cove and got hold of the back of my boat ... I thought my lovely Buca Lapis was done for. Delabole said it was the work of the little Druid...!"

Fillian leant towards him and smelt his breath. "The work of something else, I think." And he then pushed a dagger into the merchant's belly and twisted it. Bucenta's eyes bulged with pain and he collapsed onto the floor, wrenched and writhed for a while, then died.

The Emperor gestured to two soldiers, one on either side of him, to remove the body, and Bucenta was dragged by his legs towards the window and then tossed out. Delabole was not so bold now, and took a tentative step backwards.

"So, Corsulla and Macara are both dead," Fillian said. "What news of the province...?"

"It is lost, my Lord," Delabole panted. "You are too late!"

"Too late?" Fillian rose. His voice boomed with anger.

"You don't understand." He was almost weeping with fear. "The Druid is at large again. He is controlling everything that happens in the land of Geramond. Bucenta was right ... Macara went insane because of the Druid. The rebellion was the Druid's sorcery too...!"

Whereas Corsulla had scoffed at the mere mention of the Druid's name, Fillian was more thoughtful and better informed. He had met the Druid once before, and recalled that meeting now. It was as he was leaving Geramond that he saw him. As he was walking towards his ship the little man thrust himself into his path. Just an old fool, Fillian had thought at the time. But he could recall his words now as though they were only uttered a few moments ago instead of sixteen years. As though they were the only words he had ever heard.

"I am the shining light in this dark land. But to you I am the shadow in a dream. I will be forever watching what you do to him. I am crafty. I will lie in your head to ambush your thoughts. When you look at Vercingoral it is me who you will see, every step of the time you have left. I will bring you back. Oh, how badly your plans have turned out. The deeds you do will hasten what time you have left!"

Fillian smiled to himself and stepped down from his seat, walked steadily towards Delabole and put his arm around his waist. "This Druid ... is about to meet his match." He walked with Delabole towards the door. "If he thinks that his conjuring and trickery can compete with the force of the Empire, then I think it's time he felt the full extent of that force."

"I did everything I could, my Lord. I swear it."

"I was warned against leaving you in control," Fillian replied. "People told me that the local prince would not serve the empire's best interests."

"But I always did," pleaded the Governor. "I always tried to do as you would have done."

"I don't doubt it. The homes of the finest families in Repecia are staffed with your countrymen. There are more slaves in my homeland from this province than from all of the others combined." He stopped walking, half to catch his breath and half to catch his thoughts. "The thing is ... what I need to ask myself ... is whether the kind of man who can sell his own brother into slavery, is the kind of man I want running one of my territories. Do you know what I mean...?"

"My brother opposed you, my Lord. Remember? If it had not been for me you would never have conquered Geramond."

"So much for my military prowess then," Fillian chortled.

"My brother would never have surrendered."

Fillian sighed deeply. "It's just that ... he did, in the end. I don't mean on the battle field. I mean in other ways. You know, you and your brother have more in common than you think."

The Emperor reached out and opened the door. For a brief moment Delabole wondered where they were going, before realising that someone was, in fact, coming into the room to join them. When the door opened Vagor was standing on the other side of it, and when he saw Delabole his instinctive reaction was to thump him flush in the face, and with such ferociousness that the sufferer was knocked onto his back. Vagor plunged into the room and would have attacked Delabole again had he not been held back by the Emperor.

"Steady, my friend, or it will be over too quickly," Fillian said, softly and quietly so that only his servant could hear him. Then he took his hand away from Vagor's chest. "Now you may have your revenge. Don't hold back on my account. I have no further use for this man." He gave Delabole a look that was as angry and as black as a thunder cloud. "His governorship is officially revoked!"

Delabole had not bothered to get back onto his feet for he knew that he would have been knocked down again. So he snivelled and panted as he wiped the blood from his face with his sleeve. And as he did so he looked at Vagor, but he knew him only by his original name, Vercingoral. Badad had warned him that his brother would return and now he had and Delabole was not prepared for the occasion in any way. He did feel some shame; could barely look his brother in the face. But his overriding emotion was fear.

Vagor, as he was now known, was as strong as he ever had been. Sixteen years as Fillian's prisoner and slave had obviously nourished that legendary strength, and his body was lean and muscled. But he looked altogether different. That ruggedness had gone. He seemed much more refined; a completely bald head and shaven face, a well tailored tunic made of leather and rings of gold on his fingers. His face, without a beard, revealed a large scar running from his ear to the side of his mouth, and Delabole wondered when and where he had obtained such a wound, as Vercingoral or as Vagor. In any case, he knew that his brother was much harder and merciless now. Where Vercingoral had contained a bold, caring quality, Vagor, it was evident, was made of nothing but hatred, aggression and a fierce sense of loyalty to his master.

"You are about to pay the price for losing my province," Fillian said to Delabole, stepping away from Vagor. "And no amount of grovelling and snivelling can save you."

Delabole was faced with a choice. He knew that he was going to grovel, for that was what he did when all else had failed, but he was unsure who to grovel to. Both men had good reason to loathe him and want him dead, but only one man had the power to do it at this present time. What seemed like an instinctive and repentant gesture was in fact a calculated act of self-preservation. He threw himself at Vagor's feet and clung onto is legs for his life.

"My brother," he sobbed. "My good king." He kept his head down for he wanted his sobs to seem penitent and not fuelled by fright, which they were.

And his strategy seemed to work for a while. Vagor did not move or do anything at first, but looked down on Delabole. Then he looked at Fillian and then he knew that he must finish what he had started. So he leant down and with one of his huge hands he picked his brother up off the floor by the back of his cloak. When he had him on his feet again he moved his other hand quickly onto his neck and held him at arms length and began to squeeze the life out of him. Fillian's eyes were wide with glee and anticipation, and gasped with delight as Vagor tossed his brother against the wall as though no effort was required at all. He drew his sword but did not move quickly enough, for Delabole was up and out of the door with the swiftness of a spring hare.

He went out the way he came in, and was back on the deck of the ship in no time at all. But the legionaries, knowing that he should not be there, prevented him from jumping overboard. Ten of them enclosed him in a ring. Fillian and Vagor emerged from below and were let into the ring. The deck of the ship had become an arena, and in the sunshine of a spring day, Vagor and Delabole were going to fight until one of them was dead.

At Fillian's instruction, Delabole was thrown a sword. This was going to be a fair duel. And it added to the fun. Brother against brother. They were of a similar height and only two years separated their ages, but there was little doubt that Vagor would prevail, whether Delabole had a sword or not. Nevertheless, the younger brother cast off his heavy cloak to release his arms, and threw himself at Vagor, but missed. The audience cheered. Vagor responded by swiping his shorter sword across his brother's chest, catching the cloth of his shirt but not wounding him. Swords clashed thereafter. Arms strained and shoved. Delabole moved away. His brother went with him. Then Vagor seemed to possess a sudden desire to have it over and done with as quickly as possible, and grabbed hold of Delabole's free arm whilst keeping his busy arm at bay, and pulled him towards him.

Delabole knew that he was beaten and offered nothing further to prevent his defeat. For Fillian and the crowd of soldiers, on this and on other ships close by, the fight was over too quickly; Vagor was just too strong. When he had been pulled close enough to speak so that only his brother could hear him, Delabole attempted his final, most desperate performance. He knew that his brother, or rather the good king he used to be, would not have abandoned him to utter ruin and death, no matter what wicked deed he had been guilty of, so appealed to that man, not the one that was about to run him through with his sword. Vagor was a foreigner, but Delabole's plan was based on his assumption that there was something of Vercingoral left in him.

He briefly wondered what had happened to his brother to turn him into this vacant, hardhearted fighter, as much under his new master's spell as he once was under Badad's. Taken away to be a trophy of war, proof to a cynical crowd that Fillian had actually conquered the 'unconquerable' island at the top of the world. A prisoner for a time thereafter, he was sure. A combatant in the arena, perhaps. But now the Emperor's closest aid and personal guard, and that was something quite different for it meant that the strong heart and iron will that were Vercingoral's greatest characteristics were completely turned the other way so that he had now accepted a life of servitude and was loyal and obedient to his new master. Those sixteen years had turned him into Vagor; he had lived as that man and had done what was required of him. But surely not now that he was back in home waters, within sight of his own land. No-one could change so much that they would forsake everything they once held so tightly. That was Delabole's only hope, so he pursued it.

"Very well, if my time ends here and now it is only what I deserve. Fillian was right. It is my punishment. Not for losing his province but for betraying you. My only brother. My only kin.

"Do you remember me? I think you do. And you remember my

great sin. You have not forgotten and will not forgive me, will you? All I ask is that you kill me cleanly and quickly. You should have let that legionary kill me all those years ago, at High Cleugh. Then you would have been able to kill Fillian and everything would have been so different. You would still be king, with Henwen at your side." And with the mention of her name he saw Vagor's eyes flicker and mellow ever so slightly. He was pleased. "I was right. You are still Vercingoral, deep down. You've come home. Breathe the air, my brother. It is clean and cold air blowing down from the mountains of Tragara."

What Delabole did not know was that his brother had been told of his wife's sad, humiliating fate, and that the news, above all else, had turned him into Vagor all those years ago. Yet, she had not entered into his thoughts again until now. As he looked out, beyond the flotilla of ships to the grey ocean, he could almost smell her scent on the breeze, and at once her face came back into his mind as clear as on the day he had first met her. Then he glanced quickly at Fillian, who seemed puzzled as to why he was delaying. His sword dropped from his lose hand, and the Emperor grew more restless. Until, that is, Vagor gathered the hapless Delabole into his arms and sped with him to the edge of the ship and tossed him overboard. Fillian rushed over to make sure that the worthless Governor had gone down with the tide, and was relieved to see that he had. He turned and when his servant knelt before him to reassure him of his obedience, he placed his hand gently onto the top of his head and all was well between them.

Twenty

The Druid Returns

It suddenly occurred to Fogle, as the last of the bricks that had for many years blocked the entrance to the 'Red Beard' tower was removed, that he had not eaten at all that day, and it was afternoon. He therefore rubbed his rumbling belly and stood back and watched as the two youngsters tossed the last of the bricks onto the pile, then wiped the sweat off their foreheads and caught their breaths, all the while glaring at Fogle furiously for not having helped at all. Fogle replied that he had been supervising them and that he was saving his energy for the climb to the top of the tower. Then he looked up and blew out his cheeks in horror at the sheer height of the thing from close range. The tower, more commonly known simply as the 'round tower', was the highest that Bosscastle had to offer, and therefore the tallest, mightiest structure in the whole of Geramond. Of course everyone knew it was there, but no-one had taken much notice of it until now, for it stood in a part of the cove that was somewhat difficult to get to due to the narrow pathway on this side of the bay.

Because of its location, unlike the buildings around the Druim Square in the centre of the fortress, the tower fell into disuse at the beginning of the second age, ultimately to be abandoned altogether following the death of Henwen. A round tower, then, with the perimeter wall running right through it. It was evident that at some point part of it must have collapsed because it was definitely a different colour from the rest. Red stone, hence its name. And it had windows in irregular places, as though they were an afterthought, for they differed in shape and size so that no two were the same. Now that he was looking closely, Fogle could see clearly that this was the most ancient part of the castle. It was certainly the most awe inspiring. But nonetheless it looked out of place where it stood and seemed to serve no function other than what it was, obviously a watchtower.

After a dozen or so attempts at forcing the thick, wooden door open with his shoulder, Galfall attempted to kick it through with his booted foot, but still to no avail. The door was so tightly lodged in its frame that they wondered why it had needed to be bricked up in the first place, for no-one could have got in. The more Galfall thumped and kicked the more agitated Fogle became, for he was aware that they were being watched by a small gathering of people on the steps, brought here by the noise echoing around the cove, and when caught on the sea breeze, being carried over the wall into the cavities of the castle. The longer it took for the door to be opened the more the group swelled until it was a crowd, watching with interest and bewilderment, informed of Fogle's search for the Boss Throne and suspecting that he had indeed found it. Then Gonosor pushed and shoved his way to the front of the throng and came down the steps and towards them with an urgency in his stride, accompanied by Crispill and three other loyal associates.

"He'll try and stop us," said Fogle, edgily. "Hurry, Galfall." The youngster kicked and shoved with renewed energy, and Salissa helped, belying her slight frame by matching Galfall blow for blow. Fogle, at last, joined in too but the door was wedged so tightly that it did not budge an inch. And Gonosor was speeding towards them. The closer they came, Fogle noticed the scroll in Crispill's hand, and he knew instinctively that their names had been placed at the top of the list.

"Open, damn it!" Fogle cursed, kicking more frantically. They all ceased their efforts when they noticed the water in the cove swelling to become forceful and menacing. When the waves crashed against the stones and went high into the air before falling and flooding the pathway, Gonosor and his party stepped back and leant against the wall, out of danger, but unable to proceed any further. Fogle, Galfall and Salissa were getting saturated too, but their bit of the path in front of the door was wider. The trapped sea seemed determined to free itself from the confines of this false bay and slapped and soaked the stone walls, so violently that Gonosor led the retreat back up the steps to safety. Then, astonishingly easily, the door gave in and opened slightly. Fogle was the first through. They shoved it closed once they were inside.

Badad was standing in the middle of the road, in front of his horse and cart, in that familiar way that suggested he was conjuring something. He lowered his arms, straitened his robes and climbed back into his seat. Carthrall, sitting next to him, was utterly befuddled. Indeed, he had never seen anything so strange in his life. But he was not afraid. There was nothing threatening about the little Druid, even though he did not much care to be in his company. At close range Badad's smell was repellent, and as the cart got underway Carthrall leant to one side and quietly wondered when those foul robes had last been washed, or his hair and beard.

Badad had made the journey from Threeshire to Bodmiffel, via the Mor Pass, a thousand times but none so energetically and heartily as this one. The sun tried its best to filter through the trees to shed light across the forest floor, and the little man was pleased that springtime had come to this part of Geramond as it had to the Shirelands. So the cart rolled on and Badad whistled to himself merrily. They then turned onto the old coast road.

"From here to the sea," said the old man. "Have you ever seen the sea? Fresher air you cannot breathe."

"I have," replied Carthrall. His voice was soft and unsure. "I went to the coast with my father ... and my brother ..." The latter part of his statement was said in a way that was intended to offend and upset the Druid.

"You don't believe me, do you?" asked Badad, sadly. At first he had tempted Carthrall away from his mother and the farm by promising to take him to his brother. Half-way through the journey, as the boy showed signs of coming to terms with his poor mother's death, he told him who he really was. And who he really was, was the King of Geramond. A farmer's boy one day and a king the next. Badad, thinking back, did not blame Carthrall for being unconvinced. He realised that, in the youngster's mind, he was just a mad old man, and that made him chortle to himself, because apart from anything else that is precisely what he was. "Soon I will be able to prove it to you." Then, mischievously: "You have the look of your mother about you."

"Don't do this to me," Carthrall sighed. "I have heard enough of your rants for one day. Just take me to my brother. He's all I've got left now."

"That he is. Tell me, young sir, do you like to go fast...?" Carthrall was puzzled. Badad cracked the reigns fiercely several times. "Like the wind, dear companion," he shouted to the horse. "Like the wind...!" Suddenly the horse jolted and quickly moved to a gallop, pulling the rickety cart behind it. The boy nearly toppled backwards but Badad steadied him. He could not, however, prevent his filthy, grey hair from blowing into Carthrall's face. Through pools of mud and over rocks, there was nothing the old road could reveal that hindered the cart's swift passage through Ingelwitt Forest, towards the sea and Bosscastle.

Fogle had been right to hoard his energy for the ascent up the tower. Not only were the steps shallow and plentiful but they spiraled upwards at a gruelling gradient, with only minimal daylight allowed in through the thin arrow slits spaced intermittently in the wall. Galfall lead the way, some five steps ahead so that he could inform his fat friend if a particular step was worn or unstable; relying more on touch and the feel of the wall then on his eyesight. The stone felt cold and the air smelt ancient; they could hear Gonosor and his gang of thugs banging at the door, but that noise became fainter the higher they climbed so that the prevailing sound was poor Fogle's beating heart and laboured breathing, like a panting wolf was following them.

Then they reached the first level and the floor opened out into a small landing with a single door. Galfall pushed it open before stepping back to allow Fogle to enter. This was not the room; it was bare except for a bed, but it did have a window so Fogle went to look out of it to check that Gonosor had not yet gained entry to the tower, and was pleased to see that he had not. He therefore used the moment to collect his breath before trotting out of the room and pushing Galfall and Salissa back up the stairwell.

Up they went, past another three landings and three similarly dull rooms. But they did notice that on every level the room was bigger and more ornately decorated. The first had contained just a bed, probably for a guard or attendant of some sort; the latest also had a bed in it, but a much more splendid one for a much more important person. Other items of furniture, too. A large desk with a seat, a dressing table and various dishes and pots for washing. The three of them entered. It was clear straight away that this new room was the finest one so far, but it had one thing in common with the others: a roughness and a sense of abandonment, as though no-one had set foot in here since the selection of Calamthor.

Cobwebs prevailed and hung in every recess. Dust dominated everything and the floor was not covered in furs or rugs but by the rubble that had fallen from the vaulted ceiling. But it was bright thanks to the large window. The shutters were wide open and flapping back and forth in the wind. Suddenly, once the door had been opened, the wind entered the room with a revived dominance and was intent on causing havoc. Fogle, as he had in the other rooms, ran to the window and peered over the edge. Gonosor and his group had gone, either away from the cove altogether or into the tower, which was more likely as Gonosor very seldom gave up once he had started on something. But the little man's sense of dread quickly faded with the realisation that they were so high up now that it would be quite a while before the Bodmifflian caught up with them. He looked out at the view. To one side the sprawling citadel as he had never seen it before, and beyond to the verdant forest. On the other side nothing but the cold, grey ocean and the thin outline of the Bodmiffel coast. He looked down again but only for a brief moment and to impress himself with how high he had climbed.

"Look at this," said Salissa, picking up a garment from in front of the window. It was silk and finely embroidered, obviously a woman's. By the way it was crumpled it had been removed in a hurry and then discarded, as though the woman never intended to wear it again. Then the girl realised the garment had been Henwen's. This was the window from which she had thrown herself into the cove. That's why the shutters were wide open. She looked out of the window and wondered what had been so bad to make the Queen throw her life down with the same abandon as her overcoat.

"I'll wait here," said Fogle, struggling to recover his poise and purpose.

"Are you all right?" asked Galfall.

"Aye, lad. I will be soon. You two go on without me. The room we're looking for can't be much higher. Fetch me when you've found it, there's a good lad."

"What if Gonosor comes?"

"I'll shout you down."

They did as they were told, climbing further until they reached the very top level, where the door to the room was only a couple of feet away from the top step. Beside the door there was a statue of King Kanance, in full armour, standing upon the giant's severed head, whose eyes were set in such a way as to suggest that it was almost grateful to have been slayed by such a mighty, valiant opponent as him. Kanance had a serene, almost benevolent look on his face, and while one hand was clutching his sword the other was outstretched as though to welcome Galfall and Salissa to the top of the tower. The staircase did go further but only up to the roof.

They paused for a while to admire the statue, and wondered why something so magnificent was not displayed in the very centre of the Druim Square, where everyone could look at it. But this place where they were now was much more ancient and venerated than the rest of the castle, and the only place a statue of Kanance could possibly be put on view. And why should anyone be allowed to see him? Only the men responsible for the enthronement of a new king ever caught his gaze, to be reminded of their responsibilities. Then Galfall switched his attention to the large, wooden door; tentatively lifted the bronze latch and pushed. He was utterly astonished, and delighted, to discover that the door was not locked.

"Perhaps the throne has been taken out!" he said to himself in a panic, but loud enough for Salissa to hear.

"No," she replied. She pointed to the inscription on the base of the statue. "Look at that." It read: 'Be you stranger or friend, you have arrived at the threshold of eternity. Enter and see it for yourself. Touch it. But unless you are my brother in blood, do not dare sit upon it. Glory and strength to my kinfolk. Death and damnation to an imposter. Enter sons of mine. Go back the stranger, unless you have a wish for a terrible death.'

Nervously, Galfall pushed the door open and stepped over the threshold. The girl followed him in. The room was quite bleak and in stark contrast to what they were expecting to see. The Throne was in the centre of the floor, facing the window. It was made of stone and had no carvings or ornaments. There were four rows of wooden benches on either side of it, obviously for onlookers to witness the enthronement of a new king. And that was all.

Galfall walked to the front of the Throne and studied it closely. How could something so plain and unexciting have been at the centre of a myth that had endured for hundreds of years? And how could simple stone contain the power to choose a king? Not for the first time since the start of his adventure, Galfall was disappointed and he felt let down. And whenever he felt like that he instantly looked for something new to look forward to. Salissa came to stand beside him and inspected the Throne for herself. Sunlight came in through the window, and when caught in her thick, black hair her true beauty was revealed again. Her clothes were still worn and tatty, but she looked stunning to the young man's eager eyes. He had liked her from the moment he had first set eyes upon her, but now, at this precise moment, he wanted her. Whereas in the past he had been inclined to hide his feelings, he had since realised that he had been denied everything he had ever desired, and that now he must help himself if what he desired was ever going to be his. She caught his gaze and returned his smile. Then he grabbed hold of her arms and jokingly pushed her towards the Throne, making her scream and wriggle in fear. He pulled her towards him with a firm grip and kissed her. Not a quick, stolen kiss but a firm, overpowering one. Salissa wriggled some more and pushed him away with equal force.

"What are you doing?" she raged, stepping away from him.

"You know I like you," he replied. "I've given you enough clues!"

"That doesn't mean you can do what you just did...!" She wiped her mouth. She was furious.

"Why not? What's the matter with me? I'm as good as you're going to get."

Realising that his reply was not impulsive but plain nasty, she was beginning to grow uneasy in his company. That arrogance that had initially repelled her had returned.

"I don't want this," she said, quietly and mostly to herself. "I'm not ready."

Galfall stepped towards her so she retreated to the door. His face did seem calmer and more sincere but she did not trust him anymore. Then his eyes glazed over, not with sadness but with fury.

"It will happen between us, Salissa," he said, pointing and wagging his finger at her. "I will make you fall in love with me. You see if I don't...!"

At that point Fogle entered the room, panting and gasping as though he was about to drop dead. He placed his hands on his knees.

"I'm about ready for the knackers' yard!" he said.

"Are you alright, Fogle?" asked Salissa, more concerned for the little fat man than for herself.

"Aye, lass. I will be once I've got me nostrils back!" He looked up and saw the Throne. "Is that it?"

"It's not much to look at," replied Galfall, speaking to Fogle but looking at the girl. His face had mellowed again and his eyes were large, so she almost felt sympathy for him, like she would have for a dog that had just bitten her and then skulked away into its corner.

Fogle stepped into the centre of the room. His joy trounced his exhaustion. "It doesn't matter what it looks like. We've found it! That's all that matters. The Druid told me to find it and I have!"

A few moments later Gonosor and Crispill burst through the open door. Crispill laughed when he saw how uneasy Fogle was now that they had caught him up, but Gonosor was enthralled by the seat in the centre of the room, and walked around it several times, without taking his eyes off it.

The road ahead was straight and long but the trees had growth on them now and therefore obscured the view ahead. Badad pulled tight on the reigns and the horse slowed down and then stopped, so he sat down.

"Tell me, my young friend ... have you had a happy childhood?" It was an unexpected and strange question, but Carthrall was prepared for anything in the company of this strange little man, so he answered quickly.

"Most of the time."

"But life must have been hard on the High Moor! Working on that farm must have been tough, yes...?"

"Hard work never killed a horse," the boy replied.

Badad found the reply amusing. "Very true." He went quiet and Carthrall knew why – he was guilty of something. Badad would have admitted that he was if the boy had asked him. "All I will say is ... I did my best for you when you were born. I took you to the right place and gave you to the best people I could find. When I presented you to Mirrial she called you her precious gift, so I knew that you would be well taken care of and that she would raise you as her own. It was important that you had a normal, decent upbringing. And all that hard work has certainly built up your muscles, which is also important."

Carthrall, at the mention of the name, began to weep into his hands. Wilfren had always told his two sons that crying was a sign of weakness so the boy tried to be as discreet as he could. Badad handed him the reigns. "What are you doing?" the boy asked.

"You are in control of our horse now, young man," replied the Druid. "And you must decide what direction we go in. Forwards takes us to Bosscastle, or we turn around and retrace our journey back to Aldwark and the High Moor! But before you make your decision, ask yourself one thing ... was what I told you about who you really are a total surprise...? Or was it something you'd known, deep in the pit of your stomach for all of your childhood?"

Carthrall did not answer straight away. He had stopped weeping and was giving good thought to the question. He thought of Mirrial and Wilfren, and of Galfall. Badad looked at him closely all the while, inspecting him for traces of his true mother and father. His observation that he looked like Henwen was true, and as he handed back the reigns the Druid realised that he was indeed Vercingoral's son as well.

"I can't go back," the boy said. "I'd be on my own."

"And is that the only reason we'll go forwards?"

Carthrall was growing tired of the old man's persistent probing and questioning.

"I can't tell you what you want to hear...!" he scowled. His face was filled with frustration and anger in equal measure. "I'm so confused. Everything that I thought was the truth has turned out to be a lie! The people that I thought were my family have turned out to be strangers. I don't know who I am anymore."

"You're the king."

Carthrall's anger was doubled by the comment. "You keep on telling me that, old man, but it means nothing to me...!"

"It will."

"Why will it?"

Badad struggled to find an instant response, even though the question was valid and urgent. Rather than offer a direct answer, he chose a different tactic. He looked again at the boy and surveyed someone who was obviously in distress. Yet, within hours he would be entering Bosscastle with him and proclaiming this wreck of a boy to be the eagerly awaited king. The saviour of the country no less. So he knew that he had to do something to calm his nerves, to somehow reassure him. Then he remembered that he had once been very honest and guileless with Henwen, and would need to be again with her son.

"You and me are the same in a way you would not believe," he said, and continued once he knew that he had the boy's attention. "Like you, I once had a different life." Carthrall looked surprised and puzzled. "You don't think I've looked like this for all my time on this earth, do you? I know what I am. How I appear to your eyes...! How bad I smell. And do you know why? Because every minute I am awake my mind is racing with thoughts of how to bring this splintered land together, so that I don't have the time or inclination to think about anything else." His face sagged and his eyes narrowed. "And I'm tired of it."

"Why let it worry you?"

"Because I have to. It is my destiny. Do you believe in destiny? To some it is just a word but to me it is my curse."

"I don't understand."

"I used to be someone else!" snapped Badad, mixing anger with his deep sadness. "I used to have a happy life. I had a wife, you know! Oh, yes. Although it's hard to believe when you look at me now." He realised that he was ranting and being totally illogical, so he paused for breath before continuing in an altogether calmer manner. "A long time ago … too long to say how many years … I used to be called Marrock. I lived, with my wife, on a smallholding in the foothills of Tragara. I was a hunter, and one day I strayed too far into the wilderness. I knew those hills like the back of my hand, but the snow fell quick and deep and covered the land so that everything I recognised vanished. I sheltered for the night in a cave and huddled in a corner to keep warm. I knew that if I went to sleep I would die, so I thought of my dear wife for I could not bare not seeing her again."

"What happened?"

"I died!"

Carthrall was confused. "But you're here now."

"Pannona, mistress of the Druids visited the cave that night and breathed fresh life into my body, but I was not the same man at all. Marrock had died. She could not change that. But she could create Badad, and give him his mission, like she had done to countless Druids before me."

Carthrall grew restless and edged away.

"So you're a ghost?"

Badad tittered. "I am flesh and blood, just like you. Marrock had been a short-legged fellow. This is his body! I have his mind and his heart still. I have his memories. And that's the very worst thing." He did not get a tear, but was close to one, so turned his face away. "I can remember my wife!"

In no time at all Badad regained his potency and his face was once again filled with energy and vitality. "My curse has been my mission!" Then he gave more thought to his statement. "No, not my mission. That is an honorable cause. But its success is reliant on people to do what's right. So the people have been my curse. Most of them at any rate. What I'm saying is … I was created for a sole function, and so were you. If I chose to turn away from the path that is set down in front of me, I would be forsaken and would spend my days on this earth wrecked with shame and regret, and so would you be...!"

"What would you have me do?" asked Carthrall, whilst inwardly frightened of the Druid's response, but trying hard not to let it show.

"Embrace your new life," Badad replied quickly, as though he had been waiting for the question. "Without fear or dread of the days that lay ahead."

"I wish I was back on the farm."

"Do not assume that an ordinary life will make you immune from the evils of the world. If the events of recent years have taught us anything, it's that the vortex of war takes all men up in its violent swirl, not just kings! Wilfren was an ordinary man." Badad was blunt and forceful with his reply. "And so is Fogle...!"

"Who's he...?"

"Precisely! He's a blacksmith from Woldshire, and yet he will be your most loyal and obedient subject ... your defender and your champion in your hours of need, as he was mine."

It was difficult for Carthrall to imagine that the Druid had ever had such an hour. There was something about the little man that instilled in the boy strength and courage, like that was his sole purpose after all, and not what he'd said.

"We must be on our way, old man. Will we reach the castle before sundown?"

Badad, gripping the reins tightly again, smiled with joy and pride. "Oh, we may yet," he said. And the cart set off. "Tell me, my young friend ... have you ever wondered what the world would be like if you'd never been born? I mean, how would it be different if you'd never existed...?"

Carthrall, modestly but honestly, replied:

"I don't think it would be different at all."

"Something is going to happen to you that will change that forever," Badad replied. Then suddenly the trees seemed to thin out and the road before them was straight and clear. In the distance, towering above the green land like a vision of another world, was Bosscastle, swollen with arrogance in the spring sunshine. Carthrall gasped with wonder and then gulped with consternation. Badad's path may have been blighted and cursed but his was unswervingly visible.

Gonosor was sitting on a bench to the side of the Throne, leaning forwards and resting his head on his hand, his eyes were riveted on the grey stone, whilst all other eyes were fixed on him for they could see that he was utterly fascinated by the object.

"I never truly believed that it existed at all," Gonosor mumbled. "And now here it is in front of me, for my own eyes to see. An item of myth made real! It is a relic of a dim and distant age; irrelevant and ultimately useless!" He began to giggle excitedly, and looked at Fogle, which made the little man even more uneasy. "You have wasted all this time searching for a seat that none of us can actually sit on…!" Then he returned his gaze to the Throne. "But I wonder … does it contain the power legend purports it to have, or is that the myth after all and not the Throne itself…? There's only one way to find out. Does anyone care to try it out…?"

Galfall and Salissa stepped back, out of his reach. "Why don't you try it, Gonosor," Fogle said. "After all, you're the only one here of royal descent, and if anyone has the right to sit on a throne it is surely the son of a king…!" Gonosor stood up quickly and walked around the Throne, stretching out his arm but not courageous enough to actually touch it He thought about what Fogle had said, and wondered what would happen if he did sit on it. Would he stand a chance of being selected himself?

What a wondrous thing it would be to be proven right after all. A glorious end to all those sorrowful years he had spent as a banished prince. And now, not only a king of Bodmiffel but also of the Shiremen and of all the people of Geramond. Fogle would be made to yield to his authority, and the Druid, if the Throne selected Gonosor as the next king. And then he remembered his history. The forest kings had long since abandoned their claim to be the legitimate heirs of Calamthor. Their first Lord, Maldorc, had perished in his pursuit of the glory of the Throne, for he was not related by blood to Calamthor and was therefore ejected from the seat in a violent fashion. But then Gonosor wondered if that was just legend, and therefore the Throne would be docile and he could deceive the people into believing he had been selected. But was he prepared to take that risk? He did think long and hard about it.

"My Lord, we need to be quick about what we came up here to do," Crispill snorted. "Let's arrest these rogues and get them hanging by nightfall!"

Galfall, realising that he was referring to himself and Fogle, was taken aback. "You mean we're on that list of yours...?"

"Of course we are," Fogle said to him. "I don't know about Salissa, but me and you for sure."

"Why? What have we done?"

"You are troublemakers!" Crispill retorted immediately. "Disturbers of the peace!" Emboldened by the scroll he grasped tightly in his hand, as though it was the official law of the land, he stepped towards the two Shiremen. "When your people returned to their own homes in the north, this land began to revert to something like it used to be before the Repecians invaded us. Ordered and obedient. The people of Bodmiffel looked to our Lord Gonosor to take up his rightful position amongst them ... that of their king! Then you returned and now the whole of Bosscastle is giddy with excitement because of all your talk of finding the Boss Throne so that the new king can be chosen!"

"Is that the best you could come up with, Crispill?" Fogle said, scornfully.

Gonosor had gone to the window and was looking down on the crowds below, that stretched back to the entrance to the cove and then swelled into one huge throng of people that packed into the Druim Square.

"Let's give them something to see," he mumbled to himself. Crispill, hoping that he had given the order to arrest Fogle and Galfall, urged his master to repeat his statement more clearly. "I said let's give the people something to see!" Then he grabbed hold of Crispill by the tops of his arms and forced him back until he lost his footing against the base stone and toppled back into the Throne.

Apart from Gonosor, the rest of them gasped at the same time, but more through exhilaration than horror. Crispill immediately turned frigid, as though the throne had a mind and so if he kept perfectly still it would not know that he was sitting on it. Seconds passed that seemed like hours, and after a while he dared to believe that he was right, or even that the throne was not as powerful as some people believed. Seconds turned into minutes and still nothing happened. Fogle recalled the account of Boso, and concluded that his writings were fabricated and untrustworthy. Gonosor was angry that he had not chanced to sit upon the throne himself, for now the others would be proclaiming him to be the new king.

Then, like Maldorc before him, Crispill suddenly felt a jolt of pain shoot through his entire body to settle in his head, and let out a shriek of raw pain, that seemed to sap his energy and he flopped over the arm of the seat. It looked as though he was dead, so Gonosor prodded him, but as the tip of his finger touched the baggy cloth of his shirt Crispill came back to life and sat upright before standing up and stepping clear of the Throne, all the while clasping his head in his hands and gasping for dear breath. The others stepped away from him; Gonosor to the window and the others towards the door. The noise coming out of Crispill's mouth was like nothing any of them had heard before. A screech of anguish that was so high pitched that it hurt their ears. The poor man turned to each of them to plead for their help and assistance but none of them were willing. He parted his lips to speak but instead of words a thick cloud of gas escaped from his mouth and hovered around him; reddish in colour and odourless, but swirling about his whole body like chains to seal his fate. Eyes that were once full of mischief were now glowing red with pain and despair. His skin was blistering all over his body as though his blood was boiling. The slightest breath he could muster was enough to ignite the gas so that it burst into flames; then his whole body combusted and in an instant Crispill was gone to be replaced by a ball of fire. He stumbled to the window and threw himself out. The cold water of the cove extinguished him but he was already dead. Gonosor looked down and saw that the water in the cove was agitated more than it should have been, and as Crispill's body bobbed to the surface it was suddenly and violently taken down again, and did not reappear.

Then Gonosor's attention was pulled away from the swelling water below him to the crowd in the Square. He could hear a distant and tentative rumble of applause and saw a commotion at the edge of the mob. Fogle, aware that Gonosor had seen something, came to the window. The Bodmifflian's instinctive reaction was to block the little man from looking, but then with a second thought he realised that such an action was futile now.

"It's the Druid," he said.

Fogle was instantly filled with joy and stimulation. "Is the King with him?"

"I can't see," replied Gonosor. Then his face dropped even further and he released a deep sigh. "Yes ... there is someone with him."

Galfall sped towards the window but Fogle pushed him back. "Go down and welcome the Druid, my boy. Bring him up here." The youngster was more than pleased with his function. He looked at Fogle with such a flush of anticipation that gave transparency to his thoughts. "Yes, Galfall. You shall be the first to greet the new king."

As more and more people became aware that Badad had returned the cart was overwhelmed by the density of the crowd, so that the two of them disembarked and walked the rest of the way. The Druid held Carthrall firmly by the arm. The ripple of applause which Gonosor had heard had been the initial, spontaneous reaction of the first people who had noticed Badad's presence amongst them, but that had now faded and the mob had fallen silent, allowing their eyes to do the work of their mouths. They watched as Badad and Carthrall gradually cut a pathway through the Square towards the cove. They were waiting for an announcement of some sort but Badad was not ready to oblige them. Carthrall was his priority, and he leaned towards him and whispered: "Be strong."

Such was the interest now that the crowd around them grew denser and the boy actually felt quite threatened by it. When he had agreed to come to Bosscastle, even as they approached the gate, he had not expected a reaction like this. Badad could sense Carthrall's deep unease, so ushered him through the mob like a shepherd would a lamb through a field of wolves. However, he also allowed himself to indulge his mind in contemplating the possible outcome of the day: his own demise and the long awaited end to his toil and labour. He had dared to believe that he had completed his task once before, at Kaw when the boy at his side was conceived, but events then contorted against him and so it went on. And in his heart he knew that the course of his endeavour would once again twist in a new direction, but that it would be a short one this time, for the conclusion of the great event of the age was nigh. He did not linger too long on that particular notion, however, for he also knew that it would be a bloody and violent final stage. There would be no whimper. This Third Age was not about to go quietly into the annals of history. What was about to happen in the forthcoming days would be the vastest, most distressing event of them all.

The question was, would he need to be involved? While he suspected that he would, there was nevertheless just a remote possibility that the fair Lady would come to collect him. Or not. Another thought snapped into his mind, that Pannona may have abandoned him altogether. It was an irrational fear, he knew that, but it seemed very real to him then and there, and a testament to the fact that his end was close.

They finally arrived at the entrance to the cove and pushed and shoved their way down the steps. At the bottom they saw an arm sticking in the air with the obvious purpose of grabbing their attention, so they stopped. But as soon as their swift momentum came to a halt, they were separated. Carthrall took on a look of panic as his eyes darted frantically for the Druid, but the next face he saw was actually even more familiar to him. Galfall, upon seeing his brother, was at first puzzled and then edgy and concerned. Carthrall, however, was gleeful and excited.

"What's happened?" Galfall demanded. "Has something happened to our mother? Where's Badad?" The rapid succession of his questions did not allow Carthrall the chance to reply.

Badad emerged from the crowd. "Here I am. I'm here," he said.

Galfall addressed his questions at him. "What's going on? Has something happened? Why is he here?" His tone suggested that he was not altogether pleased to see his brother, or be reminded of any part of his former life. "We were expecting you to return with the King!"

"And so I have, young Gringell," replied Badad, and placed his hand on Carthrall's shoulder. At first Galfall did not realise what the gesture was intended to mean. Then when it began to occur to him he became confused and when it finally sunk in it was like all the fresh breath had been sucked out of his lungs, his heart thumped against the wall of his chest and all of the colour drained out of his face. After a moment or two he began to laugh.

"Have you gone totally insane, old man?" he said, revived once he'd had chance to compose himself. "This is my brother. He's no king!" Badad was aware that the others were listening and hanging on every word Galfall muttered.

Carthrall, though, fully understood his brother's bewilderment and initial amusement. He had had the same reaction when the Druid first started to explain things to him.

"I know! It's incredible! I don't fully understand myself. All I know it that I wanted to come here and find you. Mirrial's dead, Galfall."

The final part of Carthrall's reply took Galfall by surprise and any remaining joviality was lost to remorse and sadness. However, Galfall and his mother had never been close and he was only slightly more sad than on the occasion of his father's death. Grief was quickly overtaken by the more pressing matter of his brother's sudden appearance.

"I understand. You were on your way here to find me when the Druid picked you up." It suddenly made sense to him. "On the way he's brainwashed you! He's warped your mind into believing what he's telling you is the truth! It's all lies, Carthrall. One of his tricks!"

"There's only one way to find out!" Badad snarled, angered by Galfall's impudence and mindful that other people were listening, picking out Galfall's comments and growing restless. "Where is Fogle?"

Galfall realised what the Druid intended and protested.

"You can't do it to him! I've seen what that thing can do to people who pretend to be someone they're not. You'll kill him, Badad. But I won't let you!"

His patience all spent, Badad took hold of the youth by the neck and forced him back, all the while demanding that first he be quiet and then he take them to where Fogle was, for he knew that the throne would be there too.

Twenty-One

The Throne Decides

Their footsteps were heard before they were seen, then they appeared at the top of the staircase and came into the Throne Room. Fogle reacted excitedly; Gonosor with trepidation while Salissa was curious. Badad pushed Carthrall to the fore, and instinctively Fogle gasped with astonishment. He had expected the King to be in his father's ilk; strong and robust, immeasurable and rousing; but what he had was a boy, puny and gaunt, pretty and palpable. He was disappointed. Salissa, however, offered the courtesy of bowing her head.

"Stop it," Galfall told her. "You're making a fool of yourself."

Gonosor laughed; Fogle was appalled. Galfall knew that he had to explain. "This is not the King! This is my brother! We grew up together so I know who he is. Badad picked him up on his way to find me. He never did have a king to bring us so he has bewitched Carthrall. It's completely ridiculous. The Druid is deceiving you all."

Gonosor, liking what he was hearing, stepped forwards. "And not for the first time," he said. "For he has deceived and bewitched people before. My sister for one, who would never have betrayed her own folk had he not meddled with her mind. He tricked her into believing she was in love with that foreign king. And he turned my father's mind against me, so I was banished to Baladorn and denied my birthright, so that he could impose his will on those with lesser minds than I!"

Badad, once again, tilted his head and raised his eyes. "I am so tired of them all," he sighed. "I have done what you asked of me, my Lady. You can ask no more." And he waited, but this time she did not answer.

Meanwhile, Gonosor had turned his attention on Carthrall, and saw a familiar face staring back. Soft and kind, but set within a frame of iron, and so he began to doubt his own reasoning but did not say so.

"Is it true, Badad?" asked Fogle.

Badad sighed ever deeper, his disappointment confounded with Fogle's involvement.

"I will not explain myself here and now," he replied sadly. "I have explained my actions to the one person who deserved to know, and will not do so again to people who do not. This boy is the rightful King. Whether or not he was brought up in the Gringell household is neither here nor there! His blood is pure and his heart is good. And those qualities are all that the old throne requires." He glowered at the Bodmifflian. "And he knows it! Look at him. He has seen his sister in this boy. Ask him. He cannot deny it with a semblance of truth." Gonosor turned away and refused to acknowledge the Druid's statement. "Now, Galfall has told me that he has seen the workings of this throne for himself, which means that someone must have tested it. Who and why?"

"He was a troublemaker," Salissa said. "Who did not believe it was as powerful as people thought and so tested it for himself." Gonosor tried to stifle a guilty expression. Up until now he had afforded the girl very little of his attention, but he was nonetheless thankful that she had not told Badad what had really happened to poor, misplaced Crispill, for he was distrustful of the little man still and knew that he could lose his tongue again at any time the Druid wished or thought necessary. He did not want to go back to being a mute, especially at a time like this.

"I'm pleased you've all seen what this thing does to bogus men for you now know what to expect if he's one ..." He pushed Carthrall into the centre of the room, and quite forcibly so the boy stubbed his foot against the base of the Throne. "And if it does not happen you shall know that he's genuine." Now he glowered at Fogle. "And that I am to be trusted after all...!"

"He'll die, Fogle," Galfall pleaded.

"Sit on the throne, my young friend," Badad instructed Carthrall.

"Don't let him do it," Galfall persisted.

Then all eyes, including Badad's, fell on the fat Shireman. Fogle thought quickly though not clearly. Wilfren had told him once that he possessed many great qualities but none of them were ever present when there was a decision to be made. Nevertheless, he convinced himself that if the boy was Galfall's brother there was no way he could possibly be the longed for King. And by reaching that conclusion he knew he was doubting Badad's motives, or worse, questioning his sanity altogether. So guilt filled his round, flushed face as he took hold of the boy by the arm and gently eased him away from the throne.

Badad, rather than infuriated, was irritated. The easiest thing would have been to force the boy into the Throne and be done with it, but doubt was not a strange emotion to him either, and he was full of it now. If he did compel Carthrall to sit on the throne, and nothing happened, all well and good; but if he was wrong, if this boy was not the proper King, then he would be responsibly for his death. A murderer no less. Worse than that, everything he had ever believed would be proven wrong. So for him, as much as for Carthrall or for all the people of Geramond, this was a critical moment of faith.

Silence ensued. Awkward faces and a sense of disappointment and anti-climax. Then Gonosor spoke. He pointed at the Druid.

"None of you, except for him, ever knew my sister!" he began. Badad wondered what he was up to for he distrusted him just as much. "She possessed a beauty that defied creation itself, yet my father used to say that she had a nose that was too small for the rest of her face...!" He grabbed Carthrall from Fogle's grasp. "And so has he!" Then lifted him off the ground by the waist, carried him to the throne and lowered him into it. The others gasped with fright. Badad, quietly, was pleased.

The Druid instructed them all to be seated in the stalls, then joined them. No one uttered a word or dared to allow their breaths to be heard. Carthrall sat rigid in the seat, as Crispill had before him. They waited. Nothing happened. Fogle caught sight of Galfall and saw him sitting forwards, with his head in his hands and therefore not watching. Salissa's eyes were transfixed on the throne, her breathing was short and deep and her body was charged with excitement. Badad, on the front stall, was calm but poised to react when, if, the deed was completed. Gonosor seemed to be the most relaxed, sitting as he was with his boot resting on the bench in front. Then Fogle's bench snapped in the middle and they all jumped in shock, and Fogle was sent to the ground. Salissa chastised him. Carthrall glanced across and braved a smile.

And they waited. Galfall began to realise that his brother had been sitting on the throne for longer than Crispill had, and began to wonder. A strange sound came through the doorway. Louder as it got closer, like the wind but with a growl to it. Footsteps, coming up the staircase. A gust of wind entered the room, so strong that they had to hold onto their benches to save themselves from being tossed like rags to the back of the room. A vortex of what looked like dust to their eyes blew up from the floor and spun around the boy, before moving away. Its form collapsed, not completely, but to make shapes of men, as though they had been present all along but only now, covered in the dust, were they visible.

Not just men, but obviously kings of men. A dozen or so in the room and numerous more outside in the hallway. Grey shadows, surrounding Carthrall and stretching out their arms and fingers to touch him. He was rigid with terror, but managed to look into their faces. While they were not exactly horrible they were fearsome and angry. He looked at their bodies. While they were most certainly not living now they had clearly been proper men once; but not made of flesh anymore, just tatty rags that covered their ancient bones; faint spectres of what they once were, and more exposed the thicker the dust settled upon them, making their lower halves the faintest. Men of varying ages; some very old, others strong men and one or two no older than he was.

Each one was a vortex of dust and it occurred to Carthrall that it was these swirling clouds that made them manifest, therefore they could surely not harm him physically. They had another thing in common: a fascination with the boy, and some tried to prod him and brought their wisened faces close. One of them stepped away from the throne, a tall man who had been cut down in his prime, by the looks of him. Helmeted and heavily cloaked, with sword in hand. His eyes searched around the room before settling on Badad, who considerately lowered his head for he knew that this particular spectre was none other than Kanance, the oldest of them all, not in years or appearance but due to the length of time since his death. Galfall, too, recognised him from the statue that guarded the entrance to this room.

"Why have we had to wait so long?" the ghost snarled, his voice gravelly and tinged with a strange, foreign accent. "Any of the heirs of Lamorak could have claimed this prize…!"

"The heirs of Maldorc prevented them from coming here," Badad replied, shielding his eyes from the dust.

"There is another, still alive, who should occupy this seat before the one you have presented to us," said Kanance.

"Alive in flesh only. His mind and soul were lost many years ago," Badad told him.

"Then you would have us pass him up for this mere boy?"

"The boy is heir to both Lamorak and Maldorc. He can unite your people again."

Kanance and the others huddled together to discuss the matter, and whispers filled the room. All the vortexes then joined together to once again form one swirling mass of dust, that completely engulfed Carthrall so that he disappeared from sight. So they all grew agitated and Galfall rose to his feet, fearful for his brother and brave enough to try to save him. Then he was blown off his feet and was sent hurling to the back of the room, only stopping when he hit the wall, otherwise he would have gone on forever. Fogle grabbed hold of Salissa's arm to save her from going the same way, then pulled her to the ground where the wind was not so strong. That's where Gonosor already was, safely underneath his bench. Badad, though, had remained seated and his arms were outstretched as though to embrace and welcome the wind; and in any case he was so short that the gusts went over the top of him. The vortex swirled ever faster and they wondered what could possibly be happening to the poor boy within it. His adornment or his termination?

The vortex suddenly collapsed and the spirits drifted out of the room as quickly as they had entered it; the wind went with them and everything went calm at last. Badad tentatively stepped towards the throne. Carthrall, he had noticed, had been adorned with a crown. Not an elaborate, bejewelled thing but a plain, silver band in the old style. But his eyes were tightly shut and his body seemed to be deprived of breath and life, as though the spirits had sucked it all out of him. The others, realising that whatever mysterious power had been in the room with them had gone, came out from their hiding places. Galfall, assuming his brother to be dead, forgot about his own aching back and ran over to him and shook him until breath entered the boy's lungs and his chest bellowed and he opened his eyes, to the vast relief of the Druid.

So, in the dim twilight of a spring evening, as the darkness and shadows ensued, they had their king. But any sense of achievement was tapered by the boy's obvious exhaustion and bemusement. Badad turned to Fogle and his face was at once ignited with delight. All animosity between them was forgotten as he said: "We have our King!" Then they linked arms and jigged and skipped around the room together. Salissa went to the throne and knelt before Carthrall and lowered her head with obedience and respect. Badad, dancing still, noticed her gesture, and so did Galfall. His face was ignited with annoyance and indifference. Moreover, now that he knew that Carthrall was not his brother after all, he was consumed with anger and felt deceived by Wilfren and Mirrial. But his overriding emotion at this time was envy. Worse still, he resented the attention Carthrall was getting. All of their lives the younger brother had attracted and cultivated the attention of his parents, whilst he had always been cast aside and given little thought. Now Fogle and the Druid were drawn into Carthrall's half-light. And Salissa, too, without any regard for him or what he might be feeling. And if they had been alone in this room, knowing what he did now, Galfall would surely have killed him to be rid of the troublesome boy once and for all. But instead he ran out of the room and went down the stairs.

Only Gonosor noticed. He had not been sure how to react, so he did nothing at first. Then Badad went to the window and shouted down to the vast crowd at the foot of the tower: "We have our King!" And the crowd responded with a cheer so loud and spontaneous that it seemed real, travelled back from the tower to fill the whole of Bosscastle. The people, like Badad and Fogle, danced and celebrated. The Miffel Drums pounded once again and someone, somewhere, sounded the Shire Horn. Gonosor could hear the commotion and knew that any resistance to the new king was futile. In any event, here was Henwen's son. Her own blood. Raised a Shireman, true, but with enough of his mother about him to learn to love the ways of the Forested lands. No, this was no foreign king, but their own. Amidst cheers, the sound of the drums and the horn: the forth age of Geramond was ushered in in good style.

Twenty-Two
Terrible Vengeance

The chilly night air was filled with the sound of singing and jollity. As before, after the end of the Repecian regime, Druim Square was full of people dancing around fires. Happy people, but this time celebrating the start of something they had longed for rather than the demise of something they had detested. The new King was sitting on the balcony of the Great Hall, with the others, and those people at the base of the steps and therefore close enough to see, could not take their eyes off him for they could barely believe that he was there at all. And the fact that he was still so young did not detract from their enthusiastic admiration. All the better, in fact, for they knew that he would rule them for a long time to come, unlike an aged king who would have died before they'd had chance to get used to him. So the Druid's words were repeated over and over:

"We have our King!" Uppermost in Carthrall's mind was where Galfall had disappeared to. Whilst the others were enjoying the music and the sight of the people rejoicing, he was preoccupied with why his brother had reacted like he did.

"Has anyone seen him?" he asked.

"He'll be back soon enough," Fogle said, as he tapped his foot and clapped his hands to the beat.

"He's annoyed because no-one's attention is on him anymore," Salissa added. She was sitting next to Carthrall.

Gonosor, sitting further along, next to the Druid, was annoyed by her comment.

"Who is this girl? What gives her the right to be sitting here, in our company?"

"The same thing that gives me the right," Fogle replied, whilst looking at the girl kindly to allay her fears. "She has done her bit."

"How?"

"She saved Galfall's life for a start. And then she took him to the Western Gate and showed great courage there as she tried to distract the guards…"

"But Galfall did not open the gate," the Bodmifflian retorted. "The Druid never intended him to!"

"They did not know that. Salissa risked her life for our cause. Isn't that right, Badad?" Badad, though, had not been listening. He seemed distracted, and rose from his seat and stepped to the front of the balcony. How tired he looked now. He tilted his head and put his ear to work, and even above the din of the party he could hear something. Fogle was puzzled.

"What is it?"

"He's back," the Druid replied, sadly.

"Who's back? Galfall's back?"

Badad turned. His face, as well as tired, was set with terror. "Fillian's back!"

So terror spread over their faces too, except for Carthrall's, who did not fully understand the extent of the Druid's statement.

Under the shroud of darkness, ten Repecian war galleys approached the castle, before the swell of the sea prevented them from getting any closer. The slow beat of a drum guided them in and when it stopped the ships' oars were pulled in and their anchors were dropped. Punil, on the first ship, looked down the line to make sure they were all straight and still.

"Is this close enough?" he asked his skipper. The skipper confirmed that it was.

"Projectile is ready!" bellowed the man at the front of the ship, next to the ballista. Punil inspected it. The missile, a huge boulder, was in its sling and the cables were straight and tight, so he stepped away. Similar calls emanated from the other ships, fainter as they came from further down the line. Punil was satisfied.

"On the fifth beat, bring this castle tumbling down…!" he said, and instructed the drummer to begin. The beats were deep and certain. An arm was raised and when the fifth and final beat was counted, brought down swiftly. The cable was severed and the ballista was unleashed and the Emperor's vengeance was underway. All ten ships released at the same time. The force of the act made them sink at the front but they were buoyant enough to come back up and steady again. With a whoosh and a whistle, ten spheres of rock were sent hurling towards Bosscastle. All ten hit, and were heavy enough the shatter the wall. Stones fell into the sea but the ships were far enough away not to be too troubled by the disturbance in the water. All ten ballistas were reloaded with speed and ruthless efficiency as Punil looked upon the damage with great satisfaction.

The party in the square was brought to an abrupt end. One minute they were dancing and singing, the next, after ten separate blasts had slung shards of stone upon their heads, they were running for their lives, scattering in all directions but mainly swelling at the steps of the Great Hall, where their King was. Surveying the damage, Badad and the others saw that some of their kind had already fallen foul of Fillian's weapon, lying abandoned in the square as everyone else panicked and fled. Carthrall was dumbfounded and quietly hoped that no-one expected him to have a solution. Fogle was deeply sad that the blood and guts of the people were still being shed, even now that the King was in place. Gonosor, though animated with rage, was nonetheless helpless.

Then another ten missiles hit Bosscastle. Six smashed into the wall, three into the Bossmilliad and one went through an existing hole and entered the citadel proper; with nothing to stop it until it ran out of momentum and it dropped down on the people beneath it, crushing them and filling everyone else with utter fear. The stampede for safety was actually killing more than the missiles. Screams and howls of anguish prevailed.

"What can we do?" asked Carthrall, himself afraid and fearful for his life.

"We must abandon the castle," said Badad.

Gonosor was objectionable. "We cannot!"

"It's the only thing we can do!" Fogle added.

"We've only just got it back!"

"Then let the King decide," said Badad.

Carthrall retreated when everyone looked at him for his response, then took a deep intake of breath.

"Will we all perish if we stay?"

"Oh, yes, my Lord," said Badad. "The Repecians intend to destroy Bosscastle."

Without hesitation Carthrall said: "Then we must leave."

"Is that your instruction?" asked Gonosor.

"It is," replied the King.

"ABANDON THE CITADEL!!" roared Gonosor. His voice boomed across the square so that everyone could hear him. And those that had not yet made for the gate did so with urgent speed.

"Yes, yes," the Bodmifflian said to himself. "As before, we shall take to the forest to defend our country."

Many people did not make it. Even as Bosscastle was being evacuated the missiles continued to smash into the ancient stones, killing them indiscriminately; women, children and men. Fires continued to burn but no-one was there to tend to them, so they burned out of control and caught hold of anything that could sustain them. They retreated to Ingelwitt, and Fogle was dismayed to find himself back in the heart of that forest in the exact place where he had set up his camp of rebels before the fall of Bosscastle. That event seemed like distant history now. How quickly things change, he thought. He was so disheartened that he could not bear to spend the night there, so left the others behind and found his way to the place where the trees thinned out to present a view across the valley to the fortress. Badad, who had seen him leave, followed him.

The black sky was lit up by the monstrous fire that now engulfed Bosscastle. And he could hear those missiles still crashing into the stones, even though there was no-one left inside to dislodge or maim. His heart sank with every thud and crunch. Badad moved to stand beside him. Fogle was not surprised to see him there, but did quickly spare a thought to how old and tired he looked.

"It is the worst night," said the Druid.

"So many men are dead ... for nothing," replied Fogle, sadly. "What a waste of time it's all been! In a week or so we'll be worse off than when we started."

"Would you give up your liberty so easily?"

Fogle looked at the little man sharply. "We can't fight another war, Badad. There's no fight left in any of us. Even in Gonosor, and that's saying something...!" Badad winced with fatigue. Fogle noticed but did not comment.

"This time it's different," said the Druid.

"How?"

"We have our king!"

"He's just a boy."

"But the people will fight for him."

"They fought for another, better king, at High Cleugh ... and still lost. Face it ... we're done for. There is no more hope. But you're right about one thing ... it is different this time. Years ago, Fillian came here to conquer us ... now he's come back to destroy us completely...!" He gestured for the Druid to dare to glance across to the burning castle. "Look at what they're doing!"

Badad cringed. "I see it. But I can't stop it."

Fogle was shocked.

"You've got to help us, Badad," he affirmed, quite gruffly. "If there's any hope at all then it's you."

"Don't place such a burden on a decrepit old man."

"You're the same man you were when you first arrived in this forest and promised me that better things were ahead. Well, where are they, eh...?"

The fact was, Badad knew that there was something that he could do, but doubted whether he still possessed sufficient power to be able to do it properly, or at all. Since Carthrall's enthronement he had felt tired and drained of all his energy. He felt old, like all his years were finally catching him up all at once. He felt mortal again, as though his wrecked body could give in at any moment, and in a way he hoped that it would. But Pannona had not come for him, so he knew that he had work still to do.

As they turned to return to the camp the sky opened and released its rain. Fogle took shelter beneath a full tree. Badad joined him. They looked across to the castle and saw that the inferno was now involved in a contest with the rain storm.

"I knew you could do something," said Fogle, daring to break cover and run back to where the others were.

Badad was bemused.

"That wasn't me," he mumbled, then followed him.

The heaviest of the rain passed quickly to leave the air damp and drizzly. The people of Bosscastle were dispersed throughout the forest, not just around the periphery of the clearing. They were all wet and exhausted, touched in one way or another by the events of the night. Mainly quiet and subdued. Sleep was had only by a few. Those within the clearing picked themselves up off the ground when they saw Badad and Fogle return. Carthrall was also pleased to see them. Gonosor, though, was his usual, plain-spoken self.

"Well ... what have the pair of you decided that we ought to do...?"

"Is the castle burning still?" inquired Carthrall. He was genuinely concerned, even though he had spent just one afternoon and evening in the place. His instincts served him well enough to realise just how much the place meant to his people, and how the sight of it being raised to the ground was affecting them.

"The rain will not have extinguished the fire," Fogle replied.

Gonosor groaned with rage. He pulled his beard. "We cannot stand idly by while Bosscastle burns...!"

"It's a diversion," said Badad, loud enough for only those standing next to him to hear. He did not want everyone else to hear what he had to say. "Fillian knew that if he attacked the castle we would either flee for our lives or be foolish enough to try to defend it. In any case, we have been oblivious to what has really been happening these last few hours ... the landing of the main part of the Repecian army."

"Where?" asked Carthrall.

"Bossiney," replied Gonosor. "The only natural harbour on this southern coastline. Five miles from here."

"More soldiers than he brought with him sixteen years ago?" Fogle inquired.

"I would imagine so," Badad said.

"What happens now?" Carthrall asked.

"If we delay any longer he will gain the foothold he needs to push further inland and once again cut a swathe of devastation through your country." He paused. "But if I could only have a day or two …"

"You've got a trick up your sleeve, Druid," said Fogle. "Mind if I ask what it is?"

"I don't know yet," Badad replied. "That's why I need the time." Of course he did know what he intended to do but did not care to divulge it to the others for they would be more scared of that than of Fillian's army.

"Then we'll have to give him a reason to stick around here, won't we…?" said Carthrall.

"Yes …" Gonosor blasted happily. "That's the son of Henwen talking…! You're right, my Lord. We'll march to Bossiney and find out what he has to say for himself…!" Then he roared with laughter.

Fogle was more cautious. "Wait a minute. We can't possibly defeat Fillian in battle. If we go to Bossiney it will be like committing mass suicide."

"It will give the Druid the time he needs," said Carthrall.

"It's the only option," Badad told them. Then he placed his hand on the boy's shoulder. "All that you have to do now is convince your people to follow you there."

Carthrall's confident expression disappeared following the Druid's instruction. And he was unnerved by everyone looking at him, so he skulked away into the trees.

"What is it, my Lord?" asked Salissa, who had seen him separate from the others so had followed him.

"Stop calling me that!" he snapped. "Yesterday I was plain Carthrall and now I'm everyone's lord and master!"

"You're our king!"

"I don't want to be. I wish I'd never come here! I should have stayed in Aldshire where I truly belong."

She could tell from his tone that he did not mean what he was saying and realised that the Druid must have said something that had unsettled him.

"What's going to happen?" she said.

"Have you seen Galfall?" he asked her. She was taken aback. Why would she have seen him when no-one else had?

"No, my Lord."

"Call me Carthrall," he instructed her. "He should be here, with me when I need him."

"Why do you need him?"

He looked at her and saw the same, grimy beauty that his brother had seen.

"Why are you on your own, Salissa?" he asked. It was another question that took her by surprise. "Where are your family?"

Galfall, she remembered, had asked her the same question shortly after he had arrived in her home, but at the time she did not wish to discuss the matter with him. Now it was different. Carthrall was not like Galfall in any way. He was quieter and unassuming with not a trace of his brother's arrogance. She liked him and because he was her king, trusted him. So her face took on a gloomy expression as she began to explain.

"My mother's dead. My father … well, I don't know whether he's alive or not. You see, when I was nine years old, the Governor decided that he would be sold as a slave. That's what happened down here." She turned from sad to bitter. "Evil things happened all the time, to anyone. We bore the brunt of the Governor's vicious regime." She stepped closer to him so that he could see the anger in her face. He turned his face away, shyly, but as though he was glancing back to the camp. "When the day came to take him to the boat my mother tried to save him. Well, not save him exactly, she just wouldn't let go of his legs! So a guard pulled her off him and then stabbed her with his dagger. I was there … I saw it happen. People wanted to help her but they daren't. They just left her where she fell to bleed to death. But what's worse is that so did I. I was too afraid to go over to her so I ran home instead. Later that night I dared to go back to the cove but her body had gone. To this day I don't know where it went." She drew a deep breath into her lungs. "That's why I loathe the Repecians with every ounce of energy I have. It's why I risked my life to help Galfall, and why I'll help you. I can't bare the thought of them coming back. I'll do anything I can to stop them … even fight."

"You may have to," he scoffed. "The Druid has instructed me to say or do something that'll make the other men follow me into battle. But I've only been King for a day and I don't know what kings do to inspire their people. Anyway ... to their eyes I'm just a boy. They won't listen to me."

She realised that he genuinely felt sorry for the predicament he found himself in, and understood why he lacked the confidence to do as the Druid instructed; why he had run into the darkness of the forest. They could hear the murmur of the busy camp and could see the fires and torches twinkling in the mist. They were his own people now, yet were strangers to him.

She offered what little advice she could.

"Just say what you feel. And don't make the mistake of thinking that you have to appear to be brave and bold. No-one is that anymore. But whatever you decide to do, don't wait around here for too long. A boy or not, you are the one person everyone is waiting for. Speak to them tonight and see what happens. If it ends up that you and I go into battle on our own then so be it."

Shortly after that they both returned to the hub of the camp. Fogle offered the boy a reassuring smile and placed a friendly hand against his back and nudged him into the centre of the crowd. By now Carthrall was getting used to being pushed and shoved to where other people wanted him to be. It seemed to be an integral part of his new job, to be cajoled and prodded. Gonosor wanted him to stand on a rock so that everyone could see him, and once again he felt compelled to oblige. The very rock Badad had stood on when he had announced to the rebels that his arrival signalled the beginning of the end of the rebellion, and then exhibited Gonosor's tongue to prove the end of the strife that had plagued this land for so many years. A fact that was not lost on the Bodmifflian, who therefore kept his mouth firmly closed and guarded it with his hand.

There was a swell of applause when Carthrall got onto the rock, and a little cheering, though muted. He looked nervous and ill at ease with the situation. Badad, however, was intrigued. Now he would see how like his father he was. But there was a lengthy pause at first, as the King took in the sight of his audience. What a sad and pathetic lot they were. The men were the worst, which surprised him, until he realised that the men knew they would bear the brunt of the brutality that was certain to ensue soon after this night. He remembered Salissa's advice, and when he caught sight of her standing amidst the crowd he drew the strength to speak.

"It is fair to say that I haven't made a very promising start!" he said, quietly, almost timidly. But when they responded by chuckling he grew stronger still. "And you may well think that I am cursed, and that by coming here my misfortune has fallen on you too." Badad surveyed the reaction. "But you would be wrong. Those ships were on their way to Bosscastle long before I was. And if you think that the timing of my arrival could not have been worse, then you would be wrong again. A day or two earlier and you would have been even worse off then you are this night, for you would never have known your king…!"

Badad smiled. Yes, this was the son of Vercingoral speaking. He could almost hear his old friend's voice coming out of this young man's mouth. His face swelled with pride, his aching limbs temporarily eased, he crept away. Carthrall continued.

"For that is who I am … the King of Geramond! The king of a land that is under attack. So mine may very well be the shortest reign in history. But it won't be the last. Whatever happens over the next few days, however strong the Repecians are, this country will rise again, and one day in the future, just like we have been these last few months, the people will be free again. And when the time comes for them to rise in revolt, they will do so in memory of us here, just like we were emboldened by the memory of Vercingoral and Henwen. I'm sure that my father knew that his army could not defeat the Repecian force, as I know that we can't. But that did not stop him from going to war. And it should not stop us." Then he paused to think about what he was going to say next. What he said appalled his uncle. "I'm not going to stand here and tell you what you should do. The truth is … I don't know. Anyway, I think that in a situation such as this you should all decide for yourselves how best to survive."

This was a strange and confusing strategy to Gonosor, a man known for his overpowering and demanding personality. His way was to bully and argue until he got everyone to do as he wished, not talk in little more than a whisper or provide options and alternatives. But Fogle understood it. He had, after all, been present when Vercingoral gave his speech from the balcony of the Lampas, when he renounced his crown in favour of his brother, knowing full well that the people would not accept him and would rather he remained in power. Politics of the mind, that's what it was, and Carthrall seemed to be just as adept at it as his father was.

Torches flickered to illuminate morose faces, hanging on the young man's every word.

"All I can tell you is what I intend to do," Carthrall continued. "I shall go to ..." he had to think hard and remember the name, for he was a stranger in these parts. "...Bossiney, and seek out this Fillian ... and tell him that I am the king, and that his soldiers may very well conquer our lands, but never our hearts. And every day that his people are on our soil, my people will have their minds bent on the day when they shall be free again...! Now, if any of you should decide that you would like to accompany me, I shall be honoured to walk with you, though I cannot guarantee your safe return." Fogle smiled, for he understood what was happening. And so did Salissa. "And to those of you who will not come, do not think that you have abandoned me. You hardly know me, after all. To you, I wish you well, and hope that you find a safe place to hide. Thank you. And good-bye,"

He stepped down from the rock, relieved that his ordeal was over and that he could stop trembling now. He walked away without turning back. Then he stopped and did turn.

"I don't know the way," he said.

"Then I'll show you, lad," replied Fogle, walking speedily to catch up with him. Badad had already told the boy that Fogle would be his staunchest ally, so the sight of the Shireman striding towards him was not a surprise. Salissa was the next to commit herself. Then Gonosor, who released an almighty groan, for he did not understand any of it, even his own decision to go. Behind them, all the rest of the people. Carthrall walked at the front with his head faced in the same direction as his feet, but he somehow knew they were behind him.

Badad was not there to see them leave. Something had compelled him to venture deeper into the forest. A whisper in his ear from a familiar, kindly voice. Although his first reaction was to ignore it and stay with the others, now he was delving deeper into the darkness of Ingelwitt with renewed awareness and anticipation. Looking back, the camp torches were mere flickers of life, getting dimmer and the sound of their voices were getting fainter until finally both the lights and the noises of the camp were gone and he was alone. A bright light appeared amidst the trees up ahead; a shimmering vision of the Lady Pannona, as he remembered her from their last meeting: fragrant and stunning to look at but all-powerful as well.

"You always know when to find me, my Lady," said Badad, "For I seek your counsel still."

She approached him. "As the people still seek yours?" Then she stopped in front of him. "How much more do they think you can do for them?"

"Just one more thing, that's all," the Druid stumbled. "And you know what that is...?!"

She raised her eyes to the sky.

"Alas, the only option available. But not to you!" He seemed to be taken aback by her comment. "Surely you know that you can't help them anymore. Have you not felt the change in yourself this last day and night? Of course you have. Tell me how you feel now."

"I feel drained," he answered. "Like I am about to expire."

It was obvious to him what was happening, now that the Lady had made him say it out loud. All of the Druidic powers he once possessed and wielded had left him, so that all he was now was an old man whose expiry was well overdue. A mere mortal. The change in him since the day before was stark and brutal, like his body and mind were in the very final stages of decay; diseased and rapidly failing. But he was not in any pain. Just tired. As the realisation finally hit him that the Lady had come to fetch him, he stumbled backwards until he hit a tree, when his legs gave way and he slipped onto his backside. These, he was certain, were his final moments in this world of men, and he knew that he should have been pleased and relieved, except that he was not. Badad, like Marrock before him, was a man who was only ever comfortable in the company of those he knew well, but now he was alone and knew that he would never see any of those familiar faces again.

Weakly, he asked: "Is my task complete then?"

Pannona smiled.

"Your undertaking was to restore a king to the throne that all the peoples of Geramond could settle on. That is fulfilled, is it not...!"

"His name is Carthrall," Badad replied.

"Then your task, at last, is done."

"Then give me another one, my Lady," he pleaded. "For I do not wish to die now. They need me still. Geramond is being attacked again by those foreign hoards and I am needed here and now if they are to be defeated, so that the people of this land can enjoy their freedom and their new king!"

Her gentle, peaceable face took on a look of surprise. "Is that what you really want?" she asked him. "Another Druidic life to be spent in the company of these petulant people ... who will defy you at every stage of your journey? Just think how hard this undertaking has been and how utterly exhausted and spent you are now. Could you do it all again? Surely not, when the alternative is something altogether better."

Badad drew a breath deeply as Pannona knelt down beside him and placed her hand between his head and the scabrous tree trunk. The sight of her next to him was a great comfort.

"It's just that I worry about them, my Lady," he said, struggling now to utter a sentence in the one breath. "What will become of them after I've gone...?"

She understood his dilemma but recognised that his angst was fuelled more by his fear of the alternative than any great and genuine desire to stay in this world. "It's time for them to stand alone, without the Druids' guidance," she said.

"But they will fail without me."

"Apart from anything else, your body has come to its natural end," she said, softly, wiping a wisp of hair from his eyes. "And long overdue so the process is quickened thus. Now, don't be afraid, master Druid. You have waited too long for this moment to shy away from the prospect now that it has come. Allow me to fulfill my promise to you, my little friend, in return for all your endeavour and perseverance."

"Then if these are my last moments, promise me that you will help them, and let me slip away with a clear conscience," he said.

She sighed sadly. "I can only control the minds and hearts of men by working through a Druid. Now that I have none left I am powerless here. But don't despair, Badad. Your conscience shall remain flawless and solid, for you above all my Druids have served and helped these people best." Her voice contained tones of genuine affection and admiration. "You are the most famous Druid of them all, and men will tell stories about Badad of Kaw and how he saved the Kingdom of Geramond and nudged it into its forth age. Its golden age."

The little man was blinking irregularly, some short and others prolonged as though he meant never to open his eyes again. His breathing now was shallow and awkward. His body was lower than before so that only his neck and head were resting against the tree; his legs were flaccid and his arms were still by his side. Only the tips of his fingers showed signs of life, as he had just enough energy to scrape the dirt on the forest floor. Then, with renewed vigor as though he wanted to prove that he was as stubborn as ever he was, he asked: "How will I know? What will I see?"

"A light," she replied. "A single point of light when all else is dark. The light will get bigger until it devours the darkness, then it will fade to leave just the haze of a summer's morning in Fa-Noodar. The best way to arrive is after a long, long journey that has lasted many years, as yours has. Do not expect riches here or wisdom. Fa-Noodar has given you your voyage. Without Fa-Noodar you would never have done or seen any of the things you have. But you have not been cheated, for all your wisdom and experience will allow you to understand Fa-Noodar."

He nodded. He understood. Pannona lowered his head until it rested upon the ground, then rose and stepped back to look upon him. When she was sure that he had at last expired, she herself slipped away, although her presence would be felt in the world for some days to come.

Twenty-Three

A Bossiney Dawn

They walked out of the forest and crossed the valley. Women and children, the elderly as well as the strong. Gonosor was at the forefront for he knew the way but the King was close behind, with Salissa on one side and Fogle on the other. Before they had left the trees behind, at the edge of Ingelwitt, Gonosor had revealed something that shocked them but also gave them hope; something that had been hidden for many years, since the early days of the last Repecian invasion: a stash of weapons; swords, daggers, shields and spears, that had been concealed by Henwen's army when it became clear that Fillian was not going to be defeated and that they needed to flee into the Middle Lands, but must move swiftly and unhindered.

None of them had the protection of armour, although Gonosor and some of his set wore thick, leather coats that did at least offer a shell of comfort. Even the King wore the tatty clothes he had arrived in, and his people were dressed in whatever they had on when Bosscastle was attacked, such was the urgency in their departure. Most of them had not eaten anything since the feast earlier in the evening and none of them had rested since then. Therefore, no-one spoke or ranted as they marched. Just an assortment of desperate people, certainly not an army, who marched onwards even though they were quite certain that they were going to their deaths, for hope as well as everything else was left behind.

Gonosor fretted about what the break of dawn would bring; Carthrall was worried about the welfare of his brother and Fogle looked all around for a glimpse of the Druid, but despite his anxiety he knew in his heart that Badad would be doing something to help them, and would not let them march haplessly towards their doom.

Then someone further back did finally break the silence, and they all heard him.

"I hope we live to see another night," he said. Carthrall, to himself, muttered: "I hope that this journey to Bossiney is a long one."

The road would have taken them into the valley and up towards the castle but rather than chance that they skirted the forest until they were well clear of the fortress, and then crossed to rejoin the road. Poor, unfortunate Bosscastle, they thought, for it was still being bombarded and smashed to pieces. They could hear it being destroyed. That boom sound followed by the ancient stones crashing to the ground; and fire was still ravaging the place despite the rain, and gave the black sky an orange glow. The sight and sound of it all only added to their sense of foreboding.

Gonosor stopped. He was the first to see it. Others stood around him and looked down upon what had so mesmerised him. There, in the dip of land that sloped into the sea, the Repecian camp, that was so vast that it went up the far slope; tents and billets that had been erected in hardly any time but looked solid enough to have been a permanent scene on this landscape. Hundreds of them, aglow with the flames of the torches and fires; and thousands of soldiers roving with purpose and intent. In the harbour itself were dozens of galleys at anchor. It was a sight that made their hearts race. Fogle recited the words Vercingoral had uttered before the battle of High Cleugh: 'there lies your task. Are you up to it?' Only this time was different for the answer was clear for all to see.

Gauin Fillian awoke early. He had had a restless night and was therefore relieved that dawn had arrived outside, even though his tent was still falsely lit by the torches. He cast off his cover and pulled himself upright, lowered his spindly legs onto the ground and walked guardedly to the door to peer out. Rain dominated the morning, or rather a fine, cold drizzle that soaked everything and turned the ground to mud. He heard one legionary across the way grumble to another: "Why did he have to bring us back here?"

"Why indeed," said Fillian, to himself, as he lowered the flap of material that was the door and went back to his bed. Vagor, who had seen him, immediately went into the tent. "I wondered where you'd gone," said Fillian, groggily. "Taking the fine, spring air, eh?"

Vagor lowered his head courteously. "Forgive me, master," he said.

"I could have been killed in my bed. You're supposed to be my guard. If I'd been killed, what would you all have done then?"

"Forgive me," repeated Vagor. "Is there anything I can get for you?" Fillian pointed to his robe, so Vagor fetched it and wrapped it around his shoulders.

"Damn northern weather," said the Emperor. "It's enough to chill a man to the bone. No wonder my legs ache here." As he did every morning, Vagor inspected his master for a sign that his health had deteriorated during the night. Fillian's health had seemed to worsen by the hour during the journey to Geramond, and although he looked tired and drained, there was nothing about him to suggest that he had declined further. 'The falling sickness' the Senators had called it, showing concern whilst secretly hoping that whatever ailment it was would shortly kill him. But Fillian was made of brawnier stuff than to be beaten by an illness, even though it made for a sturdier test than anything he had experienced on a battlefield. And that was the root of his grumpiness lately: his frustration that his once mighty strength had left him and showed no signs of coming back imminently. He knew precisely who to blame: the Druid.

For the past ten years or so Vagor had been his strength. When he had first arrived back after his great conquest of Geramond he paraded him merely as a trophy of the war; had drawn great delight from the Shireman's obvious despair and embarrassment; watched in awe and wonder as he fought with his tormentors and captors. Vercingoral quickly became famous throughout Repecia for his fighting skills and for his ability in the arena as a wrestler, the Repecians' favoured sport. 'Fillian's barbarian' they had called him and marvelled at his strength and dexterity and wondered if anyone could ever defeat him, and if they ever did would the Great One forgive them for doing it.

At a dinner party at Palmatine the subject of Vagor's invincibility arose. One wise old guest, a senator, offered the explanation. "Vagor is fearless," he told Fillian, "The pain inflicted on him in the arena is as nothing when compared to his anguish at being separated from his own people, particularly his woman. And since he realises that he is unlikely ever to see his homeland again, he has no real desire to stay alive, and that's what makes him so dangerous. His spirit will never be broken in the arena. He wants to die, therefore the only way to truly punish him is by keeping him alive." And it made perfect sense. Therefore, the very next day, Vagor was told that he would not compete in the arena again but would serve in Fillian's own household as his slave.

With the memory of those early years fresh in his mind, and fully aware of his own vulnerability and of how vital his servant was to him, it was with unease that he asked: "How does it feel to be back on home soil?" He then nervously awaited the answer.

Vagor replied quickly and convincingly.

"I have no feelings for this place," he said, seemingly affronted by the inquiry. "Just a desire to get the job done then leave as quickly as I can."

Fillian, who was perched on the edge of his bed and was shivering in the cold, damp air, tried to conceal his gladness. "I almost believe you, my friend," he mocked.

Vagor went to him and once again knelt before his master. "My life is my service to you, my Lord."

Fillian rose and stepped away. He seemed agitated by Vagor's devotion rather than pleased. "Yes, it most probably is," he snapped. "For I have given you a far better life then the one you would have had as the king of the wretched, barbaric people of this island. I have shown you the wonders of the world … the power of empire. Thanks to me you have trodden the golden streets of Ramrah and dwelled in marble halls, when really you should have been knee deep in mud and ruling your kingdom from the squalor of a wooden hut!"

Vagor also rose. "I cannot deny what you have given me."

"What I have given you?" Fillian mused. "Yes. But now I am going to give you what you desire most … your freedom…!"

The servant was taken aback by the comment and was puzzled as to what his master meant by it. Fillian did not bother to explain that it was his own understanding that if he brought Vagor back to his homeland and set him free then the curse that had inflicted him almost since the day he had left these cold shores for his own home, would be lifted and his health and strength would return. Nor did he divulge that those things were more important to him than the services of a mere slave, regardless of how devoted he happened to be. He knew that his command of the Empire was under threat back home from those that would restore a republic, and therefore his health was vital if he was to keep a firm grip on his power and privileges. He had remembered the Druid's words:

'I will be forever watching what you do to him.' And: 'I will bring you back.' Well now he was back, and he knew that Badad would be aware of this new gesture to release Vagor from his slavery.

"I don't understand," replied the servant.

"It's perfectly simple, my friend," said Fillian. "You thought that you would never tread upon these shores again, but I have brought you back. Therefore, if you are so minded to leave me and return to your own kind, if that is what you want, then I will not do or say anything to prevent you ... and neither will anyone else here. You are free to make up your own mind. But you must do it now or not do it at all."

It still did not make sense to the Shireman.

"Have I offended you in any way?" he asked, cagily.

Fillian laughed. "On the contrary. You have been the most loyal and constant servant a man could wish for. You saved my life, no less. So, to my mind, if I release you then I shall be out of your debt. Consider it payback for all of your services to me."

The Emperor walked towards the rack and lifted down the gilded breast plate to his suit of armour, cast off his robe with a shrug of his shoulders and proceeded to fit the piece onto himself. Only, he barely had the strength to lift it and had to pause to catch his breath. Then Vagor stepped towards him and helped him into it.

"I didn't ask for your help," Fillian groaned. "Haven't you been listening to a word I've said?"

Vagor fastened the piece of armour tightly at the back, one strap after the other, then fetched the golden gauntlets and fitted them onto the hands. Fillian pushed into them firmly until they covered the whole of his lower arms, and closed his right hand to form a fist and smiled when the spikes protruded from his knuckles. Next, the leg harnesses, not gilded but plain iron, that were clasped around his legs and secured with a buckle. Only when this had all been done, and Vagor was fastening Fillian's purple cloak to his shoulders, did he offer his response.

"I have been listening. And if you say I am free then I truly am. So freely I have decided to remain your loyal servant, if not your slave."

Fillian was filled with glee. "Then you were telling the truth when you said that you no longer had feelings for this land?"

"It is as foreign to my eyes as it is to yours, and I shall not stay in it a day longer than I have to."

Fillian walked to the far side of the tent to collect his sword. From behind, Vagor studied him carefully. Even with his gleaming armour on he was a poor imitation of the man he used to be, and still looked feeble and sickly. Chuckling excitedly between coughs, twisting around, Fillian said: "We must turn our minds to the task at hand. Punil has things under control here. The citadel is destroyed and its inhabitants have no doubt fled into the forest like they usually do. I will leave five cohorts here and the rest will come with me into the Middle Lands ... into the heart of this despicable country. This time I know the way. We'll follow the course of the river, around the mountains and on to the city of Woldark, then Aldwark. Once they have been recaptured this land will be conquered again, and we can go home. Are you with me?"

"I am," Vagor replied.

Fillian, grasping his servants forearm, said firmly: "I intend to destroy those cities ... raise them to the ground! Persecute those residents that survive until none are left. So, I ask you again ... are you truly with me...?" Then he stepped back to examine the Shireman's reaction.

"I am with you!" Vagor affirmed.

Fillian slapped his servant's arm playfully. "That's the way, my friend. Cold heart and all that. It's not without cause that they call me a cruel, murderous brute. I have resolved to be such a man, and rejected decency long ago. Thus no man is comparable to me, for I heed not the pain of other men. I am freed from normal laws, and can be the raging beast whilst I breathe the breath of life. And the Empire is as strong and as cruel as I am for the Empire is my creation." He had a set, tough glaze about his face as he spoke. "I am that vile, slippery man that provokes fear and fright … and makes men suffer the worst trials that they will ever know. I am death itself. So I ask you one, final time: are you with me…?"

Without pause for hesitation, Vagor replied: "I am."

"Then lead my men," Fillian said. Vagor was shocked so the Repecian spoke quickly. "Be my strength on the battlefield. Be my hands as it is wielded." He pressed his own sword into Vagor's hand and held it there until the Shireman held it for himself. "For I am not strong enough anymore." The old sword was held aloft, then slashed through the air several times until it settled.

"I am honoured, my Lord," said Vagor. "I will do your bidding now, as I always have. I shall destroy Woldark with my own hands if need be. And in its place a new city will arise, built of stone and brick. It will be the capital of this province, and stand forevermore as a testament to your greatness."

Fillian smiled and sighed with joy and relief. "We will leave today … this very morning. Get yourself ready for battle, my friend."

Dawn broke suddenly and with a flurry of activity. Gonosor and some others had kept watch on the Repecian camp for what remained of the night while the others tried to capture some sleep, for the events of the next day were certain to be tumultuous. But not much sleep was had; a snippet here and there. The children slept for they did not understand. Fogle did not so much as close his eyes for a second; instead, they were alert throughout and determined to seek out a sighting of the Druid. When dawn threatened, it became clear that Badad had not followed them to Bossiney, so he decided to return to the forest to fetch him and find out what he was up to. He slipped away without anyone noticing.

Dawn meant little in the depths of Ingelwitt for just a small fragment of the spring sunshine was strong enough to penetrate these venerable branches, and Fogle had to tread carefully and feel his way through until he reached the deserted camp. There, the trees thinned and a view across to the smouldering ruins of Bosscastle was offered to his tired eyes. And what a wretched sight it was. The Gatehouse was the only recognisable part of the castle for the rest of it had been demolished by Punil's assault on it, which was still ongoing and it occurred to him that they meant to destroy it completely until all that remained was just its ruined form. So dismal was the view that Fogle could not bear to look for longer than a quick glance, and instead he walked briskly away, back into the forest proper.

All the while he called out the Druid's name, but no reply came. The trees creaked and groaned in the breeze; a hare scampered across his path, and just as he was beginning to calm down after the shock, he caught sight of someone up ahead, and stepped quietly towards him.

"Badad, is that you?" he called out. "It's me, Fogle." But he quickly realised that it was not the Druid for he would have surely answered him by now. He slinked to behind the thick trunk of an oak tree, and dared to peer out; his heart was thumping against his chest and his hands were shaking. This had not been the first time he had been caught alone in the forest with an unknown entity, but this time he meant to keep his distance until he was sure he knew who, or what, it was. It was on its knees, whatever it was, and looked to be nothing more than a mere man, but heavily cloaked so that his face was hidden. Fogle studied him closer to try and see what he was doing. Then he realised that the man was kneeling over a body.

"Oh, please no," he panted, beginning to suspect that the dead body was none other than Badad. His heart raced faster and anger began to burn in his face, before he finally stepped out from behind the tree and ran towards them, purposely screaming at the top of his voice to unnerve the stranger and send him fleeing.

The man glanced back then rose to step away but Fogle moved swiftly for such a hefty man and arrived sooner than expected, and kicked the stranger away from the body sending him soaring across the forest floor. Once there, his worst fear was confirmed; not Badad, but Marrock; just as bad for he knew them to be one and the same.

"Not you, too," he said, thinking of the time he had held old Toggett's head in his hand. But this was even worse, for he knew that with Badad dead the war was surely lost. Therefore his sadness rapidly turned to rage and he sped towards the stranger on both his hands and his feet, like the hare he had just encountered. He stopped short of him. "What have you done?" he demanded. "What have you done to him…!!?" The stranger, still on his backside, took down his hood and he was a stranger no more.

"Galfall…!" Fogle, while calmer, was nonetheless puzzled as he stumbled back onto his feet. "…. the Druid…?"

"I found him like that," said Galfall.

"What has gone on here?" Then he noticed that there was something strange about the youngster; something different as though he was unfamiliar after all: gaunt, half-starved and vacant. "What has gone on?" he repeated.

Galfall scurried away.

"The Druid has expired," he said. "His task was fulfilled therefore he had nothing to live for."

Fogle was enraged further.

"Nothing to live for? What about his promise to help us? You can't tell me that Badad strived for years and years to protect the King and bring him to the throne only to abandon him once the crown was on his head, with his new realm under attack! He has not lived his life to bring him to this end … cold and abandoned on the forest floor."

Galfall was still kneeling on the ground, propping himself up by his arms, his cloth cloak covered in bits of twig and dirt. "Who has ever decided when and how to die, Fogle," he said. "Did Toggett? Did my father? Will you or I?"

Fogle, exhausted with grief, collapsed onto his backside in front of the youngster. He raised his head and looked at Galfall again, and was even more sure that something had happened to him during his absence.

"Where did you go?" he asked. "Why did you run away?"

Galfall was reluctant to answer and pulled his hood over his face. Then he mumbled something: "I am too ashamed to say."

"You were jealous of your brother, weren't you, lad?"

This time he pushed his hood down completely. "Yes," he replied, quite firmly and unrepentantly. "It seemed that once again Carthrall had ended up with everything while I was left with nothing," he glanced at the Druid, "despite his assurances that I would amount to something. It has always been that way. My mother doted on him whereas she barely ever gave me a second thought. Now I know why. Now I know their secret. I didn't believe any of it when the Druid returned to Bosscastle proclaiming my little brother to be the King. It seemed so absurd. Even you must admit that you had your doubts. So when the throne selected him, after all that happened in that room … that we'd endeavoured to find don't forget … I admit that I was furious!" He was speaking with an angry tone, as though the pain was still real. "I had every right to be. Badad had known the truth all along, yet allowed me to believe that for the first time in my life I was the remarkable Gringell boy! All those things he said to me that morning on the edge of the forest. He told me that it was my destiny to break Bosscastle … only he didn't mean it, did he? For I did not do it. He did it himself. He deceived me, Fogle. He let me think that I was special, and all the time he knew that it was my brother that was the one, great hope for Geramond."

"I'm sure he did not mean to deceive you, lad," Fogle said.

"He tricked me! And I was angry! So I ran away, and ran and ran until I could go no further."

"Where did you go to?"

"The only place I know in these parts … Bossiney! I had been there before … with Gonosor. Only, when I got there, I saw the ships … dozens of them … and thousands of soldiers wading through the water onto the beach. I knew that Fillian had returned and do you know what…? I was glad that he had, for it meant that my little brother would not reign for very long! It meant that the Repecians would hunt him down first, and I would be rid of him once and for all! How could I have thought such a thing?"

Then Fogle noticed some marks around the youngster's neck; like rope marks. He thrust his hand forward and forced Galfall's head back to see them more clearly.

"What happened to you at Bossiney?"

Tears welled in the boy's eyes. He began to shake. "I don't know," he sobbed.

"Who did this to you?"

"The Governor," he whispered, almost too embarrassed to speak.

Fogle was unsure how to react. "Delabole, you mean?"

Galfall nodded. "He was there. I didn't see him at first for he was hiding in the bushes. When I saw him I didn't think that he was a threat. He looked a mess ... as though he had been sleeping rough for years ... like those old hawkers that used to pass through Aldwark, against whom everyone would lock their doors until they'd gone. He looked like an old man ... but dirty and spoiled."

"Why was he there?"

"He said the Emperor had dispensed with his services. He asked who I was so I told him."

"Did you tell him about Carthrall?"

He shook his head.

"He knew that there was a new king, but I didn't tell him I was his brother. In any case ... I'm not, am I? It was getting dark. He told me I could stay the night with him and share his food, but I wasn't so sure."

"But you went with him?"

He nodded.

"I was hungry, you see. It turned out that all he had to eat was two dead rats and I wasn't that hungry. But the fire was warm and the ground beneath me was soft. From there we were we could watch the Repecians as they built their camp. He was very interested in watching that. 'I am no longer strong enough to bare the burden alone,' he would say. 'Go down there and fetch my brother.' I didn't really know what he was talking about. Then he told me that he had done something terrible. When I asked him what he had done all he would say was that he had betrayed him...."

"Vercingoral," Fogle mused. "Delabole did betray him, then took the Lady Henwen as his own wife, against her will. That's what he meant. That's why he was so reviled ... that and the whole slavery business. What happened then...?"

"He began to tell me that he had hated his brother all his life, and admitted that he had always envied him his power and strength. That's when I told him that I had always resented my own brother, and he said we were the same, him and me, and that I should stay with him or else I'd perish. When I listened to him talk about his brother, and when he said he'd do anything to be rid of him, well that's when I realised that I did not despise Carthrall at all. I had been stupid and impudent but I wasn't as obsessed as he seemed to be. I remembered that for most of my life I had protected my little brother and had shielded him from harm. Why should things be different now, eh? So all I wanted was to return to Bosscastle. But by then the Repecians were attacking it and I realised that you all would have fled into the forest."

"What did you do?"

"I told him that I intended to return to Ingelwitt. He snarled something … I couldn't make out what it was. I stood up to leave but he pounced on me like a bear or a wolf…! I tried to kick him off but before I had chance to get free he …." then he stopped talking, just rubbed his neck.

"He did that," asked Fogle, looking at the rope marks. "You were lucky. He could have killed you."

"I think he did," sobbed the youngster, falling onto his side and burying his face in the dirt.

Fogle, at last, rose to his feet and stepped back. "What did you say?" he demanded. "Don't talk daft, lad. You're here, aren't you?"

Without raising his head Galfall said: "He meant to kill me, and I think he might have succeeded."

Fogle stepped further away.

"You're tired and hungry, that's all. You're confused. You've been through an ordeal but it's not as bad as you think. You're amongst friends again, Galfall." Then he stopped and asked himself what it was he was afraid of. Surely he was not fearful of the youngster? He took a tentative step back towards him and reached out his hand to pull him back onto his feet, but Galfall cowered away from him, out of his reach. It occurred to Fogle that of all the people that had been affected by the war, including himself, it was the young Gringell that had suffered the worst. A promising youth at the beginning, and full of enterprise and energy then, was now wrecked and drained as he recoiled along the forest floor, ruined by his grief and his shame.

Fogle knelt beside the youth, pushed back the thick hood that covered his face and looked at him closely. He had seen such a pallid, distressed look once before, in this very forest. Another neck wound, but this time caused by a rope rather than a blade, but just as brutal and cut so deep into the flesh that it was hard for him to imagine that the boy could have survived an attack like that. So doubt began to creep into Fogle's mind and he was now inclined to believe that Galfall was telling the truth. He therefore rose and stepped back again. He glanced at Marrock's lifeless body and wished more than anything else that Badad would return to explain what had happened to the boy, for he did not understand any of it.

"He can't be dead," he told himself. "He is not a spirit like his father for I touched him with my own hands. He is flesh and blood like the rest of us." He turned to walk away from the scene but found himself running instead. Before he knew it he was back in the clearing, where he stopped to look across the valley to the ruined castle.

"How badly it's all gone wrong," he cursed, and turned. Galfall, risen, was standing in front of him, which caused poor Fogle to jolt backwards and fall to the ground.

"You touched Wilfren with your own hands, and found that he was flesh and blood, like you," said Galfall. "But that didn't make him any less dead than he was." It seemed remarkable how calm he was now, when just minutes before he had been the trembling wreck. He held out his hand for Fogle to grasp hold of, but the little man got back onto his feet by his own means, so Galfall placed his hand by his side.

"It hasn't turned out so badly after all," he sneered, then smiled. And as his lips straightened blood began to pour from the edge of his mouth. Fogle, frightened, ran away. "I know what it is I have to do," Galfall shouted. Fogle stopped momentarily and turned. "And when I do it, you must get onto the high ground."

And with that said he disappeared. So did Fogle, as fast as his short legs would carry him.

Vagor had changed into his armour: black to Fillian's gold. They were next to each other on horseback and in the pale blue sky dotted with cloud, the spring sun endeavoured to shed warmth upon the pair of them. The camp was being dismantled by auxiliaries whilst the main part of the army was standing in formation in front of them.

"You are well rested," Vagor said to them, in that clear, booming style. "So today you will work. We will leave this place and go inland to complete our task. We will kill anyone who will dare to stand in our way, for now is the time to restore order to this province once and for all, and our pitilessness shall send out the message that the Great One will never be defeated or cast out of this land. By the time this is over, I expect all of you to be covered in the greasy blood of our enemy." Then he turned his horse, and Fillian turned his and together they led this long column of armour-clad soldiers away from Bossiney.

"They're leaving," said Carthrall, crouched in the long grass at the top of the hill.

"We've got a fine morning for it," Gonosor replied. Then they looked behind at their own army. Young, able men were at the forefront, but they looked more terrified than the older men standing behind them. At the back were the women, including Salissa. Most of them displayed an expressionless mask that suggested they were prepared to perish this day alongside their men. And that was the predominant feeling amongst these people: a determination not to be overawed or become victims of their own misfortune. Salissa, put amongst the women to give them hope and strength, for they associated her with the King, even though he had ruled for only a day, did try her best to instill into them a sense of hope, at a time when hope was lost. She said: "I am young. And I shall most probably die today. I am scared, like the rest of you. But I will tell you that I'd much rather die here today, a young, free woman, than die of old age after a lifetime as a slave…!" And the women that heard her smiled politely, but her statement did little to settle their nerves.

"Do you think we should say something to them?" asked

Carthrall, not quite sure how he should react to the situation. The truth was that he was so edgy and petrified that even if Gonosor had replied that he should say something, he would not have been able to. In any case, this was not an occasion for fine words of inspiration, for these people were not going into battle under the fallacy that victory was within their grasp, but were resigned to their collective fate, had accepted that it was for the best and simply wanted the battle to ensue until it was done with. The Bodmifflian stood upright and proud.

"Fillian!" he blasted, taking his own people by surprise with his thunderous voice as much as the Repecians down by the bay. "This land is spoken for!!" And he pulled his long sword from its scabbard. "We will defend it in the name of Carthrall, King!!"

Fillian stopped and turned when he heard the shouting from atop the hill. For the first time he was aware that the enemy had been watching them and was initially unnerved before turning agitated then angry that none of his scouts had seen them approaching the night before.

"Do they not know when to give in!?" he blasted.

"Prepare for battle!" Vagor instructed, and looked on as the column of soldiers that had been following them turned instead to face the enemy. Now that they knew they were there, all they had left to do was charge down the hill, and they did so with tremendous courage and menace, so that Fillian actually moved further back from the front, leaving Vagor in command. Once they had started to run, such was the sharpness of the slope that they could not have stopped even if they had wanted to, so they hopped and jumped into battle in a disorderly fashion. Carthrall had stayed close to Gonosor, as they had agreed, but nonetheless immersed himself in the fighting.

"What kind of people would throw down their lives so carelessly?" Fillian asked himself, riding onto the top of a hillock, accompanied by two of his guards. He longed to be in the midst of the fighting, but his weakness prevented him, therefore he cursed his luck and vowed to himself that when all was done he would hunt down the Druid and have his revenge. In the meantime, he observed in awe and amazement as Vagor, that rock of a man, pushed and slashed his way into the heart of the battle.

Outnumbered, half-starved and dazed, the Shiremen and the Bodmifflians brawled as best they could but apart from Gonosor and a handful of others, the rest were fodder for the merciless Repecian legionaries. Men were slashed to pieces before they had even had a chance to defend themselves. The air was scented with the smell of death and carnage; the ground littered with noble, yet dead people. If this was all that the people of Geramond could muster then the defence of their land would be over before it had really begun. Vagor cut through them almost effortlessly. Then, bored with those undemanding, ineffective adversaries that threw themselves recklessly into his path, he switched his attention to someone he knew would be able to give him a decent fight: Gonosor, who was only several feet from him and edging closer with every legionary he slaughtered.

Gonosor saw that black-armoured warrior coming at him out of the corner of his eye, so took in a deep breath and turned to face him, not really confident that he had either the skill or the energy to overcome him. Nevertheless, he held his hefty sword above his head, screamed as loud as he could, then lunged at his adversary. Vagor stepped out of his way and the tip of Gonosor's sword was thrust into the ground, soft and freshly churned. He just had time to pull it and turn around before Vagor, now on foot, ran towards him. The sharp sound of their swords clashing was louder than anything else on the battlefield. And it was Gonosor, fearsome and strong, that actually landed more blows, but each one of them against Vagor's iron shield, rendering them useless.

The Bodmifflian recognised the face in front of him, and was so taken aback that he actually stopped fighting and stepped back.

"I know you," he said. Vagor came at him again. The point of the sword missed but Gonosor grabbed hold of his arm and pulled him closer. "You have returned!" he said, then knocked the black helmet from off Vagor's head. A bald scalp and clean face did not disguise him at all, or change him into another person as far as Gonosor was concerned. "Vercingoral!" he muttered, not quite prepared to trust himself. "I can't believe they've let you live this long. You obviously made a better slave than you ever did a king...!" And with that said he slammed his sword against his adversary's chest, but that black armour was just too thick.

The mention of the name, and the fact that Gonosor had recognised him, only served to make Vagor more angry and violent than he already was and he hacked the Bodmifflian against the leg, cutting him down like a blade of grass.

"Go ahead, my Lord," Gonosor panted. "Finish me off. I have not been a loyal servant of yours, after all." He gasped with fear as Vagor, sword held aloft, stepped towards him, seemingly without remorse or pity. "You have waited a long time to do it, so do it cleanly and quickly. If not for my sake, then for my sister's ... who will surely be watching." Then Vagor stopped. Something snapped in his mind. An old memory, long suppressed and abandoned. He looked around him and saw nothing but death. Then his eyes sought out Fillian, his current master. "How can it be, that the man my sister fell in love with, had a son by, is fighting against her beloved people this day...?" said Gonosor. "And will murder her own brother...? What a strange day this is. I warned her about you! I told her you were not to be trusted. No Shireman must ever be trusted. Not Delabole ... not you...! Now just get on with it. If anyone is going to finish me off then it may as well be Vercingoral...!"

"Vercingoral is dead!" said Vagor, and pulled back his sword preparatory to thrusting it into the Bodmifflian's neck.

Carthrall, from nowhere, leapt onto Vagor from the side and had just sufficient strength to divert him from his task, giving Gonosor time to scramble away. Then he watched as Vagor and Carthrall fought each other.

"Yes," he mumbled, pleased with the outcome. "This is the way it's supposed to be."

Never in the history of this ancient land has a contest between two people been so unequal. With every blow the boy was sent hurling backwards. He was kicked while he was down. The hilt of the sword was smashed against his head when he tried to get up, but something stopped Vagor from finishing him off. Perhaps it was his guilt at fighting a mere boy.

"He is your son!!" Gonosor yelled. Vagor heard him, and

looked closely to inspect the boy at his feet. Carthrall had heard his uncle too, and waited for something to happen. Vagor twisted his head to get a better look, then quickly turned it to face another direction so that he did not have to look at him any more, and caught a glimpse of his master instead. When he dared to look at the boy again it was not him he saw but his mother, looking back at him with those fiery eyes. The more he looked the more he remembered about the lady, Henwen. His sword dropped from his loose grip and fell upon the ground. So did Vagor, onto his knees next to Carthrall, and he stretched out his finger to touch the boy's face. Yes, he could see clearly now. This was Henwen's son, and therefore his own flesh. Not knowing what to do, Carthrall offered up a slight smile, that made him appear even more like his mother.

"So much pain," said Vercingoral. "So many wasted years."

"I am the King," Carthrall replied, softly for he was trembling with fear and unease. "But I will gladly settle for being a prince for a while, for you are our true king! I didn't ask for any of this, you see. It was the Druid who persuaded me to come here …"

"Badad?" Vercingoral mused. "Then he did succeed after all." He stood up. "Geramond is reborn. But now we're here, and all is lost again…!"

Fillian was watching from the hillock, and was confused as to what his servant was doing in the middle of the battlefield.

"Just kill them!" he blasted. "Finish this now!" Aware that Vagor was looking at him he indicated that he expected him to do just that. He was unnerved and alarmed, therefore, when Vagor started to run back down the bank towards him, as quickly as he could so that in no time at all he was coming up the side of the hill. At first he thought that he was coming back to relay a message but when he saw the glare of anger on his face, and the sword, covered in foreign blood, he began to fidget and doubt his motive.

"I am not Vagor! I am Vercingoral … King … husband … father…!" And the sword was stabbed into the Emperor's side before his two guards had had a chance to protect him. Fillian fell from his horse onto the ground, barely alive. His last thought was that his great servant had turned against him; his last observation was of Vagor towering above him before placing the tip of his sword underneath the gilded breastplate and pushing it into his belly, not taking it out until he was sure he had finished him off and his body fell still.

The guards were not sure what to do and one looked at the other, bewildered and troubled. The fact was that Vercingoral was bigger and stronger than either of them and most probably both at the same time if they had dared to pit their combined muscle against him.

"I am a Shireman and I have just killed your Emperor...!" Vercingoral said, holding his arms out wide as a gesture for the two guards to come closer and do what he expected them to do and what they both knew they should. "You were supposed to guard him from the Shiremen! You failed." He lunged forwards and grabbed hold of one arm and pulled it towards him until the sword that arm was holding was jabbed into his own belly. The guard quickly removed it and stood back. Vercingoral staggered around for a moment or two before collapsing. He raised his head and looked across to where the battle was still raging and tried to locate his son, but could not. He did, however, find Gonosor; a sight that reminded him of Henwen, his great love, so that as he breathed his last it was his memories of her that accompanied him as he slipped away. The guards ran off.

Galfall had moved closer towards the castle. The bombardment had ceased and all he could hear was the dim sound of the battle further along the coast. The youngster was exhausted and confused and leaned against a tree to stop himself from falling. He pulled his hood over his head and would have disappeared altogether if he could.

"I cannot do it," he muttered.

"Yes you can, Galfall," said the voice in his head. "I have told you what it is I expect you to do."

"I'm telling you I can't do it!" he insisted, getting angry and looking all around the thicket for a sighting of the woman who was speaking to him. He did not know who she was but recognised her voice, for she had spoken to him once before. He did, however, know that it was not his mother.

"It is your duty. Your task. Your destiny."

He chortled.

"It was never my destiny to end up here ... like this...! I am too young to die!" The last part of his reply came hurtling out of his mouth loudly and furiously.

"You know what the alternative is. You have learned that much at least. You shall die if you do not do it. But if you do, and only you can, you will live forever more."

He was intrigued. "Immortality you mean?"

"Yes. In the hearts and minds of your countrymen."

"You're trying to trick me! Just like Badad tricked me."

"Badad has gone. You can follow in his footsteps, Galfall. All the powers he possessed can pass to you."

"I will be a Druid?"

"You will be the last of my Druids. You will be the most powerful and the most celebrated of them all."

"More powerful than a king?" he asked.

"The most powerful man in the world," she replied.

He thought about that prospect for a moment, then his haggard face broke with a smile. "I will try," he told her. She did not say anything more and somehow he knew that she had gone.

He pushed himself away from the tree and staggered further towards Bosscastle, towards the gatehouse. He took a dagger out of his pocket and held it firmly in his hand. He raised his free hand until it was touching the cold, scabrous stone, and tried to remember the words. Then he started.

"Rise again Corbilo, from watery depths. Galfall doth call. Whenever I might be minded to pull on you, I will drag you up, earth and sea all with you. Rise again, Corbilo, far from top and far from bottom, that giant of old of whom men hath forgotten...!" And he stepped away from the wall and waited anxiously for something to happen. Nothing did. "GALFALL DOTH CALL!!" he repeated, but much louder. "Galfall the Great," he said to himself.

Fogle dashed through the forest like a wolf after its prey, weaving and winding through the trees as though he knew precisely where they were. And suddenly he broke clear from the forest; the sight before him, at the coast, was one of chaos and bloodshed and he was filled with fright and dismay. As he paused to catch his breath, the ground beneath his feet began to shake. He turned to look back into the forest for that was where the commotion seemed to stem from, but saw nothing. There was a tremendous noise to accompany the quaking earth, a crumbling noise as though the very ground he was standing on was about to explode. He set off running until the fortress came into view again. That, he was now certain, was where the noise and the shudder was coming from, and he thought for a moment that the bombardment had begun again and the old castle was on the verge of collapsing altogether. It was, but not because of anything Punil's ships were doing.

Punil was on the higher deck of his vessel fervently observing the castle as it visibly shuddered, an anxious, almost disbelieving expression covering his face and repeated on the faces of his subordinates as they gathered around him. One of them panicked and demanded to know what was happening, but he did not really expect an answer and did not receive one. Stones began to crumble away from the main body of the fortress and crashed into the sea, and when that became more frequent they created a tremendous swell that disturbed Punil's ships enough for him to command that the retreat be sounded. It was. Oars were lowered into the turbulent sea and pulled and shoved fervently until the ships gradually began to move away from the coast.

Bosscastle, it appeared to their eyes, was moving and rising from its ancient foundations. Then the stones broke loose altogether; there was a strident clap of noise like sudden thunder, and they all dropped onto their bellies as rocks came hurling towards them. One ship, three along from Punil's, was directly hit and was smashed into pieces and all on board were instantly killed or sent to the bottom of the sea.

Amidst the confusion and turmoil, the battle stopped as Repecians, Shiremen and Bodmifflians all stood to observe the great event. None of them knew what was happening; all of them, to the last man, feared for their lives.

"What is it?" Carthrall asked urgently, weaving his way through motionless soldiers until he was next to Gonosor again, where he felt safest. The Bodmifflian did not answer him. They watched as the giant rose from his watery chamber, getting ever taller as he slowly brought himself upright; sending rocks crashing to the ground and hurtling through the air as he did so. When he was fully on his two legs he was twice as tall as the Bossmilliad had been, and knee deep in water; Bosscastle was utterly in ruins around him. Although they knew that the sensible thing would have been to run, none of them did. Instead, they all seemed to be utterly mesmerised and bewitched by the sight of him. Far from top and far from bottom, indeed, and as fierce-looking as it was possible for anything to be; with a head full of flame-red hair and a red beard that draped all the way down his front.

Clinging to the tip of that prickly beard, for he had been taken up as the giant had risen, was Galfall. One hand was placed slightly above the other and he slowly ascended until he was level with the giant's mouth; crawled across his thick beard and reached the relative safety of the plateau on his shoulder. The giant was aware that he was there, but did nothing to get him off.

He opened his mouth and released a huge roar of anger and irritation, not at being disturbed but because he had been suppressed in the first place.

"Where is Kanance?" he demanded. His words, from Bossiney, appeared muffled and reached them merely as a gust of wind.

"There he is!" replied Galfall, cunningly, pointing at the ships in front of him. "There is your enemy!"

Corbilo snarled with fury and bent down to gather one of the vessels in his hand, scooping it out of the water and lifting it up so that he could look closer at it. The sailors on board were scuttling about like disturbed mice in a hay barn; their screams nothing more than dim scratches of noise in his huge ear. Uninterested, the giant threw the ship towards land, and like a missile it crashed into the hillside, scattering splinters of wood amongst the people at Bossiney.

"I want Kanance!" Corbilo ranted. "We have unfinished business." He picked another ship out of the sea but instead of bringing it all the way up to his eye he bent down to examine it; ogling to see if Kanance was on board. When he was satisfied that he was not he let go of the ship and it crashed back into the water, on its hull but at such a speed that it broke neatly into two pieces and then sank. However, the disturbance it made in the water helped to propel the remaining ships further away from the giant.

The oars on those vessels were at full speed. Then Punil, a man not normally noted for his bravery, gave the instruction to 'bring him down' and so the catapults were quickly brought into use again, slinging rocks at Corbilo in rapid succession, although they were no more harmful than pebbles when they hit him around his chest and legs. They did, though, annoy him even more and he waded further and deeper into the ocean to chase them.

When Gonosor saw that the giant was going further out to sea he was initially alarmed that he seemed to be abandoning those of them that had endured the mayhem of the battle. He could detect that the Repecians on dry land were mightily relieved and he wondered what help the giant had been to them, other than to have brought a temporary halt to the fighting, so he clasped the hilt of his sword tightly again, mindful of the fact that as soon as the giant was far enough out to sea the battle would resume, and then be lost.

By the time Fogle arrived at Bossiney some fights had broke out again at the bottom of the hill. Coming in from the back of his own people, Salissa was the first familiar face he encountered. "Get everyone back up the hill," he told her. "Get onto the high ground!" She did not fully understand why but did as she was told nevertheless and ushered the women and children in her care back up the hill. As Fogle cut a path through the men he told them to do the same. Then he was reunited with Gonosor and the King.

"We must turn back," he gasped.

"Retreat?" Gonosor raged. "Never!"

Galfall wrapped his hands tightly around the soaking cloth on Corbilo's shoulder.

"The truth of this day is that Kanance is not here," he said. "Kanance is long dead."

"Then you have lied to me as he once did!" the giant retorted.

"Your purpose is broke and you are doomed to ever more misery, Corbilo." He released one of his hands and took the dagger from out of his belt. "Your fate is sealed." And he thrust the blade into the bulging, violet vein on the giant's neck. Blood did surface, but just a trickle and nowhere near enough to kill him. So Galfall blew into the wound and suddenly a small cut became a gash, that did cause the giant some discomfort. Corbilo swiped his hand over his shoulder to be rid of the troublesome pest, but Galfall was too small an opponent to be thrust off at the first attempt. While he still had the chance he stabbed his dagger into the vein as many times as he could in different places. Again and again he did this, until Corbilo's blood was discharging enough to drip into the sea, to colour it red as though a volcano was erupting beneath the waves.

Galfall said, at the top of his voice: "The Druids will always find the way!" And then he breathed on the wounds again. Corbilo released a riotous roar; his eyeballs rolled in their sockets before his eyelids closed for the very last time. He collapsed into the sea face down and was so heavy that he sank to the bottom in no time at all. Galfall was taken down with him.

The upsurge of water when the full weight of his body hit the surface of the sea was tremendous, spilled over the remaining ships of the Repecian fleet and scattered them once and for all. A wave was sent dashing towards the coast, that gathered in momentum as it went so that by the time it arrived it inundated the harbour and did not actually break until it was a good way inshore.

By that time most of the people of Geramond had made it to the relative safety of the high ground that overlooked Bossiney. Gonosor, Fogle and the King, however, were some way behind the others, and when they saw the wave coming towards land sudden panic ensued. Everywhere panic, as the Repecian soldiers realised that they did not have the time to escape the wall of water that was racing towards them, for they had been too preoccupied with searching for their commander, or even Vagor, following the fall of the giant. They found neither, of course. Only when it was too late did they disperse. The discipline and regulation that had characterised a Repecian army for countless generations turned rapidly into a situation where it was every man for himself. As

Carthrall looked back upon the hordes of legionaries, hampered by their terror as well as their armour, it occurred to him that they too were merely trying to save themselves. The thought quickly raced through his mind that it must always be far worse to be stricken and forsaken in a strange land, knowing that you would never see your home or your own people ever again. He could understand their anguish, for this was a strange land to him also, regardless of all the things he had been told. Then his thoughts changed to the fate of his brother; of whether he had survived the events of the day and whether he would see him again. As he scrambled for safety, slightly ahead of Gonosor and a good way ahead of Fogle, for he was the younger of the three and therefore fitter and faster, he said to himself: "I have lost everyone now. How quickly my life has changed. I went to Aldwark a farmer's boy and returned to be made a king! I am indeed cursed. Everyone I have loved has died. It's best not to know me." His words were especially consequential as he looked back to see Fogle in some difficulty; exhausted and impeded by the burden of dumpiness and age.

Fogle knew that he was in the way of the wave. Like in a dream, he had tried to reach higher ground but his legs felt heavy and unruly and would not take him to where he knew he needed to be. He could only look on as Carthrall and then Gonosor clawed their way to the top of the bank, but did not resent their success; was heartened to see it, in fact, even Gonosor for he knew now that he was not as frightening as he purported to be. He decided that it was futile to go any further, stopped and twisted his body until he was on his backside, with a view of the white surf as it came tumbling and whistling towards him.

Carthrall saw him, and screamed out his name and instructed him to try and escape, but Fogle did not hear him and even if he had he would have surely ignored the instruction, whether it came from a king or not. So he sat upright and waited. And as he waited a memory of his son, Callarn, came into his mind; the horrid recollection of how he had died. Below, he could see men being swamped by the water and prepared himself for the same fate. His next memory was of Toggett; he could almost hear him laughing and shouting: 'run, you great, fat lummock!" Then he remembered what Badad had said as they had buried the old man next to the signpost for the Shireman Inn:

> Travel swiftly, travel safe;
> And cast out mortal thought.
> One promise you have heard will be true;
> The land of men long gone,
> Of friends and sons,
> Will open thy arms for you.

'Of friends and sons': Toggett Took and Callarn. "Yes, they'll do nicely," he mumbled. "Very nicely indeed." He waited. Gonosor and Carthrall observed, fearing the worst. The water came up the bank of the hill and he shielded his face. Then it stopped just as it had touched the souls of his boots, and receded back to a more acceptable level. He gasped, looked up to the other two and spontaneously raised his fist in triumph. He mouthed the words: Thank you, Badad, for he was quite certain that it was the little Druid that had spared his life, and suddenly he realised that he had not wanted to perish here and now after all. There was plenty of life left in old Fogle yet, and plenty of work to do. Carthrall and Gonosor cheered, for both of them needed him still.

THE END